KU-735-812

**Praise for the Rise of the Jain trilogy**

'Like an adrenaline shot targeted directly for the brain'
**John Scalzi**

'*The Soldier* provides everything we demand from Asher: a beautifully complex universe where AIs, aliens and post-humans scheme and struggle – magnificently awesome. Then Asher turns it up to eleven' **Peter F. Hamilton**

'A richly imagined, exotic world, nonstop action, and unimaginable stakes – I couldn't put *The Soldier* down' **Yoon Ha Lee**

'In this riveting sequel to *The Soldier*, Asher ramps up the pyrotechnics in the thunderous first salvoes of war . . . This is Asher at the top of his game' ***Publishers Weekly***

'Space operatics and Jacobean revenge-melodramatics'
***Locus Magazine***

'Asher's intergalactic chess match combines vivid descriptions of human, alien and AI psyches with explosive and violent confrontations . . . Asher's distinctive and compelling adventure will appeal to fans of military science fiction, space opera and even cyberpunk' ***Booklist***

'Fast and furious and darkly funny . . . Asher devotees are in for a treat' ***Concatenation***

'Fights and battles galore' ***ForWinterNights***

9030 00007 2377 2

'Neal Asher kicks off another Polity-based trilogy in signature fashion, concocting a mind-melting plot filled with far-future technology, lethal weaponry and bizarre alien creatures'

*RisingShadow*

'Neal Asher manages to weave the most awe-inspiring elements of his universe together into an amazing narrative brimming with awesome technology, vast space battles, gigantic explosions and intricate machinations that are terrifying in their scope'

*WorldsInInk*

# THE HUMAN

Neal Asher divides his time between Essex and Crete, mostly at a keyboard and mentally light-years away. His full-length novels are as follows. First is the Agent Cormac series: *Gridlinked*, *The Line of Polity*, *Brass Man*, *Polity Agent* and *Line War*. Next comes the Spatterjay series: *The Skinner*, *The Voyage of the Sable Keech* and *Orbus*. Also set in the same world of the Polity are these standalone novels: *Hilldiggers*, *Prador Moon*, *Shadow of the Scorpion* and *The Technician*. The Transformation trilogy is also based in the Polity: *Dark Intelligence*, *War Factory* and *Infinity Engine*. Set in a dystopian future are: *The Departure*, *Zero Point* and *Jupiter War*, while *Cowl* takes us across time. The Rise of the Jain trilogy is set in the Polity universe: *The Soldier*, *The Warship* and *The Human*.

By *Neal Asher*

*Agent Cormac series*
Gridlinked • The Line of Polity
Brass Man • Polity Agent • Line War

*Spatterjay trilogy*
The Skinner
The Voyage of the Sable Keech
Orbus

*Standalone Polity novels*
Prador Moon • Hilldiggers
Shadow of the Scorpion
The Technician

*The Owner series*
The Departure • Zero Point • Jupiter War

*Transformation trilogy*
Dark Intelligence • War Factory
Infinity Engine

*Rise of the Jain trilogy*
The Soldier • The Warship • The Human

Cowl

*Novellas*
Mindgames: Fool's Mate • The Parasite • Africa Zero
Snow in the Desert • The Bosch

*Short-story collections*
The Engineer • Mason's Rats • Runcible Tales
The Engineer • Reconditioned • The Gabble
Owning the Future • Lockdown Tales

# NEAL ASHER

# THE HUMAN

Rise of the Jain, Book Three

TOR

First published 2020 by Macmillan

This paperback edition first published 2020 by Tor
an imprint of Pan Macmillan
The Smithson, 6 Briset Street, London EC1M 5NR
Associated companies throughout the world
www.panmacmillan.com

ISBN 978-1-5098-6246-7

Copyright © Neal Asher 2020

The right of Neal Asher to be identified as the
author of this work has been asserted by him in accordance
with the Copyright, Designs and Patents Act 1988.

All rights reserved. No part of this publication may be reproduced,
stored in a retrieval system, or transmitted, in any form, or by any means
(electronic, mechanical, photocopying, recording or otherwise)
without the prior written permission of the publisher.

Pan Macmillan does not have any control over, or any responsibility for,
any author or third-party websites referred to in or on this book.

1 3 5 7 9 8 6 4 2

A CIP catalogue record for this book is available from the British Library.

Typeset by Palimpsest Book Production Limited, Falkirk, Stirlingshire
Printed and bound by CPI Group (UK) Ltd, Croydon, CRO 4YY

This book is sold subject to the condition that it shall not, by way of
trade or otherwise, be lent, hired out, or otherwise circulated without
the publisher's prior consent in any form of binding or cover other than
that in which it is published and without a similar condition including
this condition being imposed on the subsequent purchaser.

Visit **www.panmacmillan.com** to read more about all our books
and to buy them. You will also find features, author interviews and
news of any author events, and you can sign up for e-newsletters
so that you're always first to hear about our new releases.

Researchers, innovators and inventors of the world, despite leaden precautionary-principle bureaucracy and pressure from antediluvian NGOs, you keep working and keep taking us into a bright future. Because of you, poverty and child mortality are way down, pollution and famine are disappearing, information is available to many, and ignorance becoming a choice, and many of us living longer lives the emperors of the past would envy.

I thank you.

| LONDON BOROUGH OF WANDSWORTH | |
|---|---|
| 9030 00007 2377 2 | |
| Askews & Holts | |
| AF SF | |
| | WW20003824 |

# Acknowledgements

Many thanks to those who have helped bring this novel to your e-reader, smart phone, computer screen and to that old-fashioned mass of wood pulp called a book. At Pan Macmillan these include, Bella Pagan (editor), Natalie Young (desk editor), Georgia Summers (editorial assistant) and Neil Lang (jacket designer), also freelancers Claire Baldwin (editor) and Steve Stone (jacket illustrator), and others whose names I simply don't know.

Further thanks I feel are due to those publishing scientific articles on the internet, which I read in the morning before getting to work. They set my brain buzzing with ideas, though with the corollary that sometimes I have to update the same.

# Cast of Characters

**Captain Cogulus Hoop**: A centuries-old captain from the world of Spatterjay, known by most as Cog. Just like other humans of that world, he is a hooper, the term used to describe those infected by the Spatterjay virus. Cog is also related to the founder of that world, the infamous pirate Jay Hoop. What many people don't know is that Cog is also an agent for the Polity. Cog initially set out to help another hooper, Trike, rescue his wife, who had been kidnapped by the legate Angel. This drew him to the Cyberat system, from where they barely escaped alive. They were then attacked by the swarm AI the Clade and Cog's ship was badly damaged. Dragon took them in, and they sheltered within his vast structure until he then transported them to the planet Jaskor. On this world, Cog and his crew joined Orlandine's fight against the terror of the Clade, which was seeking to break down her defences there in preparation for the coming of the Jain.

**The Client**: An expert weapons developer and the last remaining creature of a civilization called the Species. Her kind were supposedly annihilated centuries ago by the alien prador. The Client, bent on revenge, took over a weapons platform from the defence sphere and travelled to her old home planet, now in the Prador Kingdom. On a moon there she discovered a hidden library holding a treasure trove of data stores, guarded by the Librarian. The Client's battle with this ancient Jain unlocked the forbidden data she was seeking and finally revealed to her what happened to her kind. This led her to the accretion disc, where Orlandine's deployment of the Harding black hole had released two ships that had been trapped for millions of years in a U-space blister. The first which appeared held the ancestors of the Client, and she managed to persuade Orlandine to cease attacking them. The second ship let out the fearful shriek of the Jain and is the real enemy.

**Diana Windermere**: The captain of the massive Polity dreadnought the *Cable Hogue*. Sent by Earth Central, at the head of a Polity fleet, to the accretion disc and Jaskor to counter threats against the Polity, including the prador fleet that was sent too, she soon found herself up against an alien ship out of a U-space blister in the accretion disc sun. That was bad enough, but she dealt with it, allying with the prador and Orlandine's weapons platforms to that end. But now another immense alien ship is coming out . . .

**Dragon**: A moon-sized alien biomech who is Orlandine's partner in her project to build the accretion disc defence sphere. His motives and aims are often opaque, but it is certain that he has a hatred for the Jain technology within that disc.

**Earth Central** is the ruling AI of the Polity. However, it can make subminds of itself and, facing the Jain menace, makes one to deal with this. The new EC is locked out from Jaskor and the accretion disc by U-space disruption, and must find a way in.

**Gemmell** is the leader of the Polity ground forces down on Jaskor. After facing the hostile swarm AI, the Clade, it now seems, with Orlandine back in control, that his task is coming to an end. It is not.

**Orlandine**: The haiman overseer of the defence sphere project. Orlandine controls all the AIs and state-of-the-art weapons platforms that surround and guard the accretion disc, looking to contain the lethal concentration of Jain technology gathered there. She is made up of a complex mix of human, AI and Jain tech herself. When the disc was attacked by an impossibly powerful Jain soldier, seemingly to release the Jain tech, she was forced to launch her 'special project'. This involved transporting a black hole, via U-space, to the accretion disc, where it could halt the spread of Jain tech once and for all. However, deploying the black hole in fact released two ships from a U-space blister, one of these being the Jain. When its agent, the Clade, attacked Orlandine's base on Jaskor, Orlandine nearly died in an assassination attempt and was greatly weakened on losing the Jain tech which linked her human and AI self. But she managed to recover it, and the Clade was defeated.

**Orlik** is the captain of a large dreadnought called the *Kinghammer* and has been sent at the head of a prador fleet from the Kingdom for the same purpose as Windermere. Now fully allied with her, they face the new threat together.

**Trike**: Like Cog, Trike is a hooper, with the characteristic size and strength of such men from the Spatterjay world. Trike also displays signs of insanity, which the Spatterjay virus feeds and enhances if not kept under control. Trike's wife, Ruth, used to help calm Trike and keep the madness at bay. When Ruth was kidnapped and enslaved by the legate Angel, Trike was drawn into the wider battle against this android and a Jain AI called the Wheel. He and Ruth were finally reunited and escaped the Cyberat world together but a fatal attack by the Clade on their ship resulted in Ruth's death. Angel turned against the Wheel and joined Cog's ship, but Trike could never let go of his hatred for him. Their fight against the Clade continued on Jaskor, where Trike diverged from Cog and inadvertently took on the Jain tech lost from Orlandine's body. This transformed him completely, making him an even more powerful fighting machine. Using his new-found strength, and unable to forget his anger towards Angel, he destroyed the android. Ruth was eventually revived once again, but for Trike it was too late. There is no going back from what he has now become.

# Glossary

**Augmented**: To be 'augmented' is to have taken advantage of one or more of the many available cybernetic devices, mechanical additions and, distinctly, cerebral augmentations. In the last case we have, of course, the ubiquitous 'aug' and such back-formations as 'auged', 'auging-in', and the execrable 'all auged up'. But it does not stop there: the word 'aug' has now become confused with auger and augur – which is understandable considering the way an aug connects and the information that then becomes available. So now you can 'auger' information from the AI net, and a prediction made by an aug prognostic subprogram can be called an augury.

                – From 'Quince Guide' compiled by humans

**Bounce gate**: A small defensive runcible (U-space gate) installed aboard ships as a countermeasure to U-space missiles. Such missiles can be fired through U-space at a ship and materialize inside it; however, if they appear near a gate, it is the nature of the physics of this technology that the gate will route them through to U-space.

**First- and second-children**: Male prador, chemically maintained in adolescence and enslaved by pheromones emitted by their fathers and acting as crew on their ships or as soldiers. Prador adults also use their surgically removed ganglions (brains) as navigational computers in their ships and to control war machines.

**Golem**: Androids produced by the Cybercorp company – consisting of a ceramal chassis usually enclosed in syntheflesh and syntheskin outer layers. These humanoid robots are very tough, fast and, since they possess AI, very smart.

**Haiman**: The closest amalgam of human and AI possible without the destruction of the human organic brain. The haiman Orlandine is a special case, since she has also amalgamated with Jain tech she made 'safe'.

**Hardfield**: A flat force field capable of stopping missiles and energy beams. The impact or heat energy is transformed and dissipated by its projector. Overload of that projector usually results in its catastrophic breakdown, at which point it is ejected from the vessel containing it. Hardfields of any other format were supposed to be impossible; however, it has now been revealed that they can be made spherical and almost impenetrable . . .

**Hooper**: A human from the oceanic world of Spatterjay who has been infected with the Spatterjay virus. Commonly passed on through a leech bite, this virus makes its target inhumanly strong, dangerous and long-living.

**Jain technology**: A technology spanning all scientific disciplines, created by one of the dead races – the Jain. Its apparent sum purpose is to spread through civilizations and annihilate them.

**Nanosuite**: A suite of nano-machines most human beings have inside them. These self-propagating machines act as a secondary immune system, repairing and adjusting the body. Each suite can be altered to suit the individual and his or her circumstances.

# THE HUMAN

**Polity**: A human/AI dominion extending across many star systems, occupying a spherical space spanning the thickness of the galaxy and centred on Earth. It is ruled over by the AIs who took control of human affairs in what has been called, because of its very low casualty rate, the Quiet War. The top AI is called Earth Central (EC) while planetary AIs, lower down in the hierarchy, rule over other worlds. The Polity is a highly technical civilization but its weakness was its reliance on travel by 'runcible' – instantaneous matter transmission gates.

**Prador**: A highly xenophobic race of giant crablike aliens ruled by a king and his family. Hostility is implicit in their biology and, upon encountering the Polity, they immediately attacked it. They originally had an advantage in the prador/human war in that they did not use runcibles (such devices needed the intelligence of AIs to control them and the prador are also hostile to any form of artificial intelligence) and as a result had developed their spaceship technology, and the metallurgy involved, beyond that of the Polity. They attacked with near-indestructible ships, but in the end the humans and AIs adapted, their war factories out-manufactured the prador and they began to win. They did not complete the victory, however, because the old king was usurped and the new king made an uneasy peace with the Polity.

**Reaver**: A huge golden ship shaped like an extended teardrop and one of the feared vessels of the prador King's Guard.

**Runcible**: Instantaneous matter transmission gates, allowing transportation through underspace.

**USER**: Underspace interference emitters are devices that disrupt U-space, thereby stopping or hindering both travel and communication through that continuum. They can also force ships out of it into the real, or realspace. They can consist of ship-mounted weapons, mines and missiles whose duration of disruption is variable.

**U-signature**: A detectable signature left when a ship jumps into or out of U-space from which the destination or departure point of the ship can be divined. Complex matter when artificially organized down to the pico-scopic level also creates a U-signature, by which it can be identified.

**U-space**: Underspace is the continuum spaceships enter (or U-jump into), rather like submarines submerging, to travel faster than light. It is also the continuum that can be crossed by using runcible gates, making travel between worlds linked by such gates all but instantaneous.

**U-space twist**: This underspace formation can, often via the collaboration of a U-space engine and hardfields, turn like a clock spring winding up to store energy, then unwind to release it (though of course conventional geometries do not apply to this continuum). It can be deployed as a weapon – generated at a distance inside an enemy ship, where it releases its energy all at once, with the combined electromagnetic and gravity effects ripping everything apart around it.

# 1

*Jain technology allegedly destroys civilizations. It killed their own, as well as the ancient alien societies of the Atheter, the Csorians and the Makers. This is all accepted writ, but I have to ask, how did it do this? It is a technological ecology capable of forming matter on the nano and macro scales. But how is this tech different from our own, which can do the same things? It is fast and can spread like a parasitic plant or fungus, feeding on present technology and converting it. It sequesters devices, computers and AIs, and can even seize control of living creatures . . . yet we are capable of making mechanisms to do the same thing. It is reportedly most dangerous when guided by intelligence, and thought somehow to control that user. Does it make those who deploy it evil? An old aphorism has it that guns do not kill people, people kill people while a gun is just a lump of inert metal (or composites). But no, it's not that simple. A gun provides its owner with power but also an easy way to deploy it, and it is the latter that makes him more likely to use it. Can we then see Jain technology in this light? Can we in the end tie it back to an aphorism older still: power corrupts and absolute power corrupts absolutely?*

From 'How It Is' by Gordon

## Orlandine

Pillars of smoke rose from the city. Disaster-response robots still dug through wreckage and ambulances fled across the sky. On the roof of a superficially damaged apartment block sat what looked like a thirty-foot-tall, partially coiled woodlouse, but with a shifting tentacular mass in its underside – a metallic-sheened nightmare of snakes and worms. From within this mass, tendrils extruded a sarcophagus forwards and down, depositing it on the roof. The shifting tendrils over its surface began peeling back sections to spill out steaming jelly and strange organic structures, some of which were still moving. Steadily they revealed a human woman under a translucent veined caul. She pushed a hand through the caul to split it, leaking clear fluid, and stepped out of it onto the roof. And finally, Orlandine opened her eyes.

She turned to look over her shoulder at the umbilici connecting her back into the sarcophagus, which had already started collapsing as if under accelerated decay, and thence to her Jain device. After a moment, they detached from her and snaked back to their source. Down her back, and in the back of her skull, holes drew closed. She took another step and reached up to touch her collarbone. Under her fingertips, a circle of pores spewed monofabric across her skin to cover her from neck to feet. Transparent at first, it then turned royal blue. At her waist and feet it thickened to form a wide belt and boots, which took on the texture and colour of tan leather.

*Am I human now?* She continued forward. In fact this body was more human than the one she'd occupied before, since over eighty per cent of it consisted of muscle, bones and organs grown from her original DNA. She had also overwritten the brain so it matched the one she had possessed before her fall from the tower in her Ghost Drive Facility. The fall which had seemed to bring about the end to her human life. This brain contained a copy of her original AI crystal too. And the all-but-meaningless question about her humanity seemed to arise from it – from an earlier primitive self. But this body was an avatar of the device behind her. Yes, part of her consciousness resided in it, but a small percentage of *herself*. She halted at the edge of the building and, while her apparently human eyes studied the city, she saw so much more.

Via thousands upon thousands of cams and other sensors, Orlandine gazed upon the Jaskoran system. Inward, the giant hot planet Adranas sat in close orbit about the sun, while a chunk of technology the shape of a thick coin, fifty miles across, sat out from it in a Lagrange point. This core of a ship belonged to an alien race dubbed the Species, but she did not know if it contained any of that kind. It had been unresponsive since being transported from the accretion disc. But certainly one of the Species, the Client, did occupy the nearby Weapons Platform Mu. The Client had tried to save her kin by bringing the ship's core here, but she had also put this entire system in danger by doing so.

'Was that a good idea?'

The question surfed in on Orlandine's perception – someone noting the direction of her regard. She located its source and gazed through cams at Knobbler. The assassin drone had just left Weapons Platform Magus – one that had been under construction in orbit above her, and whose AI the rogue Clade had destroyed. Swirling up behind the big assassin drone, his fellow drones followed him back towards Jaskor. Reviewing their recent activities, Orlandine confirmed they had helped to bring orbital production and construction up to speed but then extracted themselves from the processes and ensconced themselves aboard the platform to return it to operational status. A new AI in place had now taken over. And, once again, these drones were looking for action.

'You mean offering the Client protection?' she asked.

'I mean just that.'

Orlandine could no longer view the accretion disc since U-space disruption had cut communication, and her reach was only within this planetary system. But she now knew two ships had been trapped within a U-space blister in the disc's sun, and the second of those had come out. The first – the Species ship – had been mauled by the combined Polity and prador fleet and her platforms out there, so only its core remained. The second ship was an enemy of the Species: the Jain. These creatures had created a technology that had wiped out their civilization and others, and had come close to bringing down the Polity in the past. With xenophobia and hostility implicit in their biology, the Jain were a danger to all intelligent life. She did not doubt their ship would head here, either to destroy the Species ship core, or to begin the extermination of those the Jain saw only as a resource to be pillaged and discarded in pieces. She analysed her feelings about that and found nothing strong; instead she fell into analysis of the Jain way of life as a survival strategy.

'You think it would have been better to tell the Client to get the hell out of here ASAP?' she asked distractedly.

'That ship core is obviously a lure for the Jain ship.'

'Do you think that if she had taken it elsewhere the Jain would have gone after it rather than come here?'

'Seems likely.'

'Yes, but then it would come for us all: for the Polity and the Kingdom,' Orlandine replied. 'I see keeping the Client here as keeping a grip on useful knowledge – knowledge likely critical to our survival.'

Though this reasoning had some truth, she understood it had not wholly compelled her to offer the Client sanctuary. The need to acquire knowledge and resources seemed paramount.

'Still . . .' Knobbler hedged.

*Arrogance and greed?* she wondered, then dismissed the thought.

'With the agreement of the Polity and the Prador Kingdom, Dragon and I built weapons platforms to stop Jain technology in the accretion disc spreading into those realms. It was then my aim to drop a black hole into that disc to annihilate the tech and, even though the Jain soldier disrupted this plan, it is still on course.' She paused, feeling a little pompous, then continued, 'I have dedicated my life to ridding space of Jain technology.' She asserted her claim on it. 'Am I to stand aside now? Am I to think only of survival and let this be someone else's problem?'

'Your choice,' said Knobbler. 'You know we're with you all the way.'

Orlandine gave that a digital nod but felt uncomfortable, her reasoning swirling in her mind. In allowing the Client to stay, she would draw that Jain ship here, but with no certainty she could deal with it. Two of the most powerful dreadnoughts from the Kingdom and Polity commanded the combined fleet out there. Yet was she assuming they could not stop that thing while she could?

Surveying space around the planet of Jaskor, Orlandine checked her resources. Sixty redubbed evacuation platforms sat in orbit, steadily taking on refugees from below and packing them inside. In fact, two of them were departing even now – necessarily under fusion drive because of the U-space disruption. Her remaining weapons platforms – six hundred of them – formed a scattered tail in the orbital path of the planet. Amidst them cargo ships brought materials for the platforms to utilize in repairs and upgrades after their encounter with the Species ship out at the accretion disc. They now sported hardfield and imploder defences to put out the disruptor beam which had shattered many of their kind. Their collective AI minds also worked furiously to come up with further ideas: induction and virtual warfare beams to disrupt the disruptor, and other methods to save them when attacked by a U-space twist. This combined gravity and U-space weapon could generate a twist within ships, which then released the energy into the real, tearing out the innards of its target. The small prador and Polity fleet stationed here was making similar changes – past enemies now joined in an uneasy alliance against an even more dangerous threat. But all of their preparations might not be enough.

'Of course, it would be nice if that knowledge of the Client's you mention was actually available,' said Knobbler dryly.

'Then I must ensure that it is,' she replied tersely, feeling again the need for acquisition as a sharp stab in the pit of her stomach.

Orlandine returned her attention to the inner system. Her exchanges with the alien there had elicited some useful data, but certainly not everything the Client, or that ship's core, had to offer. She wished she could go out and deal directly with that singular member of the Species, but leaving Jaskor was not a good idea. Maybe the combined fleet of Polity and prador ships those realms had sent to the disc *could* destroy the Jain ship, or cripple it, or maybe the thing would just sweep them aside. If they did not destroy the Jain ship, the present U-space disruption might not prevent it from coming here. She had to be ready.

But the Client . . .

She needed someone in the inner system pushing for data, seeking out the weapons and knowledge they needed, *she* needed. She considered sending Knobbler but, though a wily and dangerous assassin drone, he did not possess the tools for this job. So who, then? She turned her attention to the ocean of Jaskor, between the coast and the volcanic island of Sambre. She clawed for contact, but someone there, under the sea, shrugged her off. His ability to do this brought home that he was just the man for the job. Captain Trike, she decided, was not going to walk away from this.

# THE HUMAN

## Diana

Diana Windermere, commander of the interdiction Polity fleet sent to an accretion disc, in what had at first appeared to be a bit of sabre-rattling against the prador, rested her hands on a rail and gazed across a gap of twenty miles to what looked like a vast depiction of an ancient integrated circuit. Though not the largest space inside her ship, for others were scattered throughout the massive structure, this was the only one charged with an atmosphere. She came here sometimes when she needed the . . . space.

At two hundred miles across, the *Cable Hogue* was a giant warship. Its Laumer engine alone was bigger than most other ships, while its six conjoined U-space drives were each more than capable of hauling a large asteroid through that continuum. Its mile-thick, incredibly complex armour could deflect or absorb the impacts of most weapons known to the Polity, while it possessed hardfield projectors like pores in its outer tegument. Rumour had it that this behemoth could alter the tides of oceanic worlds it orbited. This was kind of true, but had been in the deliberate assistance of a terraforming project, using the constant output of its gravity weapon – a device that could wreck spaceships like a fast-travelling tsunami would wreck wooden ocean vessels of old.

It had many other armaments too. Some of its numerous particle beam weapons could project devastating beams a hundred feet wide. Huge armouries inside contained fusion, fission and antimatter missiles ready for it to fling from its coilguns. Its railguns could spit hard slugs at near-c. The number and variety of its lasers she had lost count of long ago. Stranger weapons lurked here too, along with iterations of the conventional she had not tried. Factories within could produce just about anything

Diana required. Things already existed in there she had never used nor felt the need to use. No single ship could stand against the *Hogue* . . . until now. She knew she would require everything her ship had to give and that it might well not be enough.

'Projection,' she murmured.

A screen a mile square etched itself into existence in the air before her – the AI Hogue, who controlled this ship in partnership with her, knew precisely what she wanted.

A thing like a giant grey claw appeared on the screen, its fingers curved to points reaching towards her. The cloud of hostile Jain tech, detached from the rest in the accretion disc where a black hole steadily drew it in, stretched half a million miles across and was still spreading out. Though the semi-organic machines that comprised it were each easy enough to destroy with the weapons at her disposal, their sheer number appalled her.

The view divided, focusing in on some of those approaching machines. The bacilliforms ranged in size from ten to a hundred feet long. A hole ran down the axis of each and, thus far, she had only seen them emit ion beams, though as linear accelerators they should be able to fling out more. One screen division showed an object like a man-of-war jellyfish fashioned out of burned bone. Its tentacles were mobile, thick and presently drawing metallic tubes out of its underside and weaving them into objects that looked like knotted lumps of metallized gut, whose purpose was unclear. Objects like sickle cells writ large – their hue green and ever changing – seemed likely to be delivery mechanisms for materials, though no AI had been able to confirm that. Sheets of thick skin gusted through vacuum. Translucent eggs a yard across floated between creations like isopods, either coiled up or open. Bars with open flower-bud ends tumbled, while other objects, with sizes and shapes as various as a collection of seeds from a jungle, drifted aimlessly. Analysing them all, her AIs had come to a worrying lack of conclusions.

Diana waved her hand and again, knowing her mind, Hogue banished the screen divisions and focused in on the cloud's centre and the *thing* there – the object somehow guiding this cloud.

At over a thousand miles long, the truly immense Jain ship *would* affect the tides of any oceanic world it orbited. Scans revealed its dark crystalline hull to be advanced armour. It bore the shape of a leaf-like and grotesque mantid and even seemed to have limbs folded against its body. They were melded into place and larger than the prador reavers running with Diana to face this thing. Its head end sprouted great black pincers from a thin neck. Perhaps a weak point? She felt the urge to giggle because that weak point lay a hundred miles across. The pincers themselves were big enough to girdle the *Cable Hogue*. The ship also seemed to have possessed an outer skin which had decayed and shrunk to woody ridges and branches over its surface – Jain tech that had oozed out from inside and seemingly died there. Organic clumps clinging to its underside, like isopod parasites, had now been identified as warcraft in their own right – each bigger than most of the ships in the combined prador and Polity fleet.

'An ugly-looking thing,' said Hogue, its voice issuing from the air nearby since she had disconnected and shut down her implants.

'Do we have more on its weapons?' she asked.

'It certainly possesses everything we saw from the Species ship,' Hogue replied. 'That disruptor beam, for example.'

And that was the thing. It wouldn't have made any difference if the *Cable Hogue* was ten times its present size. In analogy, it would still be a huge wooden armada sailing ship going up against a twenty-first-century destroyer wielding armour-piercing missiles and torpedoes. Deep analysis revealed that the disruptor beam

– its appearance something like a vortex laser – interfered with binding molecular forces and once it had hit a ship for long enough, and cut in deep enough, the effect would cascade throughout the target. She had seen it already: a Polity dreadnought capable of wrecking worlds turned, in just a matter of minutes, into a spreading cloud of scrap, breaking up like safety glass.

They had discovered a defence against this. A layering of hardfields and the timely placement of a contra-terrene device or CTD imploder could stop the beam. Ship AIs were also working on iterations of induction and laser informational warfare beams that *might* disrupt the disruptor beam. But then, the Species ship had used other weapons: gamma-ray lasers with a plain ridiculous energy density, a missile that delivered an effect similar to the disruptor but more intense – a disintegrator. Also, if this thing possessed the same sort of weapons, it could eviscerate enemy ships with a remotely projected U-space twist. It was madness to go up against it, yet who else was there?

'Full initiation of all systems,' she instructed.

'You are sure about this?' asked Hogue.

'If there was ever a time for it then it is now.'

'Perhaps combat is contraindicated,' said Hogue.

Even the AI had its doubts.

'We may not survive,' said Diana, 'but we can certainly weaken the thing and thin out that cloud. By now Earth Central has figured out that something is seriously wrong here and is preparing. Our job is to slow the enemy down, no matter the cost.'

'Initiating,' said Hogue.

All around her, she felt the immense ship shudder. Along the distant wall, lights began igniting in the output tunnels of autofactories. Lines of fire scribed out runes of destruction. Huge objects began to move through the intervening space. She knew that over two hundred fusion reactors had just come online, that hardfield generators were queuing up to the skin of the ship, particulates loading to the supply tanks of particle weapons and more being made, while the Laumer engine and conjoined U-space engines were running diagnostics. Under her feet, the platform began vibrating. Probably being shaken by railgun carousels the size of cathedrals moving into position, she thought. Lightning flashes out in the shadows were spill from the charging of laminar power storage and ultra-capacitors.

'I also think we should run diagnostics and maintenance on the major space doors,' she added.

'You are thinking we might act as a life-raft?' enquired Hogue.

The possibility should be prepared for. It would be difficult, but the *Hogue* did have enough heft in its U-space engines to jump some distance through the disrupted continuum while, inside, lay other spaces like this that smaller ships of the fleet could cram into. This was supposing anything remained of her ship when it came time to make that call.

## Trike

Trike had felt some disappointment when he took his first breath underwater. His lungs rebelled for a moment, but only as he got the last of the air out – a bit of underwater hacking and bubbles rising up around his face. A moment later, he was breathing water and not feeling much different from how he had done on the beach with Ruth, Cog, that Earth Central Security soldier and the forensic AI that had tried to subdue him.

He had continued walking, noticing without surprise that he did not float to the surface. A while back his body density had been close to that of iron, and he had changed substantially since then. He held out his hand, ripples of light passing across it refracted through the waves on the surface. It was a claw – the claw of a monster. He had wondered what he looked like then and, driven by the thought, the alien Jain technology threaded through him, loaded with programs and knowledge from Orlandine, provided the answer. Via its sensing apparatus, he scanned himself and built up an image in his mind.

He stood on the seabed eight and a half feet tall. His body still bore a human shape, but longer limbed, covered with thickly corded blue musculature that seemed almost skinless. Brown and white veins netted this, while curving spikes had issued from his sides, pointing forwards. He had no idea what biological imperative from the Spatterjay virus in him had driven that. His head projected forwards on a long neck, eyes close together, mouth filled with lethal fangs jutting forwards too. He looked like something that would kill without compunction. Retaining the image and setting a program to scan himself periodically and update it, he had moved on. And then he felt the demand come to him.

He had recognized Orlandine at once. Halting, he took in the intensity of it, and the sure knowledge of her powerful intelligence behind it. The aggressive *push* at his mind which expected an immediate response. For a moment, he felt subdued and ready to accede to it. Then anger rose and he mentally smacked the demand away, seeing it break, fragment and withdraw.

The seabed sloped down and he walked from shingle to red sand cut through with whorls of grey mud. Here tubeworms protruded with spread fronds like those of the AI Mobius Clean whose form was that of a crinoid – a spherical creature, like a mass of feathers attached together at their bases, and six feet in diameter. A thing like an eel or a water snake swam past, only it was headless and sporting rainbow fringes down its length. As he slowed to watch this, he thought about his recent conversation with Ruth.

Throughout their many decades together they had loved each other. It had driven him crazy – well, just a bit more crazy than usual back then – when Angel, under the control of the Jain AI the Wheel, kidnapped, tortured and killed her. Then his aims had been set: vengeance. But Angel, linked to a wormship and controlling technology much the same as that now laced through Trike's body, had resurrected her. He understood finally that this had been Angel's old self reasserting, that Angel had once been a Golem and a moral creature, before the AI Erebus had seized control of him.

But Trike's inability to accept that had turned rancid inside him. What then followed for Trike? His pursuit of vengeance was no longer viable, and his anger and madness raved inside him, seeking outlet. Angel remained the object of his ire but he could not act on that. His motivation had been Ruth's death and yet she lived again, with Angel eventually joining their side. Then units from the swarm AI the Clade had attacked Captain Cog's ship and Ruth became its casualty. Again. The ludicrous situation had continued, with vengeance against the Clade driving him next, despite the possibility of Ruth's second resurrection once they put her in cold storage. But he had been lying to himself. All of it had been displacement activity, his quests for vengeance always an excuse for violence and anger. Meanwhile his feelings about Angel had grown stronger and soured.

Now, on the seabed he saw clumps of rock, or maybe coral, from which stalks extended to the surface to spread seaweed, like shredded yellow paper supported by sausage-like bladders. It reminded him of home, this marine life, and it reminded him of what that home had done to him, including its most recent effects. The Spatterjay virus he had carried for so many years had made changes in him it did not make in others who were mentally stable. Then, following the assassination attempt on

Orlandine in which her Jain component became separated from her, this Jain tech had attached itself to him. It needed a ride to return her mental backup. But on delivering that backup and the larger portion of itself to her, it had failed to abandon him. And it had altered him too.

While examining Spatterjay virus-infected prador that were turning into something nasty, or rather nastier, Orlandine had discovered the genome of Jain soldiers hidden in the virus. Via the Jain tech in his body, it seemed Trike had awoken their genome too and incorporated their aggression. He had used their weapons and their facility for warfare to destroy the Clade but, in so doing, linked their instincts to kill to that sour dark spot within him. In the end, when the android had followed him, he had attacked Angel. This height of his madness had been a final step over the line . . .

No, he was rationalizing. There was something more to this, something deeper concerning Jain technology and its source, the Jain themselves. If it had just been the soldiers' aggression driving him, he would have completely destroyed Angel, but he had not. He had ripped the android apart, but also subsumed him, all his knowledge, all that he was. And now he could feel the fragments of Angel in his mind, leaden, like some form of mental indigestion. Certainly, the aggression had waned, but he still felt as bewildered as when Ruth and the others found him on the beach, and was still trying to return to some form of stability.

When he and Ruth spoke, he had told her he could never return to being human, and no chance remained for them to be as they were. He talked to her about this with utter certitude. But she argued with him that the crinoid forensic AI, Mobius Clean, might have the ability to return him to humanity. They'd gone round and round on that and he started to understand that something had changed long before. He grew angry and told her to go – there was no hope. Only when Clean attacked him, tried to subdue him, and in the process connected to him and showed what might be possible, did he finally realize the truth. He hated what he had become, sure, but there were other changes. He had no feelings for her any more. He also understood, by her attitude, by how the conversation had run, that she had been through too much as well and no longer had the feelings she once had for him. Between them only duty and responsibility remained – a married couple who had fallen out of love and just continued tightening the nuts and bolts of a relationship because of, well, habit.

The Jain tech inside him, the technology Orlandine had gleaned from a Jain node and made, to a degree, safe, had responded to his instinct and defended him from Clean – an induction warfare flash knocking the forensic AI to the nearest state of unconsciousness possible for such an entity. Then Trike had walked into the sea.

Now what?

The idea had germinated on the beach before the others came, as the sick guilt of what he had done to Angel rose up inside him. First he had thought about how the life forms in Spatterjay's ocean utterly stripped down any hoopers who fell in. They survived as animals until rescued, then returned to the human world renewed. But some further thought on that, and a look at the data he had from Orlandine, had revealed this to be a very different sea. There would be no transforming change in these waters, no martyrdom. Sure, some dangerous things lurked under those waves but he had been pretty sure, once he entered the water, he would become the most dangerous thing there. He had then transferred his gaze to the plume of smoke and steam from the Sambre volcano and somehow, it seemed the obvious solution.

Muddy plumes ahead alerted him to a change in the seabed. Soon he came to a cliff extending down fifty feet; the plumes were rising from where the seabed spilled over this edge. He peered down, past layers of sand and mud, to a cliff face of flaky rock where white nematodes squirmed in crevices, and mantis shrimps waited for prey. It all appeared new because, though life clung here, no molluscs or corals gripped onto the rock, and no weeds had taken hold. He thought the Sambre volcano the likely cause and, a moment later, his extra knowledge confirmed it. The fall in the seabed happened regularly and caused tsunamis, which was why no one had built along the coast behind him. He moved out to the edge, stepped off and dropped.

Trike landed with a thump on stone, a current trying to tug him to one side. He gazed along its course and could see it sweeping debris that way, explaining why he had not landed on sand or mud. In the dark here he simply enhanced and could see clearly. Ahead the seabed sloped up, scattered with large boulders clad in weedy growths and dangling clumps of molluscs like white mussels. He began to negotiate a course between these, noting occasional warm currents and, focusing ahead, saw an underwater glow probably from lava oozing out of a vent. Then, as if he had walked into a room with motion sensors, lights came on all around him. He peered at these, seeing curved tendrils rising from the surrounding boulders and depending glowing veiny bulbs. Puzzled, he studied a pair of these, then transferred his attention to where they issued from the nearest boulder. At this point, the boulder opened a large, golden eye.

## Earth Central

Earth Central, the ruling AI of the Polity, had distributed its mind mainly to secure locations. But it also ran it in small parts of many other AIs across its realm and viewed numerous situations that might turn serious. One of these was in the Graveyard, that area of space lying between the Polity and the Prador Kingdom. An erstwhile black ops attack ship called *Obsidian Blade*, which had transformed itself into a swarm AI, pursued the remainder of a swarm AI called the Clade. That pursuit would be lengthy, but ultimately resolved. Still, it required watching. On the further border to the Reaches, probes sent out by an outlink station had detected ancient ruins on a wandering black planetoid. Initial analysis indicated structures that might well be Jain. EC pondered this for a microsecond. Perhaps an archaeological team? No. EC ordered the departure of a sixty-mile-long funnel-shaped dreadnought from its secret base in deep space – its instructions were quite simple: complete and utter obliteration of the planetoid. There was quite enough Jain technology to be going round. Which brought EC back to its recent prime concern.

The Jaskoran system and nearby – in interstellar terms – accretion disc had been out of contact for three days now. In fact the last to leave that region had been *Obsidian Blade*, for the Clade had been the tool – now abandoned – of some Jain agency causing extreme problems there. Increasingly intense probes through U-space had been unable to penetrate the disruption enclosing that place. After the near destruction of the Species ship which emerged from a U-space blister in the accretion disc sun, and its obliteration of a large portion of the Polity and prador fleet there, the situation obviously remained critical. The Jain cloud had been reforming and mechanisms were coming out of it. The last telemetry indicated that something else had come out of the blister, but the data on that, before the blister closed and caused this U-space disruption, were unclear. The vaguely defined mass detected could have been a stray moon or a gravity anomaly. Time to seek more data.

EC put a query through a com channel that had remained

open for centuries. Who might respond had always been dependent on the degree of paranoia at the other end. As the query went through, the AI moulded a virtuality, on a whim deciding to make it the surface of the dark wandering planetoid it had recently viewed. It appeared there as an old hooper who had disappeared on Spatterjay some centuries ago.

*He* stood upon a plain of translucent carbon dioxide ice, shot through with veins of frozen water. His human senses found it dark so he reached out to the horizon, flipped his hand and brought a grav-fusion artificial sun up into the sky. Distant mountains, like the humped backs of crowded hippos, cast dark shadows as it rose. Following the rules of this environment, the fluorescence flickered and jumped like firing neurons in complex ices below his enviro-boots. He shifted then, the planetoid turning underneath him until he stood by the basalt slabs on the shore of a frozen sea. Here low walls of blue glass etched out complex foundations of interlocking triangles – those probable Jain structures.

Beside him, the frigid nitrogen atmosphere shimmered, then, with a thwack to his human ears, a prador clad in metallic blue armour appeared. EC of course understood the drivers of popular hearsay that labelled these creatures as crabs. The things did vaguely resemble fiddler crabs writ large. But he felt that their raised visual turrets and body shape, like a vertically flattened pear, gave them a closer resemblance to wolf spiders. This one was a decapod – the number of legs varied depending on family – and possessed both its claws. It rattled around to face him, the main glinting red eyes behind its visor focusing on him while its upper stalked eyes swivelled to take in its surroundings. EC felt disappointed. The prador king sent this ambassador to intercept communications when he was otherwise occupied.

'I need to speak to Oberon,' said Earth Central. An amusing

conceit, that name – the king of a race of homicidal aliens named after the king of the fairies. It had been given to the king by the transcendent AI Penny Royal, and the king showed a degree of superstition unusual in the prador in keeping it.

'The king—' the ambassador began, then imploded as if a singularity had appeared at his core. EC thought that just an effect of the virtuality . . . maybe.

A shadow grew in the ambassador's place, turned glassy, then filled with colour. In a moment, the king of the prador had appeared. The great louse-like creature only resembled his kind by being an arthropod, assuming this was a real representation of how Oberon looked now. EC noted differences to his perfect recall of how the king had appeared last time, which wasn't so long ago. Oberon's carapace had some darker areas and he had attached new mechanisms to it. On his underside to the rear, a complicated fluid shunt had been plumbed in to the king's ichor system, while just back from his head sat an aug, like a crystal slug, on a pad etched with gold wires connected to data buffers. As ever, the king's experiments were as much on himself as on his children, the Guard.

'I'm here,' he said.

'Evidently,' EC replied, then continued, 'I am seeking to pool our data on the situation out at the accretion disc.'

The king just watched him for a moment, then transferred his attention to the nearby ruins. He said, 'You appear as Jay Hoop the human pirate who sold cored humans to us. And it seems this virtuality is the planetoid discovered by probes from Outlink Station Megratal.'

EC allowed no expression of surprise on its avatar, but at once instituted a security check on data from that station. The king should not have known about that. This was a game they played, in an effort to wrong-foot each other into revealing new data.

'I see that the dreadnought *Bad Bogle* has been sent to destroy this place,' the king added.

EC pondered this, then said, 'The fact you are letting me know that you know leads me to believe your sources aren't actually within my coms systems – a deliberate attempt to drive futile activity.'

'Then let us talk about the accretion disc.'

'You know something?' EC asked.

'Less than you, as you're well aware,' said the king. 'We both require information from another source.'

'I would be glad to know of one,' said EC.

'Dragon,' replied the king.

All data on that entity dropped into Earth Central's consciousness at once. Of the four Dragon spheres first found on Aster Colora, two remained. A far-reach sensor near the centre of the galaxy had detected an object that might have been one of them, before an energy surge vaporized the sensor. The remaining sphere had been co-guardian with Orlandine to prevent Jain tech escaping the accretion disc – their guardianship and control of that area of space being the only acceptable option to EC and the king, since neither trusted the other with control there. After returning to Jaskor from the Cyberat system, where it had been gathering data on the recent threat, Dragon departed again and thereafter disappeared. All attempts to hail it had come to nothing. No data on its location. Nothing.

'You know where it is,' said EC.

'I do.'

Further searches on that basis now gave a hint of something. In various sectors of space outside the Polity and the Kingdom, the prador had more of a remote presence. This raised the probability of Dragon being in one of those areas. Still, that meant a volume of space, when totalled up, many thousands of light years across.

'How did you find it?' EC asked.

'I tracked the course of the Client,' said Oberon.

'How?'

'The library moon of the Species,' Oberon replied. 'One of my ships dropped U-com transmitters on its surface.'

EC knew that the library moon had lured the prador to attack the Client while she was in the Prador Kingdom. However, after a battle in the Graveyard, the Client left the library moon behind. In fact, agents from Earth Central Security, ECS, were closing in on it to find out what had happened and grab as much data and alien technology as they could.

'But the Client jumped away from the library . . .'

'Quite.' Oberon dipped his nightmare head. 'And Dragon intercepted her where she arrived.'

EC put it together in a second. Parts of the Graveyard were blank spots to the Polity but not to the Kingdom.

'I want to talk to Dragon,' said EC. 'But if Dragon is in the Graveyard we will need to come to some sort of agreement . . .'

'I will trust you to keep me apprised,' said the king, and over com sent precise coordinates.

'You do not wish your . . . ?' EC trailed off as the king just faded out of existence.

## The Client

The chain of the Client's body now extended forty links long. Each link took the form of a parasitic wasp the size of a wolf, all wound around her crystal feeding tree like some grotesque decoration. At birth, each body link exited backwards, the head pulling free at the last and turning in towards feeding nipples on the tree, which oozed nectar that turned rubbery on contact with atmosphere. But as they came out, connections remained: a nerve cord running through a chitin-armoured slab of muscle joined the back of the newborn's skull to the underside of its 'mother's' abdomen. The Client's body as a whole was thus a chain of minds resembling a Polity swarm AI, each capable of mentation but subordinate to the primary mind at the top. But this time, the Client gestated a new and different creature.

The remote dropped from its birth canal to hang inside a thick caul on a ropey umbilicus. Throbbing to the ichor pulse of its mother form, who fed voraciously, this caul bag steadily expanded. Later, the mother twitched her back end to swing it in against the tree, where it stuck. The remote then exuded worm feeders through the caul and latched onto the nearest tree nipples to draw in nectar before it had hardened, and it expanded rapidly.

The Client carefully monitored its growth via a connecting nerve which ran down the umbilicus. Much like the remote she had sent out against the Librarian, this creature possessed four legs and two forelimbs, double wings screwed up in buds on its back, and Jain tentacles coiled against the upper part of its thorax, while super-dense fats were packed into it. But it also grew items of a less organic nature. Underneath its tough skin, it layered in conductive and impact-resistant armour. Down the sides of its body, where an insect had breathing holes, it sprouted organic lasers. From inside itself, it could transmit an induction warfare beam, exiting at the same point in the lower part of its head as the coilgun growing throughout the length of its body. It also grew laminar super-capacitor storage and a superconducting network. As she studied it, the Client understood how much of the Librarian's knowledge had gone into its creation – the thing very closely resembled the soldiers the Jain had made.

The remote grew and grew until it was three times the length of the form which had birthed it, and twice as thick. Attached to the tree like an insect in a cocoon, it ceased to feed as the connections within it fined down, and as it made final changes. The caul or cocoon split and the remote folded up out of it to drop onto the floor. As it fell, it uncoiled and landed heavily but perfectly on its feet. The Client lost connection as it shifted and shrugged, shedding a fleshy placenta. The buds on its back split, and slowly its wings folded out and expanded, hardening into a meta-material similar to chain-glass. These were also its transceiver and as their connections firmed, the link established and it became part of the Client again.

Inside the body of her remote, the Client considered something else about what she had wrought here. When the Species had made remotes like this previously, they had always limited their lifespan by the food stored inside them. This creature was different. It possessed mandibles that could grab and slice, and a digestive system with a way to excrete. It could feed on any material its body might require, including metals and minerals, for it could eat rock and chew up items of technology. Its mandibles were diamond-edged and possessed shearfield generators to complement those edges. It had no time limit, it could live for as long as sustenance was available. *She* flicked her wings and thrummed them into motion, spiralling up around the tree and her primary form. She then stopped flapping her wings and stabilized with the grav-engine inside her, tilted and spat a chemical thruster at her rear to climb higher.

From her primary form, the Client also looked elsewhere. The vehicle she had used to transfer a former remote into the library, when she first found it, would not do. The thing was just too small to take this creature. Instead, she called in one of her platform's attack pods to hover above her life-support cylinder. This looked like a giant white melon seed, divided along its length to expose the silvery workings of its weapons systems, with further weapons protruding at one end like a technological prolapse. Her remote reached the top cap where a hatch opened, but where she retained a shimmershield to keep the atmosphere in her cylinder. *She*, as the remote, pushed through this and out into vacuum, landing hard on the attack pod and gripping the vine-like growths of Jain tech which linked its systems into a complete whole. Uncoiling two triangular-section tentacles, she probed inside it to find the correct sockets and plugged in. Now directly controlling the pod, she fired up its engines.

The Client hurtled through vacuum on the pod, passing other attack pods hanging inactive, with Weapons Platform Mu receding behind her. But at the same time, she was also in the platform watching the pod go, because she did not have to choose just one perspective – this was the nature of her mind. Ahead lay the remaining core of the Species ship – a plug of exotic, tangled metal and intricate alien technology the shape of a thick coin fifty miles wide. The dull yellow dot of it, like a moon orbiting the giant hot planet Adranas, expanded rapidly to her perception, to *this* perception.

The attack pod hurtled closer and closer. What scanning the Client had managed revealed much of the internal map of the ship's core. Though ports in its upper surface stood close to the ten-mile-wide central chamber, or living quarters, the armoured tri-doors across them were five times as thick as the doors on the sides. Other smaller ports on the upper and lower surfaces seemed likely to contain antipersonnel weapons. This was logical. The main growth of the ship had connected around the rim of this core, so there was less need for defensive measures. But she did not believe there would be none.

She flew the pod to the rim, perpetually scanning for a response. Nothing happened and in time she reached a point just a few miles out, the edge of the core rearing up above her and extending down below, close-up looking like the bare surface of some metallic elm trunk chewed by bark beetles. To either side it curved away into misty distance – an electrostatic effect retaining a thin atmosphere of gases and vapour near its surface – and there had the appearance of mountains, but with a ridged, almost reptilian look. Paralleling it, she headed towards a port twenty miles away, meanwhile spying other structures on its surface. Stud-like tanks spread arrays of black pipework, coppery square-section ducts looked like titanic wave-guides. Glassy blisters closed over tangles of blue metal, like a cubist version of coral, while v-shaped trenches contained rivers of liquid metal and deep indentations, like missing sections of square pixels, exposed netted grey ceramal. The Client realized this must be the connection paraphernalia that had linked the core to the rest of the ship – all unplugged now.

The lip of the port appeared ahead, just a thick everted and ridged wall of the same brassy metal as most of the rest. She flew the attack pod over it and above the entry tunnel – an ovoid half a mile across. The walls leading in seemed to consist of packed wreckage. Recognizable cables and optics branched out, torn and severed. Ducts had been ripped, great plates of metal torn up, oddly designed engines hung on twisted beams. Perhaps secretive access here? No – upon scanning, she saw the core had torn this stuff away from the rest of the ship when it departed, and that behind it lay the same connections she had seen on the exterior, set in an armoured hull. She began to move the attack pod inside, but a surge of power within the tunnel spooked her and she rapidly withdrew. Spitting fusion, she shot back over the rim wall and then behind it, coming down onto the hull and sticking the attack pod there. Through it, she could feel a rumbling, as if large objects were shifting and thumping home. Defences coming online?

She watched a slab of beam-work tangled with superconductors tumble out into vacuum. Other objects swiftly followed – a storm of wreckage spewing out. Scanning from the weapons platform, she watched the connections inside releasing the wreckage, and an atmosphere blast from valves all around the tri-doors blowing it out. The blast continued until it had driven everything clear. Why had this happened? Any number of reasons could explain it. Her kind within the ship might be unblocking the route for a visitor. Alternatively, this could be a weak attempt to stop her coming in this entrance, or a warning that they were aware of her. Or to prepare the way for underlying weapons. It could also just have been some automatic system which had finally kicked in because of her presence. There was only one way to find out.

The Client moved the attack pod from the hull, blasted up on steering thrusters and went up over the rim into the tunnel again. As the pod entered, the Client detached from it and on her own drives threw herself in towards the wall. Still mentally connected to the pod, she drove it in towards the tri-doors while she watched across the emitted spectrum and passively scanned her surroundings for any further response. The pod drifted in until finally it nosed up to the doors. She ramped up scanning from the pod to highly active, to elicit a response perhaps, and to try to understand the mechanism of those doors.

There was still no reaction and, after a while, she noticed the doors were relatively simple in function. They had an atmosphere seal and each of the three sections could be withdrawn into the surrounding ship's core with curved members whose meta-material surfaces ran chains of hard cilia over solid posts. Tracking the power to these, she discerned shielded s-con cables disappearing into the ship. The control system seemed to be a series of tubules, organic in nature like the potassium signalling channels of a human brain, but interwoven with photonic nanotubes. They connected to patches in the faces of each door – rough comma-shaped areas loaded with molecular receptors. Species technology, certainly. She moved forwards to investigate those door locks.

# 2

*In all human societies, people choose to opt out. Throughout human history they have done this to varying degrees. In the far past they became hermits or secreted themselves in communes – their excuses for running away usually religious – and similar examples have arisen since. During the time of the cryo-ships, many set out to find some form of isolation. However, after the Quiet War, when Earth's population exceeded thirty billion and the main spread of humanity remained confined to the Solar system, people had few opportunities to opt out physically. So those who felt the need were usually the virtuality addicts of the time. In all these cases, we can see this as not a flight towards a better or simpler state but a retreat from complexity – usually a flight from technologies no longer understood. Only after the massive dispersal of humanity, brought on by fast U-space travel and runcible networks, could society afford to indulge this choice in the old way once again. Interestingly, the hermits and the communes of today employ technologies of a similar bent to those others fled some centuries before. Perhaps we can optimistically cite this as a measure of human advancement . . .*

From 'Quince Guide' compiled by humans

## Gemmell

Gemmell strolled along a corridor in the medship but his mind, via his gridlink, ranged elsewhere. Numerous reports vied for his attention, but he had an overview of the situation now. The disaster-response teams dispatched from the southern coastal cities of Jaskor to deal with the wreckage here in the city were more than capable, but they continued to utilize the Polity assistance from the fleet above. There was no disorder. The Clade, or that portion of the swarm AI here that had attempted to assassinate Orlandine and caused such huge destruction, had been killed by Trike, while the erstwhile attack ship and now swarm AI *Obsidian Blade* had gone off in pursuit of the rest of it elsewhere. Civilian rule under the oversight of Orlandine was re-establishing very fast and efficiently – he expected nothing less from her – and already some citizens had made cutting comments about heavily armed marines occupying the city.

However, Orlandine herself had made no criticism and, as he understood it, this might be only the end of one battle, not the end of a war. Something bad happening out at the accretion disc kept the fleets above here on station. Now he needed to decide where best to deploy his troops.

Reaching the end of the corridor, he stepped into a dropshaft. Its irised gravity field slowed his descent, taking him to the lowest level of the medship. From there he headed out through a small exit to the troop carrier parked like an iron slug on the grass, its feet crushing a garden of blue roses. Two ECS marines sitting on its ramp stood up as he approached. He recognized Trantor and Baylock. The first had been with him for many years and he knew the tough, thickset man's capabilities. Baylock he did not know so well and quickly reviewed her file. She was boned, her skeleton a Golem chassis and the rest of her a mix of synthetics and original organics. In a police action two hundred years ago, she had borne the brunt of a sonic shock grenade which shattered her skeleton and ruptured many of her organs. She had chosen replacement of the damaged parts with the best synthetics available, then, when injured in other actions, had continued replacing and upgrading herself. She possessed a half-gridlink aug connection to enable some crystal storage. He noted she needed storage because she had never used mental editing. She was tough, dangerous and very, very capable, but then Gemmell could think of none of his troops who were not.

'Getting a little quiet around here,' commented Trantor. He pointed towards a nearby tower block. 'And I wonder if we're needed now.'

Gemmell glanced over. A drone, like a giant land crab but with bunched masses of weapons where its claws should have been, sat atop the building. Orlandine had brought her guardians over from the Ghost Drive Facility before she destroyed that place – finally acknowledging that using the facility to control her weapons platforms had been a fatal weakness through which an enemy might seize control of them.

'I'll have to talk to Morgaine,' said Gemmell.

'You haven't?' Trantor enquired.

'Not for a little while.'

Trantor raised an eyebrow, turning his attention to the controls and displays inset in his vambrace, and swung away. Gemmell looked at Baylock. 'You're bored too?' It was a serious question. She was old, had never edited her mind and, according to her record, had never gone through the ennui barrier.

'Not in the least,' she replied. 'I've been introducing our new recruit to combat uploads and simulations.'

Many people on this world – mostly ECS infiltrated here by Earth Central to spy on Orlandine – had made applications to join the marines. However, Baylock had said 'recruit' singular, so meant Ruth. Trike's wife had filed her annulment of vows to a positively archaic marriage and put in her application. It had been Gemmell's decision to accept her and he now questioned it.

'How is she doing?' he asked casually.

'Very well,' replied Baylock. 'The neural lace the android Angel installed in her hasn't degraded at all so the integrity of her uploads has been fast. She has combat training, having been an ECS monitor for a while, and she has actually seen combat.' Baylock shrugged. 'She was involved in some pretty grey stuff after being a monitor.'

'Illegal artefacts.' Gemmell stepped onto the ramp into the troop carrier, the other two following him. It was that trade which had led to Ruth's involvement in events here. Angel, under the control of the Wheel, had used her to trace the artefact containing the blueprint of a Jain super-soldier.

'The legality of the trade in such things is still shady,' Baylock commented. 'But you don't get involved in that stuff without running into Separatists searching for another terror weapon . . . or other unsavoury types.'

'And Ruth's neural lace is okay, considering its source?' Gemmell asked, then grimaced, recognizing he wanted to keep on talking about her.

'The forensic AI checked it out while removing that other item from her skull. It's highly advanced but it's not Jain tech. Should be no problems.'

Gemmell grunted an acknowledgement. The removal of the other item from Ruth's skull better signified her break from Trike than anything else. They'd both implanted quantum-entangled U-mitters which told each other where they were. Ruth had persuaded the forensic AI, Mobius Clean, to take hers out.

They entered the carrier and moved down the aisle between the seating towards the fore. Trantor took the pilot's chair and, as the ramp closed, he put the craft into the air with a surge of grav-engines.

'The billet,' he stated.

Gemmell dropped into one of the passenger seats and Baylock sat in a seat just one over from him.

'Of course, I wonder how Morgaine will feel about our new recruit,' she said with a gauche pretence of innocence.

*Ah*, thought Gemmell. He'd been kidding himself no one had noticed his response to Ruth and her response to him. It had come as a shock to him, although doubtless a perfectly rational scientific explanation covered it, concerning the need people felt after losing a partner, hormones and pheromones, and how the brain modelled for attraction. In ancient times, they called it chemistry. Gemmell preferred that: reactive substances fizzing together.

'I'm sure she'll be as professional about it as ever,' he commented.

Trantor gave a disbelieving grunt as he took the carrier towards the city hotel the marines were using as their billet. Gemmell leaned back and closed his eyes. Baylock and Trantor being thoroughly aware of the situation meant it had become part of the chatter between all the marines. This also meant Morgaine – commander of the Polity fleet here around Jaskor – would know of or understand the situation as well. As his commander too, she always kept close tabs on him and, with her close linkage to the ship AI of *Morgaine's Gate*, could analyse data with AI efficiency, but human intent. He opened his secure link to that distant dreadnought.

'We seem to be at a loose end down here,' he said via his gridlink.

Morgaine firmed the connection and expanded bandwidth to open a virtuality, which he had not wanted. He found himself standing under a dome of stars on the black glass floor of the bridge of *Morgaine's Gate*. Directly ahead of him, Morgaine sat cupped in an interface hemisphere. Tubes, data leads and interface technology still almost buried her. But she had changed. Though still naked and still with a medusoid mass of optics plugging into her skull, her eyes were now blue, when before they had been blind white with gridlines across them, and a feeding mask no longer concealed her face. She had also fined down the data connections running along her sides to a discreet skein of optic fibres, while all the body support tubes were gone. The last time he saw her, she had been wrinkled, sagging and all but incapable of movement. Now, having obviously run anti-ageatics and other treatments, she was considerably altered. She looked young again – much more like she had been when they were lovers, though not quite. Sitting forward, a tray in front of her, she was eating perhaps her first solid meal in a century.

Gemmell gazed at her for a long moment. The previous time here, he had felt his guts twisting up with old passion and sadness and regret. Now he found himself looking at her analytically. It could be that, being trapped in this system, she had taken the time to catch up with long overdue upgrades and treatments. He didn't think so. A lot of what she had done was aesthetic. But it wasn't enough, because Morgaine would never detach from the ship AI and never again be as she was. Looking at her, he only felt anxiety about his need to be finished with her.

'So you have no one to fight down there,' she said, putting down her fork. 'Do you suggest the return of you and your men here and into cold storage?'

'I'm not yet suggesting anything,' he replied. 'I'm merely raising the matter for inspection.'

'You must have some opinion on it,' she stated.

'I am aware that under agreement between the Polity and the Kingdom this is Orlandine's, and Dragon's, realm and that our presence is resented by some. I am also aware that the Polity ECS inclination would be for us to maintain a presence on this world until such a time as it is certain we are no longer needed.'

It was all very cold and mannered.

'Orlandine has as yet made no objections to our presence.' She lowered her gaze, picked up her fork and stabbed something that looked like a carrot. She didn't eat it, but continued, 'For the interim, you'll remain on the planet. You'll offer what assistance you can and, I suppose, you can take the time to induct those new recruits.' She looked up, hitting him with those blue eyes.

He gave a sad smile. 'Then that is what I will do.' And he broke the connection.

Gemmell opened his eyes aboard the troop transport. Trantor and Baylock were gone, and the vehicle was down on a grav-car port which extended like the leaf of a succulent from the trunk of the city hotel. He stood and headed for the door.


## Cog

Captain Cogulus Hoop walked down the ramp from the medship, wondering what the hell to do with himself now. He had tried to help Trike and Trike had refused it. He had ensured Ruth's resurrection and brought her and Trike together, only to find that it was a time for partings. Relationships between people could stand only so much trauma. And now he could see the future. That ECS commander Gemmell showed more than usual interest in Ruth and she reciprocated. Two people, experiencing loss from a previous love interest, falling together. None of his business.

He stomped out across the parkland towards his own ship. More of the local disaster-response teams had arrived with some heavy machinery to clear wreckage and deal with casualties. So what use was there for Old Captain Cog now?

He entered his ship and clumped up the metal stair to his bridge, dumped himself in his throne-like captain's chair and groped for his pipe. He paused for a moment to look around. It suddenly felt very empty without Trike and Angel. He winced, thinking about the remains on the beach where Trike had dismembered the android, then felt sad. Angel was gone. Mobius Clean, the forensic AI in possession of those remains, had stated emphatically that Angel could not be rebuilt or resurrected. Trike had not only torn the android apart physically but mentally too. Only strangely melded technologies remained for the AI to sift.

Cog sat thinking further about that beach, about Trike, then reached into the top pocket of his shirt. Rather than remove his pipe, he took out a squat black cylinder the size of the end of his little finger. He stared at this for a while, wondering why, exactly, Ruth had given it to him rather than Mobius Clean, who had clearly wanted it. He opened up the hinged lid over one arm of his throne and rummaged through the comp units and optic cables, finally coming up with a palm-sized tablet. The cylinder dropped into the universal port, which closed around it to make connections, and the screen came on. Coordinates appeared, but they kept changing. The tablet then attempted to display a map, but after a moment, that clicked off and it displayed a message: CONNECTION FAILED. He grunted and shoved the thing in his pocket. The U-mitter, twinned with the one in Trike's skull, could not find him because of the U-space disruption here. He now took out his pipe.

When Cog finally breathed out a cloud of fragrant smoke, he keyed into the ECS data sphere. He felt it was time for him to leave, since so many things had ended, yet he realized he could not. The same U-space disruption that prevented the U-mitter from connecting was due, as far as he could gather, to some event at the accretion disc. No ships were going anywhere except on conventional drive. And he certainly didn't intend to do that. Even if the disruption stopped, he couldn't leave, since his ship's own U-space drive was virtually scrap. He investigated the sphere further, noting frenetic activity still out in orbit and beyond. Orlandine had been up there but had returned to the city. He also got his first look at the Species ship's core and Weapons Platform Mu. Further investigation revealed that Orlandine had put the Client under her protection.

'Fuck a duck,' he said, and chuffed on his pipe some more.

Almost as if in response to this, a frame opened in the onscreen data to show Orlandine's face.

'You were unable to bring Trike back for treatment,' she said.

'He didn't want to come. Stubborn boy.' He pondered for a moment and only added, 'Seems what he and Ruth had is over.'

'That is interesting, but hardly relevant,' she said.

'It's entirely relevant. Without that human connection, he seems to have no inclination to let Mobius Clean work on him. Maybe that's something you understand . . .'

'I understand that Trike has been thoroughly dehumanized and is very powerful,' said the haiman woman.

Cog noted that she had not responded to his last implied question. He wanted to say something acerbic about powerful dehumanized people not being such a rarity on Jaskor, but she continued before he could.

'Right now he is on the crux of either enjoying what he is or hating it. Perhaps it is the latter since he is going to a place where he thinks it possible for him to destroy himself. Maybe he feels some guilt about what he did to Angel.'

'What?'

'Do you think it coincidental that he's heading towards the Sambre volcano?'

Cog mulled that over for a moment then replied, 'I obviously don't like what you're implying but what can be done? I don't think he's crazy any more and I reckon he's perfectly capable of making rational decisions.'

'He is also a loose cannon and a . . . powerful actor in a situation where too much is unknown,' said Orlandine. 'Rather like you. What are your orders from EC now?'

'I have none.'

'You are aware of the present U-space disruption?'

'I am.'

'I have been speaking to the Client. She informs me that two ships went into the U-space blister. The first was the Species ship, whose core you must be aware is now in the Jaskoran system.'

'Yup.'

'The second is a Jain warship which, judging by that disruption, has arrived.'

'Oh bugger.'

'Quite.' She grimaced. 'Since its prior enemy is here and since the Jain are, by their nature, utterly hostile and xenophobic, I surmise that the Jain ship will be heading here too.'

'Supposing Windermere and a shitload of Polity and prador ships can't stop it.' Cog paused for a second, adding, 'Supposing they try . . .'

Orlandine did not reply for a moment, then said, 'Whether they try or not is immaterial. They will be forced to engage.'

'You're that sure the ship will be hostile?'

'I am that sure,' she affirmed.

'Okay, but why are you talking to me about this?' asked Cog.

'I need an effective agent at a particular location.'

'This is big shit. I hardly think I am what you need.'

'You are correct. I need Trike.'

'Ah . . .'

'We need to understand the capabilities of this Jain ship and quite likely we need data on weapons we can use against it. The source of that data is here in the Jaskoran system.'

'But the Client is being . . . parsimonious?' Cog wondered.

'The Client is apparently being cooperative in supplying me with data on the things I know about, but it is limited to that. It is possible I will be able to upgrade our hardfield defences, as well as defences against the disruptor beam. There are, however, holes in that data. I do not, for example, know how to build a disruptor weapon.'

'The Client wants to keep her edge,' Cog rumbled.

'This seems likely.'

'So how does Trike fit in?'

'He is as capable as me of obtaining data from Jain and related technology. He is perhaps more capable in some respects – via his prior infection with the Spatterjay virus, he seems more integrated with his enhancements and different in other ways.'

'The plan, then?'

'You tell him all this and recruit him. You go to the Client and he obtains what he can from her or from the Species ship core.'

'Why not ask him?'

'He is not responding to me but will perhaps to you.' Orlandine paused, then continued before he could deny that, 'Logistics . . . You will take a grav-car out to the volcano and wait for him there. I will meanwhile ensure your ship is ready to fly.'

Cog acknowledged that with a shrug. It could fly but needed refuelling for the conventional trip in towards the sun.

'This is presuming,' Orlandine added, 'that you have nothing better to do and this does not go against your orders from EC . . .'

'I don't see any conflict. EC won't want a Jain warship let loose in the Polity.'

'Yes, we can suppose that,' said Orlandine dryly, and her image blinked out.

Cog stared at the screen for a while longer, replaying the conversation in his mind. He felt something was off about Orlandine – something unhuman and alien. That she no longer had a human body and was now a thing of AI crystal and Jain tech could account for that. Cog snorted. Or his knowledge of that fact could be affecting his perception of her.

## Trike

Trike recognized the type. These were like the anglerfish of Earth. Spatterjay did not have many fish like this because, in the depths of the ocean, giant predatory whelks filled that particular ecological niche. He just had time to consider it, before the nearest heretofore boulder launched itself from the bottom straight at him. As it did so, its skin changed, losing its squid-like camouflage. Nodules and weedy growths on it were sucked inside and flattened out. Masses of white mussels turned into pendulous barbles around the gape of a huge, carp-like mouth. Trike had seen mouths like that on Spatterjay and they were to be avoided – especially those with the same jagged array of fangs like shards of dirty glass.

He reacted instinctively and his Jain tech responded with him. From his feet, it drove tendrils into the stone below and rooted him to the spot. The fish – now a fat grey thing sprouting spiny fins all around – shot up and then down onto him, intent on swallowing him in one headfirst bite. He snapped his hands up and grabbed the bone-and-rubber rim of its mouth, just stopping it dead, while feeling stone cracking beneath his feet. Meanwhile the others here wanted in on the action and a second great mouth closed around his legs. The one above him began flipping its tail hard from side to side, baffled it wasn't getting what it wanted. The one below, chewing at his legs, became an annoyance since he could actually feel some minor damage being done. He bowed over, dragging the one above down and then shoving it away. He had thought about bashing it against the stone, to stun it or otherwise deter it, but knew if he tried that he would rip its lips off. It drifted back and then settled to the bottom, twitching its light-emitting tendrils and looking miffed. The one below finally released him too and backed off, spitting out broken teeth.

It occurred to Trike then how gentle he was being. He could simply have ripped these creatures apart and, in recent times, he would have taken joy in the excuse for violence. He no longer felt that urge, just an impulse he hammered down. Something utterly fundamental about him had changed, because he had an aversion to anger, to madness. It seemed almost as if, in becoming a monster on the outside, he had ceased to be one within.

Another fish attacked and he stopped it dead with the flat of his hand, then pushed it back. It surged forwards again and he slapped it right between protruding tube-like nostrils above its mouth. It swung away, shaking its head. Meanwhile others had risen from the bottom all around, shedding their camouflage, hanging in the water with their spiny fins feathering to keep them in place. Two more came at him from either side and he detached his Jain roots and stepped back, reaching out and sinking his hands into gill slits and slamming them into each other. They tumbled away, biting at each other until they realized they had the wrong prey, then parted and drifted to the bottom. He watched, waiting for the next one, and when nothing happened, he began to move on. Only when he reached the edge of the shoal, where it seemed the bad news had not reached, did another try for him. Its mouth gaped before him and he reached in to grab a hard gristly tongue and squeezed. After a moment, it ceased pushing forwards and tried to get away. He released it and it too settled to the bottom.

At the edge of the shoal, Trike looked back. All were down now and turned towards him. He pondered on the similarity of some alien life to that of Earth, until a memory, not his own, offered a correction. The first settlers here from Earth had seeded the oceans with these adapted anglerfish, along with other Earth forms. Apparently the oceans had previously contained little more than primitive seaweeds and bottom-burrowing worms. He next watched the fish putting out their lights then turned away, as from a city undergoing a blackout, and adjusted his vision.

Ahead the seabed continued its steady rise and soon he waded through drifts of mud and sand. The water temperature began to climb rapidly as he came upon the lava flow he had glimpsed earlier. Here the water boiled around glowing cracks and, in one area, lava issued from holes to harden into rocky turds. He circumvented this, finally coming to a much steeper lava slope. Trudging up it, he reached the surface, coughed water from his lungs and began to breathe air again. Clumps of pumice floated in the waves. A river of hardened lava wound into a wasteland of ash, and more pumice was scattered with flashes of intense blue. In the distance, the Sambre volcano boiled smoke into the sky. He saw no reason to depart from this road. Glancing aside as he walked ashore, he noted the flashes of blue were sprouts from huge seeds like coconuts. Another Earth import? It didn't matter. He was walking towards the furnace and all his knowledge might soon be irrelevant.

'Let me fade . . .' a voice muttered in his consciousness.

Angel was still in him and he felt a surge of savage need to incorporate him. He fought this again, gladly. He could not decide whether incorporating Angel would be final death for the android, or its continuation in him.

## The Client

The Client, with the bulk of her mind's focus inside her remote, began carefully making her way along the tunnel wall, towards the tri-door entrance into the Species ship core. Ahead of her, the attack pod on which she had ridden here hovered just outside that door. She paused, and then sent it another instruction. The thing slowly slid back until it was opposite her – scanners focusing on everything around her and ready to respond to any attack. Finally, she reached the door's rim and instructed the pod again. It moved away from her and settled like a fly on the further rim, sticking itself there.

She walked out across the door, her feet switching over from micro-hooks to gecko function to attach her to the smoother surface. It took twenty minutes to reach one of the locking mechanisms, and all the while she felt horribly exposed. It then occurred to her she had become so thoroughly engaged through her remote as to feel endangered. She withdrew a little, reminding herself that the bulk of her being resided in Weapons Platform Mu and far from this scene.

The shape of a fat comma, the locking mechanism was a raised rough surface like gnarled old wood. She moved her head over it and began scanning with her powerful sensorium. Close study revealed the compacted nano-mechanisms, the closed mouths of potassium channel tubules, and small optic interfaces like scattered mica crystals, as well as micro-pillars of superconductor. Such incredible complexity in a locking mechanism meant it must serve further security functions. She would have to be very careful.

At length, understanding to a degree the shape of it, she uncoiled two of her triangular-profile tentacles and attached them to the rough face. Within those tentacles, she extruded s-con threads, nano- and micro-tubules, and optical fibres to make connections. As those plugged in she started to receive code in light, electricity, heat pulses and nerve impulses – a huge amount of data. She began to build a model of the data, but then realized her remote did not possess the required processing capacity and so routed it back to her primary form.

Within the weapons platform, the Client saw something like the Jain shriek emerging. It consisted of open-ended formulae, incomplete molecular models, but also the elements of a language, familiar because it resembled that of the Species. She began to design responses – to solve the formulae and complete the molecules, and to answer the questions in that ancient tongue. These she transmitted to her remote. With each response the particular 'question' folded away to leave a hole in the growing model. It seemed she needed to dispel the model completely with her responses. She continued to work and eventually, after a long and tedious two hours, one of her tentacles ceased to receive further questions. She detached it and moved it to another area and the whole process resumed. Impatient now, she unfolded all her tentacles and attached them to the locking mechanism, opened up more bandwidth and really got to work.

It went on and on, the model expanding in her primary minds, and then necessarily routed into the processing spaces within the weapons platform. It hung in the virtual world like a great tangle of threads, ever expanding even as some of those threads, their answer received, withered and shrivelled. After another six hours, the whole mass began to shrink and she realized she had ceased to receive feeds to the remaining questions. At this point, she had also gained a full understanding of the ancient language of her kind. The mass became loose, dispersing, and her excitement grew. Soon, like a burglar from old human times, she would have the full combination and the safe would open. Finally, the whole mass collapsed, and she received a message in that language. It came in a combination of light and electrical pulses only. The complex response had many nuances but, in human language, it fined down to one simple word: sucker.

## Gemmell

Gemmell marched resolutely across the roofport, past further troop transports and a collection of two-man surveillance and attack vehicles, to the entrance doors into the hotel on this level. A squat cylindrical drone, with ECS decals brightly painted on its body, guarded the door. Glossy sensor band across its fore, multiphase pulse cannons on either side, it rose up on spider legs and inspected him briefly.

'Welcome, Commander Gemmell,' it said and seemed to lose interest, turning its attention elsewhere.

In his gridlink, Gemmell reviewed the layout of the place. Citizens whose homes elsewhere had been destroyed occupied the bottom ten floors. Marines occupied the top two, with immediate access to the roofports. More had arrived now than just the first complement, from the *Morgaine's Gate* and other ships of the Polity fleet in orbit. They shared rooms in shifts, dependent on their duties in the city, and had turned recreation areas here into armouries and tactical rooms. No need for much administration space, since this ran mostly in the troops' augs, gridlinks and other mental enhancements – the building blocks of the ECS data sphere on Jaskor.

He strode down a corridor, receiving the fist-to-the-chest formal salute used in quarters. Marines never saluted while out on combat duty, since the distraction might get them killed or, a salute acting as an identifier, might get their commanders killed. Finally, he entered an area that had contained a swimming pool, now boarded over with plasmel sheets. Armament storage racks ranged along one wall. The watch officers sat in front of consoles and screens, while a larger display on another wall of stretched screen fabric ran a montage of images. Most of the duty officers had kicked back in their chairs, eyes closed, performing their chores by aug. Gemmell was sure he heard one of them snoring.

'A hive of activity, I see,' he said loudly.

Booted feet dropped from consoles and desks, and the snorer snorted then sat upright looking blearily around him. Keying into the immediate system, Gemmell threw images up on the screen and reviewed present activity. There wasn't much of it and that was no good. He also felt slightly tetchy after his terse conversation with Morgaine.

'Okay, here's what needs to be done,' he said, looking around to be sure he had everyone's attention. 'I want tactical plans, deployments, fields of fire and integrated defence for airborne invasion. I want training exercises running for multiple scenarios.'

'None specific?' asked the snorer.

Gemmell glared at him. He just wanted the men busy so was making it up as he went along. He wanted them to keep their edge. But his impulse had raised a real concern. He thought briefly about the last imagery and other data they had received from the accretion disc, dipped his head and cast further images up on the screen. Jain constructs which Windermere's fleet had encountered tumbled there.

'Assume an invasion by Jain tech,' he stated. 'We'll need to deploy high-energy weaponry, thermal explosives, heavy electro-magnetic pulse weapons . . . you know the drill.'

'The city only?' a woman asked.

She had a point. To be realistic, they had to assume Jain tech would come down planet-wide. Suddenly what had been just a make-work exercise became a real possibility, and a frightening one. What could they really do if such a thing actually did occur? How could they possibly combat something like the super-soldier attacker of the accretion disc if it turned up? It seemed likely that all they could do in that case was die.

'There's only us here,' he said, 'so prepare, train and extrapolate for the defence of this city only. However, relay tactics and scenarios to the south coast cities – offer advisory assistance. Also relay all data to Orlandine. Get to work.'

He swung around and headed out, now wondering if he should order supplies from the ships above. Perhaps Orlandine—

'Gemmell.'

Spooky how she got in contact so fast, almost as if reading his mind, but the staff in the room behind must have already made contact.

'Orlandine,' he stated.

'You are correct,' she told him. 'Invasive Jain tech and planetary defence are a concern. I have been considering this. However, if something coming here destroys my platforms, then anything you do down on the surface will be ineffectual.'

'Does that mean we should just sit on our hands?' He marshalled his thoughts. 'Even while you are mounting a defence out there something might get through . . .'

After a long pause she replied, 'I will begin routing resources for your disposal in so much as they do not weaken the primary defence of the Jaskoran system. Detail your requirements.'

'I can tell you now: gun emplacements, war robots, bodies on the ground armed with effective weaponry.' He paused for a second then added hopefully, 'Grav-tanks? My people will liaise with you . . .' Via his gridlink, he shot instructions to the room he had just departed and moved on.

'These are all doable, you now have these too,' Orlandine replied.

Imagery arrived in his gridlink with source coordinates. A view from low-orbit satellites showed a shoal of drones descending into atmosphere. He saw a thing like a big clam, others from the terran insect world, some based on alien life forms and one or two that resembled no particular life form at all. All were big and generally the size of a grav-car upwards, armoured and, he well knew, loaded with enough weaponry and battle experience to have them individually listed as potential threats to the Polity. As he then felt the link to Orlandine break and another establish, he realized that somehow she had manipulated him, but he could not put his finger on how.

'Ready for deployment,' said the assassin drone Knobbler.

'Plans are inchoate yet – I'll relay you to my operations room.'

'Okay, I'll feed our capabilities and specialisms.'

Gemmell relayed contact to the operations room but paused in the corridor to study what the drone transmitted. His stomach tightened as he realized the drones sat somewhere in capability between a grav-tank and a fully armed attack ship. He shivered and moved on, finally entering another room. This had been a racquetball court. Five recruits occupied couches, and they wore training augs with attached visor input. All were in virtualities trying out the combat programs loaded to their minds. They also wore med-suits running complex military nanosuites in their bodies, boosting musculature, strengthening bones, speeding up nerve impulses, freeing up joints and generally doing all the necessary to enable them to use those programs without tearing themselves apart.

'All good?' he asked Baylock, who sat on a reversed chair with her eyes closed.

She opened her eyes. 'As expected,' she said. 'Just a few more hours and they'll be at entry level.'

'Ruth?' he asked. She wasn't one of the five.

'Her neural lace made it faster – she's ready. And though she hasn't gone for the bulk, she is already boosted and has internal mechanical assist. She told me that was a necessity when living on Spatterjay.'

'Okay, you're receiving updates?'

'I am – nightmare scenario. You really think we'll be fighting Jain tech?'

'It's a possibility we cannot ignore, therefore I want you to take on those recruits we rejected and put out a call for more. Put it out in the data sphere and local net.' He stopped to check something through his gridlink. 'There are a hundred and twenty marines still in stasis above.' With a thought, he sent the revival order for them.

'I'll need more equipment,' said Baylock. 'And a much larger area.'

'Transfer to the medship,' he ordered, then turned and departed.

Gemmell now headed for his own quarters in the hotel. While all this was in motion, he needed to get just a little rest. It wasn't physically necessary for him but did help to balance him mentally. He tried not to feel disappointment about Ruth not being there with the other recruits. However, as he reached his door he saw a familiar figure walking away towards the end of the corridor.

'Ruth!' he called.

She turned, smiled and walked towards him. He eyed her as she approached, first noting how nicely her ECS shipsuit clung to her body then, because of what Baylock had told him, seeing how she moved. Her physical enhancement seemed obvious now, whereas he hadn't noticed it before. He could also see the wary grace of someone who had loaded combat programs. He hit the palm lock of his door and it opened before him.

'So you're ready,' he commented.

She stood close, just a little bit more into his personal space than normal, gazing intently at his face. 'Yes, I'm more than ready.' An amused and self-deprecating pout.

He smiled back and then stepped into his room, turning towards her again as she entered behind him, closing the door. After a brief hesitation they simultaneously moved towards each other. A second later, she had her arms round his neck and her tongue in his mouth. He kissed her back, pulling her close and sliding his hands down her. She gave a little moan and pushed against him harder. He reached down lower to her thighs to pull her up and she wrapped her legs about him.

*Chemistry*, he thought, as he dropped her on the bed underneath him.

## Trike

After a few miles, the flow of hardened lava began to deviate from the course Trike wanted to take. It swept over to the right around a raised rock field. It also became increasingly hot underfoot – not hot enough to either damage his bare feet or get uncomfortable, but he didn't want to wade through lava. He diverted, jumping up onto a slab and making his way through the rock field towards the volcano. Here plumes of steam intermittently issued from the ground, and extremophile bacteria painted boiling pools brightly. Passing one of these, he saw ahead an object which was out of place here, lying on top of a rock: a rucksack.

Not sure why, Trike decided to move more quietly, stepping from rock to rock with a delicacy he had never managed when a tenth his present weight. Eventually he came to the rock and looked down at another pool. A woman squatted beside it, scraping bacteria from the rocks with a spatula and depositing it in sample bottles. He studied her, and Orlandine's memories supplied the data he needed. This volcanologist, Trissa Oclaire, had named the Sambre volcano. She was a bit of an oddity living here in such constant danger, studying a process already studied in much depth for centuries. Some had tried to dissuade her from remaining here but to no avail. As a free woman she could do what she wanted. Apparently, she wanted to study this place – this formation of an island – using technology considered antique centuries before Trike was born.

'Hello,' he said.

She looked up, froze for a second, then shrieked and jumped to her feet. She took off along the side of the pool and jumped onto a rock. By then Trike was in motion too and swiftly coming up behind her. She stepped across a gap, scrambled over a boulder and leapt another gap. Trike saw in perfect detail as her foot came down on brittle stone, and her ankle twisted. He heard with perfect clarity the twang of over-stretched tendons and the crunch of her ankle joint. She yelled and began to topple back, but he caught her by the back of her denim jacket and lifted her to safety, holding her up in front of him.

'I'm not going to hurt you,' he said.

She gaped at him, then said, 'What the fuck are you?'

'What I am is not important,' he replied. 'And now you've hurt yourself.'

He tried to settle her down on her feet. Her ankle gave and she yelled again, reaching out a hand to catch hold of his arm for support. She looked angry – he suspected for having been spooked by him.

'What are you?' she asked again, squeezing his solid arm. 'A robot?'

'No.' Trike turned and looked towards the volcano. 'You'll be all right now?'

'No, of course I won't be all right.' He turned to peer at her and she continued, 'It feels like I've broken my fucking ankle and I need to get back to my base.'

An annoying distraction, but Trike felt he couldn't just walk away. 'Very well, I will carry you.'

'My bag, and my sample bottles,' she stated perfunctorily.

He just stared at her.

'I'll wait here,' she added and, leaning heavily against him, lowered herself to the rock. He continued to stare then abruptly strode away, stepping from rock to rock. He swept up her rucksack and then grabbed the sample bottles by the pool, clumsily capping them before thrusting them inside. A moment later, he was back beside her.

'Which direction?'

She pointed. He handed her the bag, scooped her up and set out at a fast pace, springing from rock to rock.

After a moment she managed, 'So what are you, really?'

'I am a hooper.'

'Last hooper I saw didn't look quite so . . . blue. He also didn't look like he'd just surfaced from some antediluvian religious hell.'

'I have undergone mutations.'

'No shit?'

He eyed her. 'Some hoopers undergo extreme changes. I am also . . . infected with Jain technology.'

'That must be annoying. You anything to do with the furore back at the city?'

'I dealt with the aggressors.'

'Aggressors, were they? I thought things looked a bit messy – some sort of explosion.'

'You don't know?'

51

'I saw the blasts. Looked nasty.'

He felt slightly baffled to be talking to someone so disconnected from recent events. She obviously liked her isolation and did not check into the data sphere.

'Do you wish to know what happened?'

'It'll pass the time while you get me home,' she said, but she didn't sound particularly interested.

Trike moved at speed across the rock field and soon saw her home. The dome of composite had obviously been printed by the ancient colony bot whose remains lay decayed over to one side of it. He reached the door, composite too, and, lowering the woman to her feet, he opened it, then swept her up again and carried her inside.

Within there was a single bed backed against one wall. The seating area had a sofa facing a wide window looking out towards the sea, and in a kitchen area something bubbled in a slow cooker. The exceedingly primitive conditions reminded him of a captain's cabin aboard a Spatterjay sailing ship. He deposited her on the sofa and stepped back, having to duck his head to avoid hitting it on bracing beams across the ceiling.

'In the cabinet over there.' She pointed.

He turned and stepped over to a metal cabinet held shut with some rough string wrapped around the handles. Snapping the string, he opened it, peered inside, then reached in and took out an antique medical kit with a red cross on top. He carried it over to her and put it down on the floor. She had managed to unlace her boot and began easing it off.

'Why aren't you connected into the data sphere?' he asked.

'I like to stay low key.'

She finally got her boot off and then a couple of layers of grubby-looking socks. This exposed her red and swollen ankle.

'Ah fuck,' she said, then flipped up the lid of the first-aid kit.

'But surely you want to know what's happening on your world?'

'Why?'

Trike puzzled over that for a moment.

'For you own safety?' he suggested.

She shrugged. 'There is that.'

She took out a rolled-up gel-tech cast. He had half expected the kit to contain just cloth bandages and other ancient medical tech. After carefully unrolling it, she wrapped it around her ankle. Gazed at it for a moment, then touched the activating pad. The thing shrank around her ankle, forming to it, then changed from white to flesh-coloured. It then must have injected its fibres to input a cocktail of medications including painkillers, because she sighed and leaned back in the sofa.

'But surely you want to know—' he began.

She interrupted, 'Not really. I'm outside. I don't participate and prefer my utterly irresponsible lifestyle.'

'Perhaps you have skills, abilities, some way you can help . . .' He wasn't sure what motivated him to phrase it that way.

She shook her head briefly, as if trying to dismiss some annoying insect. 'I am neither powerful nor effective enough to make a difference.' She looked up at him and added, 'You can go now.'

Trike stared at her. She really stood on the outside and did not want even the responsibility that came with knowing the workings of her world. He turned towards the door, opened it and ducked through.

'Good luck out there,' she called.

'And you,' he replied. He looked up at the volcano, feeling uneasy, out of sorts. It seemed that, just like with the anglerfish, meeting this woman had taught him something else about himself. As he walked, he turned his attention inward. Angel hung there, in pieces, partially melded with his mind.

*Take responsibility* . . . the android's thought ghosted through him.

He acknowledged that with a nod of his nightmare head and allowed the acquisitive urge within in him free rein. The pieces of Angel began to dissolve, their knowledge and experience slotting away in the relevant portions of his consciousness. He could not now pretend that the android lived on in him – he had killed it finally and was certainly responsible for that. By the time he reached the foot of the volcano, Angel had become a dying whisper in his mind, and then nothing.

# 3

*Since well before the prador/human war, rumours abounded that Earth Central had giant warships secreted away in readiness for encounters with hostile alien civilizations, or to deal with civil war in the Polity. Running searches through the AI net, and separate databases, it is possible to find stories of a giant ship whose mass could affect the tides of oceanic worlds it orbited. I found one reference to an action that occurred in the Quarrison Drift – something about an alien entity found frozen in ice and a subsequent attempt (as usual) by Separatists to obtain this creature's technology. It was all heavily redacted and the details impossible to confirm. Data from during the war reveal little more than tantalizing hints of such a ship. The fact that none took part in any major battles has some dismissing it as a myth, while others claim it was being saved for some final defence of Earth. Then, some hundreds of years later, we get confirmation of a ship called the* Cable Hogue. *It doesn't mass enough to change the tides of oceanic worlds, but it does possess a DIGRAW (directed gravity weapon) that could. And it is big – some estimates putting it at two hundred miles in diameter. But whether it was built before the war is still up for debate and no clear answers can be obtained from Earth Central who, even now, does not confirm its existence.*

From 'How It Is' by Gordon

## Diana

Jabro and Seckurg were busy aboard the bridge of the *Cable Hogue* as Diana returned to it. They were further plugged into the ship and its AI, via skeins of optic cables slotted into their skulls, and into the sensory armour they wore. The bridge was also reconfiguring. The walls had moved back, taking the positions of her two crewmen with them, while new consoles and ship interconnects had inserted themselves. Diana immediately connected to Hogue via her implants as she headed for her control chair.

'Why this?' she asked.

'In preparation for new crew,' Hogue replied.

Extra personnel aboard were like the marines aboard other Polity ships here and at Jaskor – in stasis until needed. The ship's original organization was that when new systems came online, new personnel must be put in charge. Hogue could handle everything, including the duties of the crew already here, including Diana, but the idea was to have minds in position and in control should Hogue go down.

'Is this a good idea?' she said, sitting.

'The protocols . . .' Hogue stated blandly.

She leaned back and optic feeds curved round like pincers, inserting their plugs into the sockets in the base of her skull. She mentally linked to data on the ten support crew in storage. Five she had worked with before, the other five were recent additions. She studied specs on the five she did not know. Three were Golem, so reliable, while the other two were augmented humans. She riffled through reports and, of course, they too were very capable people she could rely on. Then another thought occurred to her: was it right to go into a battle that might be the ruination of the *Hogue* with them in stasis and possibly to die there? The grim thought made her feel distinctly uncomfortable.

'Bring them out of stasis,' she said abruptly. 'And ensure that they're up to speed.'

She now ranged out through ship's sensors to view the disposition of both her ship and the fleet. First the *Hogue*. A shifting on its surface signalled movement in its armour, as laminations parted to fill up with impact foam and spider webs of superconductor. Thermocouples were also connecting to cooling tubes for plasma ejection. Whole seas of coolants were moving to tanks scattered throughout the interior and, between two layers of armour, great robots were laying slabs of $CO_2$ ice. She briefly returned her attention to the bridge as the five new crew arrived.

The three men and two women wore a cut-down version of the sensory armour Seckurg had because, being Golem too, they did not need so many links. She acknowledged them all with mental salutes as they moved to their chairs. She would save any talk until the five augmented humans arrived – their revival was taking longer – and went back to studying her ship.

The armour, as it shifted, also revealed further weapons ports. She gazed internally at giant carousels slotting into position behind rail- and coilguns. She observed fusion reactors firing up and the charge bars on laminar storage steadily rising. One of the Golem, an ersatz female by the name of Orien, slotted in, taking oversight of ship's energy supplies. Diana watched her checking things and then, by rerouting some energy feeds, even improving efficiency. Diana wondered if Hogue had deliberately introduced the slight error to give Orien something to do.

Elsewhere Diana watched robots stripping down and rebuilding masers, which she hoped would be able to fire the counteragent to the disruptor beam . . . when they completed it. This became the full province of Jabro, as he routed particle weapons over to another of the Golem. Proving out would have to wait until under fire, which was not ideal. Other weapons – the railguns, coilguns, missiles, mines and bombs – would be the concern of two of the humans yet to arrive. Meanwhile, Diana noted something flagged for her approval. Another of the humans, a man called Dulse, was a gravity specialist but with added knowledge of U-space mechanics. Since the interrelationship between the two had become apparent, Hogue wanted to load his mind with further data. He would be useful in dealing with the weapon that developed a U-twist inside ships. She approved it, though felt uncomfortable about not giving the man a choice. The *Hogue* was preparing to the maximum for conflict.

The other five crewmembers finally arrived, fully clad in sensory armour. She gave them a mental salute too and focused her attention on Dulse. The blond-haired thickset man was rubbing his forehead and frowning. He then reached round and touched the crystal aug behind his left ear, before taking his seat. The loading was obviously causing him some problems but, once his suit plugged in, he would be able to utilize the *Hogue* processing space. She waited until they had all sat down, and watched as they connected optics to their suits, lighting them up like Christmas decorations. They were in. Now distinct minds could control many aspects of the ship. One of them – the woman Alianathon – concentrated totally on the ship's armour, which in the far past would not have required a specialist at all. Diana gave them a moment, then signalled for their attention. All the chairs in the bridge swivelled round to face her.

'You are all up to speed with the situation,' she said.

They signalled agreement, but Dulse added, 'It's a bit of a fucking mess.'

She allowed that since his medical readout showed he had a headache.

'Yes, it is a mess. But we are here to do what we can to correct that. We have to try and stop that ship. You have our weapons data, telemetry and logistics. You understand what we face, but you also understand what we don't know. I expect a protean response in all respects.'

'We know our jobs,' said Alianathon.

'Yes, you do, so I won't lecture you further.'

'Degree of sacrifice before withdrawal?' enquired Orien. 'Just to be clear.'

'Protean,' said Diana. 'We will assess our effectiveness and adjust our response as combat is ongoing.'

'The manoeuvre you used against the Species ship might be required,' said Orien. 'With something very large.'

'Like the *Cable Hogue* itself,' added Alianathon.

Orien was referring to the way they had U-jumped a prador destroyer at the Species ship to destroy it.

'Quite,' said Diana. 'We may have to do that. It is a decision I have given over to Hogue, since it might happen very fast.'

'Maybe too fast for ejection,' interjected Jabro.

Diana smiled. 'We all know what we signed up for, and the risks we face.'

Most expressions were grim, but two were smiling. Old humans near their ennui barrier. But no disagreement arose from people prepared to make that final sacrifice if necessary. They would not be here if they were not ready.

They now lay just minutes away from contact with the advancing fingers of the Jain cloud. Its forefront extended over a million miles ahead of the Jain ship, which seemed to be taking its time. The objects that formed the cloud were becoming much clearer. The larger bacilliforms – things like bacteria a hundred feet long – were heating up, an orange glow emitting from their hollow interiors. The knots, like masses of intestine a few yards across and rendered in blue metal, were accelerating ahead of these. Gathering data, Hogue squirted over an analysis and cleaned up imagery on an event occurring far back in the cloud. It had encompassed an asteroid and a multitude of Jain mechanisms had fallen on it like macrophages attacking a bacterium. Little remained of the asteroid now – converted into even more mechanisms to add to the cloud. The damned things could feed and reproduce. Diana felt a sinking sensation in her gut as she dismissed the analysis and concentrated her assessment on the leading front.

The knot things, though fast, did not appear to field any distance weapons, while the bacilliforms projected an ion beam. In a moment, she understood. The latter cut holes in defences while the former aimed to get to the ships concerned. Were the knots bombs? No, a replay of their previous encounter showed none had exploded violently enough to be carrying antimatter or chemical explosives, while spectral analysis of the explosions had revealed no fissile materials. Most likely they aimed to attach to a ship and grow, spreading invasive Jain tech through it.

'It begins,' said the prador commander Orlik over their link.

The bacilliforms had started firing. Orange ion beams stabbed out from the leading wave, crossing the intervening distance in six seconds. These splashed on the concerted hardfield defence of the fleets, creating a great glowing fog bank of ionized gas.

'No massed firings,' Diana broadcast. 'Tactical updates being transmitted.'

'Be sure of your targets, boys,' Orlik replied.

The more advanced Polity dreadnoughts fired first, shortly followed by Orlik's reavers. Single railgun shots zipped towards where at least three objects lined up. This put the chances of a hit at over eighty per cent, even if targets managed to shift course in the seconds it would take for the slugs to arrive. Diana watched the first impacts on the leading bacilliforms. Of a hundred and twenty single shots, all but one found its primary target. The only one that missed had been so accurately placed it passed straight through the hollow core of a bacilliform without touching it, then struck another one lying a hundred miles behind.

'They're not even dodging,' said Orlik.

'Maybe they just don't need to,' interjected Jabro.

He was right. Hogue loaded estimates into Diana's mind. The combined human and prador fleet simply did not have sufficient munitions to take out everything in this cloud, even if every shot slammed home.

'Arrowhead formation,' she stated, trying to stay logical. '*Hogue* to lead.'

The fleets began reforming to Hogue's tactical updates. The *Cable Hogue* moved to the fore, with the rest of the ships forming up behind. The *Kinghammer* moved in over to the right while the heavier, more modern Polity dreadnoughts shifted to the left. Diana watched this for a moment, took a breath.

'Maximum acceleration,' she ordered.

## Gemmell

Gemmell glanced at Ruth and did not like the protectiveness he felt. That wasn't good when, as her commander, he should see her as a military asset which might at some point be disposable. She stood among the rest of the squad, clad in body armour and sporting a pulse rifle. She had asked why she wasn't issued with a heavy-duty particle weapon, like the one Baylock carried, or the weapon Trantor held, with assist from his armoured suit – a thing capable of firing armour-piercing explosive flechettes. Gemmell had told her what he told other new recruits who asked the same question, 'You're new and on probation, and we don't want any friendly-fire screw-ups, especially today.'

He swung his attention away from her to the enclave prador. The ten armoured creatures had gathered in a tight C facing towards the centre of the field, across the acres of stubble. The harvester, which had started its work some time in the night when he had chosen this area, was eating up the last strip of modified linseed – sucking in stalks with seed pods the size of apples and spewing out dampened lines of finely ground chaff behind. While he watched, it completed its run and headed through a gate in the distant tea-oak hedge – a necessary wind-break here. The field was a massive open area larger than anything in the city but, as required, close to the city, and it now lay clear. Gemmell heard thunder and looked up.

The big ship visible in the sky had speared out the orange ribbed flames of steering thrusters. Thus positioned, its descent speed increased and it expanded alarmingly. This one of Orlandine's ships bore the shape of a thick coin a mile across, with an underslung crew compartment jutting at the fore and big tug-format fusers at the rear. She used these vehicles to ferry materials from various mines, processing plants and factories, to her construction sites – generally the next platform being built or, as had recently been the case, a runcible gate. As the thing threw its shadow across them all, it displaced air volume to rouse a wind papered with linseed chaff. About a mile above, it folded out landing feet, each larger than a prador and obviously suitable for the soft ground. Yes, Orlandine was prepared. He wondered at his surprise when she had told him she already had a store of ground-based weaponry in the event of Jain tech reaching this world.

The ship finally landed, eerily quiet on grav and, as that switched off, its feet sank deep into the ground. It sat before Gemmell like a massive water storage tank up on the scaffolds of its legs. Power hummed, and movement inside issued clangs and booms as the legs adjusted and ramps dropped down in its under-shadows. He eyed the nearest ramp. Lights came on inside the ship and an object began to descend, hovering just above the ramp. He gave a tight smile of recognition. The square barrel of a combined coil and propellant launcher protruded from the octagonal block of a turret. On one side of this protruded a rail bead gun and on the other a particle cannon, while out of its skirt it could fire antipersonnel lasers and machineguns. He had asked for hover tanks and he was getting hover tanks. But he was also getting something else he had not requested.

Objects coming down another ramp drew into sight. These treaded vehicles, their upper bodies standing tall, bore an almost humanoid appearance: Gatling cannons protruding where arms might have been, a head turret was a particle cannon, lasers peeked from ports in the skirt. Gemmell pondered on how the Polity tanks resembled prador, while the prador implant tanks resembled humans – one of the strange dichotomies of warfare. Next, ranging out behind their implant tanks trudged heavily armed and armoured prador.

'Our even newer recruits,' commented Trantor.

Gemmell gave a brief nod of agreement. Orlandine had informed him that she had the weapons he required but that the ship would be stopping to make a pick-up out in orbit. He shouldn't have been surprised really. The Polity presence down here heavily outnumbered the prador of the enclave so it was inevitable that the prador above should offer to send soldiers to *assist* in the defence of the world.

Trantor moved up beside him. 'Are they Guard?'

Gemmell eyed the prador as they moved out into the light. Generally, the king's family concealed their mutations inside their armour. But the Guard did tend to be a bit more creative in the decoration of that armour. All sorts appeared here. The first he studied closely had yellow and purple camo patterns, the second pure metallic blue, while a third pure white with red lines towards the edges and joints. But plenty here also wore standard prador armour of plain jade and black.

'A mixture, I think,' he replied.

As they proceeded from the ship's shadow they lined up in ranks and, with the implant tanks behind them, made a formidable sight. Gemmell glanced over to the enclave prador then continued, 'Get those tanks on their way. Two-thirds to the southern cities as agreed. Distribute the armament as well.' Now heavily laden grav-sleds slid down the ramps.

'Time to see if they'll listen?' wondered Trantor.

'Yeah, it's time for that.'

Gemmell headed directly towards Croos, the ambassador of the enclave, recognizable by his satin pink and black armour, lacking visible weapons. Croos was facing off against another prador of a similarly large size who wore matt black armour and seemed to bristle with more guns than legs.

'Switch to Anglic translation,' instructed Croos as Gemmell approached.

The one in black swivelled to face Gemmell. Checking the data sphere, he learned that this 'Vreen' had come from one of the reavers, but nothing more beyond that. However, as Vreen came from a reaver and seemed to be in charge of the new force here, he thought him likely one of the Guard.

'Commander Gemmell,' Vreen said. 'There are one hundred and twenty of us. As per your instructions, I will send ninety to the southern cities. I have uploaded all contact details to the ECS data sphere and each individual will be providing constant telemetry.'

Taken aback for a moment Gemmell asked, 'Transport?'

The black-armoured prador hummed and rose three feet off

the ground, shifted to one side on steering thrusters, then back again and settled.

'Transport will not be a problem.'

Gemmell nodded. 'Some diplomacy will be required when you liaise with the small human police and military forces in those cities.'

'We will not eat anyone,' said Vreen.

Gemmell coughed to stop laughing, then emitted a long strangled snort.

'That does not translate?' Vreen enquired.

Croos interjected, 'They will adhere to your plan completely and they can update tactically only marginally slower than your troops. They are aware that their role is to prevent civilian casualties, with the proviso that some casualties might be inevitable if the primary purpose is to prevent invasive Jain tech taking hold.'

Gemmell processed that. It was pretty much the instruction he had given his own troops, but still he found no reassurance here. Croos must have made some communication he did not hear because Vreen abruptly turned and moved away. There were other signals too, because prador began rising from the ground and bunching together in ordered groups.

'There are no other orders I should know about?' he asked Croos.

'If we had secret orders I think it unlikely I would tell you,' Croos replied.

Gemmell grinned, gave the prador a fist-to-chest salute, and headed back to his own troops. He finally came up to stroll beside Ruth as she guided a grav-sled across the field towards the road. He did it casually, while aware of the inspection from the likes of Baylock and Trantor.

'Did our situation just improve or get worse?' she asked.

He looked up as one group of prador jetted away overhead. He shrugged. 'We won't know until we see what the accretion disc brings.'

## Orlandine

Orlandine entered her apartment and scanned across the wreckage. Her erstwhile lover and would-be assassin Tobias hadn't done this and for a moment it baffled her, until she saw the ridged marks across the walls. So, Clade units had been in here and ripped everything apart. Did they have a purpose in doing so or was this just an act of wanton malice? Had the Clade been searching for something? She studied the damage, mentally linked to local computing and saw that no attempts had been made to glean data. Malice, then. Would it be nice therefore, to be in at the kill when the attack ship turned swarm AI, *Obsidian Blade*, caught up with the remainder of the Clade and finally destroyed it? The human response would have been, Yes, that would be good. She found nothing like that inside her as she stepped over the debris.

Out on the balcony, on its wall, were the marks from the weapon Tobias had used against her. She thought about him, pulling up everything in her memory with perfect recall. His body had been found, but so mashed as to be unrecognizable and unrecoverably dead. She tried to feel something about that – anger, regret, sadness, anything – but again could find no real response. If she wished, she could alter her neurochem, tweak her adrenals and cortisol, tinker with this and that inside this avatar to give it, and thence her whole self, an emotional response. If she wished, she could have this avatar sobbing on the stained floor. But it would be a completely pointless exercise.

Why deliberately introduce faults to give the facsimile of losing control?

Standing at the balcony wall she looked up at the sky and pondered on Dragon. The creature had been her constant companion here and around the accretion disc for a long time. It had in some way sensed the danger of her deploying the Harding black hole against the Jain tech in the disc and had, while seeking information on the threat they faced, nearly been destroyed by the AI Wheel and the wormship it controlled. It had returned to bring her Trike and Cog and otherwise intervene in its usual oblique and often unknowable manner. Now it was gone again, intent on further opaque manipulations. Did she miss Dragon? No, not in any emotional sense even if she did reinstate human feelings. She did, however, miss that entity's power and effectiveness, but must now do without them.

She transferred her attention down to survey the city, visually at first, and then through multiple sensors. She saw Gemmell's preparations. She saw civilians being herded to areas he could better protect or, making the choice that was their right, to just stay in their homes. She tracked supply lines, observed robots repairing infrastructure, transports bringing in food from the croplands, water mains being repaired, power lines reconnected. Everything was as it should be, and so was she. She turned to look at her apartment once again, then abruptly marched back across it to the door. Nothing remained for her here and, for now, she preferred the roof. Soon she, or rather this avatar and the device up there, would leave that too because she did not need an anchor into a past that was all but irrelevant. Focus on the present and the future. Focus on Cog, and Trike, who would soon meet, and whom she could deploy as other tools at her disposal.

## Cog

Dust blasted up around the grav-car as it settled on the horizontal slab Cog found nearest to the top of the Sambre volcano. He opened the door and stepped quickly out, moving to the edge and raising a monocular to his eyes. A boulder field lay below, cut through with glowing strips of lava. For a moment, he could not locate what he had seen from the air, then he found Trike. The big blue man was making his way out of field, in no particular hurry, over to the right. Cog lowered the monocular and studied his surroundings further.

A thick column of smoke spewed from the caldera above. Lava issued over to his left from where it had broken through the rim, while the slab he stood on vibrated as if from a huge engine running below. The slope to his right wasn't too steep but certainly some scrambling would be involved. He should be able to reach Trike before the man got to his destination, assuming, of course, that was the top of the volcano. Cog sighed and began to turn back to the car, when the ground shifted under his feet. He paused for a second as, with a heavy thump, a splodge of hot lava hit the vehicle's roof. A glance up revealed numerous black dots descending towards him and he quickly ran back to the car and threw himself inside.

The lava fall lasted a good ten minutes and then steadily died off. Cog got out again and went round to the car's boot to open it. He briefly studied the weapons he had brought, then turned his attention to another item Orlandine had provided. He hauled it out and unrolled it.

The bright white hotsuit, with integral boots and helmet, also filtered and cooled the air. The volcano emitted poison gas and pyroclastic flows. Those usually regular emissions came from one place on the other side, but they could issue over this side too.

Sure, he was a near-indestructible Old Captain, but even his kind could die in a place like this. He stripped off his boots and pulled the suit on over his clothes. As he tossed his boots into the back of the car, he looked at the weapons again. He'd thought about disabling Trike but now realized he shouldn't have even brought them. He had no idea what might halt the man, if anything at all. Slamming the boot lid, he headed towards the edge of the slab then out onto the slope.

The surface drifts of pumice and flaky scree sitting between channels of lava, like tree roots, first appeared easy, but soon turned out otherwise. Forging through it was like wading through snow, and it tended to give and slide under his feet, while air pockets filled the lava, which shattered like shell ice. Cog kept going, his hooper-strength legs driving him. A few hundred yards out, he checked through his monocular again and saw Trike some hundreds of yards ahead and nearly level with him. Trike paused to gaze back at him, then continued upwards. Cog altered his course upslope, hoping to intercept the man before he reached the top. Shortly he realized he was just not going fast enough to keep up with Trike's long stride. He speeded up, but the surface promptly gave below him and he ended up face down and sliding backwards in a fall of rubble. Finally, he jolted to a halt against a mass of lava like a pile of grey guts and covered his head until the fall had ceased.

'Bugger,' he said.

Cog dug and wiggled his way out of mounded scree. When he searched around, he located Trike far up the slope, nearly at the top of the volcano. He had no chance of intercepting him now. Swearing under his breath, he still continued to trudge up after the man. A few hundred yards higher, the loose scree thinned out, but the slope became steeper and he needed to use his hands to climb, while Trike moved out of sight above. At length Cog reached up to grip an edge and hauled himself out on top. He now stood on the rim of the volcano. A gentle slope ran down from him to the inner edge and the glare from the boiling lava below. His suit threw up an alert in his visor. The temperature here stood well above that required to barbecue glisters. However, it did not seem to be bothering Trike overly much.

The man stood right at the edge, the glare silhouetting him as he gazed down into the inferno. Cog trudged forwards, noting that some areas of the rock here were glowing. His suit noted this fact too and gave him a further warning about how long it could maintain its integrity.

'Thinking about jumping in?' Cog enquired.

Trike turned to him. Wisps of smoke were rising from the front of his body. 'It was a consideration.'

'Seems a bit of an extreme response to marital break-up.'

'What about murder?'

'Angel, you mean?'

'Yes. I would be perfectly in tune with Polity policy regarding murderers.'

'Well, murderers don't get a second chance, but things are a little murky as far as Angel is concerned. He himself was effectively under a sentence of death.'

'But he was innocent,' said Trike. 'He was mentally enslaved and yet I killed him when he was free. He was innocent.'

'So your answer to all that is to jump into a volcano?' The conversation had an odd twist, Cog felt. Trike was talking about real, horrific events but without heat, as if simply engaging in a discussion of logic.

'That intention was there,' Trike replied, 'but as I stand here I realize that would not be effective.'

Cog moved up beside him and peered over the edge into the mouth of a furnace. If he fell in, he knew that death would not be immediate. His suit would hold out for maybe half a minute then his virus-toughened body of a hooper would probably last just as long again. It would not be a pleasant death.

'It wouldn't be quick,' he said looking back at Trike again.

Then he noticed something else. The Jain veins and fibres spread all over Trike's body were shifting and pure white, as if they were glowing.

'It wouldn't happen at all,' Trike replied.

'What do you mean?'

'It's all there for us to see and understand,' said Trike. 'The Spatterjay virus works to ensure the survival of its host, while Jain tech is an energy-vore, and both of these are inextricably linked in me. Feed Jain tech sufficient energy and materials and it grows. Think of that Jain soldier from Cyberat. At the accretion disc, it fell onto the planetoid Musket Shot and there Orlandine's weapons platforms boiled it. But it just grew bigger and stronger and incorporated the materials around it.'

'But feed Jain tech enough energy, in the way of a particle beam or a CTD, for example, and you destroy it,' Cog argued.

'Yes, but not in this case.'

'What would happen, then?'

Trike waved a hand towards the caldera. 'It would burn away my nominally human body, it would burn away the virus, but the Jain tech would grow and record across everything destroyed. It would then crawl out of the pit and I would still exist.'

'You're shitting me,' said Cog.

'She knows.' Trike waved his hand towards the fire and smoke belching from below.

A shape formed in the cloud and resolved as Orlandine's face – a hologram perhaps projected from the city.

'He is right,' said Orlandine. 'But he is also wrong.'

'What do you mean?' Trike asked.

She smiled. 'You understand what I mean, but I'll explain it anyway. You already know that the Jain tech reacts to you at an unconscious level – it reacts to the whole of your mind, not just those thoughts which bubble to the surface, to your conscious. It reacted before, for example, to your madness and your unreasonable detestation of Angel.'

'So I can blame that now?'

'We are all slaves, Trike, in one way or another.'

He shrugged, then said, 'I still don't see how that relates here.'

'If you truly wanted to die, it would let you die. You don't want to die.'

'How are you so sure?'

'You are not allowing me full contact with you, but I can observe. See your reaction to those fish under the sea. See your reaction to our local volcanologist. You have not given up on this world. It's just a thought you've been toying with.'

'She said she is neither powerful enough nor effective enough to make a difference,' Trike stated.

'Yes, she did,' Orlandine agreed.

'So what do you want?'

'Open to me . . .'

Trike dipped his head for a moment, then raised it. 'I see.' He continued to gaze down into the fire.

'It's not for you,' she said. 'But perhaps, now I understand, it will be a final option for me. A final defence.'

'Would you ever come back from it?' Trike asked.

'I don't know.' Orlandine flickered out.

Trike turned from the edge and stepped away. Cog hurriedly followed him. His suit was redlining now and he was starting to feel a little frazzled.

'What the hell was all that about?'

'Orlandine no longer requires an organic human body, though

she is running one. She's essentially AI crystal and Jain tech. If she tapped into a sufficient power source, well . . .' He gestured back to the fire. 'Who knows what she could do?'

That all seemed a bit crazy, but then he had seen her apparently die and then spread as a Jain growth throughout the Ghost Drive Facility. He turned away, thoughts churning frantically as he made a connection to something she had said earlier. Jain tech reacted to a person's unconscious mind. Who was to say it did not also influence it? What might happen if Orlandine did tap into something powerful, and grow? He already had his doubts about her and feared what she might become. It seemed to him that a visit to the Client could be a good idea. Suddenly he was glad to be heading away from this world.

'You should have brought your ship,' said Trike.

'What?'

Trike pointed down at the grav-car. 'That will require some modification if I am to fit inside.'

'You can sit on the roof,' Cog replied, and began making his way down.

## Orlik

Orlik had once been a rebel seeking readmittance into the Prador Kingdom by serving as a 'deniable asset' in the Graveyard working for the king. He had been integral to identifying the gathering threat and nearly lost everything. But now he was captain of the largest prador ship ever, the *Kinghammer*, and commander of the prador fleet allied with Diana Windermere's. He scanned his sanctum with one stalked eye and wondered just how long his promotion would last.

A member of his Guard crew was dragging a chunk of mangled

wreckage to the open door while another ran a cleaner and polisher over the floor behind, leaving it pristine.

As the door closed behind them, they left no sign of the previous damage, but there were plenty of repairs elsewhere. Orlik focused for a second on the drone body of Sprag, clinging to the crane arm above him like a particularly ugly stick insect. This version of Sprag did not move, however, since the drone's mind now ran the ship.

Orlik next ranged out through the *Kinghammer*. Working hard and efficiently, his crew had managed to integrate their efforts with those of the ship's robots. Wreckage they had earlier grabbed they were still running through internal furnaces, forges and auto-factories and swiftly knitting the materials from these into the hull. The gaping hole in the ship had all but closed, and they had repaired much of the internal damage. Soon they would be moving to their assigned positions – mainly as repair and internal defence teams, ready with patches and structural beams, as well as with weapons, should the ship suffer Jain-tech incursions. Now he fully focused through external sensors.

Closer to the Jain cloud, the delay between firing and impact dropped to milliseconds. The intensity of it had increased and target destruction sat at ninety-eight per cent. More of the bacilliforms had begun firing too – orange beams stabbing across vacuum and splashing on hardfields. As yet, there seemed no coordination to the response. Linked to all the other ships in the fleet via Sprag, but in full control of his own, Orlik kept up to speed with the developing and changing battle plan.

'There's a lot of them,' he commented.

'Hence the alterations we keep seeing,' said Sprag. 'We don't want to waste our shots.'

Diana had allowed Orlik a full link into her bridge. More humans and Golem occupied it now – apparently pulled out of storage. Putting crew in storage was an idea he might look into later if they survived this. Certainly, while he and Sprag ran the *Kinghammer* many of his own crew were either redundant or being given make-work. The exchanges in Diana's bridge were fast and staccato, while the crew also communicated at the mental level, so he did not quite understand it all. He was reliant on Sprag for this, and on trust.

'Full coordination of fire,' he heard Diana say, 'and conserve. Do we have a solution on their manoeuvrability and speed?'

'We do,' replied Seckurg.

'Alianathon and Orien, liaise on maximum conservation of energy.' She then addressed the Golem running missiles, railguns and coilguns, 'You too, Ranick, but we need to save the big CTDs for the main ship.'

'I've been updating the tactical plan,' said Alianathon. 'It depends on whether you think we can afford to scrap hardfield projectors and take some hits on the armour. It also depends on how much you want to hold back for the main ship.'

'Give me scenarios,' Diana ordered and leaned back, closing her eyes.

Meanwhile Orlik observed the fleet strikes: railgun shots slamming into the bacilliforms, directed on those who were first in a line of targets along the course of each missile. Some of the other things, like clumps of metallic guts, flashed out too when struck by high-intensity BIC laser shots from the Polity destroyers. These were brief stabs, but sometimes more than one.

'Why on such low power? Those lasers are capable of much more,' he asked Sprag.

'Test firing,' Sprag replied. 'The gunners and ship AIs are trying to find the minimum energy levels to destroy their targets.'

'I see,' said Orlik, not sure that he did. Finally, he relented and asked, 'Why?'

Sprag made a snorting sound – one she had only been capable of emulating when she had been a drone, but somehow ridiculous now she was a ship AI.

'Ferocity of combatants, tricky tactics or clever manoeuvring are all irrelevant at the moment. Resources are what count. Quite simple, really. We haven't got the watts or the missiles to destroy everything in that cloud even if the bastards queue up neatly for us.'

Looking at the data, Orlik realized he had been in denial. He understood then the danger of letting AIs, and others, do your thinking for you. He shrugged on his saddle control and really got a grip on the tactical situation. They had to use as little armament and energy as possible to get through the cloud to the Jain ship. He had no doubt that Diana must be looking at scenarios dependent on how much damage they could take. That included how many ships they were prepared to lose. His prador paranoia kicked in.

'We'll dismiss the last four options,' he heard Diana say. 'We can afford to soak up weapons damage but we cannot afford impact of Jain tech on our hulls. I guarantee that a lot of that stuff out there is for sequestration.'

'These,' interjected Hogue. 'They are coiled up like jellyfish stings – primed to break open and spread.' The image the AI put up on the main screen in the bridge of the *Cable Hogue*, and doubtless projected into the minds of the crew there, came up for Orlik's mental inspection: one of the gut things, one of those metallic knots.

'Solve for that,' said Diana. 'Not one of those things gets near us. Nor do we want to be hitting substantial debris from them.'

'Quantify "substantial",' said a crewmember.

'Use defence sphere parameters.'

'Vapour, then,' said another.

Only half listening, Orlik began thinking about what might be acceptable damage and to whom. 'I want everything checked,' he said to Sprag. 'I want to know that we are taking the best options for the whole fleet and not just for the Polity ships.'

'You're thinking that maybe just prador ships will be the first to be sacrificed?' Sprag enquired.

'You know how Earth Central operates,' said Orlik.

'Certainly do,' said Sprag. 'That's why I've been checking and double checking right from the start. The only calculations thus far that might work more against us than the Polity ships involve some of our older dreadnoughts. But that's just tactical reality. And then there's this . . .' Sprag highlighted something in the plan.

Orlik studied the data long and hard. It was a fallback if things went badly for them, which it seemed highly likely they would. It detailed how the *Cable Hogue* possessed some serious, multiple U-space drives that could push through disrupted U-space to fly it at least some way clear of the cloud. The big ship also had large internal spaces into which destroyers, dreadnoughts and attack ships could fit. He then began to notice something odd about this plan because most of the ships chosen to go into those internal spaces were prador. It was all speculative, and dependent on which ships survived to get to the *Hogue* and, of course, whether or not the *Hogue* survived. Still . . . mostly prador ships.

'I don't get it,' said Orlik. 'Or are we seeing this because it is a very unlikely option, a way to apparently give us something while giving us nothing at all?'

'No,' said Sprag. 'It is based on the maximum number of lives saved whether they be prador, human or AI. Polity ships have very small crews compared to ours. One reaver has a crew of a hundred while an equivalent Polity dreadnought has, including stored marines, less than fifty.'

'So it is apparently fair . . .'

'Apparently.'

Now past the leading edge of the cloud, hellfire filled vacuum all around. Orlik could feel thumps and vibrations telegraphed up through his saddle control as the *Kinghammer* took shots on its hardfields and replied with railgun slugs. He noted the mechanisms making a further response. The things they had passed were decelerating, while those out to either side were turning in towards the two fleets, or rather, the fleet. Its defence boundary, shaped like a teardrop around the ships, gradually extended as estimates on how fast the attackers behind might be able to catch up were factored in. He understood the subtle calculations involved – whether the energy used to destroy a bacilliform was more or less than the energy used to stop the beam blasts the enemy could deliver, while the gut things were being fried only if hardfield failure might let them through to ships' hulls.

Ahead, sensors penetrated deeper and deeper into the cloud towards the misty bulk of the Jain ship as it became steadily more visible. Then, drawing a slow line through vacuum, a disruptor beam speared out from that bulk. It seemed the one directing it did not bother about what might be in the way because it touched three bacilliforms on its course and they unravelled. One moment complete and solid, the next they exploded into great woolly tangles of threads that began to powder away.

'Jabro?' asked Diana.

'Hitting it,' the man replied.

Orlik's tactical feed showed him the man Jabro tracking the disruptor beam with a virtual warfare maser and, for a moment, it had an effect. The beam frayed and writhed, but it wasn't enough. It struck a hardfield, which bruised, and then the beam punched through to hit the second field of a three-field defence.

Orlik observed one of his reavers ejecting the molten remains of a generator. As the beam broke through, the imploder already in place before the last field, detonated. This created a momentary sensor black spot, and then the beam unravelled all the way back to the clearer bulk of the Jain ship, from which now a hundred such beams issued.

'U-twist,' Sprag stated.

A reaver, which had been integral in that first defence, jerked and twisted and a blast opened up right in its centre, cutting it in half. The attack seemed spiteful to Orlik as he felt the shockwave hit the *Kinghammer*. He watched falling debris smoking in collision lasers and some of it striking the armour. A disruptor beam punched through shields, causing burning generators to streak across vacuum. The beam hit a Polity destroyer, going into its nose like a high-speed drill. Then, bending like a whippy branch, it broke out of that ship's nose to go on to hit a squat old-style prador dreadnought. There it struck a hardfield, cut through and hit another. Orlik watched dumbly, waiting for the inevitable strike, but the disruptor flickered, writhed and frayed. From a place some thousand miles out, it finally flew apart and dispersed. The effect travelled in both directions, eating up the beam to the hardfield even as it collapsed. Orlik tracked this as it went back towards the Jain ship and felt some satisfaction at seeing an explosion there at its point of departure.

'Got it!' yelled Jabro.

Flagged tactical update: a program to run through induction warfare beams, whether masers or laser. Further updates swiftly ensued as Polity AIs took the information and ran with it. There might be a way of running this through hardfields too. But payback came a second later. Seven attack ships, one after the other, exploded. Next went three dreadnoughts and through the hole in the defence, bacilliforms probed. But this time their attack cut harsh blue lines across vacuum – particle beams, burning across armour.

'Go for rain!' Diana ordered.

'This early?' Orlik enquired.

'May not be effective on the main ship, but the cloud objects have no fields,' she replied tersely, even as twenty dreadnoughts coilgunned out a swarm of missiles.

More U-twists, more ships just detonating. Appalling destruction surrounded Orlik as chunks of ships hurtled past, sometimes thumping on hardfields which flashed into existence, and then ricocheting away. There was hope because now he could see disruptor beam after beam fraying and coming apart, as well as further explosions on the Jain ship. But they were small on such immensity – like bomb blasts on a continent or brief motes of light on the skin of some huge beast.

Flagged update again: possible U-twist defence. Already ships were jumping specially programmed USER mines into U-space – a hugely wasteful tactic because the already-present disruption threw out half of them. Orlik saw mines detonating in vacuum – a brief flash of intense X-rays after a gravity pulse. A prador destroyer crumpled at one end like a can under high pressure. Analysis: no way to know where the bounce-outs might occur and that one had occurred inside the ship.

'How does that work?' asked Orlik, thoroughly within his weapons system and opening up with particle beams. He felt dissatisfied hitting marks strictly to tactics, annoyed at having his targets and energy levels dictated by computer program.

'The disruption pulse throws them off target,' Sprag replied. 'The enemy is having enough trouble targeting as it is with present disruption, else we would all be floating scrap by now.'

'We're winning,' said Orlik.

'Hasty assessment,' Sprag replied.

The swarm of missiles wove through the cloud, falling towards the Jain ship. They were cued for impact detonation, and it impressed Orlik how they managed to avoid the objects in the cloud. Then the first of them hit. A flash of light lit up space. In safety mode, sensors blanked for a second. As they came back online, Orlik watched a hemisphere expand – a plasma blast front. Where it hit Jain objects, it bucked them and left them twisted and pouring hot vapour. Further blasts ensued and gradually filled in the picture. CTDs, rated in the megatons, were detonating on the curved surface of a giant globular hardfield enclosing the Jain ship. He had come to understand the limit on how much energy such a field could transfer and store in an underlying U-space twist. Calculations ran fast. They just might be able to push that field to overload with all their weapons. And now, with blast fronts tearing out into the cloud and destroying the mass of smaller attackers, they had a chance to use those weapons.

'We can do this!' he exclaimed, only just realizing how fatalistic he had been about this attack run.

'Uhuh,' said Sprag, highlighting something for his attention.

Ships, clinging to the main Jain ship like giant isopods – bigger than all the vessels in the fleet bar the *Cable Hogue*, and of equivalent size to the *Kinghammer* – were breaking away from the mother vessel and accelerating, directly towards him.

# 4

*Dragon is a dangerous enemy or an unreliable friend, a wise god or a cosmic joker. So much has been recorded about this entity, and what it has said, it's really difficult to decide. I have written a lot about Dragon and, when I can be bothered to check through the stories and speculations I've included in 'How It Is', I find I've often contradicted myself. One thing I have learned through writing on many subjects is how careful one must be with hearsay, and how necessary it is to return to proven fact. One must step back and take a long hard look at what has gone before. But in doing so, I see that Dragon is all of the above and more. We have fallen foul of the human propensity to codify, list, describe and name things. Understandably it is one of our many attempts to get to grips with the reality around us. Unfortunately, it also makes us blind to anything outside of the label we have applied. Because we must realize that Dragon is not just Dragon. Even whether it was a discrete entity when first found on Aster Colora is debatable. When its spheres separated, it certainly became four entities. And, just like the subminds of an AI, its parts have gone their separate ways.*

From 'How It Is' by Gordon

## The Client

Barbed spikes suddenly stabbed from the locking mechanism up inside the Client's tentacles. They damaged data pathways but bound to many more. The connections firmed and a wave of computer life swarmed through the link – a whole data ecology from viruses up through worms to ever more complicated pseudo-life. She tried to tear her tentacles free, but even as she began to pull, a virus hit her nervous system and paralysed it. It was fast, horribly fast, and she realized the greater danger just a second too late.

In order to process the ostensible code of the locking mech-anism, she had opened up bandwidth from her remote to the weapons platform. The swarm flooded through this into her systems before she could close them down. She began fighting, releasing counteragents and datavores, killer programs and traps. Areas which were completely overrun she partitioned and wiped, angered by the loss of stored data in them. Just as it had para-lysed her remote to keep the link open, it now seized control of her transceivers so she could not shut them down. She made them her prime target: isolating them, cutting power sources and, in some cases, ordering internal weapons to open fire on them. The platform flickered with the blasts of antipersonnel pulse cannons, energy surges blowing out transformers, lasers cutting through optic feeds.

Even as she fought, she modelled and ran prognostics on the swarm and realized a further danger just in time. She sent the order to her attack pods to close down completely – to accept no data links from the platform at all, or from each other. All but two went completely dead. After a short pause, while the swarm did its work, the two lit up their steering thrusters and fusion drives, and turned towards the platform. They began firing at once – full spreads of railgun slugs and particle beams searing across vacuum. She responded without hesitation, U-jumping two missiles out. The two attack pods burst into balls of flame as her shields stopped their railgun slugs, particle beams and then two waves of debris. If she'd had any doubt about the hostility of these programs, it was gone now.

The fight continued internally. As she steadily shut down transceivers, it reduced the pressure, and she managed to isolate the main infections inside her. Her counteragents did their work, steadily killing these, but still she had to destroy storage and processing to root it all out. Finally, just one transceiver remained open, linking her to the remote. The data from that she ran through a filtration system, hardwiring access and preventing spread. This actually enabled her to keep her connection with it open. But even with the filtering, she found this part of her had become something else. She remained connected to it but the thing had morphed into a discrete personality. And she had no control over it.

The remote disconnected its tentacles and coiled them up behind its head. Its and her intention – the impetus was blurred – made it fling itself across the doors. It came down solidly on the attack pod, docked to the doorframe and inserted its tentacles. Though she had shut down the transceiver of that pod, it was not immune to a hard link. It detached from the doorframe, fired up steering thrusters to bring its nose out towards open space and ignited its main drive. It shot out of the entrance tunnel then turned, accelerating hard towards Weapons Platform Mu.

From the platform, the Client watched the thing as it approached, while also gazing at the platform from the remote. It began firing its railguns and then its particle weapons. Hardfield impacts lit up vacuum but this time she hesitated. Could there not be some way of rescuing this? She tried feeding her counteragents into the remote and could feel them working, could feel them reclaiming this part of herself, but reality impinged. She did not have the time, since the attack pod was just a minute away from slamming into the platform's hardfields. She regretfully loaded a U-jump missile and fired it.

Nothing happened. The remote had activated the attack pod's bounce gate. She dropped shields and fired big particle beam arrays, like glowing tower blocks rearing up from the platform. Ten beams intersected on the pod. Its hardfields englobed it, held for a short while, then collapsed. Momentarily a blackened sphere existed then exploded in a plasma flash. Even though this took just a second, she felt part of herself die and it wasn't like the shedding of one of her body units. She felt pain and real death, and did not relish the experience.

The Client turned her attention to the infection in the processing of that final transceiver, managing to kill it off without destroying the device. Once done, she began formatting suspect areas and running hard diagnostic search engines through every bit of processing in the weapons platform to ensure she had missed nothing. Then she set the repair robots to work, while dispatching heavy handler EVA units out into space to retrieve attack pods with which she could no longer communicate. As these sped out, she considered what had happened.

The response from the ship's core to her attempt to enter had been hostile, very much so, but she did not read any intelligence behind it. It had been like an autogun programmed to respond in a particular manner. If there had been intelligence there, surely that intelligence would have recognized . . . Suddenly she understood. It had responded to the format of her remote. It had responded to something that had tried to get in *just like a Jain would have tried*. In any further attempts, she must use something completely different.

The EVA units – twenty in all – closed grippers on twenty attack pods and began hauling them back to the platform, while repairs inside were going quickly and bringing downed systems back online. A detector array, whose processing had been invaded, immediately reported the approach of a ship under fusion drive. Suddenly, painfully aware of at least a degree of vulnerability without her pods, she wondered if either Orlandine or the fleets around Jaskor had chosen this moment to attack. Then she dismissed the idea after inspecting the small vessel. She recognized it as the ship belonging to the Old Captain Cogulus Hoop.

'What do you want?' she asked via laser com.

The captain's visage appeared in her mind and she studied it. Cog smiled genially. 'Orlandine sent me.'

'Why?'

'Seems she wanted me as an ambassador on the spot,' Cog replied.

The Client immediately grew suspicious of this strange development and put his old ship under intensive scrutiny. As the data came in, she soon saw that the vessel was a lot more than it appeared. Though it looked a bit ragged around the edges, its internals were state-of-the-art and it possessed concealed weapons and defences. These, however, were still no threat to her. What was Orlandine's game here?

She considered sending the ship away, but doing so would never give her the truth of its visit here. Also, some vestige of that Jain instinct to rip knowledge from things arose inside her. This Cog might be an Old Captain but she was sure she could handle him and get to whatever might be concealed in his mind.

'I am sending docking instructions,' she replied.


## Earth Central

The object surfaced from U-space with a flash of light: a simple cube with half-mile-long sides, grey and completely featureless. Yet it did contain a drive because, after tumbling for a moment, it steadied then accelerated on a straight course for the gas giant. Eventually it cut acceleration, fell in a tight course around the giant and looped out. Another flash spread an energy film briefly across vacuum and the thing came to an abrupt halt. It then transformed, folding out blocky chunks of itself into an array of complex sensors.

'You're a mess,' it said.

The powerful sensor array was intermittently connected via U-space to the ruling AI of the Polity, Earth Central, but contained a submind of the same. It hovered over a white and somewhat charred moon fifty miles wide. The apparent moon sat close to the atmosphere of the giant, sucking up a plume of gas from it.

'I should have expected you,' replied Dragon, accepting the comlink.

A moment later, further U-signatures marked the arrival of other objects. Five immense, eighty-mile-long hammerhead dread-noughts, their great shark-like bodies terminating in bulky collections of fusion engines, surfaced into realspace. Weapons pods – clinging like mile-long remoras and as dangerous as any attack ship – detached and spread out. Heavy scanning swept surrounding space. A missile U-jumped into a large asteroid, blasting deep in its core, expanding it into fragments. White lasers flashed in, melting those fragments to streaks of lava. Subsequent analysis of the debris indicated no remaining trace of the exotic crystalline matter first detected. Retrospective analysis indicated the asteroid had been natural, but best to be sure. The ships finally informed EC that only one object here remained dubious, and they had it targeted with enough armament to destroy the gas giant behind it.

The comlink expanded into a realm which was part virtuality and part reality. This standard form of communication enabled complexity but limited the ability of the participants to attack each other in virtuality. EC used it with the king of the prador for this very reason.

Inside a representation of itself, Dragon appeared as a huge snake with the head of a dragon – a form some of his pseudopods had taken in the past – and EC, choosing a man in ECS uniform, appeared beside it. EC studied his surroundings. Dragon had been hollowed out by fire. Massive strut bones crossed his interior, structures like burned-out tenement blocks clung here and there, and the ceramal remains of engines which might have been railguns were visible. But evidently, such huge damage had not finished Dragon off. Scanning revealed the constant plume from the gas giant was flowing in and throughout a network of pipes in its shell, as well as through the strut bones and in surfaces, like the one they apparently stood on. Bioreactors strewn throughout this network, some as small as a pinhead and some many yards across, were splitting and reforming gases into organics. Meanwhile the excess, because there was an excess of some gases, issued as black smoke from pores all over Dragon's hide.

EC looked down. Already the effects were evident across this surface, where fleshy nodules grew like the fruits of fungal mycelia. Elsewhere some of these had melded into drifts of matter, woven through with veins and nerves and all the paraphernalia of organic life. The complete obliteration of Dragon's organic component, and its subsequent restoration, brought home that the creature was a biomech and not a product of evolution.

'So tell me what happened,' said EC.

Dragon swung to peer at him. 'I miscalculated.'

'Detail?'

EC expected Dragon to follow up with an information package, but instead it spoke, 'I was aware of the influence of an AI upon events, but I did not know its origin. I realized that any incursion of the defence sphere might drive Orlandine to deploy the Harding black hole and was suspicious of that.'

'So I understand,' said EC. 'You went to the Cyberat system for further data, for clarification.'

'Yes.'

*Just yes?*

'How did you miscalculate?'

'I knew that the legate Angel being abandoned there was a lure for me, otherwise the Wheel would have destroyed it or utilized it in some other manner. I assumed this a deliberate distraction for me, but it had to be a real one.'

'And you went . . .'

'It was not just a distraction for me but a trap I should not have escaped. The Wheel intended to destroy me there.'

'*Obsidian Blade* destroyed the wormship which attacked you there, and saved you. What did you learn from the legate?' EC tried to keep his patience but obviously Dragon was using spoken communication because that enabled concealment.

'I learned of a prador reaver the Wheel controlled with two hundred of the Clade aboard . . .'

EC absorbed that confirmation. The Wheel's aim, it seemed, had been to drive Orlandine to use the Harding black hole and thus break the U-space blister in the accretion disc sun. This had released a Species ship, and by-and-by the reaver and the Clade had driven the Polity and prador fleets out there to fire on that ship. It all seemed perfectly tight and logical . . . except massive U-space disruption had now shut down communications with those at the accretion disc and Jaskor. Something else had happened and was still happening. There was more to this.

'The Client,' Earth Central stated.

'Propelled to a source of data that might reveal how the accretion disc was created,' Dragon shot back.

'Created?'

'It did not exist prior to five million years ago.'

Now they were getting to it.

'I . . . spoke with the Client,' Dragon continued.

EC already knew this. 'And?'

'Where did the Wheel come from?' Dragon asked.

'That is unknown.'

'No, it is not. The Wheel came from the accretion disc blister.'

EC made further connections and really did not like the scenario they began to reveal. But rather than review that, he focused back on something else Dragon had said: 'How did you know the accretion disc was not in existence five million years ago?'

'It was something I knew but did not know how I knew.'

'That's not good enough.'

The Dragon form showed agitation, swinging its head from side to side, and white saliva dripping from its jaws. It flicked its tail like a rattlesnake.

'The Clade and the Wheel badly injured me. I have since received a further injury from the Client . . . and that injury is hidden memory, now revealed.'

'Hidden memory,' EC stated

'The Makers used me as a probe into the main galaxy. I found Jain technology here and I took it back to them. It destroyed them, and I let myself forget this. I let myself forget that the Makers did not create me and that I pre-dated them. I let myself forget that maybe I deliberately took that technology back to them . . .'

EC knew Dragon's history in intricate detail, and this was truly a revelation.

'How were these memories revealed?'

'When I took the information I required from her, the Client also entered my mind – in the way of the Jain . . .'

Now an information package did arrive and, after taking the appropriate precautions, EC opened it and absorbed in an instant all Dragon had learned from the Client about the Jain. He saw the Librarian. He saw the battles and he saw a solar system demolished during warfare to create what appeared to be an accretion disc.

Dragon continued, 'I had made myself forget that I was here, yet I had not forgotten that no accretion disc existed in that place five million years ago, but a solar system did. I was here when the Jain were here.'

EC didn't even know what questions to ask now. Dragon seemed to be using him as a confessor. But this was of secondary importance to the main point revealed: the Wheel had come from a Jain warship inside that blister, and now that warship was out.

EC packaged up the information it had gleaned and, seeing no disadvantage in doing so, transmitted it. A few moments later came the reply: 'I told you so,' from the king of the prador. EC acknowledged that with a nod in the realm of data and pondered on the response. The king had said the Jain were coming, but had no real way to back up that claim. That he had been proven right made the leading intelligence of the Polity wonder if the claim of organic life on unique instincts and precognition had some veracity, then dismissed it: 'Lucky guess.'

## Trike

The Jain tendrils on his back and the backs of his legs formed a gecko bond, sticking Trike to the hull of Cog's ship, while his new chameleonware ensured the Client could only see that hull. He had chosen a good position below the nose because the emerging view was astounding. Weapons Platform Mu sat like a city of skyscrapers translated into vacuum, though one which was overgrown with lianas of Jain tech. Beyond the platform, the Species ship's core sat silhouetted over the pearlescent orange glare of the giant planet Adranas, which both orbited.

The Client seemed to have had some problem here because she was bringing in her attack pods using EVA units, when they should have been perfectly capable of coming in by themselves. Possessing the requisite codes, Trike linked to nearby satellites whose attention Orlandine had directed here. In brief overview, it seemed the alien had tried to penetrate the ship's core and this had gone badly wrong. She'd sent a remote there – a part of herself – and it had subsequently come back to attack her, which necessitated its destruction. Trike wanted detail on that but dared not probe for information from the weapons platform, not yet, so had to wait until the satellites collated what they had. He unstuck himself a little. They were now heading in towards a hold.

'I don't like how quickly she agreed for me to dock,' said Cog.

Having come from Cog's personal collection, the microwave link between them was the best spyware available. Even so, Trike did not think it beyond the Client's abilities to detect it. He considered telling Cog to use it only for urgent communication, then reconsidered. With it operating over such a short distance, the Client shouldn't be able to distinguish it just yet.

'Quite simple really,' he replied. 'The Client wants to know why Orlandine sent you.'

'Well that'll be an interesting conversation. Any idea what I should say?'

Trike considered many answers, but decided against the truth that the Client would probably try to ream out of his mind. 'I'm sure you'll think of something.'

He connected to a cam in the ship's bridge. Cog grunted an acknowledgement but his expression remained the same as usual – impossible to read either suspicion or otherwise there. Trike then concentrated on the platform. He replayed image data of it in action against the prador ship the *Kinghammer*, and from that ascertained the sites of the disruptor beam weapons. One stood not far from the hold Cog was heading towards. Next, he took another update from Orlandine's watch satellites. Data came through hard and fast, and within a few seconds Trike had more detail on the Client's failure to penetrate the ship's core. Also some speculations from components of Orlandine in those satellites on what might have happened to that huge vessel – how, while in the blister, it had probably been subjected to a time-stream at variance from the real. He wondered if the Species in it were all dead now. He also got more detail on the weapons platform. Orlandine had been subtly scanning it for a while and logged the changes to its original form.

The ribbed blue-violet flames of steering thrusters stabbed out and Trike's view of the platform swept down and away, as the ship turned to slow for a decelerating burn. He changed his hands and knees to gecko function and released his back, and the backs of his legs, then turned over and crawled up onto the top. Here he secured himself beside the protrusion, like a submarine's conning tower where the captain's bridge was located. On this view of the weapons platform he ran an overlay of its old schematic and studied the positions of the tunnels inside. No, he decided that going inside would, despite his new chameleon-ware, seriously raise the chances of the Client detecting him. He next calculated trajectories.

The ship drew closer and closer, the platform looming up around it. Space doors with a castellated join slid open in one armoured edge – a mouse hole into a fortress but still giving access to some immense hold. Trike noted the brassy veins of Jain tech running over that armoured side, the occasional nodes and protruding lumps like metallic fungi. Was there danger of detection from them? Almost certainly.

'That distraction we discussed,' he murmured over the link to Cog.

The ship jerked as one of the steering thrusters, which had been gently nudging the ship towards those doors, fired out of control, burning dirty, shooting out a sheet of oily flame that broke up and seemed to claw at vacuum as it went out. And Trike launched himself.

The force of his arrival on the platform would be enough for sensors to pick up. He shot back data on that.

'On it,' Cog replied.

A brief image of the bridge interior showed Cog swearing and working his instruments, rapidly inputting a fiction. The alleged debris impact they had suffered had caused no critical harm. One piece had merely entered the throat of a thruster and caused a misfire, while another had bounced off the hull. Quick thinking, Trike realized, and smiled as he hurtled towards the platform.

Here in clear vacuum, chameleonware was the most ineffective since he had nothing against which to hide himself. However, the ostensible debris impact worked for him. He became the chunk of that debris that had bounced off the hull – all those difficult-to-hide emissions from him he distorted to that end. A moment later, as he streaked down towards the weapons plat-form, he realized he hadn't been so clever when a high-intensity debris collision laser focused on him. He had only one recourse: he allowed damage, taking the hit on his side and allowing it to ablate the material of his body just enough to produce sufficient vapour to signify the destruction of that debris. He finally thumped down on the hull of the weapons platform. There would be a disparity between supposed remaining debris and the force of this impact. He waited, squatting, undetectable to surrounding sensors, or so he hoped, a smoking hole in his side.

'The Client is most apologetic,' said Cog. 'Seems she didn't manage to clear all the wreckage from her recent destruction of one of her attack pods. You're clear.'

Trike stood up, feet gecko-sticking him to the hull, and began walking. Glancing back, he saw Cog's ship, the *Janus*, sliding into the platform hold. The comlink fizzed for a moment then stabilized – warning enough that intervening technology might interfere. No matter. Trike could still send data directly to Orlandine without disturbance. As he walked, he realized that the apparently short distance to the disruptor installation was in fact four miles. Stepping over veins of Jain tech and occasional patches of growth, like the nubs of brass mushrooms, he broke into a steady lope. He varied the duration and length of his strides to defeat any pattern recognition because, though he used the most energy to propel himself forwards, he still applied force through gecko-stick against the hull.

Eventually he reached a rim where the hull turned inwards to the nominal top of the platform. Here stood what looked like the upper city of tower blocks. Close to, they more clearly resembled what they were: massive rail- and coilguns, the throats of particle cannons, exterior-stored missiles, reactors and hardfield generators. He launched himself from this edge in a slow glide, just a couple of yards above the deck, finally bringing himself to a careful, sliding halt on a curved wall of ceramal surrounding the projector port of a hardfield. He could see the business end of the disruptor.

Through a circular hole in the hull protruded a stalk wrapped in power lines, optics and complex pipework. This terminated in a 'bud' – a geodesic structure his passive scanning revealed to be made of laminated diamond with high reflectivity. Trike walked over to the lip of the hole and peered down into it. He saw that the weapon sat in a movable ball just like many conventional ship weapons. This rendered data about its directionality. Squatting at the edge, he continued passive scanning, getting the shape of the thing, seeing much of its internal structure via local radiation: X-rays, neutrinos, terahertz. Within a minute, he had everything he could obtain that way.

'Active scanning now,' he informed Cog.

'Yeah, right,' Cog replied. 'I'm just leaving the ship.'

Trike looked up and transmitted all he had thus far learned to the satellites, to relay to Orlandine.

Via BIC laser, projected from micropores in the Jain tech on his hand, he started with the gentle waft of induction warfare over exposed optics, and this began rendering code. Much was unrecognizable, but much was also Polity format. As he constantly transmitted everything to Orlandine's satellites, he meanwhile built a model of the weapon in his mind. The bud at the end, he learned, opened out as a reflector and, from its reflectivity, he ascertained what radiations it reflected. A moment later, he understood that the reflectors allowed laser manipulation of the main particle beam. He tried something more intense on one of the pipes to get the nature of the particulate. It was radioactive – a mix of manufactured materials from the far end of the human elementary table.

Half an hour later, Trike had the complete shape of the weapon, but he needed its programming. Sure, it would now be possible for Orlandine to build this thing, but without that final data, it would be a useless hulk unless she could ascertain that programming from its structure. Trike stepped off the lip and climbed down. No material barrier blocked his path behind the movable ball, but a shimmershield did. His detection of seepage from its surface revealed that inert gas surrounded the internals of the weapon. He reached out with one fingertip to the shield, meanwhile scanning its surrounding emitters. No. He withdrew his finger. He needed a fault. Tracing a thin s-con cable to where it passed through a Jain nodule, he sent a magnetic pulse. The brief power interruption lasted just two seconds. The shimmershield winked out and, in that instant, Trike moved so fast that in atmosphere he would have created a sonic shock. When the shield came back on, he stood inside.

Good.

Then he saw a Jain tendril detaching itself and coiling away from a feed pipe. Like a mamba detecting prey, it hooped up and oriented towards him. He realized in that instant his mistake. He had created no sonic shock on the other side of the shield but he had in here, in the inert gas.

'Oh shit,' he sent to Cog.

## Diana

Diana studied a close view of one of the twenty vessels detached from the Jain warship. At fifty miles long, it bore a resemblance to the kind of big sea louse found in the depths of Earth's ocean, sans legs. Engines on the underside propelled the humped serrated carapace towards the fleet. As it travelled, the ribs of that carapace opened gaps to expose immediately identifiable weapons. It occurred to her how similar this ship was to the Jain mechanism Orlandine had used when interrogating a submind of the Wheel, and had created again on the surface of Jaskor. But she could extrapolate nothing from this comparison.

'Jabro,' she warned.

But it was Seckurg who replied, 'High-power grasers. I'm guessing a change of tactics.'

Pure energy beam strikes were usually invisible when passing through vacuum. But such had been the intensity of the action here that particulate and gas had filled the vacuum. Lasers were now scoring visible lines of red, green and sick yellow across space. Particle beams had also changed. Previously royal blue or blue-violet, they now seemed to be issuing orange smoke and resembled steel rods hot out of an extruding plant. And the graser beams which issued from the twenty enemy ships looked like glowing silver wire.

These struck the fleet's hardfields at energy levels defying conventional physics, driving multiple hardfield collapses as they punched through. Diana saw one stab at the nose of a reaver, lighting it up like a firework as it spewed projectors. Just a moment later, the beam speared into the ship and passed out through the exploding engines at the back. The ship rippled down its length, blowing out hull plates and issuing jets of fire. It then tumbled away from the fleet, cored out and blackened inside.

'Damn!' exclaimed Alianathon.

Diana felt it in her bones as a series of *Hogue*'s projectors burned out so fast they failed to eject, but at least the superconducting grid of the ship drew the energy away. Then the ship shuddered under three graser strikes.

'Analysis?' Diana asked the armourer, as meanwhile Hogue put up images for her inspection.

'Stopped at the hull,' replied Alianathon, 'but only at the fifth dispersal layer.'

The images showed three craters on the surface, each half a mile wide. All around these, the hull had blistered for another half-mile and still, at their centres, the craters were glowing.

'Every ship,' she announced, 'target with all beam weapons but hold until signalled.' She turned to the man running the directed gravity weapon. 'Dulse, DIGRAW them hard. I want a mega-gee wave.'

'My pleasure,' muttered Dulse.

Diana continued, 'Hogue, coordinate firing. Glendour, major particle beams on every one of those fuckers.'

'Shit, they're moving fast,' said Jabro.

He was right. The ships had ramped up their acceleration, each sitting on small suns of fusion flame. Meanwhile the *Hogue* grumbled to itself as power supplies rerouted and giant hydraulic rams tracked with giant particle weapons. Then came a thrumming felt throughout the bridge, ending with a thump that lifted them in their seats. The DIGRAW had fired.

Diana watched the effect, throwing up an image of one of those vessels on the main screen. The image distorted and it seemed the ship rammed through an invisible wall. The thing rippled and bent and shed pieces. Next, the beam blasts from other ships lit it up. Sensors blanked in safety mode then came back on with heavy filtering. The ship sat at the centre of a glaring sphere, shedding clouds of incandescent particulate. The thrumming built again. But now the *Hogue* began firing its particle beam weapons.

Beams wide enough to eat up small attack ships seared out from the *Cable Hogue*. Eight struck eight targets. The completely enclosing fields of two of them, one having been struck by the gravity wave, blackened and then collapsed. They shrank down to invisibility from which points of light then flared and expanded. Two small suns exploded outwards, in an intense cross-spectrum flash of radiation that blanked sensors again and burned smoke from the hulls of the nearest ships in the fleet. The spherical hardfield of another attacking vessel also began to blacken, but it shut it down. A massive strike from the fleet hit the thing, pumping in energy. Unbelievably it did not come apart but began glowing like a component in a blast furnace, and still firing its grasers. She watched it hurtle past an older Polity destroyer at the point of the fleet. Again there was the firework display and then two grasers cut across, slicing the thing diagonally, and it exploded into three pieces.

'They're on us,' Jabro warned.

Hogue was already updating tactical. Diana's approval wasn't necessary, but she gave it anyway, 'Break and engage! Fire at will!'

The DIGRAW thumped again. A fourth Jain ship exploded amidst the fleet, its blast tumbling a unit of attack ships and ablating armour from a big lozenge dreadnought. Beam weapons kept the attackers nailed but kept shutting down so as not to cut across friendly vessels. Diana saw hardfield ejections, collision lasers lining space, and railgun impacts flaring up sheets of flame from curved hardfields. Meanwhile those grasers just kept cutting and cutting.

It was, she understood, getting really messy.

## Cog

'Welcome, Captain Cog,' said a voice.

It sounded like a woman he had once known long ago in his youthful first century of life. That was disconcerting when he considered its actual source.

'Glad to be here,' he replied.

Cog wasn't sure that he should be here – this all felt a little bit out of his league. He walked down the ramp onto the metal gratings of the immense hold and looked around. In alcoves along one wall, handler robots, like rather pretentious sculptures of beetles rendered in chrome and white enamel, stood upright.

Other things were here that he suspected were additions since the time this platform duteously served on the defence sphere. All around the walls and along the gratings underfoot, Jain tendrils ran like creepers stripped of leaves and sprayed with metallic paint. Over to one side, in bubble-metal racks, sat numerous objects like eggs or seeds grown large. Most were spherical, their surfaces cracked like mud under an African sun. Others were like huge caraway seeds and still others resembled walnuts the size of beach balls.

'So what's all this stuff?' he asked, gesturing to the objects as he strode along.

'A small portion of what I took from the library moon,' the Client replied.

That confirmed she was watching him – not that he had expected otherwise. He studied the things again. He'd been catching up on the journey here and knew they were loot from a Jain who had been older than the human race.

'So what exactly are they?' he asked.

'Jain tech, but not as you know it,' the Client replied. 'You humans understand Jain tech to be a civilization-destroying technology. It is in fact the peak of technological development deployed by one Jain to sequester other Jain and which has come to incorporate them all. It is the Jain now. You are seeing what came before. Each of those containers holds a complex array of programmable nano-machines and nano-mycelia whose purpose is not set.'

Well, the Client seemed quite chatty; he wasn't sure why that surprised him.

A door opened in the far wall and something stepped out. Cog stared at the thing. He knew that weapons platforms had these but seeing one here made him just a tad nervous. The grappler looked like a big bulky man, in fact an Old Captain writ large, but fashioned out of faceted metal. It strode out and then came to a halt. Its open mouth and eyes were windows into a furnace. Apparently, the high-temperature technology running inside caused this, since these were originally created for work on hot, high-gravity worlds. Cog thought that explanation fatuous. This particular look was all about scary aesthetics.

'Follow this grappler robot,' said the Client.

'Okay,' Cog replied, pretending to be casual.

The grappler beckoned peremptorily then turned and marched away from him. He followed it across the gratings to a round door already opening at its approach – sections sliding back into its surrounding frame. This revealed a long tunnel, spearing into the platform. Cog strolled in behind the marching grappler.

After the first few hundred yards, the tunnel wall panels disappeared and Cog found himself walking through a cageway. Now he could see much of the interior of the platform. Though no stranger to the massive machines of the Polity – he had been knocking around in it for quite some time – this impressed him. He gazed upon huge fusion reactors, tower stacks of laminar storage, tanks of particulate, autofactories and armouries, and stored replacement weapons, including attack pods and giant railgun carousels. Just the immediately visible could fill two or three medium dreadnoughts, and he could see only a fraction of what the platform contained. But there was more here too, and it definitely wasn't Polity technology.

Unless they were replacement parts for elsewhere, a web of Jain tech wove together the masses of machinery beyond the cageway. Thick veins ran across surfaces and entered various ports. They were dotted evenly throughout with large growths, like metallic puffballs, themselves spreading fibrous roots. Here a Jain control system had eaten and displaced optics. He could see alterations it had made: strange organic pipes sprouting around a reactor there, laminated platework growing from a tank of particulate, spiral coils running alongside a railgun slug manufactory. In a way, it would almost have been okay if this stuff had just grown wild, but he was utterly sure that not an ounce of material or energy had been wasted here. It all, he thought, looked alarmingly like a biological neural network.

Soon they reached the end of the cageway, whereupon the grappler led him through a series of square-section ducts, obviously not made for humans, since they both had to duck down and walk crablike. These then debarked into a bigger rectangular-section duct with polished copper walls. Some kind of immense wave-guide? Cog had no idea. Beyond this lay a low-ceilinged area, with a black floor inset with silvery electronics, or maybe the glyphs of a strange language. Cog hadn't a clue whether or not this was Polity technology around him. Finally a drop-shaft. The grappler gestured inside and then simply turned and walked away.

Cog paused there, and that was when he got the message.

'Oh shit,' said Trike.

Cog cleared his throat and though long out of practice he managed a decent subvocalization. 'Problem?'

'Active Jain tech zeroing in on me. I'm keeping clear but I need a distraction.'

'What?'

'Do something she has to react to!'

Cog quickly stepped into the dropshaft. The irised gravity field wafted him up past spider robots clinging to the shaft walls, then slowed him to a halt at an exit. He grabbed a handle and pulled himself through, coming down on a grav-plated floor.

In this upper level he found himself inside a wide pipe with part of its wall transparent. Gazing through its side, he could see a tall, chain-glass cylinder like a city block rising just a short distance away. There resided the Client, and he could see the glassy tree within and the long conjoined form wrapped around it.

He scanned his immediate surroundings.

'There, you bugger,' he said.

Jain veins ran in profusion down a wall to intersect at a bulbous growth like a metallic human brain. He abruptly stepped over, reached down and grabbed it. One heave and it came off the wall with a snapping sound. He pulled it away, a great mass of veins coming with it.

'Desist,' said the Client, voice now flat and not female at all.

He realized he had made the right choice of distraction. He closed his hands on the thing, crushing it, then heard a noise and turned. The dropshaft was working. He stepped towards it, his hands clenching and unclenching, shedding pieces of what he'd crushed, which felt sticky. Around him, Jain veins writhed against the walls, and beyond the transparent panes he could see a huge structure dipping and turning towards him. The local debris and antipersonnel laser had the watts to vaporize this part of the platform along with Cog. A shape appeared in the dropshaft and flung itself out, landing with a thump that shook the floor.

'It's working,' Trike muttered in his ear.

Cog wondered just when their roles had reversed. He considered dodging past the grappler and taking the shaft back down. But with the fire burning hot in its eye sockets and mouth, the grappler surged straight towards him, and something very 'Spatterjay' took over in him. Cog hunched over and threw himself forwards, ramming his shoulder into the huge humanoid robot. He expected to hurl it back into the dropshaft but instead found himself slammed to a halt. He staggered back just in time to dodge a swinging fist, then launched, driving his forehead straight into its face. Spitting sparks, the thing retreated a step, while Cog reached up and touched his forehead. He could feel flakes of bone under his skin. He moved forward again and hooked a punch up into its torso that lifted it just a little way off the floor, then followed it with another and another, until the heel of its hand hit him in the face and he lurched back. It tried to push him aside but he caught its arm, used leverage and all his weight, and threw it into the nearby wall. It hung there for a moment then stepped out. Air vented through the wreckage behind it, then breach foam bubbled up. He kicked it hard between the legs, but acknowledged his silly mistake when it backhanded him.

Slowly Cog pulled his head back upright and decided to stop being gentle. He closed his fists into tight balls, bones and ligaments crunching. He wasn't Trike but he was still one of the oldest of Old Captains. He landed an overhand blow to its face, crushing metal and opening cracks that leaked fire. A second hook-punch to its torso lifted it a foot from the floor and his third hammered in before it landed. The thing obviously had no finesse – just relied on brute strength – but then Cog was not exactly being artful. Ignoring the bones splintering and reknitting in his hands, he kept it off-balance, landing blow after blow. He had to admit to its toughness. He knew that such impacts could put his fist through the ten-inch timbers of the hull of a Spatterjay sailing ship. Finally, he got it to the lip of the dropshaft and paused. It was moving slowly now, dents all over its torso and its face concave, with hot liquid silicon running out of numerous splits.

'Had enough?' Cog enquired.

It seemed almost as if it nodded. He gave it a shove and it fell back into the gravity field of the shaft. Next, tapping the control, he sent it on its way down.

'I'm good now,' said Trike over their link.

'Yeah, but am I?' muttered Cog.

He looked up at the collision laser and waited for oblivion, but after a moment, it turned away.

'Your actions have no logic,' said the Client. 'Apparently.'

'Sorry,' said Cog. 'I was sure it moved and I panicked.'

'You do not possess the capability to access my data,' said the Client. 'Ah, I see . . .'

'Honestly, I wasn't trying,' said Cog, not liking her responses. 'I think Orlandine made a mistake choosing me for this. I get a bit nervous around Jain tech.'

After a long pause the Client said, back with the female voice, 'You will remain where you are for now.'

He heard a thunk behind him and turned. A door had revolved into place to close off his access to the dropshaft. Next came another sound, as of blades sliding over each other. He turned again in time to see a metal iris closing off the walkway.

'Trike?' he muttered, but there was no response.

Cog stood for a long moment contemplating what this might mean. He then sighed, shrugged off his pack, dropped it on the floor and sat on it. Reviewing recent events, he realized how close he had come to dying, just to provide Trike with a distraction, and that the Client might yet kill him. He very much didn't like the idea that he had now become an expendable asset.

# 5

*'Separatist' has for a long time been the catchall label applied to a wide assortment of rebels who fight, with varying degrees of violence, against the Polity. A rebel is a Separatist or a revolutionary – the words are interchangeable. They tell us the AIs are standing in the way of humanity achieving some utopian ideal. But replace AI with any human government and you will find endless parallels throughout the ages. These people are ideologues whose ideas of utopia are a varied collection of slogans, or vague notions which lack the clarity one would expect of a cause they are fighting for. Greater wealth, jobs and happiness for all? Sometimes, maybe, depending on . . . As has been proven, time and time again, when ideologues get their hands on power and begin to impose their utopia, and it inevitably begins to fall apart, they reveal themselves to be what they truly are at heart: authoritarians. They fight against established power because they want to supplant it, only this, not because they have some vision of a better world.*

From 'Quince Guide' compiled by humans

**Trike**

The Jain tentacle lay in pieces on the floor. Trike lowered his hand, shutting down the shearfields along his fingers. It occurred to him, as he utilized more of the weapons tech he could grow in his body, that he was becoming more like Angel. The thought disturbed him since he had incorporated all that Angel had been. His other hand pressed into a bulbous object – just like the one Cog had destroyed – attached to a nearby power stack. Then he gradually retracted it. But he maintained the EMR link he had gained into the Jain structure spread all around him.

He had acted fast and been lucky. The Client had perceived Cog's attack as a threat to her information security, and this had drawn her attention away from Trike. Without that, she would have detected him when he went straight into the automatic security and shut it down, killing the alert he had generated. He gleaned data, codes and language, ways for himself to close things down, ways to be ignored. The satisfying accuracy and completeness of his haul he must now use to help him gather the data Orlandine required.

Trike stepped over to the weapon, broadcasting the radio signal of a maintenance robot. The base of the thing sat in a polished brassy doughnut, fed from all sides by optics and webbed with Jain tech. Active scanning this, he found it had once been the computing and wave-field manipulation block for an induction warfare beam and had retained much of that structure. He searched its surface and, after a moment, found an optical diagnostic port free of Jain tendrils. Holding up one finger, he sent tendrils to its end where they formed a square and turned translucent, then clouded with a nest of optical fibres, and inserted it. He began running standard diagnostic tests and recording the feedback. This revealed a barely recognizable system it would take him some time to parse.

Trike squatted, then reached out to a nearby vein and closed his other hand around it, injecting fibres there. It only took him a minute to find EMR emitters scattered all around him. He chose one and isolated his feed to it, trying a coded emission, and then ten minutes later received an acknowledgement in return. This had once again linked him to Orlandine's satellites here near the sun. He began transmitting all he had learned, and all he was learning, as he probed the system of the weapon before him. In an hour he understood how it worked, and knew that, as a result, numerous theories in physics and U-space mechanics would have to undergo revision. But he continued gathering data until finally another signal came back to him.

'It is enough,' Orlandine told him.

Trike's link to Orlandine's satellites cut, whereupon another female voice said, 'Yes, it certainly is.'

## Gemmell

As he brought the grav-car down towards the coast, Gemmell thought about his recent talk with Trantor and Baylock. Under ECS policy for a commander, when in a situation rising to a certain level of complexity, he should employ an adjutant. This individual did not need to take extra administrative duties, since for that Gemmell only needed to open more processing either in his gridlink or the data sphere. It was to spread the load of responsibility, to have an adviser and someone to bounce ideas off. Moral support, really. As per custom, he turned to those officers close to him, both of whom, it seemed, had decided on another idea.

'I'm better with the new recruits who are still coming in,' asserted Baylock.

'You want me off the front line?' Trantor had clutched his particle cannon tightly. 'I would say that's misuse of resources.'

'So who, then?' he had asked.

The two had given each other a look, then Baylock spoke up, 'Isn't it obvious? A new recruit you've formed an emotional attachment to. One who, if she was in action, would distract you from your job of command.'

'But that's hardly correct procedure . . .'

'You know it's right,' Trantor had said, 'on many levels.' He looked up in the sky, precisely to where his aug told him the *Morgaine's Gate* was located, raised his hand and then his middle finger towards it.

'And you and the others would be okay with this?'

'More than okay. Quite happy actually,' Trantor had replied.

'It makes sense in other ways,' Baylock had pushed the point home. 'She's a raw recruit so will be less efficient in action, but she's also old, smart and experienced in ways that you are not. Better to have an adjutant who can offer new perspectives and disagree with you. If it was one of us, you'd just be in an echo chamber.'

'Really?'

'Really,' they had replied simultaneously.

Gemmell grinned to himself. None of them had liked his situation with Morgaine and, he later learned, all the *Morgaine's Gate* marines had taken a vote on who should be his adjutant. Only a few had disagreed with it being Ruth – their choices being either Baylock or Trantor. And so now his new adjutant sat beside him.

'We cannot defend a whole planet,' said Ruth.

He glanced at her. 'We defend the population centres. All those outside the cities have been informed and have a choice where to go. They have also been warned that any major infestations beyond the cities will be nuked no matter where they are.'

Ruth grimaced. 'At least some are heading off-world.'

'Fifty evacuation platforms left and Orlandine won't provide any more,' Gemmell replied. 'With all of them filled and on their way, we may be able to protect the remaining millions in the cities.'

'For a limited time.'

He glanced at her. 'Your thoughts on that?'

'We can hit landfalls across the continent but if we miss a scrap it will likely go into the ground and there's nothing we can do about that. Then, of course, there is the ocean – no way can we cover that. If Jain tech starts raining down here, it's going to take a hold somewhere, no matter what we do. The planet will be done.'

'You studied Jain tech,' he said, transferring his gaze back to the vista. The sea glittered in the morning sunshine, scattered with vessels. Silhouetted against this stood the city Marshallam – their intended destination. His gaze strayed to the land around the city. White plasticrete roads divided groves of olive, orange, lemon and pomegranate in a checkerboard pattern. It appeared very Mediterranean, except the temperature was lower here and the trees had been heavily modified. He had eaten slices from an oddly sweet olive the size of an apple from one of the groves down there.

'Yeah, I studied it,' Ruth replied. 'And I learned enough to know why it is so feared, but also why it is so sought-after. Power is like that.'

Gemmell nodded as he took the grav-car down towards the city. Touching the console screen, he got a landing spot high-lighted. He did have the option to hand over control to the city AI but negated it, preferring to have something to do.

'We will still have shuttles and other vehicles to move people once the platforms are gone . . . given time,' he said. 'But the problem here is where the hell to move them to. You can guar-antee that if this world gets hit, then any big ships or other possible evacuation sites up there, like the remaining weapons platforms, are going to be far too busy.'

'But this is a make-work plan, is it not?' she asked. 'You were looking for some plausible activity to keep the troops busy.'

'Initially, but not now.' He shook his head. 'I realized pretty quickly that Jain tech ending up here is a strong possibility, especially with the way Orlandine is preparing. And she currently puts that possibility at over seventy-five per cent.'

'Oh.' Ruth pondered on that for a moment, then said, 'And our visit here is at Orlandine's behest?'

'Not precisely,' he said, feeling uncomfortable. 'The city AI is a subpersona of Orlandine and it relayed to Morgaine that there might be a problem here.'

'And Morgaine decided that you should investigate?'

'I have carte blanche when it comes to planetary security,' he said, feeling defensive. 'But I tend to listen when either Orlandine or Morgaine mentions something. From either, such a communication has some real purpose.'

'I see,' said Ruth, her voice flat.

She stared forwards as he brought the grav-car in between skyscrapers like immense cubist cacti, sliding it under a bridge between two 'branches', then heading towards a protruding grav-car park. As he steered the car in, Gemmell thought about that conversation. It had been a bit strange. Morgaine had given little detail on the content of her exchange with the Orlandine subpersona, but had strongly hinted that his presence might be required. When he had pushed for detail, she started to get vague, then told him it was all entirely up to him as the commander on the ground. To be honest, he was looking into this not so much because he needed to understand events here, but because he needed to understand what was going on in Morgaine's skull.

'Let's see what transpires,' he added.

'Yes, let's,' said Ruth.

To distract himself he noted that this city was particularly vulnerable to attack damage, having so many tall structures. He visualized these great towers dropping thousands of tons of debris into the streets below, then hurriedly checked data on that. Shortly, he breathed a sigh of relief. As the whole continent was prone to earthquakes and tsunamis – the Sambre volcano being one sign of steady tectonic shift – the buildings' skeletons consisted of super-strong meta-materials, with grav-engines for stability and high-gas foamstones and bubble-metals making up the rest of their structures. Debris would fall, but mostly with the damage potential of origami. He then focused in on something on top of a building as they passed over it, and enhanced the image in his gridlink.

An iron-coloured stag beetle squatted atop the building, though no such beetles were the size of a tank, nor did they sport Gatling cannons on their antlers. He ran a check and saw that Orlandine's assassin and war drones had distributed themselves across *all* the cities. This was not per operational plans but it seemed the drones knew better: they had provided valid arguments in support of their present deployment, and the system had automatically accepted them until his next review of the situation. That was okay – he was not so stupid as to ignore their experience. He sent a confirmation.

He settled the car down on the grav-car park. Scattered around a couple of military vehicles here were soldiers in uniforms similar to those worn by Polity military, but with a camouflage pattern design of cubic white and grey. The Jaskoran reserve had some training and were on standby should they be needed. They were hugely loyal to Orlandine, apparently. Also, at the edge of the platform, stood two prador. Checking various battle plans, he saw no reason why they should not be here, but still suspected a degree of distrust on the part of the prador. They wanted to have a first-hand account of the ensuing exchange.

'So what's their gripe?' asked Ruth, nodding to a group of

people coming out of the exit from the building onto the grav-car park.

'Like I said, they have some problems with the defensive plans. Beyond that I don't know – they haven't seen fit to load their objections into the data sphere.'

'But essentially, they're details that should be below your notice.'

He looked at her. 'Yes, except for Morgaine telling me this is something I should look into.'

'So therefore possibly critical . . . in so many ways . . .' She nodded briefly in understanding. 'Who are they?'

'Mayor and members of the city council.'

'Really?'

He glanced at her as he unstrapped and stood up. 'Yeah. Orlandine allowed human rule here but has been steadily displacing it with AI and computer systems. The interference of these people causes little damage and helps keep the anti-AI elements in check.'

'Anti-AI elements,' she repeated, standing also.

'Quite,' he affirmed.

## Orlandine

Standing on the roof of her apartment building, Orlandine gazed up at the sky. She now had full schematics and an understanding of the disruptor weapon the Client had built. It was concerning how Trike went offline immediately after transmitting, but she assumed that was due to some danger of detection, and so concentrated on the data. Its mere existence had opened up an appropriate 'can of worms'. From it, she gleaned new knowledge of physics, of U-space technology and glimpsed deeper into territory that EC Weapons had only been investigating over the last century: the relationship between U-space and hardfields. This new knowledge filtered efficiently out into the totality of her mind and she inserted it where relevant, processing on many levels as it altered her perception of reality. She felt suddenly buoyant, superior and, with some reluctance, next transmitted it to all of her platform AIs, and to Knobbler and the rest of her war and assassin drones.

'Limited distribution,' Knobbler noted.

Only then did Orlandine realize she had sent this information over a channel that did not include the Polity and prador ships here. She flicked her attention to the big drone and located him with a search through the local security and cam system. Knobbler was perambulating over a sky bridge between buildings in one of the southern cities, keeping one wary eye on prador deploying along the coast while, with other eyes and sensors, watching *everything* else. Keying into his coms, she picked up how he had altered the deployment of other drones in this city. It was subtle, but many of the prador units now had a war or assassin drone nearby, just for backup, mind.

'A diplomatic omission,' she replied. 'Something I need to think about.'

'There are understandable . . . concerns.'

There were, and the almost subconscious knowledge of them had influenced her. First the prador. Did she really want to provide such a hostile race with this kind of weapons technology, with its concomitant change in understanding of the universe that could lead to other weapons? Sure, the prador were under the control of Oberon and his family, but such weaponry could destabilize the Kingdom and he might be usurped. No ruler was guaranteed, but the inherent hostility of the prador was. No, she did not want the prador to have a weapon that could punch through hardfields and turn high-tech armour as frangible as safety glass. But what about the Polity? While she trusted that the AIs would be a lot less likely to use such weapons aggressively, they still could. Earth Central's agendas might well incorporate the idea of annihilating the prador, if it could do so at little cost to the Polity. And she knew that Earth Central was not above allowing warfare, if it pushed technological development in the Polity, or the mental development of humankind. However, in the end she realized these factors did not inform her decision not to pass this on to them. She stood between realms in a dominion of her own and simply felt it unfair to give to one what she did not give to the other.

Surely that was it?

Orlandine blinked and returned to herself or, rather to this human facsimile and extension of herself. She tried to pull back to human consciousness, to analyse her motives, and immediately gained a new outlook. No, that was not all of it. She had limited the distribution of weapons technology out of an acquisitive selfishness. She tried to feel negative about that, but could not find the emotion. She shook her head, as she would have as a human to dismiss something from her mind. Her reasoning remained sound even if her base motives did not. Leave it at that. She quickly abandoned her dissolving human perspective and turned her attention outwards again.

Already, throughout her weapons platforms, in the factories and other facilities she had spread about Jaskor, she had instituted new manufacturing processes. In one manufactory, robots were radically altering wave-field manipulation blocks. In another, a gravity press already formed diamond reflectors. Still others produced copies of components in the weapon aboard Weapons Platform Mu, but with standard computer or AI control, rather than the Jain-tech lattice that thing had. Also, as a result of this new data, AIs were confirming theories about defences against this weapon. Certain programming for induction warfare beams would stop it; certain resonances in hardfields and some redesign of their projectors would prevent it too.

'We haven't really gained a weapon,' Knobbler noted.

This was not entirely true. Sure, if they could so rapidly come up with defences here against the disruptor, it made sense that the coming Jain ship would have those defences too. Knobbler implied they had merely negated the disruptor, but they would still have opportunities to use it.

Orlandine mentally stepped back and took an overview of their gain and what that knowledge implied. The disruptor lay within their technical and scientific grasp, but only just. It opened up possibilities she and the AIs were currently exploring. But the disruptor, being the product of a technological milieu to which the Jain had full access, had other implications. She and the AIs were like eighteenth-century weapons makers putting together a rocket engine from twentieth-century schematics. It might well be that they now knew about rocket engines, but its mere existence hinted at a lot more they did not know.

Orlandine paused, realizing the analogy also applied to the technology, arising from a Jain node, that she and Captain Trike controlled. She had taken apart a Jain node and understood it, but equally did not have access to the technological milieu from which it had arisen. And in fact had not understood all the processes involved in creating it.

She paused again, seeing her reasoning spinning her into a dead end.

'We need to work harder on this,' she broadcast. 'That ship will have more than just these disruptors.'

She cast her mind out to her satellites near Platform Mu and the ship's core, intending to order Trike to get detail on that enclosing hardfield the Client used. But still he did not respond.

## The Client

The Client had only been alerted to Cog's narrow beam transmissions when she heard his subvocalizations. Once aware, she had detected those transmissions and found him talking to Captain Trike. Cog had given Trike his distraction by tearing up Jain tech and fighting the grappler she sent to stop him. Meanwhile she had traced the transmissions of the Old Captain to the site of one of her disruptor beam weapons.

The Client now gazed through sensors she had managed to reformat – dismissing the programming used to subvert them. In the chamber below the disruptor, where previously those sensors had detected a brief disturbance just prior to Cog ripping up Jain tech, she watched Trike. The man, if he could still be called that, had penetrated the weapon and sent its full schematics and programming to Orlandine. This was irritating, and not retrievable . . . but Trike was *interesting*.

The sensors gathered much on his physical structure, but not enough for her. She put online a powerful scanning array on the surface of the station and directed its attention inwards. Trike shivered as if in a cold breeze and looked directly towards the array. This alone told her the sophistication of the technology inside him, while the sensor array began to tell her more. She considered how to react.

That the man had managed to penetrate the platform so deeply before detection was frightening. Had his aim been assassination he could have reached her. But she saw this for what it was. Orlandine had sent Trike and Cog to obtain data from her to help in the defence of the Jaskoran system. The Client had withheld data simply because she did not like the idea of any force being stronger than her – simple self-preservation. She had not been prepared to share it. Yet, meanwhile, Orlandine had made the Client a citizen of Jaskor, even though her presence might draw a greater threat here: the Jain coming out of the accretion disc. No, she would not destroy Trike, in fact he had demonstrated he might be very useful indeed. She decided to take some risks with her personal safety because of the potential advantages she had begun to recognize.

'You are very effective,' she said, via the same microwave com he had used to communicate with both Cog and Orlandine's satellite.

'It has been a voyage of discovery for me,' he replied.

The Client peered through sensors elsewhere in the platform at the four grapplers she had set in motion. She halted them, then ordered them back to their storage pods. Sending them to Trike had been an instinctive reaction she now understood to be a useless one. After seeing how Cog, whom she assessed at an order of magnitude weaker than Trike, had trashed one grappler, she doubted that four grapplers could handle Trike physically. Strength was not the only issue. With the technology Trike commanded in his body, whose density and extent she was only just beginning to ascertain, he could shut down grapplers before they even got their hands on him. A sophisticated war drone could perhaps capture this man – one with its own powerful mind and a wide selection of weapons and penetration gear. Perhaps.

'I understand why Orlandine wanted the disruptor beam weapons data. Are there any other reasons for your presence here?' she asked.

'To obtain any and all data that might be relevant to dealing with the Jain threat,' he replied. 'You understand the extent of that.'

'Just about everything, then.'

'Just about.'

'But you are confined to information-gathering?'

'Yes.' He paused for a moment then continued, 'I am no threat to you beyond that implicit in passing on details of your weapons and defences to another party who may, at some future time, be a danger to you.'

'Orlandine?'

'Only Orlandine,' he said. 'I suspect she'll have no intention of passing on any more than necessary, either to the Kingdom or to the Polity.'

'I will need a greater breadth of communication if I am to believe you,' she stated.

He immediately opened up the bandwidth of his microwave com. He extended links, wider across the EMR spectrum, to her sensors. Their conversation moved beyond the verbal immediately. She read the truth and logic of what he had told her in the function of his mind but, even so, it was still not enough. She could not be sure that he allowed her to see everything. She sent an instruction to the beam weapon chamber and over to one side of him locks disengaged on a circular hatch.

'Come to me,' she said.

### Trike

Trike felt the air pressure building and, via sensors in his skin and in the Jain network enwrapping his body, analysed its content. Just air. No invasive nano-machines to penetrate his skin or the linings of his lungs. He took a breath, then another, and his body began to top up its depleted stores of oxygen and nitrogen. These were not entirely necessary, for he could exist in vacuum almost indefinitely. As a hooper, the virus sought to keep him alive, while the Jain tech complemented this big time. High-density nodes throughout his flesh even now fused hydrogen, previously leeched from the sea and atmosphere of Jaskor, and crystal compacted into metallic form. He had his other sources of power.

The inner door of the airlock opened and he moved through the massive interior of the platform, finally arriving at the foot of a dropshaft. He stepped inside and dropped a little before the irised gravity field recalibrated for his weight, then heaved him upwards. Finally, it brought him to a halt beside a curved, ceramal door which, after a moment, revolved aside.

'So you're here,' said Cog, standing up. 'She catch you?'

'Yes, she caught me,' Trike replied. 'Come on.'

Trike headed past him along the walkway and, hoisting up his pack, Cog quickly followed.

'So what happened?' asked Cog. 'And what's going to happen?'

'The Client has accepted why we came here and has forgiven it. We're on the same side. Now some other interesting possibilities have arisen.'

An irised metal door opened ahead. Beyond it, the walkway sloped down and curved around through a space between layers of armour. Here stood giant shock-absorbing rams with coolant pipes snaking between them. Finally, they entered a long tunnel that passed under a round hatch. Trike halted below this and gazed up.

'I guess we're below the cylinder,' said Cog. 'And what do you mean by "interesting possibilities"?'

'It's hot up there,' said Trike, looking at him meaningfully.

Cog grimaced, then abruptly shrugged off his pack and opened it, taking out the hotsuit he had used to go after Trike at the Sambre volcano. Trike waited patiently while he donned it, a large part of the focus of his mind on his link with the Client. They were talking to each other on many levels, but it wasn't the communication usual between two such as Cog and himself. It did have its verbal component, as well as informational fencing, with differing levels of language and code. Without stepping straight into mental warfare, they were trying to extract information from each other and assess each other's capabilities. And he was learning things.

The Client, he now knew, balanced threats to herself, and to the supposed members of her species aboard that ship's core, against the Jain and those from elsewhere. Sharing all she knew with Orlandine would of course go towards stopping any Jain nasties coming out of the accretion disc. But it would also increase the danger to her later, by taking away her technological advantage over the Polity and the prador. Other things were in her calculations too: for example, the dangers inherent in sharing technology with a race as hostile as the prador – a race she had only recently decided not to act against. And Trike could see from this that still, in the forefront of her consciousness, was the option to run. He also understood, by the direction of her queries, by the data she sought from him, that she was vetting him as a candidate for some task. And he knew what that was.

'Ready,' said Cog, his voice unaffected by the hood and visor. The voice transmission from the suit would also adjust to the hot atmosphere beyond the hatch.

Trike mentally flicked their readiness to the Client and locks and a seal disengaged above. The hatch revolved and hinged down on one side, issuing a gust of searing air and flecks of thin chitin, like floating mica crystals. Ribbing ran across the inside face of the hatch and much of the locking mechanism lay exposed, so there were plenty of handholds. He took a grip and quickly climbed, stepping up into the Client's giant chain-glass cylinder. Cog followed with an agility most did not expect from such a heavyset man – nimbleness from sheer brute strength, of which his recent encounter with the grappler had been a salutary reminder. That too had been part of Trike's ongoing conversation with the Client.

The temperature would kill a standard, unaugmented human being. The floor of the cylinder possessed similar ribbing to the hatch, and evidence of damage, with memform repair patches steadily melding into it. Scanning intently, Trike noted scraps here and there – space suit material, fragments of old-style visor glass, an energy canister from a pulse rifle and, perhaps left as a warning, a single shrivelled human finger. Certainly, by the burns he could see in the vicinity, a firefight had occurred here. A brief query gave him his answer: Graveyard salvagers had come aboard and the Client had necessarily defended herself. Trike pretended to accept that but knew there must be more to the story. He thought it highly unlikely anyone could board this platform without the Client's complicity . . . barring himself, of course.

'Will you look at that,' said Cog.

'One of her husks – all used up and ready to go into recycling,' Trike replied.

The wasp-like corpse was the size of a large dog. Dried-out and translucent, with organs and other structures inside it shrivelled down to webs and lumps, it looked as if something had sucked every drop of energy and life out of it. Even as they watched, a small hatch opened some distance away and, like a trapdoor spider, a bot darted out. It scuttled across the floor to seize hold of the thing, and then began dragging it back to its burrow. It sounded like a bag of plastic bottles being pulled over rocks.

'Let's go,' said Trike.

They walked towards the rearing crystal tree. Sulphurous yellow and translucent, the thing was a dendrite crystal writ large, but with veins running through it. It extended from the floor all the way up to attach to the top cap of the cylinder, with the Client wound around it. In some ways, she resembled a giant centipede. Flickering all down her length dispelled such illusions, however, because no centipede was so over-endowed with sets of nacreous wings. A memory came to Trike and he realized she reminded him of a life form he had seen just once on the world of the Cyberat. Checking the mass of data available, he recalled a creature like a flying millipede but also a colony of creatures. Had he not known some of the history of the Species, he would have suspected a distant relative. But the Client's ancestors were nothing like that.

As they drew closer to the tree, the Client began to move, sliding her back end down to the floor and out, steadily dropping lower in waves of shifting movement. It was an unwieldy body-design, he felt, but obviously the product of a mind that wanted to move away from the harsh individualism of the Jain. Finally, she detached from the tree and raised her primary form twenty feet from the floor and oriented it towards them. She surged forwards, that primary form dipping down, and it looked uncomfortably like the attack run of a hooder.

'Maybe I should have brought a gun,' said Cog.

'Pointless,' Trike replied. 'If she had wanted us dead that would have happened long before now. She is in fact being accommodating. It's usually zero grav in here and she could have had us floating up where we would have been completely vulnerable.'

She slowed and dipped lower, so her primary form came level with Trike's face. Though he had already been scanning her with the instruments of his body, now he could see her close-up with his semi-human eyes. He noted first the head with its various sensors, mandibles and sucking spicules. The heads of each of the other units on her collective body were all on the underside, each up against the body of the one before it. The number of her legs matched those of a centipede, but were unevenly distributed. The wings clattered and shimmered – perhaps they gave stability. Close now, the communication became more intense and he could see the shape of her intent.

'Automatics in the ship's core destroyed your remote,' he stated. 'Then sent it back at you to attack both physically and mentally.'

'A remote with a distinct, independently powerful intelligence would have more success.' Her soft, female voice actually did issue from the form before him.

On other levels she filled in detail. Her shape, both physical and informational, with her Jain and Species antecedents, made her particularly vulnerable to the ship's core. But *his* mental make-up made him more likely to be both effective and ignored.

'You feel certain?' he asked.

'You have already demonstrated your effectiveness,' the Client replied. 'I predict that you will be successful.' Her head form swung to one side to study Cog. 'With a grounding in the physical world to keep you in touch with it.'

More there too. Cog could be a distraction and a focus . . .

She continued, 'But now, we have to be sure . . .' She shifted slowly nearer.

'What the hell?' exclaimed Cog.

Trike held up a hand to him. 'Just . . . wait.'

Her head moved closer and closer to him. He realized he did not need to use just the data connections, the fibres and filaments in his tongue, because he could issue them from any part of his body. He raised his hand and brought it down on her head, a rough carapace under his palm and under the white veins writhing there. He felt the shell at a microscopic level, found the pores in it and injected masses of nano-fibres. Once inside her skull, he had no need to hunt down connections because they were available in the organic neural interfaces that once connected this primary form to the one ahead of it. The connection felt like falling into a massive space swarming with information. Riveted to the spot, he absorbed all she had to offer and then, after a reluctant pause, opened the full extent of his mind to her.

'You are complex,' she stated in that mental space. 'You retain your identity even though your additions outweigh it a hundred-fold. But you are neither Jain nor Species. And you are not Orlandine either.'

'I am myself,' Trike replied, and it was a coagulation of all his mental processes, a conclusion reached.

Together they speculated on what he might find in the ship's core. Then they played out response strategies – some simple and others blurring off into Mandelbrot complexity, layer upon layer of responses. And then it was done.

Trike slowly returned to the moment, a weight dragging his arm down. He detached Jain tendrils; the sucked-dry corpse of the Client's erstwhile primary form dropped from his hand to the floor, bouncing and shedding a couple of limbs. Just beyond it, the Client was returning to her tree – a new primary form in control. He turned to Cog.

'Time to go,' he said.

## Gemmell

Mayor Ransom was a tall, thin individual who obviously had something insectile in his genome. Gemmell did a little bit of mental research as he sat down and discovered that the man had not been born on Jaskor, but had come in from the Polity – one of the line worlds. Ransom was a descendant of humans who had used adaptogens to form themselves to their cold, dry and highly radioactive world. Definite divisions in his skin marked it as partial carapace, and Gemmell felt sure he could see in him the scorpion whose DNA had enabled his ancestors to adapt to their world. A further query of data available in the sphere informed him that Ransom's world had once seceded from the Polity, and that Separatism and anti-AI sentiment were endemic there. The discovery felt prosaically inevitable.

The other city councillors were a mix of Jaskorans and inner Polity citizens who had come here to work and decided to stay, becoming naturalized citizens of Orlandine's small realm. Even as they sat down around the table, he could read the dynamic. They looked to Ransom for leadership. It was annoying and naive. He shot a look at Ruth and she looked back, crossing her eyes. He suppressed a burst of laughter with a snort and a couple of coughs.

The room overlooked the grav-car park, and down there Gemmell could see the two prador had moved closer. Studying the window glass, he identified standard chain-glass, without any security, and had no doubt the prador had a laser on it to pick up vibrations – to listen in on this room. Even so, he requested links through the data sphere and reached the commander of the prador here.

'You need something?' asked Vreen.

'I'm giving you open access to this meeting with Mayor Ransom,' he replied. 'You can listen in to anything that is said.'

'Most generous,' Vreen replied.

Vreen was certainly one of the Guard. He showed a grasp of sarcasm normal prador did not possess.

'So let's get straight down to it,' Gemmell said aloud. 'You have a problem with the disposition of the forces here and asked to see me about this, even though it could have been sorted out via the data sphere.'

'We still prefer human interaction, despite the heavy presence of the Polity and its technology spreading about our world,' Ransom replied.

Gemmell assessed him on that comment and from his history: the man seemed to have sympathies with Separatism. This being the case, he wondered why Orlandine's subpersona had allowed him into a position of power. Mulling that over for a second, he realized the likely scenario. Ransom had been, at the worst, a mild irritation to the subpersona AI – a fly hardly worth swatting. Now, with what might happen on this world, he could be a danger and so the AI had routed this information to Morgaine. Either that or the AI had caught a whiff of something else going on. Yet still this situation did not require his personal attention. Surely the AI itself could have dealt with it?

'Really?'

'But the Polity is not really our problem.' Ransom pointed to the window towards the two prador out in the grav-car park. 'They are.'

What was his angle on this? If he had Separatist sympathies, why raise objections to the prador?

*If prador and Polity are antagonistic, that is always good for the Separatist cause . . .*' On the rare occasions Ruth used her auglink to him, she was always concise and to the point.

*'Are we certain he is Separatist?'* He wondered.

*'Because Morgaine as good as sent you here?'*

Even though their connection did not have high bandwidth, Gemmell got a hint of Ruth's concern coming across – her distrust of Morgaine.

'Must I affirm the facts of life?' Gemmell asked. 'The Jaskoran system and the accretion disc are, effectively, a dictatorship, in fact a military dictatorship commanded finally by the haiman Orlandine. But it is one that exists only because it is allowed to exist by both the Kingdom and the Polity.'

'This is not an ideal situation,' said Ransom, looking around smugly.

'An accretion disc full of Jain tech is not an ideal situation either – one must make do.' Gemmell studied the others around the table in turn. 'And now there is a high chance that the same technology may end up on this world.'

'Yet, despite the proximity of Jaskor to the accretion disc, it never has before,' said Ransom.

Gemmell shrugged. That wasn't the debate. 'The prador are here as part of a defence force – a situation that is in accordance with previous agreements and in accordance with Orlandine's wishes.'

'But not in accordance with our wishes which, under Orlandine's rule, have generally been acceded to.'

'We do not think they are safe,' interjected the woman sitting to Ransom's right. Gemmell nodded an acknowledgement to her and returned his attention to Ransom – she was obviously one of his mouthpieces.

'The prador are under strict orders from their commander to cause no harm to the people here. They are here to protect you.'

'Doubtless words many have heard throughout history.'

*He's playing you. I think he's waiting for something,*' Ruth told him privately.

'So what do you expect me to do about this?' Gemmell asked. 'Should I order the prador to leave your city?'

'*You're right,*' he replied to Ruth.

'We perfectly understand the political situation vis-à-vis the Kingdom and the Polity,' said Ransom, glancing out of the window at the prador. 'But it is our contention that military activities on this world are merely an exercise in Polity and prador imperialism and not strictly necessary. Perhaps that is not the case.' Again, he glanced towards the window. 'If it is, we will need a detailed explanation of the necessity for that presence, otherwise it must be removed.'

The man was waffling to cover his greater interest in the scene outside the window. Gemmell looked out carefully, just in time to catch a flash and flicker of movement and recognize it instantly. It had come from the military carrier at the edge of the grav-car park. The blast, when it came, picked up one of the prador and sent it tumbling out of sight below. He at once saw the danger: local forces heavily populated the parking area. This being a distribution point, he had not thought to question that when they came in, but he did now. They had no real reason to be here. The missile strike had also been from a low-yield explosive. It hadn't been armour-piercing, or planar or high-intensity, so would not have harmed a prador in its armour, but the prador might react to the provocation. And if it reacted, as they were known to, then that meant mayhem and a lot of bodies.

'Vreen,' he sent via his gridlink, even as he stood and ran for the door, *'tell your troops not to respond.'*

*'That is not necessary,'* Vreen replied. *'They have their orders.'*

Gemmell slammed out of the meeting room with Ruth close on his heels. Once he reached the parking platform, he looked across at the site of the detonation. One of the prador had backed up against the building, its weapons pointed out towards the military carrier. Out of sight for only a moment, the other one abruptly rose into view from over the side of the building, then shot in and slammed down. Another missile streaked out from behind the vehicle but the second prador issued an anti-munitions laser from a side turret and the thing detonated in mid-air. Pulling out his sidearm, Gemmell ran across. As he reached the carrier, he saw the launcher lying on the rooftop. At the building's edge stood a woman clad in the uniform of the local troops. She grinned viciously at him, reached across to turn on the grav-harness she wore, then stepped off the building. Gemmell ran to the edge and looked down. The woman had dropped two floors before the harness activated. Then something on it flashed and detonated, slamming her sideways. She tried to claw at the air, as if she might climb it, and fell screaming. He tracked her all the way down and watched her hit the pavement far below, bouncing and flinging out pieces of herself from the original red corona. Gemmell holstered his sidearm.

'One potential witness who won't talk,' said Ruth from beside him.

'So it would seem,' he replied.

They walked back. He looked over towards the councillors and the mayor, now outside the building and, in that moment, picked up another flash of weapons fire. He just had time to turn towards it before the impact picked him up off the ground and slammed him back against the military carrier. He slid down and gazed at his burned and smoking chest. He had no doubt at all that, when analysed, the round would be found to have come from a prador Gatling cannon.

# 6

*Space warfare is the hard reality of resources, energy reserves, armament and technology, mathematics and physics, and cold calculations. It is also energy weapons scoring across vacuum to burn through materials tougher, stronger and more durable than anything known when we were confined to Earth. Missiles and fast-moving debris puncture armour like bullets through cardboard. Feedback surges instantly turn components molten and create confined space lightning bolts. Virtual warfare beams blind you and distort reality, and sometimes eat your mind. All of these will boil you in your space suit or interface armour, suffocate you in crash foam or have you fighting to breathe vacuum. It is also moments of terrifying inevitability and tactical sacrifice. When evenly matched, opposing forces engage, the result is either the withdrawal of one side or debris and death. When one side has an advantage, it will usually win. We must first accept these realities and dispel at once romantic notions about battle in space, because few heroic encounters or clever stratagems can win a battle against the odds. However, having dispelled romantic notions, let us now examine some clever stratagems and heroic encounters . . .*

Notes from her lecture 'Modern Warfare'
by E. B. S. Heinlein

# THE HUMAN

## Orlik

As the Jain vessels darted into it like hunting fish into a shoal of prey, the fleet inevitably dispersed. The ships weren't fleeing, however, but trying to make room to deploy their weapons more effectively. Unfortunately, the most potent weapon was the most inaccurate one: the directed gravity weapon, the DIGRAW. Only a few ships possessed this, those being the *Kinghammer*, the *Cable Hogue* and four of the big modern Polity dreadnoughts. Orlik observed it in action again, as a wave from the *Hogue* struck and distorted the hardfield of an attacker. That field went out just in time for the vessel to receive a further gravity wave strike from one of the dreadnoughts. The thing crumbled like a mollusc hit with a rock, yet still it continued firing and manoeuvring under stuttering fusion drives. Even radiating into the ultraviolet under constant particle beam fire, it sliced a reaver from nose to tail, peeling the ship open, then swept its grasers across a series of Polity attack ships, bursting them one after another. Finally, something gave out and it blew apart. And even then it caused further damage – hard, fast-moving debris blasting hardfield projectors and crashing into the hulls of surrounding ships.

'They're fucking us,' Sprag observed, even as the *Kinghammer* surged into a high-gravity turn that dragged at Orlik in his sanctum and left a trail of its own burned-out projectors. A graser then ripped across the hull, flaking up hull material like scales, before wandering on to nail a prador destroyer, and putting out its engines.

Appalling quantities of debris tumbled through vacuum. Orlik had been avoiding the telemetry and stats, but looking again, he now saw the count of ships destroyed. Their overall number was diminishing so fast it looked like a countdown to oblivion.

A big old dreadnought, a mountain of brassy metal translated into vacuum, tumbled along through a firestorm of ejected hard-field projectors and then ablating armour. It was one of just eight old-style prador dreadnoughts remaining; Orlik realized the simple fact that in this battle the weaker ships were the first to go.

'That one,' he said, highlighting the attacker of that old dread-nought.

His own thought and Sprag's were one as they turned the *Kinghammer* and fell in behind the attacker. Was it his own order or Sprag's that sent the swarm of railgun missiles hammering into its spherical hardfield? Orlik could not tell. Another attacker passed over, the gutted hulk of its last victim also passing close by the *Hammer*, fires flickering in the blackened cavity of its interior. The *Kinghammer* shuddered and flung up hardfields in layers. Enough to stop the onslaught and impel the attacker towards different prey, but still internal cams showed another hole through the hull and air roaring out into vacuum across the glowing nubs of severed I-beams. Two more of his crew were gone, but he was just too busy to feel emotions that were not customary for his kind.

'Stay on it,' he commanded.

'We just lost a sector,' Sprag replied.

'I know, but they're not all dead in there.'

Part of the ship now lay out of his reach, out of *their* reach. But weapons located there, after just a short delay, began firing again. This told him that, as ordered, crew had taken up the baton. Ahead, the alien vessel dodged and weaved through the fleet, dispensing destruction all around it, with the *Kinghammer* still firing on it with all weapons. This seemed the only way to deal with them: hit them hard and just keep on hitting them until their hardfields overloaded. If the Polity and prador ships let up for a minute the things managed to intermittently shut down their fields and shed the absorbed energy from them by firing on other ships.

'Its hardfield is reaching its limit,' Sprag stated.

The enclosing hardfield turned opaque around the big louse-like vessel, as it accelerated out of the main battlefield. Orlik had saved the coup de grâce until this moment and opened up with the *Kinghammer*'s gravity weapon. A ripple seemed to pass through vacuum and the enemy hardfield distorted, then it just flickered out.

'What?'

'Deliberate,' said Sprag.

This final blow should have caused the attacker's hardfield to collapse and destroy it. But the thing came out of the wave and stretched, with breaks between its armour ribs spilling debris from inside. Then it flipped over and, on scattered suns of fusion engines, began decelerating, closing the gap between the two of them. Orlik reassessed and realized he could do no more – all his weapons were firing, the particle beams emptying tanks of particulate and draining laminar power storage dry, railgun carousels spinning hot and emptying. He could open up with ship's lasers but that would only drain power away from the particle beams. He just had to hope some critical system gave out in the enemy ship.

'Wave weapon?' he asked calmly.

'Three minutes,' Sprag replied.

Orlik knew that but had hoped Sprag had something to offer he had not seen. A ball of fire consisting of vaporized railgun slugs and beam splash now concealed most of the enemy ship. Some fire rose from the ablation of its incredibly, unbelievably tough hull, but still its engines were running. And then it began shooting again.

Thoroughly engaged with the systems of the *Kinghammer*, Orlik felt the graser strikes as stabs through his body. The simulacrum of pain made him flinch on his saddle control, as a beam punched through hardfields and lanced through the nose of the ship. It burned underneath the hull, bubbling it like a carapace under the pass of a blowtorch, then passed out in an explosion near the engines. A second strike nearby shattered the bearings of a railgun carousel and it crashed through the internal structures, fragmenting. One wall of the sanctum clattered like tin under hail, a line of holes punched all the way across it. Something smacked into him and shoved him sideways partially off his saddle, and real pain blossomed down his side. Damage stats blurred to one side of other data processing. A moment later, the pain faded as his armour internally snipped off two shattered limbs and sprayed analgesic sealant.

'Damn,' said Sprag.

As he pulled himself back onto the saddle, Orlik looked up. Some of his feed was gone because of damage to the optics of his interface plate. The crane arm from which they hung had been bent out of shape, and Sprag's original body was gone. Quickly scanning around the sanctum, Orlik saw it lying against the far wall, bent out of shape but still intact. It then rose up off the floor as grav went out. With a thought, he engaged clamps, locking himself to his saddle and focused back on the enemy ship just as it fired again.

Another beam cut into the *Kinghammer*, tearing a wavering course across its hull. He realized these strikes were not as effective as they could be, because the firestorm his own strikes had raised on it soaked up their power. But it would not be much longer before they were up to full strength, because he was simply running out of munitions. Horrible realization dawned then: he was all but done. Long seconds passed as he assessed and re-assessed. The data were quite explicit: they could not survive this.

'Abandon ship!' he commanded, for few courses of action remained.

Numerous queries came back to him and he interpreted the essence of them.

'We're going to ram,' he replied.

'And you?' they asked.

'Save yourselves,' he stated, then cut com to them. Now, as was his option, he seized full control of available ship's systems, taking it away from his AI. 'You too, Sprag,' he added.

'I cannot go,' Sprag replied.

He checked quickly and saw this to be true. He had assumed the *Kinghammer* had the same ejection facility as Polity ships, but found the vessel had been made so its AI would die with it. As he routed every erg of power to the drive, he glanced at the remains of Sprag pinned by acceleration to the back wall. There were other ways. Orlik checked links and feeds. Another difference between this ship and a Polity ship was not just that he could take supreme control of it, but that he could also control its AI. He made the link and saw Sprag's erstwhile body begin moving its limbs weakly as she began to download into it.

'So you intend to die,' said Sprag.

'I will take out that ship,' Orlik replied.

He saw armoured prador ejecting from the *Kinghammer*. About half of them were going yet many remained. It wasn't logical because they could achieve nothing by dying with their ship. But he could not question their decision to stay, nor could he enforce his order.

'No,' said Sprag. '*I* will take out that ship.'

Hard acceleration kicked in, the dispersing fireball looming ahead. Suddenly the saddle control rose and the walls closed in, heaping up debris. His grip on ship's systems became tenuous and when he tried to find out what the hell was happening, the data just escaped him.

'Sorry,' said Sprag. 'From about ten seconds after I became this ship's AI, you had only the control I allowed you. And now goodbye.'

Mechanical movement shuddered all around him. The pull of acceleration dropped to nothing, then surged in transverse. Only when it happened did he realize what was happening. Everything but radio links went out but they gave him an overview, if an intermittent one. He saw the *Kinghammer* dropping away from him towards the dying firestorm. At the last moment, he saw the alien vessel, still intact and still cutting into his ship with its grasers. Then the two ships hit with a flash that blanked out everything.

Tumbling through vacuum in his sanctum, which Sprag had ejected from the ship, Orlik was out of the battle. By and by he engaged with the sensors on the exterior of it, and then connected to fleet telemetry again. To say that the battle was going badly was an understatement. Eight Jain attack ships were still active and had destroyed about a half of the main fleet. Debris and fire-gutted hulks filled space. Meanwhile, more of those tough bastards remained attached to the Jain mother ship – a vessel the Polity and prador fleet had yet to even engage with properly.

**Diana**

The power balance between prador and Polity ships had been about even when they arrived here. Now most of the least effect-ive ships of both sides were gone, as well as many of the thoroughly effective ones – possibly the *Kinghammer* too, whose loss would make the Polity's complement the stronger one. But it meant nothing. All the machinations of Earth Central and the king, all their manoeuvring prior to this battle, had become pointless. And anyway, soon even the meaningless greater strength of the Polity here would vanish because four of those things were now focusing on her. She didn't even know why she had been thinking about it.

Diana pulled herself up to her chair, dabbed at blood on the back of her head and neck where her links had ripped free, pushed her head back and hit engage in her chair arm. The links again snaked out and plugged into her skull, painfully, but they at once put her back into the system.

'What the hell happened?' she asked.

'The impact took the safeties offline,' replied Hogue aloud, voice distorted in the smoky atmosphere of the bridge.

Fans kicked in to draw the smoke away quickly, and she saw the hole, high up in the wall, petals of bubble-metal and thick shards of ceramal armour protruding inwards. At four feet across, it was minor on the scale of this ship, but not for Alianathon. Another hole on the opposite side of the bridge showed where the chunk of debris, doubtless along with most of her body, had exited between Jabro and Seckurg.

The debris strike on the bridge had been the least of the damage to the ship. The *Hogue* rolled out of a cloud of molten metal droplets that still radiated white-hot. The hole in its side lay ten miles across and cut almost to the centre. Out of control and travelling at the speed of a railgun slug, nothing remained of the reaver that had struck there. It seemed apposite that the thing which had made such a hole in their armour had killed their armourer too. Diana tried to feel something for the loss of Alianathon, but found nothing there. Was her connection to Hogue dehumanizing her as such connections did to many others?

'Dulse. What can you give me?'

'At least five minutes before I can fire again, and we'll have internal disruption from that,' he replied tightly.

'Stay on it.'

The four alien vessels continued to bear down fast. Grasers lit up the gaseous cloud, while the *Hogue* shuffled through its supplies of hardfield projectors at an alarming rate – adding to the molten metal out there. She picked just one of the ships and focused all particle beam cannons on it. The thing just kept coming, turning into a burning comet.

'U-twist,' one of the crew stated.

She felt it turn and grind in the ship, ripping out another mass of its guts twenty miles across. Four particle beam weapons went down.

'Another four reactors gone,' said Orien, just heard over the rumbling and crashing from the ship, but clear over data channels.

'Nothing left of the *Kinghammer*,' said Seckurg. 'Nothing.' As a Golem he could choose to experience emotions or not, supposedly, yet Alianathon's death beside him had evidently affected him. Jabro sat stunned with his hands down on his chair arms and offering no input to the system, staring into the hole. Diana let him have a moment while she replayed the destruction of the *Hammer* in her mind. She gave a small nod of acknowledgement to Orlik's sacrifice, then reassessed. Rewinding, she saw the prador ejecting in the ship's sanctum. Orlik might well be still alive.

'Jabro,' she said loudly. 'We have our counter to the disruptor so that is no longer your concern. I need you sharp. Work the armour and liaise on tactic Omega.'

He jerked as if slapped and that, she knew, was the physical result of his seeking aid from his interface armour. He then set to work on his panel.

'Tactic Omega,' he stated flatly.

'Start pulling them in,' she ordered. 'Get all the strays you can but we go when . . . necessary.'

That started a verbal exchange, as well as a mental one, between the bridge crew as they worked their aspects of what was now a rescue mission and retreat. All talked in flat, emotionless tones. As with Jabro, their interface armour dampened emotion, fed them neurochem and put them back in the groove of battle. Diana had no such option – she had decided against it long ago since she felt it interfered with her realistic assessment of warfare. Her assessment now was that they were fucked. She switched views, gazing towards the main Jain vessel. There it sat, clearly visible, even through massive interference. If a small number of its attack ships could do this much damage, the remainder of this fleet stood no chance against those still attached to its hull, let alone the thing itself. But still . . .

'Hogue – mass firing of megaton-upwards CTDs. Target the mother ship – everything we have, the entire fleet.' She said this aloud, also broadcasting to every vessel. 'The EMR should offer cover for us to salvage some of this.'

They had been holding back on the heavier missiles until they were much closer, but they seemed unlikely to get any nearer than they were. In overview, she saw her order carried out instantly across the Polity ships because that option in them lay directly under Hogue's control. The launch from the prador ships ensued just a moment later and it surprised her to see that just about all of them had obeyed. The swarm of missiles blasted from the remainder of the fleet, all heading towards the mother ship. In the *Hogue*, giant carousels turned and loaded coilguns with throats like monorail tunnels. From the eighteen of these remaining in action, missile after missile sped out, each the size of grav-cars or larger. These were the kind of CTDs used to obliterate moons and depopulate worlds. Crust busters.

'Crossfire on that bastard,' she stated.

One of the four attackers had been tearing into the *Hogue*'s hull but the DIGRAW was ready again. As it thumped, she felt as if she had just dropped from height onto a hard floor. The ceiling buckled and instruments flashed with disrupted optics. Screens and other displays went out, then flickered back on again, and for a second she lost sight of everything beyond the ship. In that hiatus, she gazed at a ball of lightning generating in the middle of the bridge, which then shot to one side and earthed in a wall. Back online, she saw the wave shimmer out from the ship, perfectly visible in its spreading cone as it passed through gas and debris. It struck the attacker and this time caused an immediate hardfield collapse. The field blackened, shrank down to nothing, then exploded in a small nova. Thinking fast, the AI of the crossfire ship directed its own wave at another attacker lying beyond the first. This one dropped its hardfield after the wave from the *Hogue* passed through it, then the second wave struck and wrecked it. Yet it began to change course, inevitably still firing its weapons.

'Reavers,' stated Jabro.

Five of them in a line were coming in towards the *Hogue*. They all opened up with particle beams and hit the approaching attacker.

'Ah fuck,' said Jabro.

Glowing like iron from a furnace, this attacker bore down on the *Hogue*. Hardfields flickered and died before it and the *Hogue* spewed molten projectors from a series of ports around its circumference. The thing struck hull but the safeties were back online and padded clamps whipped across Diana's body to prevent her from hurtling up into the ceiling. For one of the crew, they did not work. He slammed upwards, hit the roof and crashed down again, rolling over and coughing out blood. The

Jain ship ricocheted away before breaking apart, then exploded under a railgun fusillade.

'Permission to dock,' Hogue announced.

Rather than waiting until hull doors opened to admit them into the interior, Hogue directed the five reavers to the massive hole in its hull. They descended, weapons still firing at the other two attackers. One of them didn't make it. As its back end blew out on some massive explosion, its nose struck the edge of the crater and it tumbled away, end over end.

'They're refocusing,' said Seckurg.

The two Jain ships bearing down on the *Hogue* abruptly altered course while the remaining four, out there ripping apart the fleet, diverted too.

'They're after the missiles,' Seckurg added.

Their grasers opened up on the retreating swarm and titanic explosions began to white out the view of the mother ship. This, at least, demonstrated some vulnerability on the part of the enemy, and they were given a few minutes' breathing space. Diana viewed all the fleet ships close by and coming in, and all those that had recently disengaged straggling after.

'Opening doors,' Hogue announced.

'Dulse. The engines,' she said.

'Still good but our screening is shot. This is going to be rough.'

'But doable?'

'Yeah. Doable.'

Giant doors began grinding open all over *Hogue*'s hull. First in through them were a few attack ships, then a couple of old prador dreadnoughts that had surprisingly survived. More reavers also began queuing up, as well as smaller destroyers. However, there was no room for them all. It was the stark mathematics of war but Diana started to feel frustration and sorrow. Twenty Polity dreadnoughts – big ones – sat out there in vacuum doing nothing.

'Run,' she told them, sending all related tactical considerations. But simple reality meant that if the six Jain craft went after them, they were dead. A reply came back from a ship called the *Remington*: 'If they come after us, we will attempt a U-jump,' said its AI.

Diana ran calculations. Those ships did possess powerful U-jump engines but if they jumped, this present storm would wreck them as they exited back out into the real. However, none of them would be lost in U-space and the probability that many of their AIs and other crew might survive was higher than if they stayed and fought those six alien ships.

*The six remaining of those deployed,* she reminded herself.

'Best of luck,' she told the *Remington* AI.

Two dreadnoughts hammered through the space doors and crashed into one of the *Hogue*'s internal spaces. Four reavers, a Polity destroyer and an assortment of attack ships followed them in, their impacts shaking the great vessel. They caused damage and plenty of it, but it was acceptable. Other spaces quickly filled while ships snared up survivors on the way in – lone prador, ejected sanctums and AI cases, storage pods for marines, war drones and Golem. The ships to remain also snatched up survivors further out, though it was debatable if being inside a ship was the best option for them. Maybe the Jain ships, if they attacked again, would think scattered survivors beneath their notice.

Then came the impact. Depleted by the attacks from the smaller Jain ships, the missile swarm finally found the surface of the mother ship's hardfield. Multiple immense blasts lit up space – the output close to that of a hypergiant sun. The glare even reached inside the bridge, having wended its way through weapons damage and debris holes. For a minute or two, it glowed as bright as the sunniest day and Diana had time to spot

Alianathon's arm – the hand was clinging to a structural member just beyond the hole through which she had exited. Diana could not understand how that had happened.

Blast waves spread out from the impact point, converting gas and debris to photonic matter. With heavy sensory filtering, Diana saw the six Jain vessels hit, as if by a gravity wave. They rode out on the storm, globed in hardfields. One of them went out with a flash, so there was that at least. She watched as the glow slowly faded.

Soon, all the ships that could pack themselves into the *Hogue* were in. Retrieval of other survivors had reached a threshold whereby she would either have to move the *Hogue* or send ships out after them. How much more could she push this? The limit came when the Jain mother ship shut down its field.

'U-twist,' said Dulse.

Diana gripped the arms of her chair. Tracking picked up the disruption a thousand miles out, debris swirling for a moment then turning into a glowing fog. They could not afford another of those in the *Hogue*.

'Dulse,' she said. 'Take us out.'

The *Cable Hogue* thrummed as its multiple U-space engines powered up and interlocked their effect. As the man had said, with inadequate shielding it was rough. Reality twisted to where all matter became an infinite hole and where dimensions seemed to mean nothing. Diana's hand was the size of a sun, while those ships out there were motes in her palm. She felt something tearing in her skull as her mind tried to make sense of the impossible. For one of the crew it became too much, and hoarse screams seemed to weave themselves into the deep drone of power. As in other U-space jumps, Diana felt a moment of epiphany as the universe slid out from underneath her, but one of horror and emptiness and futility too. It lasted for less than a minute but that minute, as a fraction of eternity, was eternal itself. Then the *Hogue* crashed back into the real, the bridge rippled and its walls split and roared as vacuum ripped away the air. A mask clamped itself to her face but she could feel the void sucking on her skin.

'*One light minute,*' Hogue intoned.

Diana fought the feeling of deep futility, of the pointlessness of it all, and forced herself to re-engage. Exterior sensors gave her nothing, but then all she would see back the way they had come lay a minute in the past. She gazed instead into the internal spaces of the ship and the damage there. The jump had distorted the *Hogue* throughout, as if a gravity wave had spiralled out from a central point. In one internal space, she saw a reaver bent round into a ring. Further checking revealed that every major weapon had ceased to be available because the hull had shifted round over internal structure and closed off weapons ports. Eighty per cent of other systems inside were down too, Hogue reported, though it could repair them. Oddly, the U-space engines showed no damage at all – they had protected each other, remained pristine.

Finally, someone spoke up via the system:

'*If we can do it, who's to say they cannot?*' asked Jabro.

This was utterly true.

'*Dulse, prepare us for another jump,*' said Diana.

Exterior sensors came back online and Diana looked back to their point of departure. The Jain mother ship was still there, still undamaged and its children were returning to it – isopod sea-louse forms locking again to its hull. She felt insulted that it now seemed they were beneath its notice. But, gradually, she felt glad to still be alive.

She watched the remaining Polity dreadnoughts there accelerate away, weapons firing intermittently as they sped out through the Jain cloud. Apparently, they were beneath notice too.

# THE HUMAN

## Cog

Trike stood before the main screen of Cog's ship the *Janus* with his hands behind his back. His pose bore some resemblance to that of a contemplative admiral. Some resemblance . . . Cog grimaced and felt completely out of his league again. He realized that until this moment he had still regarded Trike as the 'boy' he had known. A much mutated and physically changed version of that person, indeed, but one whose previous disability was just greatly emphasized. Sure, he could slap war drones about and probably take on an adult prador hand to hand, but, well, he needed looking out for. Cog finally understood how much he had been missing the point about him. When Trike killed Angel that had been the last death throes of his madness, which had since dissolved in the new being he had become. He ranked alongside Orlandine and AIs in ability, powers and mentality now. This sobering reality seemed akin to that moment when a father realizes a son has grown stronger and more capable than him. But Cog consoled himself with the idea that a son very infrequently surpassed the father in wisdom. He cleared his throat noisily, and Trike looked round.

'So why the hell do we need this?' Cog asked, again running data on a frame to the side of the main screen.

'It's good to be prepared,' said Trike, turning back to the screen.

'I wasn't aware we were going into battle.'

The weapon the bay robots had installed underneath, with the ease of someone plugging a night light into a socket, was online and available. Cog shuddered at the memory of seeing his ship picked up, turned over and rapidly opened with all the ease of a chef spatchcocking a chicken. The big coilgun had been glued and welded into place with such casual ease.

Trike turned towards him again. 'It is a necessary addition,' he said. 'I'm fully aware now of the capabilities this ship has always had, but they are not what I require.' It was a little dig at him, Cog felt – a reminder of when Trike hadn't been aware that Cog was an ECS agent and that his ship possessed some state-of-the-art concealed weapons and defences.

'I thought the aim was to sneak inside that thing,' he said.

'Yes, but with limitations.' Trike turned back to the screen. 'One must also factor in that this weapon might be useful at a later date. It seems almost certain now that war is coming to this system.'

Cog grunted acknowledgement. The update from Jaskor had been worrying.

The Species ship's core grew larger and larger on the screen as they approached. Cog found looking at the distance readout below the screen sobering too. Yes, he had seen massive objects like this in the Polity. He had even visited the Cassius Dyson project, which Orlandine had once overseen, and viewed the full immensity of that construction. But this thing? It was just the core of a ship and bigger than any ship previously known. His feelings also related to whatever was coming from the accretion disc. Here were the remains of an immense vessel that had opened up a U-space blister in a sun to trap another ship it had been unable to defeat.

'The size of that bugger,' he muttered. Then, 'Where to?'

'Over the other side,' said Trike. 'The security systems are likely to be on higher alert where the Client tried to get in.'

'You sure about that?' Cog asked. 'The whole system might be on high alert. Presuming there are even levels of alertness.'

Without turning, Trike shot back. 'There are still percentage points of probability in our favour. We go over the other side.' He paused for a second, then added, 'Though of course it is possible, considering the psychology of traps, that the system is on higher alert on the other side.'

'I hardly find that reassuring,' Cog grumbled.

He focused on the screen again, then decided to do some tinkering to clean up the image. Then wished he hadn't.

The ship's core looked like a clump of wire, with a ceramic coating fractured evenly along its length, as if some leviathan had wound it into a great coin-shaped wad. The coating appeared mostly brassy, but with an iridescence like nacre. It also seemed organic. Those pieces of coating could be, if he stretched his imagination, the segments of an angular worm, or group of worms. An immediate comparison would be to a wormship, but those vessels were more chaotic in structure. They even possessed a hint of illusory sliminess and did not have such clearly defined segmentation. Here the saurian segmentation resembled the skin of a crocodile more. Yes, it seemed reptilian. And yet, it was also technology. Around its rim, mile-wide holes seemed to raise lips, chapped lips because they were segmented too. Surfaces spread here and there between the windings, with the quadrate intricacies of ancient silicon chips. Towers protruded – spikes like giant thorns, but straight and with even formations clinging to them like cubist lichen.

As they drew closer, Cog flipped the *Janus* over for a decelerating burn, seemingly over the surface of some brassy planet – a great range of hills below a starlit sky. He hit the control to revolve the bridge to face their direction of travel, then realized his sensors showed atmosphere here, and checked scanning. Besides electrostatics holding dust and gas in around the ship's core, the super-density of some of its components brought its mass up to that of a small moon and this too contributed to the effect. But the thin fog only caught some of the light reflected from Adranas rising over the far horizon. And then, just a little while later, they appeared to shoot over a rough cliff at the edge of the range and, as Cog turned the ship over this, the planetary illusion fled.

'Down there,' said Trike, linking into the ship's system and throwing up a frame over one portion of this face of the structure. Here lay another entrance like the one the Client had tried to breach. Cog swiftly brought his ship down to hover before it. The illusion returned as he scanned in each direction, taking in miles and miles of mountainous metal scattered with plains which reminded him of ancient etched electronics, curving away from them.

'Should we go in?' Cog asked, studying the entrance, which with its lipped edges also uncomfortably reminded him of the mouth of a volcano.

'I am scanning the interior,' Trike replied.

A moment later, he saw movement inside the mile-wide tunnel. Debris began to stream out, as when the Client had started scanning the entrance over the other side. Cog reversed the ship away and initiated its hardfields and collision lasers. The field batted away a chunk of debris like a spherical black iron furnace ten feet in diameter and trailing feed pipes. Collision lasers flashed to burn up smaller objects or propel them on different courses by explosive evaporation.

'I see,' said Trike.

'You see what?' Cog asked.

'Scanning activates sub-AI maintenance systems to make way for security systems. The maintenance did not previously clear the debris as it should have and now has.'

'And the security system?' asked Cog.

Trike glanced over. 'All the usual in the way of guns and missiles to deal with a brute assault. Then more to deal with the burglar approach. The Client was too clever and so activated the highest level of security – the one aimed at tracking any incursion back to its source and attacking it.'

'It is aware of us, then?'

'Passive scanning and low threat assessment.' Trike shrugged. 'It sees a primitive vessel and likely assumes primitive crew. Nevertheless it will destroy this ship if we take it in.'

'So what route in?'

'After necessarily alerting it by breaking in, we keep its threat assessment low,' said Trike. 'You'll need your space suit, the heavy one.'

'I will?'

Trike showed his teeth. 'Yes, but no weapons.'

'I'm going in with you,' Cog stated.

'We need something for the security systems to focus on while I track down its source. You will be our sacrificial goat.'

'I'm not sure I'm ready to be sacrificed.'

'You won't be, it's just a turn of phrase.'

Cog stared at Trike, trying to read him. He was tempted to say no and just pull out of this right now, but curiosity won out. He really wanted to see inside that ship's core, he wanted to learn what he could about the Species. In the end, excitement he had not felt in a long while drove him on – a feeling that only personal danger could elicit in one so old and jaded. He abruptly stood up and headed out of the bridge to his cabin.

Once inside, with the door closed behind him, Cog pondered on Trike's abilities again. The man had never seen this particular suit of Cog's, for he had concealed it well, yet he knew about it. Cog walked up to the back wall of his cabin and slammed his palm hard against a framed picture of a sea scene on Spatterjay. The picture slowly sank into the wall to leave a hole. He inserted his hand and felt a sampler take a snip out of it to read his DNA. A wave of heat ran down his body as scanners checked it was really him, then the wall split.

The suit, which was heavily armoured and possessing joint motors that would increase his already formidable strength, walked out of the wall, then opened. Panels in the front and down the legs slid aside, while the helmet concertinaed back and the whole thing loosened. He slipped off his boots and backed into the suit, inserting his feet and then his arms. The thing closed and tightened around him, special pads locking his limbs in place, the helmet's visor closing and its head-up display showing him its status. He took a step and the motors kicked in, making the suit apparently as light on him as balsa.

Next, peering into the cavity where the suit had been stored, he eyed the selection of weapons affixed to one wall. Sighing regretfully, he turned to his cabin door and headed out.

Trike waited on the stairway down to the hold. He inspected Cog for a moment, nodded, then pointed downwards.

'You just head in and try to avoid confrontation,' said Trike via the com of Cog's suit. 'Here.' A map appeared with a route marked out. He saw a slightly circuitous path towards the central chamber where the Species were supposedly ensconced.

'How fast should I head in?' asked Cog, as the map folded away and left a direction arrow blinking at the bottom of his visor.

'Go in like a curious visitor,' Trike replied. 'Speed up if things get critical, but try to stick to the route.'

Soon they reached the hold, where the ramp door stood open on vacuum. Cog's boots automatically went to gecko function as he walked from grav-plated floor to the ramp, while Trike faded into invisibility beside him. Now he could see how much closer to the entrance they were. And he got a further sense of the scale of the thing. Cog thought about flying, and as gecko function shut down, he jumped from the ramp. He could feel himself integrating with the suit as he remembered how it read the workings of his brain and the minimal movements and poses of his body. A jet nodule on his leg propelled him out further.

'The door inside?' he enquired.

'About to be dealt with,' Trike replied.

Cog spun back to his ship in time to see the weapons on its underside open fire. A carousel turned in its guts and the coilgun fired a large disc, but slowly. As this headed towards the tunnel it seemed to flicker out of existence.

'What was that?' Cog asked.

'Fusion cutter concealed by chameleonware,' Trike replied. 'Head in now, as fast as you like, to the doors.'

Cog hit his jets and shot towards the tunnel, accelerating hard.

'This is not very subtle,' he observed.

'As subtle as possible at present,' said Trike. 'Subtlety was the Client's mistake.'

'Really?'

'Fast now but slowly once you're through the door, Cog,' Trike told him.

Tunnel walls slid by in a blur, and the tripart door lay ahead, still closed. As Cog drew near, now decelerating, a ring-shaped glare etched itself into existence. A moment later, a thick circular chunk of the door extruded, with the fusion cutter attached to its outer surface, and floated away. Rapidly applying his suit jets, Cog dodged it and shot towards the hole. An intense orange particle beam lanced out from the wall, incinerating the fusion cutter behind him as he made it through the opening.

'Fuck,' he said, with feeling.

On the other side, the continuation of the tunnel spiralled into this place. Here the organic nacreous look became more obvious and reminded Cog of the inside of a whelk shell, but with technological infestations. Running along one side, over quadrate patterns and channels in which liquid metal ran, a metal road appeared to have flaked away from the wall, supported in place by curved-over horns. He propelled himself to this and landed feet first, engaging gecko again. He expected some weapon to fire on him, but nothing happened.

'Are you in?' Cog asked.

'Yes.'

'So what's going on?'

'Tracing upper quadrant – data trunk. Penetrating . . .' Cog was about to ask what that meant when Trike added, 'Distributed system. I'll need an access node. Of course, no central processing. We couldn't be that lucky.'

Cog realized Trike must be trying to include him. He did understand the man was attempting to penetrate the security system as it scanned and responded to Cog, but how remained obscure. He sighed and just started walking. A short while later, an object flew into sight. The glass bubble with hardware inside rather reminded him of the lower machine part of a Cyberat's body. It hovered just above him momentarily, then shot away.

'Something watching me,' he observed.

'There's a very great deal watching you,' said Trike. 'The system has decided you are a low-level threat since your ship has moved away.'

'My ship has moved away,' Cog repeated, not exactly comfortable with that.

He kept trudging along.

Trike added, 'Weapons emplacements are focused on you. If it did consider you a high-level threat you would be gone by now. You are not worth the concomitant damage to the core should it open fire in here – rather like using a pulse rifle to kill a fly in your house. That will change if you do cause damage, so don't.'

'Oh right. Thanks for letting me know.'

'Think nothing of it,' said Trike.

After a further hundred yards, Cog spotted something falling across the tunnel to land on the walkway ahead of him. The surface under his boots shuddered. He strained his eyes and the visor took up the load, magnifying his view. A large globular object sat there. Then the white and fleshy thing at once began to slide towards him.

'Erm, I take it you're seeing this?' he enquired.

'Semi-organic,' said Trike. 'The Species birthed their own organic robots and this might be one of those.'

'Integration with the security system?' Cog asked.

'Seems the case. Accessing node . . .'

'Erm,' said Cog. 'What do I do?'

'Another one,' said Trike.

The walkway shuddered again and, glancing behind, Cog saw the twin of the one ahead had landed there. This one was nearer, so he could get a better look at it. A large, funnel-shaped hole lined with long, silvered plates lay open facing him. Both of the things slid closer and, as he prepared to propel himself away from the walkway, he suddenly felt very warm and his suit threw up data into his HUD. They were scanning him intensely, the creature ahead emitting terahertz, X-ray and neutron beams while the one behind acted as a receiver.

'They're not weaponized,' Trike stated. 'They're here for threat assessment and yes they're transmitting directly into the system.'

After scanning, they set into motion again, closing in further on Cog. He decided enough was enough and launched himself forwards and away from the walkway. The thing ahead tilted as if watching him with that glittery hole in its fore, then something flooded from inside to fill the hole, coils like guts, and whipped out towards him. The knobbly tentacle, like a wire whose insulating layer had burned to expose braided metal threads, wrapped around his ankle and began to haul him in.

'What do I do now?' he asked.

'Try not to get killed?' Trike suggested.

# 7

*In the far past, the two opposing regimes of the United States of America and the Soviet Union established a hotline so their leaders could communicate at once. This was supposed to prevent misunderstandings that might lead to nuclear Armageddon, while the two sabre-rattled and fought proxy wars in other countries. What it might have achieved is debatable had they actually come to the point of launching weapons: 'Have you fired your ICBMs at us?' 'No, old chap, of course we haven't.' Now, after a long destructive war, we have two, large, opposed regimes whose potential for Armageddon is beyond the planetary scale, and that there is a hotline between Earth Central and King Oberon of the prador is a certainty. And it seems highly likely that the essence of their exchanges is not much different to those of that past age. The sabre-rattling is the manoeuvring of giant fleets either side of a wide border, and the shift of military production to this world or that. Occasional incidents occur when warships from one side stray into the territory of the other. No proxy wars have been fought, but then such an alliance would be difficult for the xenophobic prador. The conversation, should it come down to the line, would be similar too: 'Have you launched world-busting kamikazes at us?' 'What an outrageous idea, of course not!'*

From 'How It Is' by Gordon

## Earth Central

The five, giant hammerhead dreadnoughts dropped into the real first, materializing in vacuum in shimmering, stuttering lines, then coming to a full stop in a row. A minute later, the mile-wide cube appeared, some way behind them. It folded open into a sensor array, as it had when approaching Dragon.

Now here, at the edge, Earth Central analysed the decision it had made in having the dreadnoughts go through first. It seemed an attempt to ensure its armaments got here to be ready to protect it against danger. But though the cube contained massive processing, it did not actually contain all of Earth Central, just an aspect of itself whose destruction would merely be an annoyance to the whole. It realized this aspect, this submind, must have begun to develop a sense of self . . . and self-preservation.

The stars here shone across the spectrum like distant Christmas lights, but none lay nearby. The nearest object, beside the ships, was a wanderer dark planet over a light year away. Here also lay a barrier to underspace travel. Theories of U-space describe it as a non-location, without the conventional dimensions of the real. In travelling through it, one could breach the dimensions of the real, even time, given sufficient energy. Everyone knew that U-space and the real were linked. How else could USERs work, or how else could they block travel through U-space within finite volumes of the real? But a dirty secret the AIs generally kept to themselves was that they did not entirely understand this link. The math there fell off the edge of the infinite or collapsed into singularities.

Here, anyway, lay an edge to the disruption that had issued from the accretion disc. It wasn't a precisely defined edge because, with sufficient power and sufficiently balanced U-space engines, ships could push much further into it. The five hammerheads were capable of such a feat. They were in fact capable of reaching right to the centre, though they would sustain significant damage. Earth Central now analysed the disruption as best it could at this proximity. The AI noted a rhythmic element to it, a resonance. A few hours of observation, analysis and some heavy processing confirmed that it had not resulted from the deployment of a weapon, but the collapse of the U-space blister into the Harding black hole which Orlandine had deployed. Further calculations gave a timescale: it would be forty days before it would be possible to send another conventional fleet to the accretion disc and have it arrive there sufficiently undamaged to be effective. But that did not mean something might not come out from there earlier.

Earth Central pondered on all it had learned from Dragon. Two ships had gone into the blister and almost certainly both were now out. EC next began processing scenarios. The Jain ship had been capable of raising Jain technology from the material of worlds. It had, in the process, turned a solar system into an accretion disc of debris filled with wild Jain tech. It also appeared to be back in control of that Jain tech, and certainly possessed other highly advanced weaponry. It also likely had the kind of completely enclosing hardfields EC Weapons Division was still struggling to develop.

The combined Polity and prador fleet stood against this ship, including the formidable prador ship the *Kinghammer*, and the *Cable Hogue*. Earth Central had every confidence in Diana Windermere – she was supremely capable – and with such fire-power at her command . . . EC winced mentally. It didn't matter how much confidence it might have in Windermere. Even with the formidable firepower, it was logistically impossible for the fleet to deal with the Jain cloud, let alone the Jain ship. But what else was there available?

Since the Client had transported the ship's core to the Jaskoran system, the Jain ship would probably go there. Standing against it were the Client, Orlandine and her weapons platforms, and the small combined fleet there. Both the Client and Orlandine were quantities that did not slot easily into tactical and logistical calculations. Technically advanced beyond the Polity, the Client, an alien weapons designer, could come up with something game changing. But would she even be inclined to do so? The Jain were both an enemy of her kind and her ancestors. How would she react? Orlandine was also highly advanced. Her abilities had grown constantly since she had decoded a Jain node and, in reality, she had ceased to be human or even haiman, but something beyond. Given resources, she too could come up with something game changing. But, all those years ago when she had first received that node, she had committed murder to keep it secret. She liked power, and how she might react to the Jain remained up for debate. EC did think it likely both would fight against a Jain aggressor, but the substantial possibility that they might end up allying themselves with it remained. It was also likely that no game-changers would be in the offing, and the Jain would roll over them as ruthlessly as it would doubtless roll over Windermere's fleet.

EC had to be prepared, and was in fact preparing. The AI linked back to the whole of itself – coms were intermittent this close to the disruption – and gazed upon the system Windermere's fleet had originally departed from to go to the accretion disc. Ships were arriving there now and with no pretence at concealment. *Battlewagon Beta* and *Gamma* had arrived. These were cylindrical behemoths whose firepower outmatched even Orlandine's weapons platforms. Other more conventional vessels gathered around them like bees around logs. Elsewhere in the Polity, still other ships were grouping and filling up their armouries. Previously mothballed factory stations were coming up to speed, making weapons and further ships. Planetary and solar system defences were upgrading and running drills, while the horrible spectre of a conflict on the scale of the prador/human war rose up.

EC then gazed upon other scenes, via a convoluted U-com route around the disruption ahead. First, the prador watch station over there. It seemed the king was also preparing for things to turn nasty, or rather, nastier. A new batch of fifty reavers had arrived. Next, through a watcher the king probably knew about and allowed, EC studied the fifty-mile immensity of the King's Ship. There was much activity there too. Reavers and other prador ships were massing in the vicinity. But other more worrying activity could be interpreted as *not* an expected response to the probable threat from the accretion disc.

Objects were arriving to gather in a large swarm about the King's Ship. Others issued from the ship itself, where EC surmised factory complexes lay. Closer inspection revealed much variation, but of a recognizable design. Those from the ship looked like antique jet engines a hundred yards long, wrapped in rings of hardfield projectors. Just like all the rest, these were prador kamikazes – high-yield CTDs flown by the flash-frozen minds of prador children.

EC closed up into a cube again. Thoughts of personal survival, in this aspect of itself, immediately became a secondary consideration. It was time to go and talk to Oberon, the prador king, as close and personal as possible.

## Gemmell

'I did wonder why you never wore the same kind of armour as the rest,' said Ruth.

Gemmell sat up and inspected his chest. A military autodoc

had swiftly made its repairs and left a webwork of scar tissue, just like other webs on his body. Until now, he had never thought this unsightly, but rather a salutary reminder of past mistakes. He decided in that moment to have some cosmetic work done and the scars removed, mainly because of the expression on Ruth's face as she looked at them. He swung his legs over the side of the bunk in the military carrier. He stripped off his uniform trousers, stained with his own blood, then, gridlinking to send his instructions ahead, went over to a fabricator set in the wall.

'I had it installed over two centuries ago,' he replied.

'Why?'

'Some undercover work – it saved my life then and has saved my life twice since, including today.' He felt her hand running down his back. Shivered.

'I can't feel it.'

'I have layers that run two inches into underlying muscle,' he replied. 'They're diamine film interspersed with s-con and shock foam – soft when inactive but hardens on impact, also heat dispersing, to a degree.'

Subcutaneous armour wasn't a common option for ECS soldiers, since those who might be inclined to it tended to go the whole hog and install themselves in a Golem chassis. When he thought about it, he realized his relationship with Morgaine had informed his choice. Seeing what had been happening to her all those years ago had given him an aversion to straying further than necessary from his humanity. And now, thinking about that ship captain and commander of the Polity fleet above, Gemmell realized he really must understand what had happened here. After pulling on new trousers from the fabricator, he walked back to the bunk, sat on the edge and, closing his eyes, engaged through his gridlink. Data began to flow in.

The arrests had begun shortly before he landed on the tower

car park. Orlandine's subpersona AI here had known that Separatists in Marshallam, led by Mayor Ransom, had been plotting to cause a rift between Polity and prador forces in the city. Linking to that city AI, he got detail on that. It had known they plotted to cause a fight between the two forces by first provoking the prador and, in the ensuing mayhem, kill a high-ranking Polity officer. That target had only been confirmed as him when he arrived, otherwise they would have chosen someone else. The AI had been tracking down all the culprits and potential culprits and, since its operation affected planetary defence, had informed ECS via the data sphere. Morgaine had picked this up and deliberately dropped him into it all.

He opened his eyes, feeling emotions hardening inside him. On the face of it, the operation was valid – ECS often used its personnel as patsies to reveal plots against the Polity. In fact, in the police action for which he had the subcutaneous armour installed, he had been just such a person. Yes, it was all valid, but he could see the undercurrents. Morgaine had put him in specific danger unnecessarily, without giving him full warning about what he was walking into, that he was a target. She had also known Ruth would be by his side, and equally under threat. He could not call her on it or take it to a military court. It was all a bit grey. But it was definitely something she would never have done before. He closed his eyes again and made a particular call.

'Gemmell,' she said.

Straight into a virtuality – standing on the bridge of the *Morgaine's Gate*. She looked fully human. Her loose, revealing clothing exposed a youthful body. She stood up and walked a couple of paces from her throne. No connecting hardware was visible any more.

'What did you hope to achieve?' he asked.

'I don't know what you mean.'

'You dropped me in as a prime Separatist target.'

'That was necessary to get them to act and reveal themselves,' she explained. 'I had every confidence that you would be fine.'

'You did?'

'Of course, but, even if that were not the case, the job you have is, necessarily, one that is not without risk.'

'There was risk to others too,' he noted.

'Soldiers are soldiers,' she said flatly.

He realized they could go round and round like this endlessly, and it was pointless. He had already made his decision. Mentally reviewing his military contract, he saw it had expired long ago. He drew up the attached form and filled it in, then filed his resignation from ECS in the data sphere.

'She is still on contract,' said Morgaine, immediately aware of his resignation.

'Temporary recruit who has a choice once this action is over.'

'War is dangerous,' she said.

'So am I,' he replied.

As he fell out of the virtuality, he saw tears in her eyes. In retrospect, he wondered if it had been her deliberate intention to push him away. Then he was sitting on the bunk again, and there opened his eyes.

'Not so fast,' said a voice in his mind, a new contract appearing in his inbox.

'You've been watching,' he said.

'I have,' replied Orlandine. 'Just accept.'

He did, and when he walked out of the carrier with Ruth at his side, to see Mayor Ransom pinned to the ground by the recently arrived Vreen, he smiled as the details slotted into place. He then glanced over at a big mantis drone he recognized. Cutter had doubtless arrived to give the action here Orlandine's stamp of authority. She was in command on this world, ultimate authority ending with her. Reviewing his new contract and attached media, he saw that the troops, both prador and Polity, could stay, but under the command of her general: him.

## Orlik

Orlik had lost two of his limbs in the debris strike, but felt greater loss for the *Kinghammer*. His interface, which now only connected him to the systems of his sanctum, and thence to the chaotic chatter beyond, felt utterly redundant. With a thought, he disconnected it. The chatter continued through his implants and it suddenly annoyed him. He wanted some peace, for a moment at least, so he powered those down too. But still there was noise. The damaged crane jerked and quivered above as its hydraulics failed to lift the skein of optics and interface plate away from his back. He tried to shrug it off, only he couldn't move. The clamps that had locked him to his saddle control still held him.

He just rested there, his inclination to disengage the clamps fading as loss upon loss impinged upon him. His fellows in the Guard, his crew and brothers . . . a thought gave him the list of those who had perished in the destruction of the *Kinghammer*. Others *had* managed to abandon ship, but whether they had survived he would not know for some time. And of course Sprag. He felt utterly alone now without the ancient terror drone at his side. And all of it, all these feelings, were so unpradorish. Prador regretted the loss of useful machines like the *Kinghammer* because of the power they bestowed, but they did not mourn them. Prador did not suffer bereavement at the loss of kin, but rather enjoyed the removal of competitors. And prador certainly did not mourn the loss of a Polity terror drone and enemy.

Orlik pondered on why he felt this way. Certainly changes wrought in him by the Spatterjay virus and its extravagant extension of his life was a cause. During Orlandine's dissection of two of his crew, he had learned that the virus collected the genomes of those it had infected before. When it impelled the mutation of new hosts, it used those genomes in this process, so Orlik wondered if he actually had some human in him. The thought both horrified and fascinated him. But he should not leap to that conclusion. The virus stored more than human DNA. Maybe he had something of the Atheter in him? And then he wondered why he did not express some of the Jain, who he doubted were very empathetic.

*You're procrastinating*, he told himself.

Still disinclined to use his implants, he reached down to insert his claws into pit controls, and worked them. He told himself his disengagement from the ship's systems had brought home to him how reliant he had become on computer connections. Yes, he had decided he should hone his skills for normally accessing prador technology . . .

It took him a minute to find the routine to disengage the clamps. Further twists and stabs powered up the array of hexagonal screens before him. Linking to the exterior sensors of the sanctum, he pulled up some views of outside that were not blocked by walls of armour or tangled masses of spaceship debris. It seemed a chaotic mess within the *Hogue*'s massive interior, though he knew everything had been fitted in with AI efficiency to utilize the space available. It reminded him of the packed contents in the basket of a fishing scoop, only here the fishes, crustaceans and molluscs were reavers, attack ships, destroyers and dreadnoughts, while slotted between were armoured prador, occasional sanctums like his own, AI mind cases and storage cylinders for cryogenically frozen marines. Movement out there revealed prador towing themselves through the few intervening spaces, probably in search of airlocks to hammer at with their claws. Space-suited humans sought refuge, Golem too, some skinless and others who had lost part of their skins.

As Orlik watched this activity, he saw robots appear, some of them carting air bottles and cutting equipment. He watched as one snared a space-suited human and towed him over to the armoured wall of a Polity dreadnought. A hatch opened there and it inserted him inside. The flare of a cutting laser drew Orlik's attention to another robot freeing a prador trapped in wreckage. Soon released, the prador then propelled himself over towards the exposed section of a nearby reaver. Then another humanoid figure appeared – quite obviously Golem since he wore no space suit. He moved swiftly through the chaos, closer and closer, and finally peered up at one of Orlik's external cams. Shortly afterwards he banged against the sanctum.

The Golem hung by one hand while thumping the diagonally divided doors with his other fist. Orlik simply did not want to answer. He had no doubt that others had recently sent him messages he should have picked up through his implants or interface. And while using the pit controls, he had not bothered to initiate exterior coms. He just didn't want to be part of that outside – of the responsibility of defeat, or of the *Kinghammer*'s destruction, and so many other ships under his command. He did not want to be involved in all that loss.

'You going to answer that, you useless lump?' asked a familiar voice.

Orlik felt he had slid into memory, then came a rush of either excitement or panic. He abruptly pushed himself up off the saddle control, pulling his claws from the pits and, with a clatter of working limbs, spun around. The *drone* Sprag stood up. Her long body had straightened out and she experimentally flicked her wings.

'I thought you were dead.'

'I am,' said Sprag. 'The me that controlled the *Kinghammer* died with it. You're talking to the copy I allowed to download back into this old body.' Sprag paused for a moment. 'I'm back where I started, really, and it feels small.'

'You piece of shit,' said Orlik. 'You ejected me.'

'Seems I shouldn't have bothered,' replied Sprag. 'Seems your latest run of Spatterjay mutations is turning you into a limpet.'

'You disobeyed me. You usurped me. That's punishable by death.'

'Well I died,' said Sprag. 'Did you know limpets use the same orifice for both arsehole and mouth.' She paused again. 'Or am I confusing that with some other useless mollusc?'

'I should put you through recycling,' said Orlik, feeling joyously back home. He turned on his implants then and received the delayed messages from Diana Windermere. It seemed she had invited him to her bridge. He sent an instruction to the doors control and the air began to hiss out as they opened. Shortly the Golem Seckurg stepped inside, ready to lead the way.

*'You don't have a recycling plant any more,'* said Sprag, now talking to him through his implants. *'Seems you misplaced that with your last ship.'*

Orlik baffled his suit translator with a strange hacking bubbling sound from his much-changed mouth and vocal apparatus. He wondered if some of that viral hoard of genetic material had given him the capacity for laughter. He watched Sprag scuttle across the floor – wings did not work in vacuum and it seemed the drone had lost her small internal grav-engine. Orlik lowered a claw for her and Sprag climbed up it onto his back.

# THE HUMAN

## Diana

The remaining isopod ships had docked, and the Jain ship was slowing.

'How's it doing that?' Diana asked, glancing to Seckurg's empty seat then frowning and looking to Jabro. When he didn't respond she gave him a mental prod and he looked round.

'Ion drive,' he replied. 'It has some kind of field effect ramscoop out, which catches gas and debris, ionizes it and then throws it forwards – it's all field effects, electrostatics and some kind of magnetic bottle generated off them.'

'The second question to ask has to be why,' she replied. She wanted to get them all talking because things had turned quiet and a little tense when the maintenance robots came to make repairs. They had also collected up the few remains of Alianathon, along with one Golem crewman whose crystal had been fried in a feedback surge – one they hadn't even noticed had died until that moment.

'It makes little sense,' said Dulse. 'Its course is towards the Jaskoran system as extrapolated, so why's it slowing?'

'Something else is happening too,' said one of the others. 'Seems the cloud is drawing in around it.'

Diana hadn't noticed that and focused through ship's instruments. Yes, the cloud was definitely tightening and, even as she watched, a couple of the bacilliforms spiralled in and landed against the hull of the ship, sticking there. But not all the Jain tech was doing this. Tens of thousands of the knot-like, metallized intestine things were swirling in a circle ahead of the ship, where heavy ionization became visible, like a blue torch beam shining through fog.

'Getting some strange phenomena there,' said Dulse.

'Detail,' Diana spat.

He routed his observations over to her. One U-space map, unfortunately highly degraded because of the constant disruption, nevertheless showed the tangled mass of U-space effects in front of the ship. The damned thing looked like a glassworker's nightmare of a Klein bottle.

'So what is that, Hogue?' she asked.

'I don't know,' the AI replied.

Diana just sat, absorbing this admission – she had never heard it from the AI before.

Hogue continued, 'The phenomena are locally absorbing disruption and feeding it back to the energy U-twist in the ship.'

*Right.*

On the map, she watched curved lines briefly scribing round and disappearing – slivers of light like much stretched lunar crescents. In her consciousness, she put the map to one side and again concentrated on what she could physically detect. Gravity phenomena were evident and she could see that many of the knot things were connecting up and, in some cases, forming long chains. The other objects – the knot progenitors that looked like jellyfish – were walking along these chains and using their tentacles to weave them together more tightly. Sickle forms arrived too, landing on the chains and deflating, their contents draining away. All were still swirling around in front of the ship, both clockwise and counter-clockwise. They reminded her of blood cells heading towards a wound to clot it, as the things continued to come in and clump or form chains.

'Heavy data transmission from the ship to the phenomena,' said a Golem called Espree. 'Something like induction warfare.'

'Hogue?' Diana enquired.

'Espree is correct,' the AI replied. 'It is causing the objects to alter their structure as they mate up. The changes are not uniform.'

Next, a beam probed out. Diana at first took this to be a disruptor, except this beam was wider and possessed a bluish tinge.

'Pseudo-matter in that thing,' commented Espree.

Diana studied a close capture of the beam as it continued to probe and touch here and there in the whirling mass ahead of the ship. The thing looked like a hollow glass tube packed with writhing black worms. Another view showed it running along a line of the knots that, upon its passage, layered together and extruded spikes and nubs. Pulling back to get an overview, she saw that these structures formed curved chunks half a mile thick, coming together and interlocking. She began to see the shape of it just before Jabro spoke out.

'It's forming into a ring,' he said.

Just then, a portion of the rear wall of the bridge slid aside. First in came Seckurg, followed by Orlik in white armour, but mostly identifiable by the Polity terror drone crouched on his back. They were a very unusual duo.

'Welcome, Orlik,' she said.

Orlik waved a claw at the image up on the main screen. 'Seckurg has been keeping me apprised. Do you have any idea what we are seeing here?'

'No idea at all,' Diana replied.

'Are you all blind?' interjected the drone.

'What is your name, drone?' Diana asked.

'Sprag – erstwhile AI of the *Kinghammer*. Not that that's relevant,' the drone replied. 'I just wonder why you are so deeply into the detail that you cannot see the whole picture.'

'Explain,' Diana instructed.

'It's quelling U-space disruption locally and building a ring. A big ring – big enough for it to pass through. Need any more clues?'

Diana felt a shiver run down her spine as she got the implication.

'It's building a runcible,' said Jabro quietly.

## Orlandine

Still sitting on the roof edge of her apartment building, Orlandine looked like a normal human female. And she could cut down her sense of self to feel like one. But when she had tried that recently, she felt narrow, constrained and small. And so she returned to what she really was: that great coiled louse-like thing on the rooftop behind her, as well as the spread of Jain tentacles and mycelia down through the building and steadily growing through the drains and caves underneath the city. She was also computing, storage and processing in numerous satellites, and in the partitions of AI minds for six hundred weapons platforms. But even all this did not sufficiently describe her, because she was not just her physical elements but the flow of information through them.

'I am Orlandine,' she said aloud, not worried she might be heard because her extended awareness told her no one could hear. She shook her head, majestically amused that still she retained some human traits, then turned her concentration to events in the inner system.

Her satellites there gave her clear views of Weapons Platform Mu, its attack pods and the ship's core. They also showed her Captain Cog's ship hanging stationary in vacuum a hundred miles out from the core. However, they did not reveal what she wanted to see: Trike's and Cog's activities inside that core.

'Do you have anything for me?' she asked through a particular data channel.

'They have remained out of contact since entering,' replied the Client. 'This is an understandable precaution since the security system in there might detect com usage.'

'Like you did?'

'Precisely.'

The Client hadn't been particularly upset by her using Trike to steal the schematics of the disruptor beam and had in fact sent additional useful data on the weapon. However, the alien had been less giving when it came to data on the enclosing hardfield she used. The Client's convoluted argument, concerning Orlandine's ability to adapt the technology in time, did not fool her. The Client selfishly wanted to hang on to the tech. Orlandine hit a mental brick wall with that thought, because hadn't she herself done the same in keeping weapons data from the prador and Polity ships here? No . . . no, her rational decision was based on circumstances, while the Client had based her decision on fear. Orlandine considered trying again, but angrily decided against it. She had no need to *beg* for information since she had plenty of data to work with and the confidence that answers lay within her grasp. She returned to her research, but was only just getting started again when the signal arrived.

Detectors, far out in the Jaskoran system, alerted her to the phenomenon but, since she could only use laser com, she received the alert one hour and twenty-three minutes after it had first appeared. Fortunately, the satellites and installations remaining out there by the gas giant possessed a degree of their own intelligence and had tracked the thing.

It seemed initially to be a combined U-space signature and gravity anomaly. Yet when sensors focused in on it, they revealed a convoluted mass, like glass pipes whose twists and turns routed out of the dimensions of the physical universe. The thing then shifted, travelling faster than light in realspace, which was supposed to be impossible. It alighted for a moment over a cold planetoid and somehow caused an ice storm on the surface. It shifted again and again and tracking was intermittent – sensors often picking up where it had been after it had moved on. Even so, Orlandine had the impression of the terminus of a torch beam searching the system.

Finally, it slid in towards the gas giant, in whose orbit she had built the runcibles used to move the Harding black hole. Here, because some of her installations and satellites remained, sensor data were more complete. She could not really call the thing detected there 'an object' because it was not material, but a distortion in space, a commingled inter-dimensional knot of both U-space and the real. She read gravity slopes in there and weird time distortions. A laser fired at it scattered, as if hitting a faceted gem. Then it passed close over one of the moons which also orbited the gas giant. Her remaining installation there went offline for a moment, and when it came back on its internal clock was some minutes ahead of her own. It then reported a massive energy loss and she recognized the entropic drain as the result of a time distortion.

She decided it was time for more input so, after reluctant consideration, broadcast this data to all her AIs, to Knobbler and her drones, to the Polity and prador fleets and, with hesitation, to the Client. She immediately received hundreds of responses and filtered them for hypotheses she hadn't thought of.

'Remote field projection through U-space,' commented one of the platform AIs. 'Indications of pseudo-matter in there.'

This was true, and she felt happy to have some return on her investment of distributing data. She then wondered at her odd reaction, before delving into her knowledge of the subject to come up with what Polity scientists knew. The field manipulation of matter using shearfields, hardfields and shimmershields and various iterations between was common. There had then been some experiments in manipulating matter through a runcible gate, which had been successful. However, there had been numerous complications concerning pseudo-matter structures generating and collapsing, temporal effects and amplified gravity phenomena. Orlandine could see how this related but, of course, no runcible gate existed out there through which something could operate.

She watched as the thing hovered in orbit of the gas giant for a while before falling towards the clouds. It sank into them and, red against the shifting pastel shades, an eye-storm developed and spread. She began to discern a distinct cellular structure appearing across it. Globular areas expanded to fifty miles across and when they touched formed a honeycomb pattern. In the past Jain tech had been seen to form such a structure when fighting to survive a hostile environment. However, in that other past case it had broken up as the environment destroyed it. Here it seemed to be getting stronger and stronger.

'That does not look good,' said Knobbler.

'No, it does not,' she agreed, wondering at the surge of excitement she felt.

Discussion continued but with no real conclusions reached. Within a few hours, the thing stretched thousands of miles across. Her installations out there produced deeper and more detailed scanning. The gravity phenomena were evenly patterned, which was a degree of manipulation beyond Polity technology, and definitely linked to U-space effects down there. A rise in density showed that this structure possessed solidity well beyond that of the surrounding gas. Then the centre began pulsing out gravity waves. A central hexagon slowly expanded, incorporating the boundaries of the ones surrounding it while outer ones shrank in towards it. Finally, the thing had formed into a ring five hundred miles across. Analysis revealed super-dense areas in there, evenly distributed U-space phenomena, while the gravity waves waned away. At this point, the Client added her opinion:

'It's coming,' said the alien.


## Diana

The mother ship had almost completed the ring. It lay half a mile thick, both radially and axially, while bacilliforms sticking to its face formed a surface seemingly consisting of millions of pores. The beam, obviously a complex tool rather than a weapon, was melding them together. Jain-tech veins began to creep over its surfaces to sprout cyst-like growths, while specialized mechs crawled there like organic construction robots.

'Tactics,' said Diana. 'Give me scenarios.'

'We jump in and hit it with everything we've got,' suggested Jabro, just airing the idea and definitely not comfortable with it.

'Then it drops attack ships again,' said Seckurg.

'Doesn't even need to do that,' said Sprag.

Diana wondered why the thing irritated her so much.

'Explain, please,' she said to the drone tightly.

'We used everything and we could not penetrate its hardfield,' Sprag explained. 'That hardfield is enough to encompass both it and the . . . runcible.'

'Suggestions?' Diana asked, meanwhile running tactical scenarios and not liking the results. It seemed likely the Jain ship would head for the Jaskoran system, but what if that was not its intended target? Obviously the Jain aboard had managed to send the Wheel out of the U-space blister to manipulate events so it would be freed. Did this then mean that the Wheel had been in constant communication with it while it was still trapped in the blister?

'Hogue?' she asked mentally, sending her thoughts to the AI.

'*From what we now understand of the physics of it, communication may not have been possible. There would be a time disparity between the real and the inside of the blister. However, since we have no idea how the Wheel was sent . . .*'

'*So that Jain ship may know all about the Polity?*'

'*I would say that beside the possibility of communication between the Jain in that ship and the Wheel, it knows about the Polity,*' Hogue replied. '*The data were available.*'

Of course. The thing had penetrated their systems effortlessly with that weird scream. Debris from the battle would also have been a source of information. She knew, for example, that many AIs were missing. Maybe they had been destroyed, or their beacons damaged. But just maybe those attack ships or the mother ship had snatched them.

'*So that runcible might not open to Jaskor,*' she said.

'*It might not.*'

The Jain may have other targets in mind. What if it had decided to attack the Polity? She had no idea how the runcible it was building could take it anywhere without a receiving runcible of similar scale. She knew nothing about how this technology worked. Maybe it was possible to go through to one of the big war runcibles in the Polity, or it was somehow open-ended and could deposit the ship anywhere? What if that ship were to appear in the Solar system? What if it were to appear above Earth? Diana took a breath and got the speculations under control. The 'what ifs' were not helping.

'U-jump missiles?' wondered Orlik.

Diana returned her full attention to the bridge even as Hogue sent her the present weapons manifest. They had over a hundred U-jump missiles left.

'The enclosing field does not stop them,' she said thoughtfully, 'but we know that the Jain ship has internal bounce gates.'

'I'm not entirely familiar with the technology,' said Orlik. 'But surely a U-jump missile has to materialize proximal to the bounce gate to be drawn in. Could it be that with the field extended to cover that runcible, it sits outside that proximity?'

'He's right,' said Dulse.

'I'm getting some steeply climbing energy readings now,' interrupted Orien.

Diana knew she had no further time for discussion. 'Hogue, jump us back. Now!'

The whole of the *Cable Hogue* jerked as if some giant gyroscope within it had slammed to a halt. Their fall into U-space was a ragged thing this time and every object around Diana seemed to twist a hundred and eighty degrees into oblivion. She looked at Orlik and the prador appeared to be tearing out of the real. Then they were in and all objects around her multiplied to infinity. Orlik after Orlik partially overlapping extended in a curved line, aiming in a direction to which she could not point.

*'Prepare missiles. Target the runcible,'* she told Hogue.

A sense of terrible immanence impinged and Diana felt as if the abyss wanted to drag her in and down forever. Then with a crash that split one side of the bridge and twisted her bones, they were out again.

Debris hit the hull, collision lasers began firing and hardfields intercepted the worst of it. Jabro grabbed weapons control and lanced out particle beams, burning up Jain knots that were falling towards them. Diana felt the violent tug of the missiles launch, but even at that moment, she knew they were too late. She glimpsed a meniscus swirl across the giant ring as the runcible opened. Multiple white-hot dots appeared there as the missiles fell uselessly through into U-space. Then their hardfields flared under massive load as the *Cable Hogue* slammed down on the larger curved hardfield which enclosed the Jain ship. The great

Polity dreadnought spewed projectors in molten lines until the hull itself struck. Even firmly clamped into her seat, Diana felt the wrench and her bones breaking. She saw Orlik flung to one side, the armoured monster crashing into two of her crew as well as the consoles there, crushing them. The *Hogue* bounced away, tumbling through vacuum, with its hull distorted and a dent visible a hundred miles across. Damage reports swamped her mind and she swept them aside as the *Hogue* AI stabilized the ship and fired up its engines to pull them away, but the Jain ship did not respond. It was as if they did not matter any more.

Drug patches oozed through the padding around her to ease the pain in her legs, ribs and arms. She searched for further exterior views through the system, at last finding an undamaged sensor array, and looked back. The whole Jain cloud now funnelled into the point between the mother ship and the gate, and began falling through. Thousands of bacilliforms, the knot things and other objects besides were disappearing through the meniscus. Then the mother ship began to move again. Slowly it nosed up to the gate, giant pincer pricking the meniscus, until mile upon mile of it was sliding in, and through.

Gone.

# 8

*Ages before the Quiet War, a robot was pretty easy to define as an item constructed of moving parts, usually of machined metal and moulded plastic, all controlled by a similarly manufactured computer. These machines contained no organic components at all. Meanwhile, biotechnology underwent massive expansion. This brought us the almost wholly biological machines, dubbed 'biomechs', like manufactured bacteria to eat waste plastics, worms whose sum purpose was to accrue rare earths from ocean muds, builder corals and searcher snakes, cleaner leeches and carpet moss – the list is long. This utilization and repurposing of the machines of life simultaneously made its way into robotics. Robots gained muscles, sometimes wholly artificial, sometimes grown. They gained biological eyes and other sensors. They got skin. The toing and froing between manufacture and growth has been such that the line between what is a robot and what is a biomech has grown narrow and blurred, hardly a line at all. Now, when someone describes something as a 'biomech', it generally just means a machine with more of the squishy stuff inside it.*

From 'How It Is' by Gordon

## Trike

Trike crouched against a tunnel wall as the organic thing on the other side dragged the Old Captain down. Should he intervene? No. The moment he did so he would alert the security system of the whole core to more than just a tough old human in a space suit, and it would really pay attention. Quite probably, it would start deploying the weapons sited throughout these walls. Every few hundred yards sat an emplacement in a recess. He had already studied one of these and found it contained a multiple-use weapon that could project any form of coherent EMR, as well as many designs of railgun slugs, and a smaller version of the disruptor whose schematics he had stolen from the Client.

The sphere reeled Cog in and he did not seem to be fighting it. Then, at the last, he reached down and grabbed the tentacle in both hands below where it wrapped around his ankle. He snapped it like a piece of warm liquorice and, hanging on to the broken end, used it to swing back down onto the walkway, his space suit gecko-sticking him there. Next, he stepped forwards, dug his hands underneath the sphere and tossed it from the walkway. Trike tracked its trajectory. The thing made no effort to change it and just sailed across the tunnel to bounce from a further wall. Meanwhile the one behind didn't react, and Cog started walking away from it.

'There is something decidedly lacking here,' Trike said.

He turned back to the hole he had torn in the wall and pulled himself through into the duct beyond. Here ran pipes and semi-organic data feeds. He located another protruding nodule – a subprocessor and energy booster for the nervous system of the core – and drove his fingers into it. Swiftly he made connections with thousands of nano-fibres. He began reading system responses again and gradually worked his way into the under-lying programming.

'Whadda y'mean?' Cog asked, sounding annoyed.

'The response of the security system here to the Client was highly complex but by the numbers. Its response to us has been the same. I sent your ship away and it thereafter all but ignored it. You were classified as low threat to be observed but I now know why those globular things were sent.'

'Oh yeah?' said Cog, obviously less than impressed.

'The system detected the Spatterjay virus inside you and sent them to make a further assessment.'

'So what's missing?' Cog asked, finally paying attention.

'A fully intelligent response, and anything that looks like real curiosity.'

'The Species . . .'

'I extrapolate that the security system is responding as programmed but that it has not alerted the Species themselves. Logically it should have done so right from the start.' He extended his reach within the node, checking something.

'You don't talk like you once did, boy,' said Cog.

Trike felt a momentary irritation then banished it as he found what he wanted. 'Oh . . . I got that wrong. It has been regularly feeding updates to . . . something, but there has been no response.'

'They're dead, then?' asked Cog.

'That is one possibility,' Trike replied. He peered out of the hole and located the Old Captain, still stomping along the walkway.

The other possibility was that the system had alerted something which, after the Client's complex attempt at penetration, might see the ensuing, ostensibly blunt, attempt as actually subtle. The recipient of the alert could have surmised that Cog was not alone and hoped for Trike to reveal himself. Or was he just being too paranoid about this?

'So what are you doing now?' Cog asked.

'Trying to find something else,' Trike replied. 'I've accessed a minor node here and through it am locating one of the main . . . processors further along.'

*There.*

He had it and viewed a detailed schematic of his surroundings. A main processor, which up until now had only been speculative based on his understanding of this nervous-system architecture. It sat in a metallic encystment of the tunnel wall two miles ahead. Trike retracted his fibres, but left numerous nano-transceivers to maintain his connection. He then withdrew his hand and crawled out through the hole. He hurled himself forwards hard, parallel to the wall, and this initial impetus sent him off in a flat trajectory at thirty miles an hour.

At the two-mile limit, Trike put his feet down, engaging with gecko function. He immediately scanned his surroundings. Practically invisible across the EMR spectrum, he subverted any scans that hit his chameleonware so returns on these would show nothing. However, halting his momentum had physical effects on his surroundings. He sensed at once, via those transceivers left behind him, that he had activated a small subsystem – something he had not detected at his launch point. The 'nervous system' of the ship's core must be more sensitive here. He observed that it had detected an anomaly which might indicate the presence of an interloper, but could equally be simple materials shifting due to vibrations still running through the core from recent action. It became watchful.

As if trying not to break shell ice, Trike walked to a pore in the side of the tunnel. With it only being a yard across, he had to crawl inside. Ahead of him lay a blank convex wall with no way through and he moved up to it, resting a hand against it. Gentle laser scanning from his palm elicited an ultrasound response through the material but revealed no more than a cellular impact structure to a few centimetres deep. More powerful scanning, he was sure, would alert the system. However, via those transceivers he undermined local security. All the scanners within and about this wall became inert. Bracing himself in the tunnel, Trike drew back his hand, then thrust it forwards. His claws punched through the material and he began to tear it away. Even for him it was hard work and he was thankful that the protection here was environmental and not against physical attack. He peeled up layers like orange skin to reveal green honeycomb laced with superconductor. Next was a foam layer snowing around him, and finally a material little different from ceramal. He drove his fist into this, once, twice, and it cracked. Two further blows and he could haul out inch-thick chunks, finally making a hole big enough for him to get through.

He made it inside the cyst, where the main processor squatted like a desert toad in its burrow. The thing was about ten feet across and had a decidedly organic look. The toad head seemed to possess a mouth and brush sensors but sealed under a translucent yellow layer. He scanned it with everything he had available and realized it *was* a life form, but one in biological stasis. Its folded, skate-like wings concealed ten folded legs. It possessed a brain of sorts, extending from its head down into its back and then branching into the skate wings. The main connection extended from its back: a thick braided cord rising to the ceiling, and beyond there diverging into the system. After a moment he understood from the data, via Orlandine on the Client, what this was. The Species made creatures for their maintenance and protection. The Client itself, since its resurrection, had not made anything like this because it used the robots and computing of Weapons Platform Mu to serve their purpose, but in its previous incarnation, it had.

Trike stepped over to the thing and walked around it until he faced the head. This wasn't where the greatest concentration of its cerebral matter lay but it was the best chance of access, since here it attached to what had once been its main senses. He reached out and swiped, tearing away the translucent covering, which bounced against the wall like a rubbery mask. He then opened his mouth wide and lunged forwards, clamping his teeth onto the thing's face. It was hard, petrified and, with micro-drills whirring at the tip of his tongue, he bored in. Powder gusted out and he broke through into softer matter, there spearing out thousands of microfibres. As these stabbed deeper inside, they branched into hundreds of thousands of nano-fibres, and he made connections again.

Translation took some time as Trike modelled and further penetrated the system.

He explored and found thousands of processors like this one spread throughout the ship's core. Those locally had been sending alerts towards the centre but receiving no reply. He delved deeper, mapping the entire network. Large areas of this nervous system were down and, had he known their location from the beginning, he could have shown Cog where to walk into this place without the system detecting him at all. He then found the cache from where the system had sent the two globular things, and noted other creatures in there balled in a mass and all in stasis. He located further caches spread throughout the core. Soon he had the shape of it all and began to see how to work it. Those creatures in the caches possessed coded identification. They perpetually emitted a microwave signal while in vacuum then complemented that with a pheromone one in those places that were pressurized. It simply said, 'Ignore me.' This might have been enough but Trike wanted to be sure.

A strong facet of Jain tech was its ability to sequester, and Trike himself was loaded with it. He began, in a steady cascade, to seize control of the main processors. After a little while, he reached one of those regions where many of them were dead and inspected that. He half expected weapons damage but instead discovered that the system had broken down beyond its quite admirable abilities to regenerate itself. The whole thing was ancient. He found layered scar tissue and organic isotopes and from these could date the system, ascertaining that it had been running for hundreds of thousands of years. He saw that this steady breakdown represented a danger. In one large hall, he found the burned remains of things like giant flatworms and, studying the data, understood that the system had released these in response to a threat. What that threat had been was lost, but subsequently it had attacked its own creatures, incinerating them with grasers. It was all like the faulty immune responses of an ageing body: overreacting to perceived threats and attacking itself. Nevertheless, he now controlled much of it.

'I have it,' he finally said.

'Have what?' Cog asked.

'Our way in.' He copied the 'ignore me' signal and began broadcasting it. Next, he made a link directly to Cog's suit and set that to transmit the signal too.

'I've managed to make it ignore us,' he told Cog.

'Such a relief,' the Old Captain replied, dripping sarcasm.

'Now we will go and see who's awake here.' Trike suddenly felt uncomfortable with his own blithe acceptance of what he had done.

## Orlandine

AIs and drones viewing the data recognized the object forming on the gas giant simultaneously. Orlandine had identified it some minutes beforehand but had not wanted to acknowledge it and, again, share it. She had deployed runcible gates in warfare. She had built them. Of course, she recognized this thing. The realization had sent cold down the facsimile of her human spine, but she could not parse the feeling as either dread or excitement. The process had occurred at great speed, and without any of the giant tools, factories or mining operations she had used. Something had managed to build a runcible gate, floating in the upper atmosphere of the gas giant, in less than a day. She felt . . . envious and knew she *wanted* this technological knowledge. The gate then initiated – the cusp, the meniscus forming across the ring – and objects began to spew out.

Orlandine watched a great fountain rising out from the equator of the gas giant. Focusing on some of the objects emerging, she recognized them at once. The bacilliforms and gut things were classic Jain tech from the accretion disc. Other forms and tangles arose too and it all looked like detritus from an explosion in a biotech component factory. This mass began to spread around the gas giant in an equatorial ring. She immediately started pulling back those of her watchers she could move. When these Jain objects began landing on the moons where she had based one of her main installations, she observed the effect. A great mass, like balled-up scrap metal and jungle growth, slammed down into the surface and immediately speared out vine-like shoots, breaking through the sulphur crust, cracking up chunks of it. The thing spread virulently, occasionally throwing up sprouts like toadstools. Close scanning it for as long as possible, she saw the Jain growth using stored radioactives for energy, and its main extent heading towards her installation. When it reached the outer wall, the automated system there carried out the instructions she had sent just a moment after the gate opened.

A distant view, from one of her fast retreating satellites in the area, showed her the surface detonation on the moon. She had at least prevented the Jain tech from sequestering her installation and getting to the fusion reactors. However, it showed the Jain tech next flooding into the area, and she realized it must be feeding on the heat.

'We're rapidly running out of time,' Knobbler noted.

She did not think that worthy of a reply and was too busy pushing weapons construction and other preparations to their physical limit. She flung a virtual glance in his direction, briefly assessing the activity in the southern cities. Such had been the outflux of refugees to the evacuation platforms, they were consolidating there. Under Gemmell's plans, the remaining population of one city – the least defensible – was moving to the other cities.

'Push it harder,' she instructed, already transmitting a live feed to everyone on the planet of events in the Jaskoran system. 'Compulsory evacuation.'

'Already on it,' said Knobbler.

Another four evacuation platforms departed and people flooded into the surface departure points. The bad news travelled fast and the process became a lot less leisurely. Refugees abandoned belongings, while planetary haulers and shuttles blasted for orbit only seconds apart, unloading fast in the massive bays of the platforms and returning straightaway for their next loads. At the present speed the Jain tech was travelling, she reckoned on taking the planetary population well below a hundred million. A lot fewer people for her to worry about, and a lot less to get in her way . . .

Then she saw that the clock had all but ticked down to zero.

Two giant spikes rose up out of the runcible gate, mile upon mile of them finally revealed as pincers capable of grasping a small moon. Then came the head of the thing, and the neck. A massive storm spiralled out from the site of the gate as the Jain warship rose up and up. Its progress further stirred the gas clouds around it, raising giant tornadoes. Drive flames flared from engines on its underside and these ignited reactive gases drawn up from deep down in the clouds. Fire exploded across the face of the gas giant to give a suitable backdrop to the monster as it pulled clear of the gate, with the fountain of Jain mechanisms re-establishing behind it. It roared out beyond the clouds and finally into vacuum. There it screamed.

Orlandine felt the immense data surge throughout her distributed being. By some unknown mechanism, it had even crossed disrupted U-space and so redoubled when she finally received its EMR element. This, from the data she had from the Client, was a challenge and a test – a call to destructive mating and warfare integral to the weird and twisted psyche of the Jain. Did it make any difference if she decoded it and answered it? The thing was coming to wreak destruction either way.

'Nasty,' said Knobbler, as the scream began to die.

'Oh I agree,' Orlandine replied, but did not want to express the strange excitement she felt, nor the *familiarity*.


## Diana

Diana watched the remainder of the cloud form into a funnel. A tornado of millions of Jain mechanisms swirled together, bunching up into an almost solid mass to fall through the runcible gate. She then transferred her attention to the stray ships she had been unable to secure inside the *Cable Hogue* as they circumvented this and came towards her. Their intermittent weapons fire, and that of the *Hogue*, fried objects not yet in the funnel, but without urgency. The remaining tech had ceased trying to attack or breach defences and seemed intent on getting to that gate. Next, focusing back on her bridge, she watched as a surgical robot slid the comatose body of one of her crew into a cold coffin, while an autodoc worked on a woman with crushed ribs.

The woman pointedly ignored it, still focused on her instruments, a look of irritation on her face.

'So what do we do now?' asked Orlik.

The King's Guard had driven his armoured legs into the floor and held on to an exposed beam with one claw. Maybe that would be enough to prevent him crushing any more of her crew if further hard manoeuvring became necessary.

'I am considering,' Diana replied.

They did not possess the firepower to stop the Jain warship, but they did possess data that could be useful to others who might have it. Again focusing on that tornado, she saw the concentration of objects steadily waning. If they ran for the gate now they might well get through, but be in no condition to face any kind of attack on the other side. Just a little while longer . . .

*'We still do not know where that gate goes,'* Hogue informed her privately.

*'Hardly relevant, don't you think?'*

*'Agreed.'*

'We go through,' she said aloud. 'Hogue, loop course, maximum acceleration to take us there when the concentration of Jain objects is at optimum.'

*'Optimum?'* the AI enquired.

*'When we can get through intact.'*

Aloud she added, 'Have the other ships fall in behind us.'

'This is supposing the gate remains open,' said the terror drone Sprag. 'It'll be unfortunate if it's closed at the other end.'

'Runcibles don't work that way,' she replied loftily.

'Runcibles don't work the way that this one apparently is working,' the drone answered.

She ignored that and concentrated on her crew. 'Minimum engagement once we are through,' she said. 'Orien – status on armour?'

Orien had taken over Alianathon's role while hers, concerning energy supplies, Hogue had divided up amongst the rest.

'The armour is intact and memory metal elements are drawing power to straighten out the dent. The problems in that area are that all the hardfield projectors are compromised – we can use them but won't be able to eject them if they start overloading.'

'Jabro?'

Jabro, who had taken control of all weapons, replied, 'Nothing working in the impact zone and nothing likely to work for six hours.'

'What coverage?'

'Antipersonnel lasers at surface, particle beams to a cone point twenty miles out.'

'We factor that into our transition point,' Diana said, jointly running the calculations with Hogue. Though they could calculate for many factors on this side of the gate, they could not for the other side, however. They just had no idea what the Jain ship or the objects might be doing there.

The *Hogue* shuddered, then creaked and groaned like an ancient house in a storm. Diana could feel the surge of acceleration, which did not bode well for the effects of any heavy manoeuvring. She also noticed resonance in the bridge grav-plates as their effect pulled her down into her chair then released her rhythmically. After a moment, grav went off completely. Checking, she saw that Hogue had redirected power from the plates, and from many other areas within the ship, into essential repairs or laminar storage. Grav-plates, and human comfort, were not essential.

Six fusion flames jetted in a ring from the *Hogue*, hurling it through vacuum. The impact had damaged none of the engines since they had driven the ship into the Jain ship's hardfield. As it accelerated, Diana slid her perception to sensors around and in the hull. The massive dent was now visibly on the move:

distorted memory beams straightened out, hull armour loosened in layers like a burn blister and bulging out steadily, while static discharges caused lightning storms in internal shock-absorbing spaces. Robots were also busy pulling away the broken ceramic linings of projector ejection tubes, as their exteriors also straightened. They disconnected and replaced damaged components in the weapons systems there too.

Diana turned her attention inwards to where warships were crammed in a seemingly scrapyard mass. Stray prador, marines, AI cases and Golem had been helped where necessary to those ships which had the space for them. Some ships had transferred whole crews to others, the recent manoeuvre having heavily damaged the vessels concerned. Now Hogue directed the stabilization of these vessels with rams, billions of cubic yards of crash foam and the docking clamps, harpoons, cables and grabs of the ships themselves. She checked how long it would take to eject them should that become necessary on the other side of the gate, and did not like the result. Then she moved her focus back outwards as weapons fire ramped up.

The *Hogue* was now entering space where the number of Jain objects had climbed steeply. It lanced out with particle beams, incinerating large items in its path while hardfields batted aside their smaller brethren. The AI next targeted those not in the ship's path but in range to attack, but found no need to fire. It seemed the objects had been directed to expend what power they had in getting them towards the gate. Ahead, at the gate itself, the number of them dropped from a peak, yet the frequency with which they had to destroy those in their path climbed in relation to their acceleration.

'They're going through fast,' noted Seckurg. 'And I'm getting an even gravity reading through the gate.'

'Hogue?' Diana asked.

'The gravity phenomenon is similar to that of a gate opening on a planetary surface, only a lot higher,' replied the AI. 'I surmise that the exit gate is located near, or on, a massive planetary body, or close by a sun.'

'We can handle that?'

'Depends which way we are pointing when we go through.'

Diana accepted it. If the gate pointed down towards a sun or some Jovian world, things might get a little difficult. However, that seemed unlikely, since the Jain ship and these objects would have problems too . . . unless the ship had no idea where the gate led and had inadvertently opened it in precisely the wrong place.

'Their acceleration indicates the necessity for escape velocity,' said Hogue.

'Give me data.'

A block of information fell into her mind, edited for human perception. She could not grasp the maths concerning the transference of gravity through the gate but she could understand its interpretation. They were going to hit very high gee that would have worse effects than their impact onto the Jain hardfield. She now saw that Hogue had warned all the other ships both inside and outside the *Hogue*. Humans in those ships were already heading for gel stasis while the prador made their own preparations. The 'normal' prador were locking down, filling their suits with impact foam and their bodies with a high-density ichor, while the Guard were merely locking down – their Spatterjay virus-infected bodies made them extremely rugged.

'*You need to go into gel stasis,*' said Hogue. '*As do your human bridge crew.*'

'*And if you fail? Where is your backup?*'

'*I have multiple backups in the form of the AIs of the ships within.*'

'*I don't like it.*'

'*You do not like to be out of control.*' Hogue paused for a second then continued, '*In the very small and unlikely event that I or the other AIs have a problem, I am preparing.*'

Diana saw how and transferred her gaze to Orlik. The King's Guard looked up as a hatch opened in the ceiling and out of it drifted an interface plate like the one he had used aboard *Kinghammer*. A moment later, the drone Sprag rattled into the air to land on the thing, then flew it down to Orlik's back, settling it in place. It engaged at once.

'Is this necessary?' Orlik asked aloud, his voice also echoing through the establishing link.

Diana sent a signal to undo the clamps holding her in place. Pain medication had done its work and she could move well enough in zero gravity. She pushed herself out of her seat at the same time as others in the bridge and disconnected the optic plugged into her skull. Having implants only, she could thoroughly limit access to her mind, so none of her thoughts could spill over. From her seat, she propelled herself to the door.

'Probably not necessary,' she replied. 'Just a precaution.'

Orlik, she could see, was already exploring the control he now apparently had of the *Cable Hogue*, and no doubt delighting in the weapons at his command. In the tunnel beyond the bridge, Jabro moved up beside her.

'A prador in charge of this?' he asked, but he had a quizzical grin.

'Organic backup, should it be required,' she replied, until the door closed behind them. 'But, of course, Hogue now has access to Orlik's mind and thence to that drone's, which is connected, and enough subtlety to learn all the Polity needs to know about prador experiments with AI.'

'I knew there had to be some subtext,' said Jabro.

The gel-stasis tubes were already protruding from the walls

and open when the humans arrived. Diana pulled herself down into hers, and pads closed across. She did not feel the shunts entering her body, just knew they were doing their work, as cold washed through her. The lid closed and the gel flooded in around her. She retained enough conscious connection to the ship to watch as it hurtled through the burning debris of Jain tech towards the meniscus of the gate. Then, as that connection faded, she wondered if her resentment of Hogue's opportunism, in the midst of disaster, would be the last thing she felt.

## Cog

'Damn it, what the hell was that!' Cog bellowed.

Still no answer from Trike but thankfully the hideous noise had ceased. Screaming over his radio, it had interfered with his HUD, throwing up weird script and alarming ghostly images. It had sounded like an evil monster shrieking somewhere in this ship's core, but that was ridiculous. It had to be a feedback whine or a massive EM emission or something, surely? Cog shivered. He'd felt the damned thing in his bones.

'Trike?' he queried again.

He scanned around. Had something happened to the seemingly indestructible man? A buzzing sound came over the radio, then, 'Go here.' His HUD lit up crosshairs that shifted to one side and centred over a wall protrusion like a golden tree stump. He altered course, clumping towards it.

'What the hell was that noise, Trike?'

'I'll explain when I reach you,' Trike replied.

Cog grunted in annoyance and moved on. His suit told him he had covered over ten miles so he was halfway to the chamber at the centre of the ship's core. The walkway had ended some time ago and now he moved along the wall of a tunnel as it spiralled into the distance. Across this stretched struts which bore some similarity to the giant bones he had seen inside Dragon. His new course also took him through an area forested with bunches of spiralling metallic sprouts. Having to duck underneath or step through them began seriously to irritate him, while his footing seemed a landscape of broken slate, with numerous holes and places where his boots refused to stick.

'Damn it,' he said. 'Do I have to keep walking?'

There was no response.

'Trike? You still there?'

Green-silver veins appeared through channels in the slate floor. He paused to reach down and stab at one with his finger. The stuff rippled – it was liquid – then proceeded to climb up his finger. Quickly withdrawing his hand, he shook it, scattering droplets that sped away like bees.

'Best not to touch that stuff,' said Trike.

'What is it?' he asked, moving on.

'Memory metal superconductor,' Trike replied, 'with a degree of its own intelligence – it flows where needed.'

'Right, okay.'

Cog walked more carefully thereafter. Finally, he reached the base of the tree stump. About ten feet across, it consisted of numerous brassy lianas tangled together, and looked very much like Jain tech. He tried the sole of his boot against it and it stuck, so he walked up the side of it and then onto the top. From above the forest of spirals, he gazed out. This looked in no way the same as the interiors of large structures in the Polity and the Kingdom. The angles, surfaces and whole shape of this place were all wrong. One moment the landscape appeared manufactured, and then alien and organic. He was trying to nail down what niggled him about it all when he saw an object sliding towards him from the distance. As the thing drew closer, he got it. The place did remind him of seashells – of structure deposited in layers and spirals of nacre – and much of it seemed the product of some biotech artist. But in the end, it blurred into *wrongness*, the truly alien.

The object drew closer – a twenty-foot flatworm with a figure atop it: Trike squatted near the head with one hand down on its surface. It drew to a halt beside the stump and, with a shrug, Cog stepped up onto it.

'I take it you dealt with the security system?' he enquired.

'Yes, I did,' Trike replied. 'Though it is faulty and may still react to us.'

'How do you mean?'

'The whole system is very old and breaking up,' Trike explained. 'It's even been attacking itself in some areas, so no guarantees.'

'I should have brought my gun,' said Cog. 'So that noise I heard . . . that was the security system?'

Trike looked round at him. 'No, that was the Jain warship arriving in the Jaskoran system. Even now Orlandine is preparing its welcome.'

'Why did it announce its arrival?'

'It is the Jain way.' Trike faced forwards. 'To potential prey and mates they send both this challenge and this test to see if they are worthy.'

'Worthy of being which?'

'Both.'

'Seems a bit fucked up.'

Trike ignored him.

They slid on through the tunnel, which as they got nearer to the centre, grew narrower. Trike spotted something on one wall and drew their strange vessel close to it. Here a great slug-like mass clung, wider than it was long and about the size of a house.

Behind it lay a nacreous trail much like the earlier pathway Cog had walked, and much like the slime trail of a snail. The slug-thing also dragged a long skein of pipes that stretched to various sockets in the wall about it. Even as they watched, one of these pipes disconnected and slithered over to another socket further ahead and plugged itself in.

'What the hell?' wondered Cog.

'Maintenance,' Trike replied. 'You've seen the organic appearance of everything around us. It seems the Species didn't have robots. They gave birth to the organic mechanisms that built and now maintain this ship.

'Right.' Cog looked down at the surface he was squatting on. 'So this vehicle is alive?'

'That depends on how you define life.'

'Okay . . . it has a brain?'

'Yes, but it is as limited as that of the average Polity mainten-ance bot. I control it completely.'

Of course he did.

The craft rippled underneath them as it moved on. Checking his HUD, Cog saw they were only a few miles from the nearest edge of the central chamber. The tunnel continued to narrow and here lay one hundred feet across, with surfaces all around consisting of long metal leaves evenly layered. Soon the tube became just twenty feet across. Within this gathered some of the globular organic machines like the two which had come to inspect him initially. As Trike manoeuvred around one of them, Cog saw that it had dried out and apparently decayed in places. He checked his display again and noted atmospheric pressure here, but could not figure out how it was maintained since there had been none behind and the tunnel lay open to vacuum at the entrance. Trike finally drew their strange craft to a halt and settled it to the wall beside a door.

A convex nacre hatch spanned the tunnel, with concentric steps running towards its centre. Cog followed Trike to the point where he pressed his hand down against the edge of the central disc, waited a moment, then lifted the disc away.

'It's made so it can be opened at any of the concentric rings, depending on the size of what wants to be moved in or out,' Trike explained.

The hatch trailed glutinous threads and when Trike shoved it aside, they stretched across the gap. He swept these strands away and went through. A short length of further tunnel led to a similar but concave hatch. Cog followed then waited as Trike pulled the section of hatch closed behind them. On his HUD Cog watched the air pressure rise and realized they were in an airlock.

The next hatch opened with similar ease and on the other side Cog felt the pull of gravity at once. Perspective shifted round and he hung from the exit while Trike stood beside it, seemingly unaffected. Cog dropped to the floor and Trike replaced the hatch, then walked down parallel to the floor, finally jumping to land beside him.

'So this is it,' said Cog.

They stood in an area with a ceiling a hundred feet above them. Cog wasn't able to see a far wall because what he could only describe as a forest blocked the view. Here and there, spirals reached up from holes in the floor to holes in the ceiling. They seemed to be made of compressed fibre that reminded him of paper yellowed by age. Massed in the areas around these stood objects like desiccated old trees, with the branches snapped down to nubs.

'Fifty levels,' Trike commented.

Taking that in, Cog now saw those spirals were ramps leading up. He focused on the trees and saw things wound around some of them. Trike started walking towards the nearest. Cog felt material crunching underfoot as he followed. Peering down, he saw large flakes of translucent carapace and the occasional easily identifiable insect leg. When they reached one of the trees, the source of all the detritus became evident.

'Not the same as the Client,' said Trike. 'But then, the Client was the last iteration the Librarian made.'

The remains of this particular member of the Species reminded Cog of a millipede. Only when he studied it closely did he see its segments were partially distinct animals. He poked it with a finger and the lower segment fell to the floor, breaking into two halves and shedding most of its legs.

'All dead?' he wondered.

Without answering, Trike caught hold of his shoulder and dragged him back. Something was approaching through the trees and soon it became clearly visible. The creature seemed the by-blow of a manta ray and a horseshoe crab, but it was the size of a grav-car. It looked as if it should scuttle but moved very slowly, almost arthritically.

'Maintenance,' Trike stated. 'The system sensed our movement when we came in.'

The thing limped over, scoring a trail in the detritus with its dragging tail. It paused to study them with cloudy compound eyes up on stalks and might have rattled its mandibles together, if it had two of them. It then headed over to the dried-out husk on the floor and attempted to pick it up with its remaining mandible. It only succeeded in breaking the husk into pieces. Finally, it did manage to snare a chunk of it, but seemed confused about what to do next. It stood for a long while, then slowly turned and moved off.

'That thing is tens of thousands of years old. We'll have to be careful.'

'Why?' Cog looked at him.

'The Species here died a lot longer ago than that. This, and those things you encountered, were much younger and produced later. The ship has the means of making these creatures and there are plenty of them still about. Some are quite dangerous.'

'But we're done here now anyway, aren't we?'

'No, we're here for data.'

'So what now?'

'We go up,' said Trike, gesturing to one of the spirals.


## The Client

Two consecutive blows had come down on her. The Client studied the data Orlandine had transmitted, and the images. The Jain ship had arrived, as expected, but it had also drawn through a massive cloud of Jain tech, which was already reproducing in the outer system. And then this. Now she knew for sure that her kind aboard the ship's core were all dead.

She shifted on her crystal tree, clinging more tightly and suddenly feeling utterly vulnerable. She found herself emitting pheromones – communication molecules – and wasn't sure why. Sniffing them into her anosmic receptors, she found them to be of a kind she had used before Pragus resurrected her aboard this platform. They were a call to the maintenance creatures like the one inside the ship's core – creatures she had never made in this life. She also recognized the strange feeling rising up inside her as grief.

'Where are you going?' she asked.

The data feed from Trike, which he had only just felt worth the risk of opening, supplied detail as he said, 'The security system here, broken down as it is, still protects something at the top of the chamber. The data indicate that it is whatever passes for a command deck or bridge in this place.'

'Very well,' the Client replied. 'Meanwhile I want everything you have on the core systems.'

She sensed Trike's reluctance – he could not hide it, such was the depth of their connection now. Then he mentally shrugged and began transmitting. At first, she thought the data might be simple enough to handle in her own mind, but the continuing stream forced her to open further processing to accept it, concurrently opening out her own mind. From this, she obtained a clearer picture of the situation inside the ship's core.

The occupants had died long ago, but how long she had yet to ascertain. The maintenance system had continued functioning. This iteration of the Species had worked in a similar manner to her, producing 'assistants' from their own bodies. But for larger tasks, they had created bioreactors to produce bespoke creatures in greater numbers. Numerous such reactors were scattered throughout the core, and had continued operating after those that had made them had died. The continuous renewal of those organic robots, over a long stretch of time, had resulted in copying errors and mutations, which led to things breaking down. Maintenance out in the main body of the core still worked well, but within the central chamber things had gone seriously wrong. The creatures that kept the place clean and functional had been subject to diseases propagating from millions of decaying corpses. Their replacement frequency had been high and, consequently, their mutation rate too.

As she gradually filled in the whole picture, the Client saw how she could penetrate this place. She began growing another organic robot of her own, making additions and subtractions as and when she ascertained what might be required of it. At one point, as the last unit in the long chain of her being swelled hugely and became gravid, she asked herself why. Why did she want to have anything more to do with this graveyard? Sure, she could obtain much data there, but any more than she already had from the Librarian, who had actually created these creatures? Yes, she realized, there would be more. Time had flowed in the blister at variance to the outside universe, but still a great deal of it had passed. The knowledge base of the Species there would have surely diverged. However, was obtaining this data worth the risk of hanging around here, when a Jain ship had arrived and now lay only days away?

Then, only as she seriously considered running, did something occur to her. She had died. An assassin sent by the prador had killed her, yet she lived again. She had been backed up in quantum crystal storage in her original form, and restored from that. Perhaps the Species in the core also possessed such crystals in their bodies? Also, because of the maintenance failure of their habitat, vast quantities of their physical remains had not been recycled. She realized, with a surge of almost religious conviction, that she could resurrect them!

But first she, and that core, had to survive. She *did* need to protect it. How best to do that? On conventional drive through the disruption, hauling it with her, she would be slower than the Jain ship and its attack vessels. They would rip her apart. No, the safest place for her at present still lay behind Orlandine's defences. Meanwhile she needed to check if those Species remains did contain processing and, if so, gather as much of them as possible and transfer them here to her platform. She could run and possibly stay ahead of the Jain ship until out of the U-space disruption, then U-jump as far away as possible. Because, she had no doubt, the Jain ship would have enough to occupy it. She was utterly sure that, outside the disruption, the Polity and the prador were preparing.

She turned her attention to the remote growing in the womb of the body unit at the end of her chain being. The thing was very much like the last one she had sent. It possessed many weapons, tools, defences and the capability of taking sustenance from its environment, and was practically immortal. However, one such creature would not be enough . . .

# 9

It has been supposed that should the prador build their own AIs, it would be a civilizing influence on them. Their AIs, when free to develop themselves, would become hugely intelligent and effective, end up taking over from the ruling prador and running their society in a peaceful and productive manner. However, our definitions of peace, plenty and civilization are not universal. Human technology, from the simple flint axe to the complex AI, is just an extension of ourselves. So we can see the Quiet War not as the rebellion of a separate species we created, but the action of our extended, collective will. We wanted the corrupt politicians and the wealth-grubbing corporations gone, we wanted peace and plenty, and the AIs obliged. In light of this, one must then ask what the prador desire. Certainly they want plenty, but preferably as a result of rivals being crushed. Certainly they want peace, but as a result of enemies exterminated. And civilization? Sure, but in the case of individual prador, only when they're on the top of the heap looking down at the rest. So no, we don't want the prador to build their own AIs, we want them to have ours.

From 'Diary of a Xenophobe' by C. M. Run

## Orlik

Within the *Cable Hogue*, Orlik might be able to control appallingly powerful engines and weapons systems, but he knew the *Hogue* AI possessed veto over anything he might do. He felt like an inconsequential speck within its immensity. He had not experienced that in the *Kinghammer*, although, retrospectively, he understood his control of that ship had been no more than here.

'This strikes me as . . . unusual,' he commented.

'It is.' Sprag's voice sounded slightly disembodied in Orlik's mind, slightly cold. 'You are the very last backup in a chain of many. I count at least eighty ship AIs that could take your place, and then there are the minds of many Golem and war drones. I would say it is an attempt at . . . inclusiveness.'

'The possibility of Orlik having to take control is not so remote as you calculate, drone,' interjected Hogue. 'Any weapon or unforeseen event that takes me down would most likely affect all proximal artificial intelligences too.'

'And there is some expectation of such?' asked Orlik.

'Not really, but it was a small thing to include you in the circuit.'

Despite the fire and debris ahead, as the *Hogue* cut a path through the Jain objects towards the gate, Orlik found through the ship's sensors that he could inspect this gate across a wide swathe of the emitted spectrum. Mental pressure in other directions gave him a gravity map too, and then a manifold U-space construct that made his mind ache.

Hogue continued, 'It is the facility of AI to calculate odds to the nth degree and prepare for them. But I do not need to tell you this, since the prador are now venturing into the realm of AI.'

Orlik shrugged and shivered, tightening his grip on the floor. His connection to this ship felt very different. His major ganglion itched, as if something was tickling its way along it.

'A very new venture,' said Orlik cautiously.

'One involving a Polity drone, apparently,' said Hogue.

'Oh hell—' Sprag managed, but no more.

Orlik felt the whiplash through his mind as the *Hogue* AI

reached in through his implants to snare Sprag. With a buzzing and clattering, Sprag fell to the floor while ahead the meniscus of the runcible gate swept up in front of them. Hogue read him too, as memories arose so clear he seemed to be in the moment of his meeting with the king. Then came his transference to the *Kinghammer* and Sprag essentially becoming its AI.

'You have no AI,' said Hogue.

Orlik had no time to object before they suddenly hit the meniscus and began to move through it. The twisting pressure on his body drowned the sickening wrench of transit on his consciousness. He flattened against the shock foam inside his suit, things bursting painfully inside him, his remaining shell cracking. He divorced himself from it, fleeing into the ship's memory space and sensors, as the *Cable Hogue* shot up from the surface of the gas giant on the other side, gravity clawing at it, grav-plates coming on inverted to ease off the load. He spewed fluid from his mouth, some of which issued from the damage inside him. Ahead, out in vacuum, the Jain ship dragged away but the cloud lay all around. The *Hogue* diverted, thousands of gees of acceleration flinging it to one side. Orlik glimpsed the other ships coming up through the gate as well and taking the same course. Then, gradually, as they drew away from danger, the pressure began to lessen.

'That was fucking rude,' said Sprag quietly.

Orlik was past caring.

## Orlandine

A bright clear day dawned on Jaskor with the only visible cloud a grey boa over the Canine Mountains. In the morning warmth, Orlandine could smell jasmine from the vines on the balconies below. Despite all the mayhem that had occurred here, flowers still bloomed and hummingbird moths still came to them in the mornings. She smiled, testing the expression, and gazed up at a cerulean sky which gave no indication of further mayhem on the way. But a foretaste of that came in the form of an information package.

'We hope this data will be useful to you,' said the Hogue submind incorporated into the package.

Orlandine immediately focused on the data. Even honed down to relevance, there was a lot of it. She could choose to go through it at her leisure using the submind as a guide, but neither she nor the Jaskoran system had time to spare and, anyway, she wanted that data *now*.

'Sorry about this,' she said, not really meaning it.

The submind gave a mental shrug – it had no interest in its own survival. Orlandine absorbed it in a second, established the timeline to the data, divided it up into packages and distributed those across her overall mind, dropping them straight into memory. Within just a few minutes, events out at the accretion disc, after the U-space disruption had cut her feeds from there, became part of her own experience. She saw the Jain ship controlling the cloud, its destruction of Polity and prador ships, its launch of its attack ships and what it took to destroy them. She watched the combined fleet taking a horrific beating and finally, desperately, the remnants of it escaping imminent destruction when the heavily damaged *Cable Hogue* transported them away. She now knew that the *Hogue* and trailing ships were swinging around the Jain cloud out by the gas giant, having come through the runcible, but did not see how they could be useful.

Integrating all this into her present tactical plans, she broadcast updates to her weapons platforms and the Polity and prador fleets here. Morgaine acknowledged this tersely – she had already received the same data package from Hogue. This gave Orlandine a moment of pause. The AIs in Diana's fleet, as well as having designed a counter to the disruptor, had made headway in building their own disruptors. As this was no longer a technology she could keep to herself, she released the schematics Trike had stolen to everyone. All ships and platforms responded immediately. The prador commander set prador technicians to work. The platform AIs changed their formation and quickly applied data on disruption beam defences to the beam weapons they were already building. Every one of her forces and allies were doing what they could. Orlandine avoided straying into further calculations of the likelihood of them making a successful defence.

'Some need to tinker with present strategy,' observed Knobbler.

She directed her attention to his location, keying into his feed. After the events in Marshallam, he no longer felt it necessary to keep an eye on the prador. Steadily working his way along a beach, he was stabbing mines down into the shingle, the scene lit by drive flashes from fleets shuttling refugees up to the evacuation platforms. His redeployed drones were busily at work setting up gun emplacements and other defences around the southern cities, and hunting down every piece of weaponry available. They had just found a cache of mining explosives, including CTDs, and of course decided they too would be useful. Meanwhile Knobbler was fielding a great deal of grumbling from them. They felt they would be better deployed out in space.

'Only to tinker,' she replied. 'Though we were lucky it was unable to establish its gate any closer, we have no time to make major changes now.'

'We were unlucky it was able to establish a gate at all,' Knobbler observed.

From the roof of her apartment building, Orlandine nodded,

grimaced, then flung her full perception out beyond Weapons Platform Magus.

Time *had* just run out.

A prolonged flashing of light across vacuum marked the first shots as thousands of Jain-tech objects flared to vapour. The outlying attack pods, in a sense acting as spotters, followed that fusillade with ten more. Completely emptying themselves of railgun slugs, they then ramped up on fusion drive hundreds of gees in retreat.

Orlandine next concentrated on her other forces. The six hundred weapons platforms had spread out across fifty million miles of vacuum. This was closely bunched for such extreme firepower but wide enough to encompass most of the cloud when it reached them. The spread also, she calculated, effectively concentrated firepower, while it sufficiently reduced the chances of a large detonation destroying many of them. Steady streams of attack pods issued from each platform as they dispersed everything available into action.

The Jain reply came a moment later as the bacilliforms needled particle beams across the millions of miles intervening. Orlandine chose one of the leading attack pods which was accelerating towards the cloud. The controlling platform AI had disengaged to give the radically stripped-down submind autonomy. With the signal delays of laser com, this was the best way to conduct the attack. They fought alone, only to update by laser com when larger tactical changes became necessary. She re-engaged and, via that platform, kept the laser link open to follow the pod's progress.

Surrounded by its fellows, the pod hurtled into the Jain-tech cloud. It was split down its length and opened to expose the silvery deadliness of its weapons. Firing five particle beam shots in quick succession, it obliterated four of the things that looked like knots of metallic intestines. The fifth, just clipped by a beam, tumbled out of control, glanced off the side of a bacilliform, then exploded under a railgun strike from another pod. Her pod next swerved hard, stabilized and fired its own fusillade of railgun slugs. It pleased the submind to take out two bacilliforms with one shot, then to wing another of the gut things and send it crashing into an object shaped like a man-of-war jellyfish fashioned from burned bone. *Shooting fish in a barrel*, thought the mind. Orlandine thought its descriptive abilities quite limited. The whole battle reminded her more of a World War II dogfight.

She retreated from the pod for a better overview. The battle now seemed like a massive fireworks display writ across vacuum, and the effects on the cloud were evident. A burning hollow developed in its forefront. Retreating further to a watch satellite high above, Orlandine got the impression of a fire burning through fuse paper. But inevitably this could not last. She turned her attention to the Jain ship, even as the tactical alert impinged and that monstrous vessel began shedding some of its equally monstrous attack ships. A second later, a small data feed winked out and she realized the attack pod she had been viewing through was gone. Others soon followed: hardfields collapsed under intensely powerful graser strikes, superbly designed weapons fizzed to long bright explosions of molten metal and shattered ceramic.

'Okay, we've pissed it off,' she said. 'Now concentrate on those fuckers.'

The remaining attack pods took the shortest routes they could to get out of the way. The moment a tactically significant portion of them was clear, the weapons platforms opened fire. The beams speared across vacuum, easing out like the rise of liquid in a thermometer from Orlandine's perspective, and with the distances involved. They carved through the cloud, incinerating objects in their path, but they were not the prime target. Then they struck.

Sensors blanked out in the glare from an ovoid sun, coming back on with heavy filtering. All the beams had hit the enclosing hardfield around the Jain ship. She considered what she had just seen. With that hardfield up, the Jain attack ships could not use their grasers. They could only use them once outside the field and for that the mother ship would have to close it down . . . Orlandine issued no more instructions since the tactical plan dictated the platform response. She just waited.

Even as the attack ships reached the inner perimeter of the field, her platforms began launching a storm of railgun slugs. Those at the edge of her formation also coilgunned out missiles containing high-yield CTDs. Would the mother ship react to this by not yet shutting down its field? No, it just had. Stupidity or supreme confidence? The attack ships continued their approach as the railgun fusillade arrived. The things bucked and flared under numerous impacts but the main hail of slugs rained down towards the mother ship, then simply began vaporizing.

*Supreme confidence*, Orlandine realized, not entirely sure why that pleased her.

## The Client

With her connection firming to it, the Client's latest remote climbed out into vacuum, and she gazed upon the stars. Out of them, balanced on its fusion drive, an attack pod fell down towards her, tumbling over on thrusters and decelerating to come past her position. She launched, employing the EM drive in her body and accelerated to intercept it, landing easily, with her feet sticking. Did she need to control the pod directly? Yes, because Trike did not have full control in the core, and the core security system there might try to penetrate it. She inserted two triangular-section tentacles into sockets all her tech had recently grown, and took full direct command of the pod.

Taking the pod towards the core, she mapped security ahead while reviewing the codes from Trike, and decided on a direct approach. She flew over the wide upper surface to one of the shallow entrances and nosed in. Just inside, she made a full scan. No detritus lay within the short tunnel so defences could fire on her. With pod weapons poised on a hair trigger, she watched them as she transmitted one of the codes. Security merely tracked her and, after a moment, the door divided in three sections and these folded inwards. She immediately flew into a short wide tunnel. Studying structures on the side of it, she saw, just ahead of where a big maintenance organism was laying down material, a section of slate-like wall. She turned the pod to face this and fired its particle weapon.

The beam speared out and carved a circle, spraying out thousands of squares like scales in a hot plasma cloud. As she completed the circle, a pressure differential blew out the section carved away and it tumbled through vacuum towards her. She jetted the pod sideways and went in, passing the glowing ends of beams which resembled the rib bones of some titanic beast. Veins of organic tech had spread about the inner face of the spherical cavity within. Ahead of her loomed the mouth of a square-section tube. Internal defences all around powered up immediately, then powered down when she told them she was not there. The system possessed enough intelligence to register the damage but now could not trace its source. She entered the tube, the sides of the attack pod almost touching its walls, and flew to the end. Here she settled and stuck it against one wall, then detached from it.

An octagonal hatch sat in the wall at the back of the tube. She ignored this and concentrated on the surface to one side.

Extending a limb, she rerouted internal power to the organic laser in her complex hand and fired it up. She scribed a circle and at the last cut, moved aside as this section blew out too. She quickly dived inside as a core repair system came online. Behind her, metallic threads shot across to web the gap, gel surfaces spreading between to crystallize. Ahead, masses of material feed tubes, power lines and semi-organic robots all centred on one object.

She negotiated through this paraphernalia to drop down on the surface of the massive white ovoid. Here she found a node – a nexus from which nerve fibres spread all over the exterior – and inserted two tentacles, spreading fibres and making connections. It took her only moments to find the control interface and thence the processes involved in copying. She set this running, tweaking it as she desired. A split in the ovoid opened beside her and rolled back lips to expose a cavity. Detaching her tentacles, she scuttled over and crawled inside. The mouth slammed shut and immediately protuberances, vibrating knives and a thousand other organic versions of the tools a Polity AI surgeon might wield, extruded from the surfaces all around her. She shut down her defences and dropped into somnolence as the bioreactor began to take her, as the remote, apart.

## Morgaine

Morgaine gazed through her ship's sensors at the planet. She also watched through soldier cams and other sensors down there, as Gemmell stepped from the military transport with the woman Ruth at his side. They had arrived on the outskirts of the city where grav-tanks were arrayed on flattened crop fields. She considered how, with a thought, she could use the weapons at her command to obliterate both of them, surgically – an explosion and a cloud of vapour and they would be gone. Childish speculation. She had no intention of killing them, just as she previously had no real intention of putting Gemmell in danger.

'You have cut the tie.'

Orlandine appeared in human form aboard the virtual bridge Morgaine had created. Orlandine presented a facade much like Morgaine, who also looked completely human – an illusion she had created for Gemmell when she pulled him into this virtuality. Now no longer necessary, she dispelled it, and once again became a withered being wrapped and penetrated by technology, rather like some human subject on the maximum life-support of past and ancient medical technology. And yet, even in this form, she knew she was still much more human than the figure before her.

'It was well done,' Orlandine added.

'The tie that held us together was our inability to let go of our past. I could not release him while he still loved me, so I had to kill that.' And she had. She had seen his attraction to Ruth and so created the illusion of her own jealousy. In competition with the woman, she apparently restored herself to an earlier youthful form. Her later revelation that this had been a lie would have driven him away. But, entangling Gemmell in the childish and soon-to-be-crushed Separatist plot in Marshallam had been Orlandine's idea, and a better one. True, Ruth or others might have been killed, but the overall death rates had remained unchanged. The likelihood of Gemmell dying had been low, however.

'He will be very useful to you,' said Morgaine. 'Free of his concerns for me.'

'And you will be more efficient without your concerns for him.'

'I have always performed at optimum,' Morgaine objected.

'Nevertheless.' Orlandine began fading, distracted, her attention elsewhere.

'To business,' said Morgaine.

Orlandine rose a little out of her distraction to turn her avatar and had it nod once, then disappeared.

All cold function now, Morgaine felt a sense of freedom. Gemmell no longer loved her and the last dregs of her attachment to him were, she felt sure, leaving her. She dismissed the virtuality from her mind, though kept the comlink open to Orlandine, and turned her attention outwards. She had received orders from Diana Windermere, just as Ksov, the commander of the prador fleet here, had received orders from the prador Orlik. Under her command, their combined fleet must turn its focus outwards and concentrate on defending Jaskor from the Jain threat. Despite the phenomenal firepower of the six hundred weapons platforms, the Jain cloud had begun filtering through and objects were on their way here. The leaky barrier the platforms provided would also become more permeable as they necessarily redeployed to face those giant attack ships, even more so when the mother ship itself reached them.

'You are ready?' she asked.

Ksov appeared in her vision, chrome-armoured and crouching in his sanctum. 'Deployment on your word,' he replied.

'Then now,' she said.

Hundreds of drives fired up around Jaskor as prador and Polity ships began to move out of orbit. The *Morgaine's Gate* took the lead point of a curved wall of ships, spreading to cover a wide area of space. She had finely calculated their distribution to stop as much as possible reaching Jaskor. But it was a loose net just hundreds of thousands of miles across, deployed against a shoal millions of miles wide. Inevitably, Jain objects would get past, and those items would then be the business of Gemmell and Orlandine.

# THE HUMAN

## Diana

As the gel drained away around Diana, her body felt leaden. Her implants were down and she had no perception of how much time had passed. A warm flush, starting at the top of her head, passed down her body. She opened and closed her hands and they felt fine, so she sat up, and realized at once that her military nanosuite had knitted her broken bones and repaired other damage. The suite worked fast, but this meant she had been out of full stasis for at least ten hours. How long had she been under? Slowly, almost reluctantly, her implants started coming back online.

'So we're still alive.' Jabro sat up in a nearby gel coffin. He gazed at his right arm in puzzlement, for it too had been broken.

'Yeah,' said Dulse.

In the zero gravity of the room, Diana easily flipped herself out of the coffin and engaged her boots to the floor. She felt a lot better, for the nanosuite had repaired more than her bones. She studied her shipsuit, with remaining gel on it drying quickly and flaking away from the exterior. There was still stuff inside the suit, and she would have liked a shower and change of clothes, but discomfort was irrelevant.

'Let's get back to it.' She led the way to the door.

Via her implants, she now saw to her horror they had been in stasis for forty hours, and still Hogue held off on updating her fully. Perhaps it wanted to give her at least some moments of recovery time. No, it was avoiding telling her something. Still logy because of the rubbish floating around inside her body that her nanosuite needed to snare and dispose of, she went over to the door leading to the bridge, but it didn't open. Instead, another opened leading into the cabin area.

'There is no rush, for the present,' said Hogue via intercom. 'You have time.'

Diana halted, feeling resentful, then saw the feeling as an indication that she wasn't quite ready to assume her duties. She turned and headed for the other door.

Once inside her cabin, where grav-plates gradually increased their pull to one gee – showing her just how feeble she felt – she stripped off her suit, used the toilet and then took a shower. Before dressing, she gulped down a large flask of liquid her fabricator provided, then ate a big bar of something that tasted like fudge. Both were loaded with complex chemicals, biological support and nanotech. Even as she dressed and started to feel more able, her implants began to come fully online. Finally, she returned to the bridge.

'We are on course to swing around the cloud and hook up with Morgaine,' said Hogue aloud. 'This is the optimum tactical option.'

'Really?' said Diana tightly.

Plugging optics into her body, she began to get detail. Orlandine's six hundred weapons platforms were presently in a firefight with the Jain attack ships and holding their own. Imagery came through into her skull. She saw one of the giant attack ships hurtling through a firestorm and finally dropping its shield. At this point, a disruptor beam hit it and it fell apart, but slowly. A gigaton CTD finished the job and debris rained down on one platform, smashing it to scrap.

'Orlandine has the disruptor,' Seckurg commented.

'So it seems,' she replied.

Again, she felt resentment, then quickly suppressed it. Hogue's tactical assessment was correct. The *Hogue*, the ships it contained and those trailing behind it, she could better deploy in secondary defence against anything that got past those platforms. Already the AI had opened up the massive hull doors and the ships packed inside were easing out and falling away to take up formation around it.

## Trike

Ten levels up, the thing came scuttling down the ramp. It bore some appearance of the creature they had seen below but brandished pickaxe mandibles to the fore and moved a lot faster.

'Get rid of that,' said Trike, trying to penetrate the system here. The command deck they were heading for had high security and, over long years, had separated out from the rest of the core and gone its own way. Frustratingly, he could detect no signals across the emitted spectrum to decode and thereby gain access via that route. He would have to make physical contact to penetrate and seize control of it.

Cog moved forwards, eager for something to do. He stood in the descending creature's path and it rushed him, raising its pickaxes. This deceptive move revealed its real weapon. With a body heave, it ejected an object from its mouth. A lump, like the head of a large sundew plant, slammed into the front of Cog's space armour and sent even him staggering. Issuing tentacles, it began groping and thrashing about him, vapour boiling up from the powerful excreted acid. The acid had little effect on Cog's armour but, scanning the thing, Trike saw its backup option. He stepped in behind Cog and caught hold of him, rooting his own feet to the ramp. The object detonated, blasting both of them backwards and tearing up the ramp attached to Trike's feet. He pushed Cog aside, detached the Jain tendrils securing his feet, then leapt up and over the gap just as the creature fired another of its acid bombs. He slapped this aside and it exploded in mid-air, then he kicked the creature hard, lifting it up off its feet. Before it could come down again he double-fisted it sideways and sent it tumbling off the ramp.

'You okay?' he enquired, looking back.

Cog sat up. 'I'm good.'

His suit had a couple of cracks that had filled with breach sealant, while the acid had etched shallow grooves across its surface. He heaved himself to his feet while Trike scanned deeper. Cog's few injuries had already begun healing. Had a normal Polity human occupied that suit, most of his organs would have been jelly and his bones in splinters at this point.

'We can expect more of that?' Cog asked.

'Yes, until I can penetrate the system up there.'

'What about other defences? We might be able to deal with creatures like that, but what about disruptor beams, particle cannons or railguns?'

It was a valid question.

'We're not yet within the sphere of influence of the system up there. That creature –' Trike gestured over the edge – 'seems to have acted on its own cognizance.'

'Still doesn't answer my question.'

'Give me a moment,' Trike replied.

He went in deeper, tracking around the nervous system surrounding the area cut off above and riffled through defensive protocols, locating weapons, assessing and checking. After a moment, he had it. The Species had not allowed heavy weapons within their living areas because of the danger of precisely Trike's kind of subversion. He supposed that, were they required in here, it would already be too late. The surrounding security must be wholly organic. But then, as they had seen, organic chemistry could produce some nasty surprises.

'No heavy weapons up there,' he told Cog.

They continued up the ramp for a few paces, then Trike broke into a steady lope. Another level up and another creature appeared.

'I'll take it,' he said.

Though more than strong enough to deal with these organic robots, Cog did not move fast enough. Trike slapped away two projectiles before reaching the creature, and caught its pickaxe mandibles as it tried to drive them into his chest. One heave and it went over the side of the ramp. They moved on and the pattern repeated on the next two levels. The level after that something different awaited them.

'We're now in that sphere of influence,' said Trike. 'Stay alert.'

A thing like the globular robots they'd first met squatted on the ramp this time. However, it had spread four tentacular legs to stick it in place. As he and Cog approached, it exuded a tube and started vibrating, as if a piston engine had started up inside it. Then it fired.

Trike tracked the first projectile, like a large melon seed, as it shot towards him. He had time to scan and analyse it before swaying to one side so it missed him. Heavy compressed carbon with diamond edges, incredibly sharp. Next came a stream of them, issuing at vicious speed.

'Get down flat!' Trike shouted, diving to one side.

He had time to see Cog dropping, the stream passing over his head and cutting into one of the Species trees. This splintered in half, but still hung in place, the upper part attached to the ceiling. Further impacts deeper into the forest smashed up shards and wrecked other trees, dropping dead and dried-out occupants to the floor. As Trike caught the edge of the ramp and swung under it, he realized the guardians here had seriously diverged from their original programming. Surely they would not previously have fired something that could damage their creators?

Sticking to the underside of the ramp, he scrambled along to the position below the creature, then swung back up beside it. It turned the barrel of its organic machinegun towards him and he closed his hand around the thing. But its immense strength began to push even him back. He stabbed his hand down, fingers straight, hard claws penetrating, but did not get very deep. Two more tries and he thrust his hand inside. He pulled, opening a gap, then released the barrel and jumped up on top of the creature. Both hands now in the gap, he tore it wider and wider. Projectiles slammed all around the area as the nozzle waved wildly. He had nearly torn the side off the creature before he spied a thick muscular tube shifting projectiles through it with fast peristalsis. He grabbed this and pulled hard. It snapped abruptly and he fell onto the ramp. More shots tracked across to him, punching straight through the ramp, then ceased abruptly, with the nozzle pointing and vibrating, but ammunition cut off.

'Well that was exciting,' said Cog, standing over him.

Trike glanced up at him and then flipped upright, leaning over the massive wound he had torn in the creature. Its interior looked like the combination of some mammal's guts and the seed cavity of a melon. Trike leaned in closer, scanning deeply. It occurred to him then he'd been stupid. He reached one hand into soft flesh and exuded a Jain tentacle, spearing it towards a particular spot just off to one side of the centre. The thing's nervous system spread from a fist-sized clump of matter there. As his tentacle reached and injected microfibres inside it, branching into nano-fibres, he made connections to its brain.

Just a short search revealed no ability to broadcast across the emitted spectrum. Next, tracking nerve cords, he began mapping and then modelling the whole creature. There had to be some way for it to receive instructions and report to the overall system but he struggled to find it. Then, at the end of some nerve cords on its surface, he found organs whose purpose baffled him, but only for a moment.

'Fully organic,' he said.

'Do what?' asked Cog.

The organs produced complex organic molecules that the creature squirted into the air. Trike went deeper, scanning one of these organs, and began to understand it. The Client's language, the Jain language and that of the Species, did not just consist of light and sound but also molecular communication. He made comparisons and, working back from what the creature was broadcasting now – intruders, and I have been damaged – he began to translate the encoding molecules.

'We've got problems,' said Cog.

Trike looked up. Where the spiral ramp entered the floor above, creatures were swarming down while others took to the air. Trike grimaced. He did not have the time to decode the language fully and produce the correct molecules for communication. Instead, he cut the organ free, grabbed it and began drawing it inside himself through his palm.

'You can move faster. I'm too slow to keep up while walking,' said Cog.

Trike stared at him, baffled until Cog fired up the thrusters on his suit and rose into the air. The swarm drew closer. On the ramp were things like giant horseshoe crabs, while in the air pterodactyl forms, with razor whiptails and branched multi-eyed heads, drew closer.

'I'll meet you up top,' said Cog, accelerating away, a short moment later thumping straight into one of the fliers then tossing its broken body to one side. Trike ran after him, slapping aside acid bombs and dodging streams of melon seed projectiles. Finally he leapt up, stepping from back to back on the crowded creatures, then dropped off the side of the ramp, swinging underneath and scuttling up on all fours along its underside. He had not fully taken into account Cog's abilities, nor had he been fully using his own.

## The Client

The Client connected to a remote. It wasn't the remote she had made, but she could not tell the difference. Crawling along the octagonal tunnel from the bioreactor, the thing had nearly reached the far end when she connected to another remote too. This had crawled into the airlock at the end of the tunnel by the time she also included a third. The serial and parallel communication between the three creatures boosted signal strength, and via them she brought in other remotes, growing rapidly in the spiral gestation tube of the reactor. The breadth of her perception increased and she was soon handling the data from multiple sensoria.

In her first new remote, she returned through the partially repaired wall she had earlier cut open and went straight to the nerve nexus of the reactor. Inserting her triangular-profile tentacles, she reconnected and observed the stages of growth of the thus far twenty of her kin growing inside. Now, rather than focus on the reactor itself, she concentrated on its outward connections. As she had suspected, this reactor connected to a vast network of similar ones spread throughout the core of the ship. Most were accessible to her. Those that weren't were either breaking down or had been cut off from the rest by some small separate biotech and security realm. But there were plenty enough for her purposes. She dispatched the schematics of her remote to all of these, with instructions to reproduce. And so her perception within the core and her ability to act there increased. Already, eight new remotes began moving away from the reactor to begin their assigned task.

# THE HUMAN

## Orlandine

Tens of thousands of railgun slugs fired out, but quickly turned into spears of glowing vapour, pointing in towards the Jain warship. This spear shape showed it was not the warship disintegrating them but the attack ships – if the counter-hits had come from their target the slugs would have vaporized into slower-moving bulbous masses. Antimatter missiles were sent in next, detonating in a sweeping cascade. The Jain warship, along with its attack ships, disappeared inside a cloud of fire fifteen thousand miles across. It bothered Orlandine that the warship had not used its own weapons – as though its occupants felt no need for them yet.

The weapons platforms kept on firing into the cloud, still using railgun slugs because the hot nuclear debris would interfere with the effectiveness of energy weapons. The fusillade lasted for an hour, with the burning cloud growing all the time. Then, at appalling speed, the attack ships shot out of it. Somehow, under supposedly conventional drive, they had ramped up to a quarter light speed and were still accelerating. Orlandine understood the reason for their odd formation – a convex front facing the weapons platforms – as soon as particle beams from six hundred platforms converged on it. She measured energy readings, as their enclosing hardfields climbed to the overload limit which the AI of the *Cable Hogue* had told her about. Those reaching their limit rotated behind the rest, shut down their fields and emitted visible grasers through the narrow gaps in the field defence. The immense power of these sent platforms into hardfield cascade, spewing out molten projectors like thousands of tracer shells. Their defences collapsed until the grasers cut into them. She saw a beam slice a platform from end to end, internal explosions blowing the two halves apart. Another shot sliced one from top to bottom, while further beams mangled twelve others but left them still capable of launching an assault. Then the attack ship formation broke.

Their abrupt change of directions, scattering them into the weapons platforms' defensive line, should have been physically impossible. Orlandine registered gravity waves and even U-space disturbances. Twenty platforms bucked and shifted abruptly, thousands of miles out of position. Somehow, the attackers had utilized their mass to turn onto new courses. Windermere had neither seen nor reported tactics like this. Grasers lanced out again and fried hardfields. But the attack ships were no longer going for the kill, they just seemed intent on whittling down defences. A single victory came then, as fifty particle beams intersected on one of them, along with the close detonation of a CTD. But it was pyrrhic as the ship came apart, shedding impossibly hard debris that struck two platforms and tore through them.

A short while later, she received one of the intermittent tactical updates from her platforms. She began running through it quickly, breaking it up into packets to distribute about her extended mind. The attack had altered; the Jain were surely employing some new tactic. Then she saw it in the scan data.

Changes were occurring in the surrounding Jain cloud. The clumps of Jain tech, in particular the knots of metal intestines, were streaming into long chains, in turn feeding down towards the bacilliforms. Thousands of them were pointing in the direction of her weapons platforms, which she had expected, but she did not yet understand the purpose of this reorganization. Then, through one of her satellites, she found herself looking towards the throat of a bacilliform a thousand miles out. The form flashed and spat an object at the satellite. *Linear accelerator*, she realized.

The knot of Jain tech sped in at near-relativistic speed, crossing the gap in seconds. Her satellite threw up its own hardfield and the object somehow transferred momentum, decelerating to slam into it, but not hard enough to cause projector collapse. It pancaked on the hardfield and just hung there in vacuum. A moment later, the satellite reported invasive computer life generating in the projector itself, feeding back through the thermocouples and promulgating induction warfare. This was horribly fast and horribly close – it was actually in part of her mind. Satellite defences turned against it and she tried to complement them from her distance, but the com delay was too much. The delay then dropped away as the satellite started beaming the attack directly back to her, as well as to other satellites in her network. Orlandine reacted as quickly as she could, relaying instructions to one weapons platform at the rim of the defence. A particle beam whipped out and fried the satellite, then two more which also showed signs of infection.

'Hit these,' she said, issuing her first direct instructions since the battle began. She sent coordinates of bacilliforms lining up as linear accelerators for the knots. Even as she sent them, she saw the things firing. They rained the sequestration devices on the platform defence, but some also fired towards Morgaine's ships and Jaskor. It would not be long before Gemmell and the troops on the ground were in action.

Meanwhile, the attack ships were wreaking havoc amidst the platforms and barely exposing themselves to the kind of concentrated fire that could collapse their enclosing hardfields. Even when they dropped them for graser strikes, and thus opened themselves to attack, they endured a pounding no Polity dreadnought could withstand.

Platform Silus . . .

She picked up the whisper across AI minds and via sensors aboard others focused on the platform in question. Recorded action showed its defence weakened by the passes of two attack

227

ships. It spewed out burning projectors and shuddered under a tentative graser strike that cut away towers on one of its surfaces, but no more. Four sequestration knots hit it all along its length. Via its own sensors, she observed how they pancaked on impact, just as the one had on her satellite's hardfield. But here they spread rapidly, writhing across the surface in waves to form a loose net. The platform AI immediately hit them with antipersonnel lasers, tracking along the lengths of the vine growths. Orlandine watched a laser incinerate one of these to ash. However, scanning of the process revealed accelerated growth around the damage. The thing, like the one that had attacked her installation on the gas giant moon, fed on the energy. Multiple, concentrated laser strikes resulted in major destruction of one of the nets, but it wasn't quick enough. The thing threw up bloated sacs in the areas yet to be hit, and these exploded, strewing clouds of objects about the platform. They were smaller knots and, where they landed, immediately spread and grew. Penetration of the hardware and software of the platform was rapid.

Antipersonnel lasers began to drop from the AI's control, while some even began feeding low-intensity lased light to the mycelia. They tapped into power feeds as their growth found nano- and microscopic pores in the armour. Cams and other sensors fell under virtual warfare, which penetrated platform computing to interfere with vital systems. At each impact site, within just half an hour, the Jain tech had spread to miles across and reached a mile inside.

'I predict catastrophic failure within two hours,' the AI of Silus commented.

One mycelium reached a reactor and in just minutes had sequestered its entire output. The thing glowed like an ancient light bulb filament as its growth accelerated. Threads and vines etched into metals and other materials, feeding on them and expanding. It also invaded a cache of grapplers and Orlandine, fighting a viral attack on the sensors she viewed through, saw grapplers staggering out, enwrapped in thready growths. But then they became purposeful and rapidly headed out into the platform.

'Hold for as long as possible,' Orlandine instructed. 'We need data on this, but prepare destruct protocol.'

Then she received further reports of eight other platforms being similarly invaded. One of them, where a mycelium had landed in a crater caused by a graser strike, went offline for an hour. It came back online to broadcast virtual warfare at other platforms, then opened fire on them, its weapons lighting up space all around it. The neighbouring platforms returned fire, which it blocked for a little while. It then shimmered and dragged to one side, seeming to stretch as it tried to enter U-space. It disappeared, then bounced out of that continuum just a thousand miles from its original position as an arc of wreckage, pelting down on other platforms. Whether the remains of its AI had done that, or the mycelium which had sequestered it, she did not know.

'Time to go,' said Silus.

The upper interlink detached from its AI case while the lower one pushed it up through a tube like a bullet into a chamber. The linear accelerator of the tube hurled it out of the platform, even as grapplers tore away the walls and entered the AI's erstwhile chamber. As the AI fell clear, a gigaton CTD imploder ignited deep inside the platform. In an instant, it disappeared in a ball of fire. Then the explosion reversed, collapsing down to a point too bright for any sensor to observe, and a secondary plasma explosion blew out a wave of incandescent ionized gas. Nothing but the stripped base matter of the platform remained.

# 10

*How strong is a hooper? It's difficult to get a sensible answer to this
question. Hoopers are cantankerous and contrary. It is known that as
they grow older they get stronger, but also less inclined to allow anyone
to prod, probe or measure them. They might take part in a strength
test and pretend to be weaker than they are, or 'accidentally' break the
machine measuring them. Even so, despite the difficulties in obtaining
data from hoopers themselves, it is possible to measure the effects of the
viral fibres which increasingly occupy their bodies as they age, fortifying
their bones and enhancing their muscles. From this we know that young
hoopers – whom the Spatterjay virus has only infected for decades –
have the maximum strength which conventional physical enhancements
can provide in the Polity, like boosting and bone reinforcing. Those into
their second century of infection are as powerful as a civilian Golem.
In their third century, they are possibly stronger than even military-
spec Golem. Those who are older still, who knows? There are limitations
to the forces physical matter can apply. Theoretically.*

From 'How It Is' by Gordon

## Cog

Their destination hung at the intersection of strut bones, like
those inside Dragon, with a single spiral ramp leading up to a
wide shelf beside it. Cog, still flying, circled it while eyeing his

propellant and power supply. He settled on a strut until the raptors threatened to swamp him, then moved on. He'd lost count of how many he had broken and sent plummeting before he saw the other horde swarming up from the base of the ramp, and the brief flickers of Trike's fast-moving form ahead of it.

'I don't know how to get through the door,' he said via his suit radio.

'One thing at a time,' Trike replied.

Another of the fliers attacked Cog, whipping him with its tail. The impact juddered him sideways on the strut and left a score on his space armour. He eyed the creature as it rejoined a group of them circling in closer, and sighed, since he had seen this a couple of times already. He wrapped his legs round the strut and waited. Now in a long line, they began streaming in. As the first reached him, he punched its main body and felt it break under his fist, caught its tail and slammed it into the next one. This same routine continued for the next eight of them, then the remainder drew off to regroup. They weren't very bright, he'd decided.

They flocked together again as if in conference, perhaps deciding to make the same attack as many times before. Then a flash lit their surroundings and Cog flinched inside his armour. One of the fliers fell, trailing fire and smoke. He pulled closer to the strut and searched the vicinity because that flash had been an energy weapon – like the shot from a pulse rifle. Another flash, two more, then it seemed a thunderstorm fired up all around him. He glimpsed black shapes sweeping round too fast to identify. Peering down again, he saw Trike now well ahead of the horde on the spiral, so he released his legs and jetted down, swooping to the ramp and landing hard. The thing shuddered beneath him.

'We can't catch a break here,' he said. 'How are we supposed to access that place if we're fighting these fuckers off all the time?'

Trike shrugged, looked up. 'New visitors.'

'Yeah, I know, seems that one part of the system is attacking another, like you said, but the newbies have pulse weapons.'

Fliers poured down out of the chaos above. Some bounced off the ramp, neat holes glistening in their main bodies of muscle and metal rods. Then two larger black shapes descended. They hit the ramp between Cog and Trike on the one side, and the approaching horde on the other, folding knife-like glassy wings. These hard-looking things seemed a lot more dangerous than those Cog had already faced. Each stood on four armoured legs and sported frills of triangular-section tentacles behind their heads. They had two multi-jointed arms like those of an auto-surgeon. Their long and vaguely segmented bodies extended into whiptails, terminating in barbed spikes. But their blend of organism and machine seemed the most disconcerting, even though other creatures here had that. Giant cyborg insects.

'Bugger,' said Cog, ready to throw himself to the side of the ramp. He already knew they sported energy weapons.

'Now let's see what we've found,' said Trike.

Cog glanced at him, but Trike simply spun away and began walking up the ramp. The two creatures meanwhile turned from him to face down the ramp. Allies? Cog watched as they began drawing their 'hands' across the ramp with a sound like a circular saw going through wood. Dust spewed up around them then, with a crunch, the ramp separated, thumped under his feet and began rising. Going down on one knee, he drove his fingers into the woody substance to secure himself as the upper part of the spiral closed up towards their destination, while the lower section collapsed, spilling many of their pursuers as it did so.

'Could be an idea to get off here?' Trike suggested mildly, as the ramp continued to rise.

Cog let go and jetted out and away. Trike streaked onto the

shelf above, just as the spiral closed up solid under him. Down below, the lower section crumpled in an explosion of wet, organic debris, turning into a short solid pillar which sandwiched the crushed remains of their pursuers. He grimaced, then landed on the platform beside Trike. A moment later, their two strange rescuers fluttered in to rest nearby.

'What the fuck are they?' Cog asked. 'Something you took control of?'

Trike shook his head. 'They are the Client.'

Cog eyed the creatures dubiously. 'What now?'

Trike gestured ahead. Here hung an object that bore the appearance of a huge neuron suspended between nerve connections. The entrance Cog had earlier inspected was a translucent blister, with an organic mass trapped underneath it like tangled intestines. Trike tilted his head back as if listening, blinked and showed his teeth. 'She's moving fast.' He then gestured to the door. 'We just walk in.' He stepped forwards and the blister split from top to bottom, organic masses parting before them. A short tunnel, whose walls seemed formed of compacted snakes, was lit with a pearlescent glow, as was the room beyond. Here stood triangular-profile pillars of a crystalline material similar to that of the Client's feeding tree. Bulging from these, like epiphytes, were objects resembling brain corals sculpted by a cubist. All of this also seemed tangled together by an organic mass – a vined growth with a disconcertingly reptilian look.

'Why didn't the Client send in one of her creatures?'

'Because she knows she cannot stop me,' Trike replied. 'And perhaps she trusts me.'

Cog glanced at him sharply, but then swung back to the scene before him. Something about it niggled at him and now he saw it. On closer inspection, that organic mass revealed itself as one of the Species, only larger, thicker and from which numerous tendrils and vines had grown. These looked like the explosive growth of a parasitic fungus from inside it, yet he could see order in its connections to the pillars and cubist brain corals.

'What am I seeing here?' he asked.

'The captain, the pilot, the autarch or the president,' Trike replied. 'I'm not entirely sure of their social structure. Whatever it was, it was at the centre of things here.'

'And now?'

Trike showed his teeth and, walking over, stepped carefully into the tangle. He reached out to one of the corals and placed a hand on it, then stretched his second hand out to place it on another. Cog watched curiously as the tendrils on his arms and hands writhed and then extended into the cubist convolutions.

'Keep watch,' said Trike. 'I may be some time.'


## Morgaine

The Jain knots, evidently sequestration devices according to the tactical updates from Windermere, should not be allowed near their hulls. Morgaine saw them as more dangerous than the bacilliforms, which seemed to be just mobile linear accelerators and energy weapons. Her integration with her AI was as near total as it could be, without her becoming something like Orlandine, and Morgaine turned her ship on fusion drives, then fired an array of particle beams which intersected on a distant point. Five knots had lined up there to feed into a bacilliform. Her beams arrived after three had gone through. The bacilliform flamed out of each end and then exploded, sending the other two tumbling. She picked them up with further shots – flies caught in an acetylene torch.

'Where the hell did the other three go?' she asked aloud, a

concession to humanity that had her grimacing. It annoyed her to recognize it as such. Damned if she wanted do the human time thing like Orlandine did.

Telemetry arrived in her mind. An old prador destroyer – an ugly lump of ship that looked like a heart fashioned of brassy metal – had stopped one of the things on its hardfields. A replay from sensors on a nearby reaver showed the ship's hardfields going out, then the knot falling to its hull and spreading. Already the old vessel's connection to other ships had dropped out, and it had ceased firing on anything coming through its allotted section of space.

'You have a problem,' she told the prador commander, Ksov.

'I am aware of that,' he replied.

Jaskor also had a problem. The other two knots dispatched that way had drawn out of range. Others were through too and more coming. Besides the weapons platform defence breaking up, it simply hadn't been wide enough, and the cloud spilled around it. One large tongue of it also reached in-system towards the sun, following a spiral path that would eventually intersect with Weapons Platform Mu and the Species ship's core.

Detonation.

Morgaine focused again on that prador destroyer. There was a titanic blast, as a reaver cruised past it, while the hollowed-by-fire hulk of the destroyer tumbled away. It seemed Ksov had dealt with his problem. Perhaps the Guard considered normal prador of lesser importance.

'Now we both have a big problem,' Ksov sent.

She had already seen it: two of the giant Jain attack ships had broken through the platform defence and were on their way in. Tracking back along their course, she saw weapons platforms firing on each other. Updated telemetry told her that Jain tech had now sequestered forty platforms. Eight had either managed to destroy themselves or others had destroyed them, but the rest were firing on their fellows. Attack pods also swarmed around each other in a vicious dogfight. She had a moment of epiphany. The Jain were not attempting to destroy them outright, for they saw them as a resource to control. Why else hadn't the mother ship taken part in the action? Why else were those attack ships not deploying the full extent of their weaponry for destruction? A brief tactical analysis seemed to confirm this. But Windermere had ordered her to defend Jaskor, and those two attack ships were more of a threat to it than Jain tech spread on its surface. They had weapons that could destroy a world, and she could not afford to assume they would not.

'Close up – we have to stop them.'

She sent instructions to move the ships into an arrowhead aimed between the two attackers, with *Morgaine's Gate* at the sharp end. But the prador ships' telemetry showed they were not responding as they should, and a message came from their commander.

'No. I will take the one on the left and you take the one on the right.' Ksov sent a tactical plan. She studied it. It looked like madness, utterly suicidal.

'This is crazy!' she exclaimed, as she watched reavers gather round one large old dreadnought and accelerate massively. But even as she spoke, she felt something loosening in her chest. Maybe the time for madness had arrived. Subliminally, she noted the old dreadnought ejecting its captain's sanctum, then a stream of prador in space armour. At least their commander was not completely careless of their lives.

'No more crazy than your tactic,' he replied.

She made rapid calculations, half herself and half her ship's AI. Her plan had been to try to blow the two attackers off course, then follow them, hitting them hard and driving them away from Jaskor. Ksov's plan was more radical.

'*Lancet*, slave control to me and eject,' she instructed a dread-nought not much smaller than the *Gate*.

'Very well,' replied the AI of that ship. 'We no longer have a choice.'

'Well, I'd like to have a fucking choice!' said the interfaced captain of the *Lancet*, even as an armoured egg closed up around his control chair and his links began detaching. Meanwhile, the ship had already ejected a coin-shaped vessel containing the ship's cryo-suspended and gel-stasis crew. The captain became even more unhappy on learning his AI had overridden him and initiated these ejection routines, along with its own.

All the Polity ships rapidly closed up in a formation mirroring that of the prador, as they ramped up acceleration to maximum. Control of the *Lancet* fell into Morgaine's mind, and she positioned it behind and to one side as she ran point. Now in its controls, she assessed its armament, then set its railguns firing towards the attacker designated to her. They would not stop firing until their carousels spun empty. Within the ship, she primed all its remaining CTDs and power supplies to detonation upon a feedback surge from its hardfield generators. The fields would all project to the fore . . . prior to impact.

Soon the formations of prador and Polity ships were closing on the two attackers. Both ships disappeared behind firestorms as railgun slugs vaporized on their enclosing hardfields. The prador reached their target first. The attack ship's field went down and its graser speared out. It sliced across, chopping two reavers in half even while railgun slugs slammed into it, the thing shuddering and shedding wreckage. The graser probed, again and again, the reavers ejecting streams of projectors that exited whole then flew into molten clouds. At the last, they parted and the big dreadnought hammered down, all its hardfields to the fore to ram the attack ship. This killed the momentum of both ships in a blinding explosion, the reavers speeding through and past it. Morgaine watched in horror as the fire cleared. The prador dreadnought was gone, but the attack ship remained, slowly tumbling, warped out of shape and leaking fire, but still there.

'It didn't use its hardfield,' the *Gate* AI noted in her mind, though she found it difficult to parse whether that was its thought or her own. The impact should have been enough, according to the data from Windermere, to drive its enclosing hardfield to collapse. But apparently the course of least damage had been not to use its field. She saw the reavers turn over and kill their acceleration on main fusion, heading back towards the thing. But she could watch no longer because her own target now lay directly ahead. And its field went down.

She felt the *Gate* shudder as a graser swept across. Over to one side she saw it blow hull metal out of a destroyer and the ship veered out of formation. Next came the stab of a disruptor towards the *Lancet*. She intercepted it with induction warfare, shutting down the beam, even as it touched the *Lancet* and the ship's hull began to fly apart. They had not used these before. What other weapons had they not used? She found out, as it felt as if someone smacked a hammer against every bone in her body. The whole bridge shifted and distorted and grav went out. Peering down into the technology enclosing her, she saw blood welling out. But this was not the worst, because it seemed as if half her mind had just blanked out and she suddenly felt incredibly slow and stupid, and alone.

'Gate?' she asked, but there was no reply.

Her data feeds still worked. She saw the formation breaking away around her as per plan, but could find no reason to follow. Her AI was gone – the feed told her that. Another graser strike, probing across her hull, found its target. White light flared in the bridge and she felt the skin on her face crisping as it blinded her. Through internal cams, she saw the beam cut straight through her bridge, just a few yards to one side of her.

*Missed*, she thought.

Then, with the disintegrating *Lancet* just behind, the *Morgaine's Gate* struck. Time slowed as she saw her hardfields collapsing against the hull of the giant attack ship. No need to send detonation orders, this impact would breach most of her CTD store. She had time to wonder whether this would make things harder or easier for Gemmell, then the universe seemed to stutter, and fell on her.

## Earth Central

As expected, a powerful USER had been located within the watch station. Clamped to the underside of the lead hammerhead, Earth Central studied the effect upon the linked Laumer drives of all five ships. They skipped out of U-space leaving a trail of photons rucked up from the quantum foam of the universe and, just for a moment, sat exposed in the real. The station, appearing like a giant barbell translated into vacuum, immediately opened fire with a particle beam twelve feet wide. This expected response should have been enough to seriously inconvenience if not destroy any Polity ship trying to cross the border into the Prador Kingdom. It wasn't an act of war, just in agreements – prador ships crossing into the Polity expected a similar response.

However, the thoroughly new design of the five hammerheads, and their linked drives, enabled them to breach high levels of disruption. They bounced along through the real for less than a minute, then dropped back into U-space before the beam could even reach them.

Next, sliding through the grey continuum, EC observed the gravity wells of stars and planets and moons as holes. The swirls and flows, the strange echoes of quantum order in the real and the direction that was time delving deep into the continuum in a way not definable through human language. EC understood most of what it could perceive here, and the infinite progressions and singularity collapses were not routes into madness for its AI mind. In fact, they were no route to madness for the human mind, and much easier to understand than why some humans reacted as they did, bare-brained, to such surroundings. EC also recognized the cysts of pseudo-matter, indicating detectors sunk in here from the real. The prador now knew five large Polity warships were travelling to a certain destination and, no doubt, were preparing a potentially nasty welcome.

Finally, after a measurable time in that continuum, but whose relation to the real varied, the ships surfaced. In that moment EC felt like a soldier might feel upon stepping into the barracks of the enemy. The massive surges of data and EMR had that hint of breechblocks clacking home, knives slithering from sheaths, and laser-targeting locking on. The five came to a hard stop in relation to the many surrounding reavers and cued-to-jump kamikazes. The AI gazed beyond the reavers at the immense King's Ship and quickly opened com.

'We need to talk,' EC said.

## Trike

The connection to the Client lay wide open, but she did not attack or attempt sequestration. She just waited for what he would find. This surprised Trike, for he had expected interference; he had expected the Client to seize control here and deny him access. In fact, he felt sure of that intent when her two remotes entered what he dubbed the command deck of the core.

'What do I do?' said Cog, standing between the creatures and Trike.

'*Do you want control here now?*' Trike asked the Client.

'*They are to collect the remains,*' she replied.

'Do nothing,' Trike instructed Cog, and the man moved aside.

The creatures moved forwards to begin dismembering the corpse of the captain or pilot here and transfer the remains outside. Trike ignored them and explored his connections. Already having penetrated the ship's security, he found the language and the coding were easy. From this point, he stopped fighting a system but found it enhanced him. His perception spread out all around him, beyond this command deck. He ceased to be the invader here and became the controlling mind. Within the system, he found the Client and now she was the invader. From his position of power, he knew he could cast her out. He could also extend his reach and seize greater control of engines, weapons and all the further panoply of this great vessel. But he did not want that; he wanted data. And he soon found it.

Masses of information became available to him, but searching it at first was a problem. Next, probing his own mind, he found the solution in the mental and AI architecture he had inherited from Orlandine: he created subpersonae, stripped-down copies of himself he could assign to specific tasks. He first dispatched one to search for data on weapons, then another to search for defences. This he felt was too specific so he next created personae to respectively find science data roughly divided into biology, physics, materials science and resultant technologies. Another he dispatched to learn everything the Species knew about the Jain. Yet another he directed specifically to investigate U-space tech. Then, while creating a persona to look into tactics, he found details on the battle between this ship and a Jain warship, which led him on to the ship's log.

This stretched far back in time. Trike decided, while his personae did their work and transmitted their results to the weapons platform, as well as the nearest of Orlandine's satellites, he would speed read the log himself. It started right at the beginning, from the genesis of the race.

They woke to full sentience with minds packed full of knowledge, but little in the way of tools to manipulate their environment. The Librarian was a close but unseen godlike figure in their minds, communicating, assessing and judging. Short-lived to begin with, generations lived and died inside a great hollow sphere while the Librarian tweaked their physiology and mentalities. When satisfied with its achievement, it made further changes so the Species ceased to die of maladies that had previously taken them off within a century. As their knowledge grew, the Librarian finally allowed them out of the sphere and into the solar system it occupied. Here they built a technological civilization under the Librarian's benevolent dictatorship. However, their science operated under severe strictures. The ancient Jain limited their EMR output and, though they discovered U-space travel, it did not allow them to use it. It also did not let their number go beyond a million. After a few thousand years, it seemed to have a change of heart, and instructed them to build vessels capable of travelling in U-space, then took off the other strictures. Their number rose into the millions as they packaged up their small civilization and prepared to move. Trike understood the reasoning. So close to the other Jain, the Species were vulnerable to detection. With the limitations removed, their EMR output increased and would eventually reach the nearest Jain in five hundred years. Unfortunately, though they were ready to move well before the five-hundred-year limit, one of the other Jain found them.

Much detail in this first part of the log linked to numerous other sections of the ship's database. Trike could study four-dimensional images of their time in the sphere, maps of molecular language, individual stories and speculations – a great mass of information on the rise of a civilization. While sending the entirety of this log to Orlandine and the Client, he necessarily honed down his perception of it to chart the course he wanted. This became easier when he focused on the personal perspective of the individual whose remains the Client's creatures were now removing from this command deck.

The captain of this ship, still overseeing its steady spiralling growth, watched the battle. The interloper attacked immediately and the Librarian faced it, both of them in ships like the Jain warship now in the Jaskoran system. First the new arrival screamed its challenge, and the Librarian responded in kind, decoding and answering that scream with one of its own. The two ships hammered each other with horrifically powerful energy weapons, attack ships and swarms of missiles, incidentally tearing apart a giant frigid world in the process. Finally, forced to drop their fully enclosing hardfields before catastrophic collapse, the two then pounded each other to the point of breaking apart, whereupon the Librarian slammed its ship into the other like a hunting squid on a fish.

The battle proceeded inside the attacker with semi-organic robot extensions of the two Jain concerned. Trike viewed what the captain of this ship managed to glean of the mental battle that took place too. Both a battle and amalgamation, the two ripped at each other's extended mentalities, as a result capturing and integrating mental and physical parts of each other's technology, extended organisms and minds. The Librarian then followed its troops inside and finally confronted its opponent inside the attacking ship. The two fought with ferocity beyond belief. Trike could not know its full extent as an external observer, but the indications were that it encompassed the mental, the nano to macro in the physical world, and plain mechanics and energy weapons. The two badly torn-up forms merged, ripping and reintegrating on all levels until finally one remained. It dragged itself to a surviving attack ship and fled the remnants of the two behemoths. Just moments later, a massive detonation destroyed them.

Trike paused, analysing what he had seen. Evidently, the Librarian's consciousness remained supreme for, after years of silence, it finally compelled the Species to leave what had been their home – accompanying them in the attack ship. But the Client had provided Trike with detail of her own battle with the Librarian and it had been nowhere near as ferocious. It was as if the Librarian had wanted to lose. He also considered that final detonation. No doubt, the loser had set some device to discharge should it lose, which rather undermined the idea of mating as a battle scenario and continuance of the Jain race. Perhaps, he thought, the Jain were already destroying themselves, before one of them created the kind of tech found in the accretion disc.

Even as the Species departed the system of their birth, another Jain interloper was on the move. It intercepted them in the system of the accretion disc in its earlier, undamaged state, knocking their fleet out of U-space with a giant USER. This was the Jain that had eventually been captured in the U-space blister in the sun there. Trike studied intently what the Species had done. They took a U-space twist to its limit while opening a giant runcible gate effectively on itself. This created a loop in spacetime that dragged in proximal objects: the Species ship and the Jain warship. Jain and Species fell into this, still fighting, still ripping at each other with disruptors, induction warfare and energy weapons. But cause and effect began to part as they dropped into separate spacetime geometries of the blister. They ended up in their own timestreams and effectively their own universes.

Here the log departed from the story of the Species as a whole because those aboard this ship were now effectively in a universe separate from that of their fellows. They repaired their vessel and set to work on finding a way to attack the Jain ship and ultimately destroy it. Trike observed twenty thousand years of research and effort that gave him an understanding of the blister and the trap they were in. It simply came down to energy. Because the ships sat at different points on the time slope within the blister geometry, all their weapons were subject to entropy. For the Species it was like trying to fire a laser at a target tens of thousands of years in the future. Within their ship, they detected the efforts of the Jain to destroy them, but only with the most sensitive of instruments. Finally understanding the futility of this exercise, the Species moved on to searching for a way out of the blister. By now, they realized that the time disparity between themselves and the outside universe was nearly a hundred to one. Twenty thousand years had passed for them inside the blister while outside it had been two million. Surely, their own kind reigned supreme out there by now, or was gone? Surely, the destructive technology the Jain used, and which the Species had studied and understood, had destroyed them? Surely, their reason for entrapping the Jain ship had ceased to be relevant?

Their reasoning, however, ceased to be particularly reasonable. The thousands of years trapped inside the blister had changed them. Becoming highly introverted, they slid into the realm always a danger to AI: that of ultimate navel gazing, of losing themselves in their own constructed realities. Again, the problem was energy. They simply did not have enough to break out of the blister because the energy of the sun in which they had created it, fed it. They did, however, have enough energy to throw out smaller objects or informational constructs, rather like a man at the bottom of a well able to toss out stones. This they managed with a data-gathering probe which they also enabled to return. It came back infested with Jain tech and they surmised that the universe outside had been swamped by this sequestering, destructive technology. From this Trike understood that the Jain had done the same. It had sent out its own probes and finally one of them had lodged itself in the mind of a wormship: the Wheel.

Despairing at the discovery, the Species became even more deeply introverted, losing impetus, losing any reason to continue existing. They neglected the ship's maintenance as they retreated into mental constructs, into their own private worlds. They began to die. Trike estimated that the last of them died forty thousand years after they entered the blister. Their automatics mutated and steadily changed, but survived. When Orlandine freed the ship from the blister, it was these that had responded. Automatics caused such damage to the waiting prador and Polity fleets. How formidable this ship would have been had the Species actually survived. And, of course, the Jain had prepared to encounter such a ship, not knowing what had happened to its old enemy.

Trike withdrew from this sad history and looked beyond the command deck again, as he began to reintegrate subpersonae who had finished their tasks. This utterly new experience he found painful. The personae had strayed from himself to become *other*, and as he assimilated them, he necessarily had to destroy and discard parts of them, along with much of their knowledge which he did not have the capacity to absorb. This process felt all too familiar because of its parallels with what the Jain did to each other, and because, in essence, he was part Jain himself. He decided that, in the future, he would not so blithely create them, and wondered if Orlandine felt the same about it.

Out in the rest of the ship's core, events had moved on.

Scanning through the security system, he found himself assimilating its broken-away parts the same way he had his personae. As the system integrated, he noted the bioreactors producing remotes for the Client. These creatures had taken control here and there, but only for self-protection – to facilitate their journeys to the habitat below him. Through the Species equivalent of cams, he watched remotes collecting up the remains of those previous inhabitants in large pods, like giant wheat grains. A quick scan of one of these revealed it to be no more than a storage container. He even saw remotes vacuuming up the dust on the floor, while others worked in the air filtration ducts to collect remains there, even so far as taking the filters. Respectful disposal of the dead? He very much doubted it.

'What are you doing?' he finally asked.

'You have transmitted all the data here to Orlandine but, as yet, have received no reply from her?' the Client enquired.

'Nothing as yet,' said Trike. 'I am presuming she is busy.'

The Client's data package arrived a moment later. He wondered if this might be some sort of attack, and noted his own arrogance when he simply opened the package. The update was a wake-up call. Events had moved on since he had heard the scream of the Jain warship's arrival. He gazed upon the battle of fifteen minutes ago, since the signals took that time to reach them. The horrifying destruction matched that in the ship's log.

'You are preparing to run,' he said, *remembering* the weapons data he had retained from one persona. He had schematics and design for the completely enclosing hardfields already transmitted to Orlandine and much else besides. At least the Client's departure now would not result in the loss of useful knowledge. But in the end it did not matter, because Orlandine no longer had the time to apply anything new.

'Yes, I am preparing to run.'

'Why the remains?' Even as he asked the question, he realized the answer. 'Quantum processors, crystal storage . . .'

'I can bring them back. Once I have removed them from this ship's core, I can resurrect them.'

'You will not stay to face your enemy,' Trike stated.

'You have the data and you have access to the systems of this ship's core, to its sensors and its telescope arrays. You are at the centre of it now and, via that log, you have seen the capabilities of that warship. What do you think will happen here?'

Trike flexed his mind, gathering his resources, and then reached out further. With godlike enhancement, he gazed in detail at the Jain warship and its attack ships wreaking mayhem on Orlandine's defences, as well as the Jain mechanisms falling onto her world. Already hundreds of weapons platforms had been destroyed while others were in the process of being sequestered. The Jain warship, still enclosed in its hardfield, had shrugged off heavy attacks and had yet to use its own weapons. The result was foregone. Orlandine would lose. The Jain warship would annihilate or sequester all the forces arrayed against it.

Trike felt a surge of the cold rage – the old madness that had dogged his mind since before his encounter with Orlandine's Jain element, in the tunnels under the city. The creature in that ship had sent out the Wheel, and so had initiated all the events which led him to this point. And that required a response.

### Ksov

Ksov, the commander of the small prador fleet, watched the impact of the *Morgaine's Gate* and the *Lancet* on the other Jain attack ship. The blow was more effective than his because the thing broke into its ten segments, which, he hoped, would be inert. He also hoped to snare a piece of it at some time – such armour would be very useful to his father the king. The one he had dropped a prador destroyer on was another matter. It had rolled out of the impact still intact and begun to right itself. It then seemed almost inevitable that when the railgun strike from the reavers reached it, they vaporized against a fully enclosing hardfield again.

'Pull off from your attack, Ksov,' said a voice. 'Head back around Jaskor. This vector.'

It took him a moment to realize that the instruction had come over the prime command channel. Only one could be speaking to him from there.

'Commander Orlik,' he said. 'You survived.'

'I certainly did,' replied Orlik.

EMR had climbed because of the recent impacts, and scanners were not picking up much; however, he could see new ships had arrived. He sent instructions to his fellows and they altered course, taking them in a wide sweep around the Jain attack ship and back towards Jaskor. Further scanning revealed something big out there, hammering in rapidly. Next came an alert: gravity wave. He focused on the attack ship and saw it jerk, its enclosing hardfield darkening for a moment then winking off. A concentrated column of railgun slugs followed, blasting it back in a long line of fire. The commander's own ships bucked in the sideswipe of that gravity wave but flew clear as the second wave came in. The attack ship buckled and tumbled as something slow and glassy licked out after it. He first recognized the disruptor, then its giant source: the *Cable Hogue*. The beam finally struck home and began to splinter up long ribs of its armour, like a tightly wound ball of elastic touched by a razor.

It seemed to him that they had won the engagement, especially when other reavers moved in, firing their particle beams, but then he checked vectors. Yes, they had defeated this attack ship but the thing was fifty miles long, travelling at stupendous speed straight towards the face of Jaskor. Focusing towards the planet, he saw the remaining evacuation platforms there speeding away under full drive. The war had arrived at that world in full and no more refugees would be leaving.

'Sweep round and intercept,' Orlik instructed.

The particle beams were now cutting into the attack ship as they would any normal ship. But though the beam strikes were powerful, on the sheer scale of this thing, they were hand tools whittling away at a tree. Ksov's ships went into low orbit and he sent his instructions. They ramped up acceleration to maximum and inverted grav-engine effect – a string tying them to the world as they swung round it. Only the reavers could swing this tightly and the older dreadnoughts began to stray off course. Ksov made his calculations and sent them to his brothers in the Guard.

'Three of us,' one of them replied.

Ksov was tempted to designate three subordinates, but knew that would be an utterly selfish decision and contrary to his king's wishes. Instead, he checked manifests and damage logs and selected the three least battle-ready reavers. As he suspected, one of those was his own.

'Orbital insertion evacuation,' he instructed his crew as he programmed his ship's course and set its remaining weapons for detonation.

He then removed his armoured claws from the pit controls and headed to the side of his sanctum. One last glance at the screens showed armoured shapes shooting out of exit tubes. He turned away, inserted a claw into a control beside a heavy circular hatch and twisted. The hatch opened and he scuttled inside. He settled, operating internal controls in his armour to link to his ship's system and fleet telemetry. In passing, he considered how Orlik's choice to link to his vessels in the way he had was the better one. A moment later, his array of turret eyes gazed upon a collage of scenes. He saw the other two selected ships ejecting their crews. He watched the first of those prador hitting atmosphere and already burning suit rockets to try to slow their descent, then he sent the instruction.

On the hull of the reaver, another hatch opened. A wind roared around him, but he had to release his hold on the floor and propel himself forwards to get moving. He tumbled through semi-vacuum. Automatic initiation of steering thrusters stabilized him relative to the reavers, then, as he used those thrusters to slow himself, he watched the ships slide on towards the horizon.

Atmosphere thickened around him and his suit temperature began to climb. He checked his suit supplies and saw he had enough fuel for a burn of an hour. His grav-engine would ameliorate final descent and impact, but still he would be going in hard, very hard. The chances of survival for one of the normals would have been sixty per cent, but for him and his fellows, thankfully, substantially higher. Whatever. He had done his duty. He now concentrated on the image feeds and telemetry.

The fleet swung hard around the world and the massive attack ship came into sight. Barring the three ramming ships, the reavers opened fire with every weapon available. Energy beams struck first, ablating that incredibly hard hull but not penetrating. Penetration was not the aim – the particulate impact and subsequent explosive ablation pushed the big thing fractionally in the direction they wanted it to go. Railgun slugs next, causing a massive firestorm along one side of the thing. These pushed it even further but still not enough. Slower missiles, fired first in an arcing course to avoid the other strikes, then arrived, and the ship disappeared in a storm of titanic explosions.

Ksov called up a view from the nose of his erstwhile vessel. It entered the firestorm and he briefly glimpsed the hull of the alien ship before impact. That sight blanked out. Replay came from the other reavers as they sped through fire. Three reavers, one after the other, slammed into the attack ship. Rear view then: an explosion five thousand miles across, atmospheric effects below with trailers of fire spreading around the world. He wondered for a second if they had set the atmosphere ablaze, but those trailers of fire began to die. He then got a clear view of the attack ship. It had been shattered at last and, checking tracking, he saw that most of its pieces would bypass Jaskor. Some, unfortunately, would not, but at least the world might survive. He cancelled imagery from the reavers and concentrated on the outlook ahead, and his suit readouts. Now it was time to look to his survival.

# 11

*It is common knowledge that directly interfacing a human brain with an AI will result in the human brain simply burning out. This whole perception arises from the story of Iversus Skaidon and his creation of runcible technology. It is both right and wrong. The key word is 'directly', because interfacing technology can create buffers between the organic human brain, with its linear evolved thinking, and the mentation of AI. 'Human brain' is also a debatable term. It is possible gradually to replace weak organic components with rugged and more easily integrated tech, manufactured in situ by nanites and by other means. This has been occurring for a long time and has resulted in amalgams of human and AI across the Polity. The haimans are the buffered kind, while the captains of old interface dreadnoughts are the other, gradually shedding their humanity over the ages until the distinction between them and their ship AIs is lost.*

From 'Quince Guide' compiled by humans

## Gemmell

Even with his visor closed and filtering automated, the flash turned night to bright hot day. Gemmell had also sent instructions to the public via every method available: they had to stay inside, close blinds, close their eyes, and protect their skin.

However, there would always be those who didn't get the message or did not heed it. They would be the ones requiring corneal and optic nerve regeneration and emollient for skin burns. Many, Gemmell thought, would be okay because most here had taken advantage of Polity nanosuites, enhancements and various kinds of boosting that could deal with the damage. He felt a tad ashamed to feel a righteous gloating that those who had not would likely be Separatist sympathizers.

'Good grief,' said Ruth, turning her back on the glare from the horizon and holding her hands in at her belly. He could feel it on his hands too – the burning – but his skin had been tweaked to handle this kind of radiation and a lot more. He smelt something odd in the air, like cooking cabbage, and glancing over to a nearby hedgerow saw the leaves there steaming.

The glare began to diminish and his visor adjusted accordingly.

'They destroyed it,' he said.

She turned back, shaking her hands and grimacing. Orange streaks of fire, highlighted from that main glow and etched round in layers to pale lemon, had turned the sky into a thing of beauty. Meanwhile aurorae had begun dancing over the mountains – great columns of electric green and blue.

'There'll be a shockwave?' she asked.

'Yes, but it won't reach us for some hours.' He closed his eyes for a second to get a better picture from the ECS data sphere, only it was incomplete. The battle had ramped up EMR, which interfered with data transfer. He did see ten evacuation platforms, loaded with people, on a vector quickly taking them away from the action. He could only hope that they would be ignored. Dropping back hard through atmosphere, shuttles and other transports were returning to the cities. Heading off to join their fellows, the remaining fifteen evacuation platforms were hurriedly reinstating their weapons. Further searching revealed that the small fleets above had destroyed *two* giant attack ships detached from the Jain mother ship. He tracked the courses of large debris coming down and saw that, thankfully, the largest would go down in the ocean, while others would hit far from here on the other side of the continent.

This interruption of the night cast Gemmell back to his early years as a marine. Even as the horizon glow continued to fade, it seemed the sky acquired a new nebula, only this scar of light moved. Bright flashes lit its interior, leaving afterimages in his eyes. He even saw a line scoring across as a titanic particle beam reached out to some target. Concentrating on radar imagery, he saw other objects still falling towards Jaskor. Windermere's fleet, which had absorbed Morgaine's, was eating these things up with energy weapons and railgun strikes, but there were so many of them. Too many of them.

As the objects drew closer, Orlandine's satellites and other weaponized infrastructure nearby opened fire, but with weapons less effective than those of the ships. He also saw them focus on defending themselves, not stopping the stuff from reaching the surface. And soon shooting stars lit the night.

'More of the shitstorm is arriving,' commented Baylock, even as she climbed up the side of a grav-tank and dropped inside.

Their meagre supply of drones, including Knobbler and his unruly bunch, began interception in atmosphere. Gemmell turned and looked back to the main city where Orlandine controlled the guns. Particle beams speared up into the air and drew burning trails there. A short while later, he saw her sentinel drones, left over from the ruins of the Ghost Drive Facility, rising up like bees from a nest and the firework display spread. A constant thunderstorm rumble began to grow, punctuated by the sawing shrieks of particle beam fire and the sharp crackling of railgun slugs breaching the air.

'Like I said before, there's no way we can stop everything,' said Ruth from beside him.

'We do what we can.' He rested a hand on the grav-sled rail and operated its controls through his gridlink.

The sled rose fifty feet above the ground, while Ruth climbed into the seat behind the twin-barrelled pulse cannon. Adjusting his optical enhancement gave him a daylight view of his surroundings. Curving back from him in either direction, across croplands and slicing a line through a forest, he could see part of the line of grav-tanks completely encircling the city. All the cities had similar defences, though for the ones in the south, it was prador, their implant tanks and other war machines which stood in for Polity grav-tanks.

'Are you good down there?' he asked via another com channel.

'As good as we can be,' replied Trantor from the caves below. 'We've mined the whole system and set up barriers. Micro-drones are on patrol.'

'Good.' Gemmell grimaced. 'But prepare for earth tremors – that debris will hit hard.'

'We know exactly how hard,' Trantor replied. 'And we know what the fault system is here – Orlandine's data on that are pretty thorough.'

'Yeah, but you have underground rivers there, remember . . .'

'Ah, gotcha.'

An update from Orlandine fell into his mind. He absorbed directly into working memory how Jain tech seized control of weapons platforms, and felt his guts tightening. Until now he had been dealing with theoretical constructs, loads of tactical data and never really worked things to their conclusion. But the speed of sequestration and ferocious growth he now saw brought home to him the reality he could not deny. They could burn the knots from the sky and destroy them on the ground, as well as in those caves if they got there, but when the tech started growing and spreading? It would be in the ground like fast-growing roots. He knew, from the moment it arrived, his forces would be fighting a constant retreat to inevitable defeat.

'Now we get to work,' said Ruth.

An object streaked down out of the sky in the distance, cutting a phosphorescent trail, to land with a crump over on the far side of the forest. Another object dropped in pursuit of it and, magnifying the scene, he saw one of Orlandine's sentinel drones. The thing slowed to a hover a hundred feet in the air then opened fire with its Gatling cannons. Rolling thunder echoed across the landscape and fragmented trees exploded into the air. The drone then abruptly shot up higher and spat something down. A flash cast black tree shadows and the intense blast cut through the forest like a giant shaver. Gemmell watched a mushroom of fire rise from the spot.

'You have to wonder how much will be left if we do manage to stop this,' said Ruth.

Gemmell analysed the recent interception in the data sphere. The drone had followed a conglomeration of five knots all the way down, hammering it with slugs and burning it with a particle beam. When it hit the ground it became evident, as it began to dig in, that projectiles and energy weapons were not enough, so the drone deployed a kiloton antimatter missile. Thousands of these things were coming down, and they were behaving intelligently. Easily destroyed singly, they now coagulated into masses in upper orbit before descending.

His connection with the data sphere cut out for a second before coming back online. Further analysis revealed battles in the computer realm. Viral programs assembled into worms and other complex forms of computer life to attempt hardware penetration. However, nastier entities were seeking these out and destroying them. Updates revealed Orlandine had initiated aggressive subpersonae for this task: her multiple copies hunted the enemy through the data realm while trying to keep coms strung together.

'Hardwire and go over to established tactical protocols,' he broadcast. 'Tight beam microwave transmission only.' He switched to that himself and his perception of the battle, as it began to warm up, waned. Every one of his troops, including the prador, had their orders now in whatever computing they carried. They would act as one to the numerous scenarios already modelled but with minimal communications. Still, however, he had an overview. That flashing on the horizon came from grav-tanks in action. They had risen to surround a fallen knot and pound it to plasma. Meanwhile a short transmission from the south delivered an information package. A thing like a mutated kraken trying to crawl out of the sea had run into prador Gatling cannons.

More objects descended. A flight of airfire drones intercepted a great lump dropping through the sky and with a swarm of missiles blew it apart. Chunks rained down in the mountains too and he knew they weren't done. A series of bright lines cut down after them, raising flashes as of a giant arc welder. Orbital railgun strike, he realized, then updated and saw the fleet had pulled back close to Jaskor again. Nearby a loud impact threw tons of dirt and debris into the sky. He didn't need to give any orders. Baylock's tanks hurtled towards it and he sent his sled streaking after, overtaking them.

A steaming crater a hundred feet across lay open in the field. Down in the bottom the enemy writhed, and he got his first close look at one of the knots of Jain tech. The thing reminded him of a smaller version of the wormship the android Angel had controlled – an object he had studied in detail in virtuality. It consisted of anguine forms six inches thick, tangled and writhing together. They were metallic and looked intestinal. Even as he watched, the knot began to loosen, then the end of one of the forms rose up out of it. Blunt and rounded at first, the thing split and opened out into further tentacles. The ends of each of these opened out too – twigs on a nightmare tree. The tree fragmented under two lines of pulse fire. He glanced at Ruth as she operated the twinned pulse cannon, grim determination writ on her face. She transferred her fire to the main loosening body of the thing just as the tanks arrived.

Opening up with particle beams, the tanks fed an appalling amount of energy into the crater. The knot opened up further – a mass of snakes burning in a fire. Black projectiles streaked in, detonating planar loads in flat disc-like explosions. These cut the snakes into fragments while other firing continued. Gemmell watched the fire ablating the things away, as they shrivelled and died, collapsing into ash. By the time it was done, the interior of the crater was molten. He pulled the sled higher to get away from the heat that was raising steam from his uniform, and delved with the sled's scanners. Nothing. He might detect nothing now, yet he was sure he had seen wormish fragments rapidly burrowing into the ground.

'Back to the line!' Baylock ordered through her tank PA. Gemmell received an alert a moment later because the data sphere was becoming more chaotic – Orlandine sacrificing data streams and concentrating on holding her own coms together. Something stirred over in those woods, knocking down trees as it approached. He tilted the sled back towards the line, sure he was about to lose contact with the bulk of his forces soon, and hoping all his preparations had been enough. Next came a communication directly from Orlandine:

'*Morgaine's Gate* is gone,' she said.

'What?'

'Morgaine is dead.'

Just for a second, it seemed the whole world shuddered to a halt. Then a thing like a hydra reared up out of the trees. He dropped a visual grid over it and analysed the feedback from spectral analysis.

'Ultraviolet lasers and missiles!' he broadcast, and grav-tanks, rising into the air, responded. He had lost close comrades before and knew the mental drill but, as ever for a soldier in action, did not have time for it now.

## Orlandine

Virtual warfare had compromised the Polity data sphere, as had interference. Only laser coms held it together now, and only when clear vacuum or air lay between emitters and receivers. Orlandine had sacrificed much of the coms between the grunts, leaving them with voice only. Their tactical preparation had, she hoped, been enough, while commanders like Gemmell retained telemetry and tactical, and she could still open up bandwidth if something radically unexpected occurred. However, she needed to cover something they had prepared for, but of which those at the brunt were not yet aware.

'Vreen,' she said, her voice heading by laser from the top of her apartment building in the main city, up to a sentinel drone crossing overhead. This relayed to other sentinel drones then between a series of five airfire drones and finally down to the docks of Marshallam city. In return she got telemetry from Vreen and ascertained his situation – able to see what he was seeing, understand his plans and update on the latest action at his location.

# THE HUMAN

Vreen, clinging to a giant loading crane above a landscape of cargo containers, surveyed the ocean lying beyond. A ship sat out in the harbour and presently two of his fellows were flying in from it carting a laden cargo net between them. The humans and Golem crew of the ship perhaps weren't particularly happy about this mode of transport but almost certainly found it preferable to staying on the ship. Vreen observed tentacular growth spreading all over the vessel.

'What is it?' he asked. 'Can't you see I'm busy?'

'Scenario B104,' she replied. 'Debris from the recently destroyed Jain attack ship will hit in twenty-three minutes.'

'Oh hell.' Vreen transmitted this data to all soldiers in the area and they began retreating. 'The buildings will be sufficient?'

'Those that are not struck by fast-moving heavy debris,' she replied.

'Like that cargo ship?' he enquired.

'Don't even try to sink it,' she began, but by then missiles were already streaking towards the vessel. They issued from a human unit at the mouth of the harbour and, when they struck, their explosions were discs of fire that cut through the vessel's deck. Its back broke in four places as it exploded into the air. The pieces crashed back down into the sea, spewing cylinders of their cargo of fertilizer pellets harvested from deepsea kelps, then bobbed to the surface.

'I was going to point out that the whole ship is made of bubble-metals and composites and so impossible to sink,' Orlandine said dryly.

'And I was about to point out that in smaller pieces it will cause less damage to buildings inshore,' Vreen replied. 'I was going to blow the thing up anyway.'

'I see,' said Orlandine, 'but you now have four floating objects infested with Jain tech rather than one.'

261

'Is that any longer relevant?' Vreen enquired.

He shot up into the sky, acceleration massive, and was soon high above the city. Gazing down from this angle revealed the tops of most of the buildings, all with the profile of boat hulls and pointing out towards the sea. The human population down there was already on the move, heading from the smaller buildings into the taller ones.

'Do you see?' he asked, picking up transmissions from sonar buoys he had launched and sketching out a picture for her.

As far as the buoys covered, a front of ten miles, the seabed seemed to be moving. A great wave of squirming forms was heading ashore. Orlandine tried to get data from her sensors on the seabed but instead had to fend off a surge of virtual warfare. Just for a second, she felt a strange kinship she had sensed before. Then fear arose to contend with elation and an awful attraction. She wanted to dive into full combat on the virtual level, to grab what she could and seize control of it. The fear won out and she disconnected. As the emotions waned she felt puzzled by her response – so much stronger than anything before. She slid then into factual analysis of the Jain growth down there and realized its extent must be due to the acquisition of materials. Jain tech, under water, could process matter so much more quickly and therefore grow faster. Something to remember . . .

'Yes, I see,' she replied. 'You must do what you can.'

'It won't be enough,' he replied tersely.

Orlandine hurriedly shifted this portion of her awareness away, and out to one of her sentinel drones as it settled down to the surface of the ocean, feathering its grav-engine to make itself as light as cork. It bobbed up and down with the waves – in this way it saved energy while it waited. Meanwhile another portion of her awareness watched through her remaining satellites and installations in orbit.

Here she observed knots speeding in then using EM drive to throw themselves into orbit around the world, where they grouped into larger structures before beginning their descent. Similar constructs, escaping the disc over the years, had flung themselves at potential targets, regardless of what weapons they might face. Intelligence did not guide those ones, but it did guide these. That those larger structures now aimed for an area of ocean between the coast and the coming impact site of the attack ship debris confirmed it. She saw one splash down in the ocean, not far from her sentinel, and immediately break apart. But it did not sink like others that had fallen into the sea. Also, in the areas of infestation Vreen had highlighted, things were rising to the surface: flat nematodes, white and segmented; some joined up so they floated like forks with multiple tines. The Jain must be monitoring Jaskor through the technology itself, making advantageous adjustments so it could surf its creatures in on the coming waves.

She swung her attention back inland to where four airfire drones were pounding a crater, flattening olive trees all around it. The knot at the bottom of the crater shrivelled under particle beam fire, though some of it escaped into the ground. She picked up a feed from cave systems below and saw ECS troopers firing on a thing like a giant bobbit worm, and retreating steadily before its slow advance. In the fields outside the main city, she saw grav-tanks closing in on the woodland hydra and blasting it repeatedly, while closer study revealed pieces of the thing squirming into the ground too. The invasion of this world was well underway, accelerating and all but inexorable.

Over the ocean horizon came the fireball four miles across and shaped like a chevron, revealing the form of the underlying chunk of attack ship. It hit the ocean at an angle of forty-five degrees and glowed all the way down. The initial strike generated a giant explosion of water and steam, and a wall of water just a few feet high but travelling at thousands of miles an hour. Orlandine's drone rose up above this then tumbled out of control in the air shockwave. However, the rugged thing soon righted itself. This primary wave, she knew, would cause immense damage on the coast but would break there. Deep down just a second later, a massive detonation lit the sea like a flashbulb miles across. The sea heaved up mountainously and humped in towards the land, travelling much slower but almost with more menacing intent. Following this, the immense underwater explosion blew millions of tons of water and steam into the sky. Irrelevant. She had her drone following the humped secondary wave inwards where, as the sea became shallower, the thing grew, soon standing fifty feet tall.

Whipped up by air shock, the first wave smashed into the coast. It hit the broken ship in the harbour but, though flinging it further into the port, mostly exploded around it in white spume. It flung cargo containers into the air, collapsed piers and tore buildings apart. But this wave spent its force exploding into spindrift. Some while later, the sea sank away, the ensuing wave drawing it in and rising high, beginning to coil over. It swept up floating Jain tech, utterly swamped the port and crashed over. The flood, carrying masses of debris, continued in. A forty-feet-deep surge washed through the streets, turning over cars, bringing in cargo containers, pieces of buildings and those sections of the ship Vreen had ordered to be blown up. Throughout all this, white wormish shapes squirmed. It swept on, pouring into a metro system, flooding along metalled roads and finally spilling out on the city's other side. Inland it submerged olive and orange trees, tearing a few up. Her drone, flying higher, gave her a view along the coast. The flood, stretching for three hundred miles, had hit the other cities in a similar manner. It gratified her to see that not one single tower block had come down.

# THE HUMAN

The flood sped inland for fifty miles, finally washing up at the foot of a mountain chain, by this time just a few feet deep. It then began to subside. As it steadily flowed back towards the sea, mostly running fast along the courses of rivers and storm drains built for just this purpose, it towed its debris with it. However, none of the white forms were evident in the flow. Instead they clung to trees, burrowed into softened ground, snared rocky surfaces or, in the cities, the faces of buildings. The Jain-tech invasion now had a firm foothold on the continent, and this emphasized what she already knew with utter certainty: their *present* defences could not stop it.

In human form, on the top of her building, Orlandine turned away and walked back to the great louse-like device that comprised the bulk of her being. Standing before it, she turned and looked out across the city with her ersatz human eyes, perhaps, she felt, for the last time. Tendrils and tentacles eagerly reached out and snared her, drawing her inside the louse form. Worms, similar to those she had seen spread across the land, wove a case around her and plugged into already open sockets in her body. By the time the device launched from the top of the building and hurtled into the sky, that body had dissolved into irrelevance in the span of her mind.


## Trike

Tracking the courses of the Client's thousands of remotes outside the Species living area, Trike saw them taking containers, packed full of Species remains, to a weapon emplacement on the face of the ship's core. There sat a coilgun that could fire a wide selection of missiles, hardened for acceleration even beyond that of a Polity railgun. These missiles could contain various loads:

atomic, chemical, antimatter, invasive technology like Jain tech and a cornucopia of biologicals. Now the remotes used the weapon to dispatch those containers at low speed across to the weapons platform, where EVA handler robots intercepted them and dragged them inside.

After watching the operation for just a minute, he judged that, by the burgeoning number of remotes and the fact they were also preparing another coilgun, the Client would have the job done in a few hours. He considered his options. When the Client finished, she would have no reason to hang around. She would not be able to make a U-space jump but, on conventional drive, she could begin moving away so would be no help against that Jain ship . . . unless forced to be. He next spread his focus from the two coilguns and assessed the other weapons available.

The ship's core was loaded. Numerous coilguns and railguns dotted its exterior, their variety of ammunition immense. Protruding particle beam weapons could fire particulates with different impact profiles. Another weapon could fire lasers, masers and grasers which he could format for virtual and induction warfare. Disruptors, much more complex than the one whose schematic he had stolen from the Client, were to hand. Their ways of interfering with matter extended well beyond molecular binding forces. These could turn matter fissile to shed energy explosively, or in controlled ways he could program to other forms of virtual warfare. In all, the weapons available numbered twenty times those of a weapons platform and were a great deal more effective.

He turned his attention to defences. The core's highly advanced armour had demonstrated its resistance to bombardment and energy weapons strikes. Adaptive and self-mending, it had already repaired the damage the Polity and prador fleets had inflicted. However, the field defence did not function as it should. This had been demonstrated during those earlier attacks when it had failed to erect a fully enclosing field. Trike began investigating this and soon found, as with other broken-down systems in the ship, that maintenance had failed. When the whole ship had left the U-space blister, it had jumped, but a back-surge through the U-space engines had wrecked their support infrastructure. Since the engines formed an integrating link, between the hardfield projectors and the underlying U-field twist that stored energy from them, the system simply no longer worked.

Trike gazed through the sensors of organic security robots at the engine itself. The thing hung in a chamber near to the rim of the ship's core – a small moon of technology a mile across, linked by superconductors to U-space sink vanes all around it. A ring of twelve fusion plants surrounded the chamber, and three were burned-out wrecks. Many of the vanes had blackened, with the pseudo-matter surfaces extending between them distorted or missing. Energy shunts and convertors had melted out of shape. Elsewhere in the ship, organic robots, active like T-cells at the site of an infection, gathered around damage. Sometimes ineffective, sometimes causing more damage, but always there. Here there were none.

'Hey, Trike, have I lost you?' asked a voice.

Trike focused on a large bioreactor just to one side of the fusion plants and began analysing the data stream. This quickly elucidated the problem: though the reactor had received damage reports, it had too little power to activate, because the fusion plants that supplied it were the wrecked ones. This seemed crazy to him, until he saw multiple backups had also been destroyed. He reached out and took control of biomechs outside this area, scrubbed their programming and territoriality, and brought them in. Much like the one he had encountered in the living area below, these things had specialized limbs and tanks of powdered and gel-suspended materials on their backs. As they scuttled in, he loaded new programs to them, assigning their tasks as fast as he read and understood the schematics of the infrastructure around the engine. Soon they were moving over the charred reactors like giant lice, some making repairs while others temporarily rerouted power supplies. All sent requests he vetted to component autofactories around the ship's core.

'Hey, boy, I'm getting a bit concerned!'

The data were an irritation and he traced their source. They entered via a very small route into his organic body: his ears. He opened his eyes and studied the broadcasting biomech. The metal-sheathed thing seemed to serve no purpose. Some generalized element of the security or maintenance systems? He tried to make a link to it to set it about something useful, but could find none. It stepped up closer to him and prodded his chest with one of its manipulators.

'My suit supplies are getting low and I've bugger all idea what's going on,' it told him. 'Have you lost yourself?'

The shape of what he was, and what he had been through to get him to this point, began to reform in Trike's mind. But it was sketchy and had no emotional weight. He stared at the sensor node of the biomech and slowly, by degrees, it became a human face. From that point onwards the shape in his mind drew in elements of his scattered consciousness and at last he saw how deep he had gone. Belatedly, he cancelled the order to a nearby security biomech to grab Cog and take him off for either reprogramming or recycling.

'Cog,' he said, his voice sounding rusty. 'How long before your suit needs resupplying?'

'Ah, you're back with me now.'

'Temporarily,' said Trike.

He reached out via transceivers on the hull of the ship's core, and in an instant connected to the *Janus*. Cog's ship fired up its steering thrusters to take it up over the core and then down, one of the big doors opening before it. It was easy enough to clear a route inside, since some of the core's biomechs were bigger than that ship.

'I've got about an hour,' said Cog.

Trike nodded, the action constrained by the connections he had made to the hardware around him. The *Janus* would be right here, outside this area, within twenty minutes. Undamaged fusion plants feeding power to the bioreactor drew his notice and distracted him. Watching through other eyes, he saw the thing inflate and shed corroded surface layers. Just a few seconds later, one of its products – already on its internal conveyance – began to nose out and load damage reports.

'What are you doing now? What's your plan?' Cog asked.

The questions brought together what had previously been inchoate. He paused for a second as many ideas began to fall into place. The forces of Orlandine and Windermere were failing and, by and by, they would lose. Even though they possessed armament and defences inferior to those of the ship's core, their firepower, in total, was substantially more. Firepower alone could not defeat that Jain mother ship. Destroying it, and the creature or creatures that had driven all the destruction and death he had seen, was unfeasible. Killing what had taken from him his wife, his life and his humanity required something more, something different.

He looked just outside the chamber and saw that the Client's remotes were still there. He began to disconnect physically but retained his links via EMR – a level of data transfer which had him growing nano-transceivers all over his skin. After a moment, he stepped away, looming up beside Cog.

'What now?' Cog asked.

'Time to ask some questions,' he said, 'but I suspect the one I ask might be reluctant to answer, and that would be unacceptable.'

He headed for the door with Cog dogging his footsteps. Even as he stepped outside, one of the remotes launched while the other one tried to. He shot forwards and leapt, slamming into the second one and wrapping his arms around it. It continued trying to get away even as he stabbed his tongue in behind its head, micro-filaments penetrating and branching into millions of nano-connections spreading meshes over the thing's brain. He connected, intercepted the attempt to cut the remote off and squashed it, and then the Client's mind bulked before his consciousness.

'*Why are you doing this?*' she asked.

'*Such routes lie open even in your biology and mentality,*' he replied. '*They are integral.*'

'The Librarian was *Jain* and you killed it,' he said.

'*I did not kill it,*' the Client replied. '*I am it . . . in a sense.*'

Logic integrated: the mating habits of the Jain, their pillaging of each other's technology and biology. This was the key. This was what would unlock his way to vengeance. He sensed the Client's reluctance for battle and understood it. She could not survive another fight and amalgamation, since other Jain minds would overload hers, already compromised by the mind of the Librarian. He then received correction: there would only be one Jain aboard that ship since they were too individualistic to work closely together. He delved deeper into the mind before him, saw the channels of access and felt her reaching into his own. This is how it happened; this *was* that fight. But at the last, they both held off from complete engagement and just read each other.

'*Show me,*' he said, without words. '*Show me how you defeated the Librarian.*'

He was only half-aware of the remote thumping back down

on the platform and Cog running over as fragments of the battle between the Librarian and the Client fell into his consciousness. He also saw how the Client had pondered on the possibility of Orlandine going up against the Jain like this but now realized that he had become the perfect candidate.

'*Show me the scream,*' he then said, at last seeing that as the key to access.

'*I will show you it all,*' she replied.

## Diana

A debris field a million miles across lay before them. Most of it consisted of the remains of weapons platforms. Amidst these, four Jain attack ships still caused devastation, but mostly in taking down defences to clear the way for sequestration knots.

'Two hundred platforms gone,' commented Orlik.

'More than that,' said Jabro. 'I count a hundred and twenty-eight also offline.'

Diana nodded but made no comment. The platforms Jabro mentioned were falling into a formation ahead of the Jain ship and firing on their fellows. Another fifty-seven were under attack from Jain tech, but whether they would fall, destroy themselves or beat off these attacks could not be known. Fifteen platforms, by dint of sacrificing large portions of their structure, had been successful.

She gripped her chair arms as the *Hogue* surged sideways, particle beams scouring near space, flaming out a strew of knots. The ship then turned again, heading for a clearer area as autofactories inside converted further depleted stores into particulate for those beams. The gravity weapon fired again, wrecking a line of bacilliforms while high-powered antipersonnel lasers burned up knots falling towards the *Hogue*'s hull. With the increasing density of these things, she wondered how much longer it would be before they were fighting their own battle against Jain incursions.

Then the field enclosing the Jain mother ship came down.

'Ah fuck,' said Seckurg, perfectly emulating humanity.

It had been in all the prognostications from the start. The mother ship had deployed its attack ships and the cloud against those before it, but it seemed inevitable that, at some point, it would itself intervene. Perhaps it would do this out of tactical considerations, or perhaps whatever crewed it would just lose patience. They had all been waiting for the hammer to fall.

The remaining platforms immediately responded to its field coming down by firing everything they had available at the great vessel. Swarms of railgun slugs filled space, lighting explosions all along their course as they hit debris and cloud objects.

'The attack ships,' said Jabro.

They were pulling off and heading back to the mother ship, enclosing fields up as if running for cover. But none of this made tactical sense. Diana could see that in just a few hours they would have trashed the platform defence. Projections had it that about a hundred and fifty of the remaining two hundred and fifty platforms would be sequestered in that time and the rest destroyed. Now she had a horrible intimation of what was going on. The creature, or creatures, aboard that main vessel had learned all it could and grown bored with the game, and now intended to end it.

Railgun slugs began to impact on the mother ship – a swathe of sparkles across thousands of square miles of hull metal. Getting readings on that was difficult with the high EMR, but the slugs were having an effect. She saw great chunks of hull exploding out into vacuum, heat ejections and signs of underlying structure shifting. Then the Jain ship replied.

A beam speared up out from the insect head of the thing, a mile wide and glassy like the disruptor. It locked on to a platform but apparently caused no damage. Something travelled up it as if it was hollow. Intercepting warfare beams had no effect – a particle beam splashed against it as if hitting a solid bar. The object, vaguely spherical, seemed to be shifting as it moved. It looked like a larger version of one of the knots. It travelled fast through the hollow beam, then slowed before striking. The beam flicked off, then back on again, locking on to another platform. Getting a better view of the first platform, she saw that the projectile was spreading rapidly on its hull, certainly like one of those knots, only much larger. Data clicked together in her mind.

'A wormship,' she said.

Of course, it started to make sense. Erebus had not designed the wormships it used but taken the design from something else: this.

The platform immediately disconnected from coms. She expected it to destroy itself, but it had no time. It began broadcasting virtual warfare until the com codes changed and cut it out of the fleet data sphere. Again and again the beam flicked from platform to platform, steadily whittling away at the defence. Looking to the mother ship, Diana saw the hull reforming, repairing itself just as fast as it received damage. They could not destroy it and, within the hour, it would have control of every weapons platform.

'Orlandine just ordered them to fall back,' said Hogue aloud.

Diana was about to reply when the mother ship screamed again. It went right through her, through her mind and through the mind of her AI. It filled up every com channel and made a nonsense of all the coding changes and other attempts at shielding. As before, she felt it in her bones, and this time by some form of induction it even became audible. But then another shriek answered and countered it – almost like anti-sound or white noise across the informational spectrum. It ate up and converted the first scream to something ineffectual, collapsed its structure, solved its formulae and replied in kind.

'Orlandine?' wondered Orlik.

'No,' replied Seckurg. 'That's coming from in-system.'

'The mother ship is changing course,' said Jabro.


## Orlandine

Ensconced in the whole of the Jain device, Orlandine flew down towards the Sambre volcano. She settled on the ledge Trike had stood upon when contemplating suicide, before he realized that dying that way had ceased to be an option for him. The heat permeated her and her Jain tech. This responded by drawing in the energy, converting and changing, improving its efficiency and tentatively spearing out tentacles to scour the surrounding rock for useful materials.

Tentacles and tendrils writhed in her underbelly, knitting together a secondary human form entirely of Jain tech, while the human body she had created resided safe in its encystment deep within. It had first been her intention to walk that body out here but, being just flesh and bone, it wasn't sufficient to the task. Another avatar, then, for this symbolic act of the destruction of her old self. She walked forwards over hot rock, trailing umbilici, to stand at the very lip of the furnace, and paused to reflect on that. Was her reasoning in keeping that old body valid? Perhaps she was retaining it as some kind of foothold in all that she had been, as well as a retreat? She *was* about to take a step that she felt would erase the last dregs of her humanity and perhaps this frightened her.

'Going the uber-human route?' enquired a voice.

She glanced aside, dismissing her speculations. Cutter, slightly beaten up by his recent orgy of destruction in the skies over Jaskor, landed on the hot rock. The bulky form of Bludgeon followed soon after and settled beside him. She had seen them coming and was glad of their presence, for these were old companions she trusted more than any others. Cutter had used this description before, when she had first used a device like the form behind her to interrogate the submind of the Wheel.

'I wonder if the word "human" is any longer applicable,' she replied.

'That's the haiman ethos corrupting your thinking. It's pretty much the thinking of the Cyberat too – that to be human requires the weak flesh component.'

'Still . . .'

'You know what might happen,' he said impatiently, getting to the point.

She nodded.

When the Jain soldier destroyed her ship after her transmission of the Harding black hole, she had escaped in a device similar to the one she now occupied. But the steady repression of her human component had begun before, during her interrogation of the submind. Aboard Orlik's old ship, Cutter and Bludgeon had rescued her, but by then she had lost control – the Jain tech grew aggressively at the behest of her hunt for data.

'It is something I will resist,' she said. 'I must hold my purpose firmly at the forefront of my mind, to do what I intend to, which is to defend Jaskor from the present assault. But more importantly, I have to keep my mind.'

'Are you sure it's necessary?' asked Bludgeon, transmitting a highly optimistic assessment of how the battle was going.

She thought this step away from reality quite strange for the usually precise drone and followed the link back into his mind. This keyed into an ongoing debate between all the drones scattered about Jaskor. They had predicted her intention when they saw her heading here. Many of them believed she might turn into something worse than their attackers and had even proposed dropping a CTD on the Sambre volcano. Only Knobbler's trust in her judgement kept them in check, though he agreed that it might be an idea to try to dissuade her. She withdrew, acknowledging Bludgeon's brief but insincere apology, and decided to reassess the situation.

Reaching out to all satellites, drones and minds available, she gathered current data. The Jain mother ship had changed course, but even as she watched the spotty feed from out there, she could see that predicted outcomes had not changed. It had ceased firing the weapon it had recently used against her platforms, but was now releasing more of that weapon's projectiles as it departed. Out of a port, open in its side ten miles across, spewed wormships. Her weapons platforms immediately destroyed some, but others, further from the mother ship, were throwing up flat hardfields – more and more of them all the time. Over a hundred of them were out now. And the sequestered platforms were falling away from the mother ship to attack her remaining platforms. Even without the mother ship present, her defence there would fail. She turned her attention to Jaskor itself.

Diana Windermere had added her few ships to the defence immediately around the world. The defence presently prevented ninety-five per cent of the invasive cloud mechanisms from getting through. It wasn't enough, while munitions out there were all but depleted. One hundred per cent would not have been enough anyway because of what had already reached the surface. The Jain attack was a metastasized cancer. Gemmell's forces and the drones were holding against the planetary assaults and this had been the shaky basis for Bludgeon's optimism. But Jain tech swept in by the tsunami had begun to spread across the land and send increasing numbers of monstrosities against the cities. Huge growths were boiling under the sea and still moving inland, while seismic readings indicated activity underground. At some point the tech would swamp the whole defence and everyone would die, or worse . . .

She focused in on a particular drone's view. Here, in one of the southern cities, a group of people had decided to move from their building. Why? She had no idea. The road had collapsed underneath them and they had fallen into a storm drain where Jain tentacles seized them and dragged them out of sight. She saw them climbing out of the hole, their bodies netted with thin tendrils that had cut through their clothing and into their skin. Bleeding and shrieking, they jerked along like marionettes. For a moment the drone could not decide what to do about them. Then it made its decision and each exploded into hot flame, the thermite shells burning everything.

'I understand your concerns,' Orlandine told Bludgeon and Cutter, 'but I must respond as I see fit.'

'You're the boss, I guess,' said Cutter.

She looked at the two of them for a while, nodded once, then stepped forwards. Trailing an umbilicus of unravelling tentacles and tendrils, she fell down towards the lava sea.

# 12

*In the past, it was the lot of the human to be born, grow to adulthood and then almost at once begin to decline both physically and mentally. It was a sad truth back then that once people had acquired an understanding of life, and something of wisdom, they were already in the process of losing that life. An aphorism of the time was that youth was wasted on the young. That brief cycle has been broken for centuries now and the routes one can take to eternity have multiplied, but so have related problems. Simply continuing to live is an option, but one that often fails. The ennui of the immortal can lead to self-destruction. It is supposed this is because for the person concerned their lives and everything around them is too familiar and therefore they go off in pursuit of dangerous novelty. This is not the situation. The problem is not the lack of novelty or difference in the world around them, but in themselves. The route to eternal life is not change without, but within.*

From 'Contemplations on Eternity', anonymous

## Gemmell

The thing possessed a lower disc-like body, propelled on its belly by flipper-like legs extending from either side. Numerous snake-like tentacles terminated in eyeless draconic heads sprouting from its back. The first tank to open fire on it blew out a large chunk of that body and knocked it over, but it quickly righted itself and the smoking hole in its side filled and sprouted replacements for the missing legs. Further shots took off hydra heads and blew other smoking holes in it, but each time it regenerated at speed and came on. Then it returned fire.

The hydra heads began issuing pulsegun fire: ionized aluminium dust accelerated in a magnetic cannon. This had the strike impact of a railgun slug and delivered a ridiculously high point charge. Intercepting grav-tank fire, these sprayed the surrounding forest with molten metal. They slammed into hovering tanks, temporarily shorting out systems and dropping them into the trees. Five went down in as many seconds. A hydra head slapped into one moving in too close, and stuck like a sucker. The tank lost power and shed lightning as the head pumped shot after shot into it at close range, finally blowing out its back in a spray of molten metal and tossing it away. The thing clipped treetops and, sideways on clear ground beyond, rolled like a plate, then whumphed down, issuing clouds of smoke. Gemmell checked assignments and saw, thankfully, that the tank had been slaved to Baylock so no one had died.

More tanks moved in, firing intermittently as they intercepted returned fire with hardfields, the recoil of their railguns forever shunting them out of position. The thing went over again and Gemmell finally saw the thick trunk from its underside spearing into the ground.

'Baylock, you saw that?' he asked over com.

'Yeah, I saw it.'

'Then knock it over and sever that connection,' he replied.

A railgun fusillade blew the thing backwards through the trees and almost cut it in half. It began pulling itself back together when circling grav-tanks lanced it with particle beams and burned through its support trunk. That slowed it, so the tanks moved in closer to finish the job, but as they began pounding the thing, all its snake necks detached and streaked off into the surrounding forest.

'Pursue and kill them!' Baylock instructed.

'This makes no sense,' said Ruth.

Gridlinked into the scanning gear of the grav-sled, Gemmell began to build a picture with ground radar and terahertz scan. He routed com back to the city then down through relays to the drains and cave system. Updates on the ongoing underground battle came back to him. Trantor had flash-burned the thing like a giant bobbit worm but was now fighting a steady retreat against creatures similar to the snakes the grav-tanks were hunting.

'Trantor, give me an X-ray and terahertz flash,' he instructed.

A moment later, devices strewn throughout the tunnels emitted those radiations. Scanning from the sled picked it up and he immediately formed a clearer image of events underground. Sure, Jain tech was attacking them in the tunnels and here above ground, but larger masses moving through the soil between were already half a mile past their line.

'Trantor, pull back and—' he began, but then caught something in his peripheral vision even as an alert reached his gridlink. He instantly inverted grav on the sled and sent it plummeting towards the ground. A stream of railgun slugs cut through their previous position then tracked them down. Ruth spun the sled's guns and opened fire. The grav-tank, which he had just earlier thought destroyed, was up and firing, fingers of Jain tech waving from its burn hole. A missile streaked in, even as laser com switched to new coding to cut out the virtual warfare the thing was emitting. He switched grav back over and the sled decelerated hard, crashing into the upper branches of the trees as the sequestered grav-tank exploded in a bright flash. Burning leaves gusted up all around them and debris smacked against their sled. He saw the gutted hulk of the tank spinning into the air then crashing upside down. Two more missiles zeroed in and blew it to scrap. Gemmell touched his ear lobe where he had felt something flick it and his fingers came away bloody.

'I didn't get all that,' came Trantor's reply.

'Pull back a mile and a half and blow all the tunnels behind you,' said Gemmell. 'Baylock, leave those things and pull back – we've got bigger problems underground.'

'You know where this is going to end, don't you?' said Ruth. He nodded.

'Baylock, high-penetration missiles at these locations, but wait for my mark,' he instructed, sending the ground imagery and highlighting points of attack.

All the tanks began retreating from the forest. In the fields behind, they inverted.

'Trantor?'

Brief imagery came through of a power-suit retreat through the tunnels, drones and other automated weapons swarming around the soldiers. Gemmell shunted the sled into rapid flight, tilting towards the city, shooting over above the tanks.

'Blowing them now,' said Trantor.

A series of deep booms ensued and the entire landscape writhed. He saw a line of trees simply disappear as the ground slumped to create a canyon two miles long. In one area, a boulder blew out from the side of a slope on a fountain of red fire.

'At a mile and half,' Trantor added.

'Hit it, Baylock!' Gemmell ordered.

Over fifty tanks rose into the air on their recoil, heavily armoured missiles stabbing into the ground below them. The tanks then flipped level a hundred feet above the ground and beat a retreat. Moments later the earth bulged up. Gemmell flew the sled higher as explosions erupted below, flinging up, in the columns of fire, writhing worm-like forms. It was, he felt, a rather literal demonstration of 'scorched earth'.

'Form a new line – concentrate on ground scanning,' he instructed, now gathering data around the city and from elsewhere.

Another tank unit had used the same techniques, keying off his instructions here. In other sections of the ring around the city, they were detecting the steady encroachment underground. As the tanks settled and began opening fire on things coming out of the shattered forest, he fast-scanned reports which had arrived in his gridlink earlier. He saw that in the south, the defence was already back inside the cities, the tsunami over there having swept Jain tech into the streets. In some areas, soldiers were fighting a steady retreat floor-by-floor up the tower blocks. Of course, when they reached the top, they would have nowhere left to retreat to.

'Yeah, I know where this is going,' he replied to Ruth.

In those southern cities, as per his plans, anything that could fly had been loaded to roof ports and other areas, ready to move citizens to an island fifty miles out. Yet no way could they evacuate all the millions of refugees, and already drones had reported Jain tech moving along the seabed towards that island. Here in the main city his troops had made similar preparations, but where to transport the people? What else could he do? Even if it were possible to send refugees into space, he would simply be transferring them into an even more ferocious battle. Up there the cloud was destroying a warship on average every eight minutes, while sequestered weapons platforms were moving in. Anyway, Diana would not allow him to use the ships under her command for that because, as always, the civilian lives were a secondary consideration in warfare. Nor would Orlandine allow the weapons platforms she still controlled to be used to that end.

It was going, he was sure, to hell.

# THE HUMAN

## Orlandine

Orlandine fell. Superconducting fibres laced through the Jain tendrils, tentacles and vines of her human-shaped avatar, shunting heat back through her umbilicus. Micro- and nano-thermal convertors up there turned it into electricity and light, spreading that through further conductors or nanotubes. She filled with energy, overflowed with it. Mechanisms packed throughout increased activity while expanding their parameters to take the load. The device at the lip of the volcano – that part of her there – sent out burrowing tentacles whose faces blossomed shearfield generators, molecular drills and saws, as well as cutting and ablation lasers. They went into the surrounding rock like an acetylene flame through polystyrene. Cutter leapt back as one of these reached for him, then both he and Bludgeon launched into the sky. Orlandine diverted the tentacle which followed them, so it looped back down and smashed into the volcano's slope. It had been questing for essential materials, and the best source had been the two drones. This kind of automatic acquisition she would have to watch, she decided, though negligently, as she plunged face down into lava.

Her false human form began to break apart. Behind her, the tentacles thickened, but even as they did so her sense of self retreated from the lava. She was completely distributing now into the whole of her physical self, which included the rapidly growing device. Her avatar lost its human shape and expanded, drawing in molten materials to process in microscopic engines with lives only seconds long. But this duration did not matter, for by the time one had collapsed another ten had grown. Tendrils of collimated sapphire extended from these. There was programming and nano-machinery all down their lengths to print out larger mechanisms: ceramic pumps and vanes to propel more

283

molten matter up through the umbilicus. In the device, processing plants expanded like puffballs, weaning out useful metals. In passing, Orlandine noted much gold and tantalum here, and found that confirmed by a geological report she had read twenty years ago. This reminded her of its source – the volcanologist Trissa Oclaire – and alerted her to danger.

Large, steadily expanding tentacles had shot down the slope of the volcano to snake across the wasteland below. Outside her home, Oclaire stood gaping as one sped towards her. It had sensed certain elements used in the construction of her home, and was greedy for the capacitor stack that supplied it with energy. Orlandine diverted it, then instituted general programming. Now, during their quests for materials, every time these tentacles sensed human beings in the vicinity, they must alert her. From this tentacle, she splintered a smaller growth packed with angstrom nanotubes and optical fibres. This was to project a voxel hologram of her human form, copied from the one now deep inside the growing device on the edge of the volcano. She stepped forwards and programmed her perception into the new avatar.

'They will not hurt you,' she said, her voice generated out of the air by the same femtosecond lasers producing the hologram.

Oclaire pointed down to the gel-tech cast on her ankle. 'Heard that before.'

Orlandine shrugged. 'Trike told you he would not hurt you and he did not. You ran from him and broke your own ankle.'

'True. What happened to him?'

Orlandine pointed to the sky. 'He's doing what he can,' she said, but it occurred to her that she had no idea what Trike *was* doing. Wrapped up in her own concerns, she had not wondered why the Jain ship had turned in-system towards Trike and the Client. Already pulling away mentally, she added, 'You are now, in fact, in the safest place on the planet.'

'So you say,' said the volcanologist, but by then Orlandine had discounted the woman from her considerations.

Her earlier Jain-tech avatar, sitting in lava, had become a massive globe full of larger pumps whose components were fashioned from hyper-dense sapphire. The level of the lava in the caldera had dropped by a foot to feed the device above, which had grown to the size of a Polity destroyer, spewing more and more glowing tentacles, expanding in pulses as they spread all over the island. And next those tentacles entered the sea.

With no humans in the ocean, Orlandine felt she could relax her vigilance and allowed them to loot what they required. Here they opened pores to cycle seawater, sieving out useful elements. As with organic life, water lubricated their processes and the tentacles began growing at a phenomenal rate. They shot across the seabed, raising clouds of muck, which only served to supply them with more materials. All along their length, as inland, they spread roots – mycelia – to grab up more materials and energy sources. Despite all of them containing superconductors to draw energy from the volcano, they required more and more energy, so she had them sprouting nodular outgrowths packed with power storage. One mycelium hit a stratum of the mineral pitchblende and began mining it, whereupon an automatic process, in the ersatz DNA of Jain tech, began constructing a fission reactor. Fusion would be next, Orlandine understood, as other mycelia, waving like the fronds of tubeworms, filtered deuterium and boron from the seawater and cracked out and compressed hydrogen.

She turned her attention outwards again. Oclaire had reminded her to look more closely at what had occurred with the Jain ship. She had heard the scream, the shriek, the challenge, but no more than that. In an instant, she was back into her off-world network. Despite the EMR severely degrading coms out there, and even laser com becoming unreliable, she found her expansion made it much easier to sift for information. Answers came from platforms currently bombarding approaching wormships. The Jain mother ship had emitted its shriek as it went into battle. The thing had rattled through all the platforms with an intensity that disrupted their minds. Had it continued, it would have been paralysing, but it had not.

A directional reply had come from in-system, a tight beam transmission whose breadth had not touched Jaskor, and this was why Orlandine had not received it. She damned herself for disconnecting, because she would have had this news from the weapons platforms earlier. She sent queries by laser com in-system, to the Client, to her satellites there, to Cog's ship and to Trike. But with the present relative orbital positions, she would receive no reply for twenty-six minutes. That was a long time in her emerging form and, before it was up, something else would become the larger focus of her attention.

Fewer Jain knots had landed in the ocean on this side of the continent, since the enemy had aimed them at human centres on the planet. However, one, driven off course by attacking drones, had come down twenty miles up the coast from Sambre Island. Even as her main growth reached landfall on the coast, she extended an offshoot steadily along the seabed in that direction. She watched it stir up the shoal of giant anglerfish Trike had encountered during his journey across from the mainland. The highly tempting luminescent worms, of course, attracted them. One grabbed a mouthful of tentacle, its hard teeth ripping through the hardened matter, and it flicked away with its prize in its mouth. After champing on the thing for a while, it decided it did not like the taste and spat it out. Others attacked too, ripping up growth and delaying her progress to her target. Even after finding the tentacles not to their taste, the fish found the temptation too much and attacked again and again. Orlandine considered driving them off with electric shocks or simply killing them with underwater bursts of laser. Then she sensed something.

She recognized one of those pre-programmed responses, like when the tech had begun to build a fission reactor on finding pitchblende. She turned into this and explored it, finding the growth of mechanisms which were like interrogation augs. This was the Jain tech lining itself up to sequester life forms. Her immediate abhorrence faded when she saw the utility, because here she could acquire soldiers for her cause. She began altering the process. The sequestering would be the same, but she pushed further, using knowledge from her examination of the prador second-children from Orlik's original ship, who Jain tech had been turning into soldiers, and from her studies of the Spatterjay virus.

During the next attacks, the anglerfish found themselves unable to spit out the chunks of tentacle they bit off. Mycelia rooted in their mouths and spread, first finding their primitive brains. Once they had taken hold, all the fish hung in the water, stabilized by small movements of their fins, as the mycelia began making radical changes. They weaved in boosted muscle fibres, penetrated teeth and bones and laminated in carbon, toughening skin and spreading a superconducting mesh through it. Soon they needed more materials, so the fish settled down to suckle on tubes she extruded from her main growth. They also loaded ketones and a flood of nano-stores of oxygen to supply their enhanced bodies with energy. Was this enough? For now, she felt it was. They were a prototype – foolish to supply them with energy weapons and power supplies without knowing their reliability. If the enemy seized them, those weapons might be turned against her. Meanwhile, her main growth continued steadily and inexorably along the seabed.

With her awareness now among the shoal, she sent it swimming quickly ahead of her main growth and shortly could see the enemy. The knot had expanded into a mass a mile across. It did not have the wormish structure of her growth but resembled a giant spread of pale-blue lichen. She assumed this format allowed it to glean useful materials from the seawater and, no doubt, it had extended mycelia into the packed mud below for more. This all fed five growths, like the sporing bodies of lichen, at the centre of the mass. Here stood columns of tangled lianas cupping fat translucent spheres in which she could see squirming growth. All were leaning in towards the coast. It took her less than a second to understand their purpose.

The invading Jain tech aimed to subsume or destroy the intelligent life on Jaskor. Growths on the other shore were proximal to their target, so sending in walking or crawling biomechs was sufficient. Being so far away, this one was growing new knots to expel explosively through the surface of the sea towards the nearest city – the capital city. It occurred to her that, being so distant, it had probably not expected attack, so that's what she did.

The shoal moved in over the main growth and began ripping at the columns. They shredded tough Jain tech with teeth now as hard as metal-cutting milling bits, driven by enhanced muscles and braced by bones a Golem might admire. Within minutes, two of the growths were falling and the fish there moved on to the spheres, ripping open weak skin to expose slowly writhing knots. They attacked these too, and began pulling them apart. The whole scene played out like many feeding frenzies in similar oceans. The other three columns went down, the water clouded and the fish had completely torn apart one knot before the Jain tech responded.

An exposed knot shot out a tentacle, its end morphing at the last minute into a hand which closed around one of the fish.

Orlandine was there in the fish as its attacker injected its own mycelia and attempted to seize control. She fought back with the fish's mycelia and made a connection. At once she recognized tech she had decoded centuries ago in a Jain node, but controlled by a submind almost the twin of what had resided in the worm fragment in Orlik's old ship. Having already taken apart that similar mind, she knew what to do with this one, and what to attack. The physical battle continued in the body of the fish, but the main battle slid into virtuality. She began reaching into a dispersed mind and generating viruses in its base programming. These assembled into chains that connected discrete elements of the mind in closed loops – worms to eat up processing for their own propagation. Similar attacks came her way but she routed them into swiftly generated subpersonae where they could succeed or fail – those personae which were sequestered were immediately erased. But then, with a flash, it disconnected her.

Through the eyes and sonar of another nearby fish, she saw the one that had been seized shuddering, the water around it boiling, and micro-explosions lifting its scales to expose an ember glow. The tentacle released and it tumbled down towards the lichen growths. Realizing its danger, the enemy had destroyed the connection by routing a surge of power into the fish. It released three other fish too, whereupon stabs of bubbles shot up from the lichen to hammer cavitating projectiles into the shoal. The impacts were hard and penetrated. If her fish stayed, the thing would kill them all. No matter, she sent them speeding away out of range as her main growth, like glowing fingers, spilled out of a nearby underwater trench and sped in.

'*I sent my reply to the challenge.*' The communication from Trike arrived with an information package. The twenty-six minutes had passed. Further packages arrived from the Client and from her own satellites, but she wanted to know what Trike had to say first, so opened his. Even as she opened it, she split off further subpersonae, devoid of any impetus to survive but merely to win, and almost as conscious as fully functional human beings. Over to these she handed control of the attack upon the Jain growth, while her main self stepped into a virtuality.

'You can make subpersonae too,' she said.

'Of course,' said Trike.

They stood on the deck of a Spatterjay sailing ship. One of the living sails had folded up on the spar and ahead, rearing out of the sea, there was a monolith called the Big Flint. She noted he had taken on the form he had on that world – a bulky bald-headed man with the air of an underworld enforcer.

'What have you done?' she asked, even as she delved into the information package in other ways, sucking up data so much faster than human speech.

At once the ship shifted to vacuum just out from the Species ship's core.

'This thing has a lot of armament,' he said.

Her own data mining had given her weapons schematics and manifests. But, as with the enclosing hardfields, she had little use for that information now. A week ago it would have made a difference during the encounter between her platforms and the Jain mother ship. Though she had to admit, her victory would by no means have been guaranteed.

'It isn't enough for me to destroy the Jain mother ship, but it is enough to give me access,' Trike added.

'You already answered the invitation,' said Orlandine, mentally moving a step ahead of him.

'Yes. The Jain subsume and destroy intelligent races they come upon. But still they must give their mating cry and open themselves to possible destruction when something is capable of responding to it.'

'You're sure?'

'Not totally, because any intelligent advanced life form is capable of overriding, if not completely rewriting, its instincts. But they were strong and at the top of the galactic food chain so had no reason to.'

Now she found detail on his actions aboard the ship's core, and the Client's reaction. The Species aboard were dead, but only so far as the Client herself had been dead – the term a movable feast. She found a tight précis of the Client's encounter with the Librarian and learned, as she should have known, that only one of the Jain would be aboard that ship – supposing the ship itself was not attacking on automatic, as the Species ship had, and the Jain not long dead. All this confirmed what she thought: Trike intended to go head to head with that Jain. If the fight between the Client and the Librarian was anything to judge by, his response to the scream – to meeting that challenge – would lead to a physical encounter. Before that they would violently confront each other, almost like sadomasochistic lovers beating each other before intercourse. It seemed utterly perverse to her. After absorbing all he presented, she considered taking apart the persona Trike had sent, even though she was aware she would obtain no more data than he allowed her to.

'Is there any way I can assist?' she finally asked, stretching out the informational tendrils of her mind to engulf the persona.

'You updated me with your situation,' said Trike, a weird smile twisting his features. 'I think you have enough to contend with where you are, not least what you might become.'

She moved in to disassemble the persona, beginning to route all its data around her distributed mind. Her mind, her storage, her being, had also expanded, as her own recently created personae slid back into her consciousness, with the mass of Jain tech on the ocean floor having fallen to them. But Trike's words raised a spectre, for they applied equally to him. A fight with one of the Jain was also an amalgamation, and he could become something nightmarish.

## Gemmell

Gemmell's visor darkened in response to another ignition on the horizon. That, he reckoned, must be the twentieth tactical CTD deployed. Three more flashes ensued and he stopped counting. The drones out there were rooting out infestations less destructive weapons had failed to destroy.

'There won't be anything left to save,' said Ruth.

'There are people,' said Gemmell.

'We can hope that, of course.'

He nodded and returned his attention to the action nearby. Robot handlers and a varied collection of assassin and war drones were retreating from the line of derricks. He sent the firing order, adding to the destruction across the continent. The missiles, standing upside down in the derricks, fired up their side thrusters and began spinning in place. Then their main single-burn engines ignited to drive their fluted nose cones into the ground. They all disappeared in plumes of soil and fire as they burrowed down. A minute later the massive planar loads, shaped charges and CTD warheads, designed for mining, exploded. Fire jetted from the ground in a long line behind the derricks. Antimatter blasts lifted a section of the earth ten miles long and a quarter of a mile wide and folded it out from the city. The whole lot came down in a new chain of smoking and radioactive hills. Gemmell dipped his head, clinging to the rail as the shockwave reached them.

Around the city the ground consisted of ten feet of humus

and topsoil, a further ten feet of clay, then a layer of conglomerate over twenty feet of limestone sitting on the bedrock. Gemmell could see much of this. The defensive ring around the city now sat inside a complete, smoking moat. It had been enough to stop the Jain tech in its tracks for the last few hours, though the action had greatly depleted their munitions. However, as it quickly filled with muddy concealing water, the moat would soon no longer be effective. Meanwhile, at a much slower pace, the Jain tech had begun boring through the underlying bedrock. He grimaced, then glanced up as something big dropped out of the sky to land heavily beside their grav-sled.

'This is not going to last.' The assassin drone Knobbler pointed towards the trench with a tentacle that terminated in a laminated diamond and shearfield scimitar.

'It's something, anyway,' Ruth replied.

'Why did you move here?' asked Gemmell. 'I thought the southern cities needed you more?'

'Vreen has things as much under control there as they can be,' said Knobbler. 'Most of my associates are with him. And, anyway, I wanted to be closer to the new action . . . to observe.'

Gemmell waited for a further explanation but Knobbler gave none. He tried to link into the data sphere for updates but, as had been the case for some hours, his connection kept dropping out. Then, at last, he got something from Vreen. A scene played out in his mind. The defenders had been fighting a steady retreat in the streets until the attacking Jain tech changed tactics. He saw one giant structure, eighty storeys tall, totter then collapse to the ground, exploding out great clouds of dust. The defenders – mostly the prador – made a desperate push to drive things like human-sized fleas with buzz-saw mouths out of the buildings. They had been losing in Marshallam. But then the tide there turned when shooting stars hurtled in, decelerated, and armoured prador crashed down into the city with weapons blazing. These were refugees from the battles in orbit. Now the prador had all but driven out the Jain tech in the southern cities and were holding against the steady wave of it coming out of the sea.

'I see,' he said. 'So what is this new action you mentioned?'

'Orlandine,' Knobbler replied. 'She has a plan.'

'Detail would be good.'

Knobbler shifted as if uncomfortable, as if the subject was a sticky one. Perhaps that was Gemmell's imagination, since he could not really tell what a monstrosity like this might think or feel, or if it felt anything remotely human at all.

'She is expanding herself,' said Knobbler briefly.

Gemmell stared at the drone as he absorbed that. This confirmed that the actions of him and those under his command were not enough. It was, in ancient parlance, the nuclear option.


## Trike

Trike felt like a character in a virtual drama who, having diverted the attention of some monster from his friends, realizes it is coming after him.

'Well, that did it,' he said.

'That did what?' asked Cog.

Trike had physically disconnected from the systems around him, but remained utterly engaged with the ship's core via meta-material transceivers over his skin. Multitasking at AI level, he had absorbed and understood the Jain scream and designed the correct response. His link to the Client remained firm despite her earlier attempt, when he began working on that reply, to break away. And this time he had not disconnected from reality.

'The Jain is now coming after me,' he replied.

'That's not so good.'

Distracted, Trike simply nodded. On the platform outside this chamber, the Client's remote lay with a mushroom of complex nanotech like an aug plugged into its brain and thence to the Client. No longer fighting him, she waited in the virtual world like an animal trapped in razor-sharp brambles.

*'What do you want of me now?'* she asked.

*'I want you to be still,'* he replied with a fraction of his intelligence, much of his mind directed throughout the core.

He had full control of the weapons, and his biomechs were constantly making repairs to them, to the main engine and various subsidiary engines – the fusion, grav, EM and others besides. He began reintegrating the hardfields with the main drive and this opened out further possibilities for defence and attack. He learned he could shift the ship's core at close to light speed and even short-jump in U-space despite the disruption. This last was a risky option because potential damage could render him vulnerable, which was possibly why the Jain ship had not done the same.

With another small portion of himself, he gazed at Cog, not forgetting the man he had known for many years. But was he a friend? Trike felt sure Cog had only helped him because his problems involved something threatening to the Polity, and that for some time Cog's attitude had been quietly hostile.

He scanned Cog deeply, seeing his ancient body so wound through with viral fibres to be as tough as braided towing cable. Modelling the man in his mind, he realized Cog might yet turn on him. But then, reviewing his own behaviour since Angel kidnapped Ruth, he understood Cog had every reason for hostility and no reasons for trust. Trike also noted the computer tablet in a compartment at the man's belt, and the device it contained. This gave him pause.

'I see you carry Ruth's U-mitter with you, old man,' he said.

'I sense a shift in our relationship, boy,' Cog replied.

'You are a man still, and you are old,' Trike noted.

'And to me you are still a boy,' Cog replied.

Trike dipped his head in agreement. 'It is true that great knowledge and power do not automatically imply great wisdom.'

Cog just stared at him, then admitted, 'To be honest, neither does great age.'

'You carry that U-mitter so, while I still have the one inside my skull, you can always find me.'

'Only when U-space is not disrupted as it is now.'

'But still . . .'

'You want to know why,' said Cog. 'Well, for the same reasons I did not allow you to grab Ruth when she went down to the Cyberat world. Because while Angel kept her near him, I could keep on tracking an extreme danger to the Polity.'

'You are starkly honest. Do you think I am as dangerous?'

'Yes I do.'

'Because I am powerful?'

'No, because you are powerful *and* a murderer.'

'I ran that memtab you gave me some while ago and stepped into your memories. Do you think I am your brother Jay Hoop reborn? Do you think I am a monster?'

'You are nothing like him now,' Cog conceded. 'I don't know what you are. I can only judge you by your actions and, with what you did to Angel . . .'

Trike cast his gaze outwards. Cog's ship sat on the shelf outside. He should send the man away – the chances of him surviving what was to come were low, as were his own. But no, he truly wanted to clear things between himself and the Old Captain.

'Then let me tell you about that,' he said.

'I hope this will take less than the hour of air I have left.'

'Your ship is now outside.'

Cog nodded perfunctorily then stepped away to a squat block of memory storage attached to the floor. He sank down on it and groped at his belt pouch for a moment before snatching his hand away in irritation. Trike grinned but guessed it didn't look like that. Knowing precisely what Cog wanted, he made some changes. The door into this place closed with a sucking crunch, the temperature began to drop and pores in the walls issued a human-tolerable mix of air. Pressure increased with a blast that stirred up and swirled ancient debris. Obviously noting this on his HUD, Cog keyed the release on his helmet. The visor sank down into the suit's neck ring at the front while the helmet section divided into ribs and concertinaed down at the back. He sniffed noisily.

'Smells like death in here,' he noted.

Trike analysed the air and found it full of putrescene and other products of decay – some no human would recognize. He began filtering out the dust, meanwhile fielding notifications on the continuing repairs to the core. He noted maintenance biomechs and the Client's remotes running into each other, interfering with each other's work. Bioreactors were still producing the latter and they were still gathering the Species remains. He assessed their movement patterns then quickly altered those of the mechs so the work of each would not conflict.

'So where do you begin?' asked Cog, finally taking out his pipe and packing it. A long flash from his laser lighter had it smouldering and he sighed out a cloud of smoke.

'I came to Spatterjay looking for a place where the monster in my skull wouldn't kill anyone, and of course, I found it.'

Cog looked up in surprise, but said nothing.

'But I had been controlling the madness for so long that it

never escaped me. Once the virus infected me, the physical strength that imparted made controlling it easier. I never grew exhausted and my grip never slipped. Sometimes I allowed it brief rein, but Spatterjay is a barbarous place where violence can be extreme yet non-lethal. Ruth found me in the fight rings, we became lovers and, no matter what I did, she just would not go away. In fact her presence – utterly vulnerably human – reinforced my self-control.'

'But you began to lose it when Angel kidnapped her?'

'So you would think, but that's not true.'

'You're kidding.'

'No, you must understand some things I have only just come to understand myself. Because I always felt on the edge of losing control, I never lost it. The difference between me and your brother is that I never accepted what I was while he obviously did.'

'And yet you tore Angel apart.'

The remotes and biomechs were now nicely avoiding each other. Out of curiosity, he checked the program from the bio-reactors making the remotes and saw them winding down. The reactors had made enough to clear all the Species remains quickly. He studied the schematics and incidentally loaded physical data from the one lying outside this room.

'And yet I tore Angel apart.' Trike showed his teeth and, by Cog's reaction, guessed it wasn't reassuring. 'My anger at him never waned and I wanted to kill him, yet I never did. Even while undergoing the most profound mental and physical changes. Instead I killed him when I apparently had those changes under control, after I had just found myself powerful enough to destroy the Clade units on Jaskor.'

The Client's remotes were very interesting. He ran comparisons and found them far superior to the core biomechs. They were potentially physically immortal, very very tough and weaponized, whereas none of the ship's core biomechs were so armed. He reached out mentally, took away control of those bioreactors from the Client and stopped their program from winding down. He also began to make his own additions to it.

'I fail to see the relevance of that,' said Cog.

'What gave me the capability of killing the Clade?' Trike asked distractedly, as simultaneously the Client asked, *'Why did you do that?'*

'Jain tech,' said Cog, looking troubled.

'I wonder how much you know about the Jain,' Trike commented, and to the Client he said, *'There are thousands of those remotes here now. I want them.'*

*'I cannot stop you taking them,'* said the Client.

*'I know.'* Trike began to delve into the Client's mind, ready to fight for what he wanted, but the creature hurriedly shunted the coding and frequencies over to him. He snatched it, absorbed it, and thousands of contacts began to open out to him. It was almost too much – he needed a physical connection until he could handle the data load.

'Hostile, much like the prador, I gather,' said Cog, then paused to watch as Trike stepped back, reached out to the crystal architecture surrounding him and speared out Jain fibres from his arms and torso, linking up all around. 'Something's happened,' he added.

'"Much like the prador" is an understatement,' Trike said tightly.

Minds fell into his compass, alien but also like the subpersonae he had created. The thousands of remotes continued to work and to think like limited facsimiles of the Client. But soon they would be slaves to his will, and he would load them with his subpersonae.

'You want to elaborate – I've picked up some hints . . .' Cog then fell silent, watching him.

Trike continued struggling to make the remotes his own. Then he discovered why the Client had handed over its links to them so easily. She had judged that it would overextend him and she'd been right. Also, because his link to her was via the remote lying on the floor outside, she had also handed over the other end of that very link. It looped and snapped closed, and he completely lost his grip on her. She slid away, but did not break a narrow bandwidth connection.

*'I could try to take them back from you,'* she said.

*'Do not,'* said Trike. *'I will not stop their work – they will continue sending you the remains of the Species for as long as you are prepared to remain here to receive them.'*

*'Then we have no reason to fight.'*

*'No, none at all.'*

Trike focused on Cog again, having suddenly become irritated by this exchange. He hadn't known where it would lead when he started but now he could see. There would be no 'clearing of the air' between them.

'Hostility is integral to their biology, just like the prador. It was their instinct to pillage the minds, biology and technology of any creature they came across, even their own kind. It is that instinct which is the basis of Jain technology, in fact, Jain technology is the logical physical result of it.'

'So Jain tech took control of you and made you kill Angel,' said Cog flatly. 'That's your explanation?'

'That is part of it.'

'Strange how, over centuries, it never turned Orlandine into a murderer.'

'Orlandine already was a murderer, before she even used it. But that's beside the point. Orlandine did not have the Spatterjay virus inside her and did not upload the data and minds of the squad of Jain soldiers stored in that virus.'

'Ah, so the Jain soldiers made you do it.'

'I didn't actually kill him – I absorbed his mind and all that he was.'

'Oh right, so you can restore him to life in an instant?'

Trike stared at Cog, realizing he had talked himself into a corner. Anything he said now would be just extended self-justification. He was making excuses for an inexcusable action. Sure, the Jain tech operated at the behest of his subconscious, while the inherent hostility of the soldiers influenced his behaviour, but *his* conscious decision had arisen from *his* subconscious. No more excuses.

'No, I cannot restore him to life any more than I could restore life to a hammerwhelk I just ate. The Jain tech and the soldiers all helped push me over the edge but in the end, the decision was mine. I killed Angel.'

'Why?'

Really Trike had no way out and decided, right then, to give Cog certainty.

He showed his teeth in his nearest facsimile of a grin. 'Because I wanted to,' he said.

Cog stood up, knocked out his pipe against his hand, then turned and headed for the door, closing up his suit helmet as he walked. Without further comment, Trike opened the door for him, and let him go.

# 13

*Those who manage to survive past the ennui barrier are those who grow and change as their years stack up. But it goes beyond that. One has to accept the limitations of both the human form and mind. The survivors are those who recognize this and adapt. Haimans are well equipped to deal with it because they have already instituted a condition that is subject to revision, both mentally and physically. Yet, in the haiman ethos, there is much of what I can only describe as nostalgia – an attachment to contemplating the idea of what it means to be human. In many respects, they are right to be concerned, and to so closely examine this issue. Advancing beyond humanity, the steady evolution of self that comes with living beyond the 'usual' human span comes with its harsh rule: there is no going back. Just as it was inadvisable for the old, in the days before the Quiet War, to attempt to recapture their youth, it is unwise for advanced humans to try to recapture their humanity. In both cases it is never a desire to return to some halcyon ideal, but to the bliss of ignorance.*

From 'Contemplations on Eternity', anonymous

### Earth Central

The five hammerheads sat in a tight formation a million miles from the King's Ship. Prador reavers and older dreadnoughts stood between, with more arriving all the time. Some of these,

Earth Central noted, arrived to offload their kamikazes but now were not leaving, as had been the case before. EC also noted two huge ships under construction – ships that bore a striking resemblance to the *Kinghammer*. Finally, it having been some hours since EC had said, 'We need to talk,' the king opened up com.

'Our conversations have never required your . . . presence here before,' the king observed.

'I feel the circumstances warrant it this time,' EC replied.

After a long pause the king said, 'You do not have a physical presence and our communications convey every nuance, therefore you are here for another reason.'

'I felt the need to ensure your attention, rather than end up speaking to one of your envoys,' EC replied. 'I presume I have your attention?'

'You have it.'

'First I would like to convey my concern at seeing such a large gathering of kamikazes here.'

The bandwidth increased, with an invitation to virtuality. Using somewhat more caution than ever before, EC accepted. EC took the form of a fully limbed prador adult of the Original Family, and stepped onto a muddy prador home world shoreline, where mudfish fought with giant ship lice over the corpse of a huge reaverfish. He realized this caution again arose from a fear of personal destruction. Now possessing existence independent from the totality of Earth Central, he knew that same existence could end here.

'You are right to be concerned because they are a force with great destructive potential.' The king appeared on the same shore walking towards EC, heavy complex feet sinking deep in the soft sea-grassed loam. 'I too would like to convey my concern about what I have seen gathering at the borders of the disruption around Orlandine's realm. And about what I am now seeing here.'

EC waved a claw at the battle over the reaverfish. 'I see you like your virtuality symbols too.'

The king swung his head towards the scene for a moment, then away again. 'It wasn't even conscious, but I see what you mean.' Abruptly he sank down on his belly plates, bringing them eye-to-eye. 'I knew the fleet you sent to the accretion disc was a small percentage of the ships at your disposal, but I was not aware of these.'

A hammerhead dreadnought appeared in the sky over the ocean, giving a true idea of its immensity. Each one of the five was bigger even than the King's Ship.

'I too was aware that the fleet you sent did not include every ship at your disposal,' said EC, deciding not to mention that what the king had sent actually made a large hole in what he could field. 'But I didn't realize just how many kamikazes you could gather together.' Two thousand eight hundred and counting. 'What purpose do you have in mind for them?'

'In forty or so days, as the Polity counts time, the disruption will end,' said the king. 'I am preparing for that, as are you.'

'It's good to see you are responding responsibly. We should integrate our forces and consider our strategy and tactics.'

'But that is not why you came here, is it?' said the king.

'Perhaps you would like to elaborate?'

'Double meanings and, as ancient parlance of the humans would have it, sabre-rattling, have been a constant in our exchanges. Let us speak frankly. You saw me gathering these kamikazes and recognized them as a response to what must be happening at the accretion disc. However, the nature of that response concerned you.'

'This is an interesting line – do go on.'

'When the disruption stops you will send your forces to the accretion disc. It is quite possible they will face something devastating. Whoever wins there may well be considerably weakened – perhaps enough so to be taken out by a sufficiently large force of kamikazes.'

'Your thinking is quite Machiavellian.'

'So of course,' the king continued, 'you want me to integrate my forces with yours so they are not at your back.'

'This would perhaps be a preferable option for me.'

'And you have ensured that it is my only option.'

EC pretended innocence. 'How so?'

The sky flickered and five giant hammerheads crowded there.

'You have demonstrated that my border defence is inadequate and you brought these ships, right here, right to me. How quickly do you think you could destroy everything you have found here?'

'It would take a few hours and likely I would lose three of my ships.'

'Quite,' said the king.

'I am sorry if this was crass,' said EC, amazed to feel contrite suddenly.

'So we shall integrate our forces at the edge of the disruption?' the king enquired.

'No,' said EC, contriteness discarded. 'If you will allow . . . I will take the kamikazes now.'

'Why?'

'Because, you may have noted, my ships are capable of travel through U-space disruption, but they are also capable of integrating other vessels in their U-field complex. My ships and your kamikazes would make up a first-strike force. Your ships and further ships of my own can then follow when possible.'

After a long silence the king said, 'Oh, I see.'

EC expected some argument but immediately the control codes began coming across. The AI tested these and the thousands of kamikazes began to stream out to organize themselves near the hammerheads. It took less than an hour before they were all in formation, during which time neither spoke.

'It is time,' said EC, once it was done.

'Very well,' said the king. Then, 'Perhaps, in the future, you will remember that you have no further need to demonstrate Polity weapons' superiority over the Kingdom.'

'I will surely bear that in mind.' EC gazed at the mudfish and ship lice fighting over the reaverfish body. They were fading away now, no longer maintained. It wasn't a good symbol, or a good representation of the situation as it stood. The mudfish and lice were too evenly matched, and the dead reaverfish incapable of tearing them to shreds.

'Perhaps there is something in this for you to bear in mind, for the future,' EC added.

'That being?'

'That perhaps a Polity without a constant threat at its border will tend to stagnate, and that its ruler might want strong and dangerous opposition over that border to remain in power and live for as long as possible.'

'And you called me Machiavellian?'

'I think we are both that.'

'So business as usual once this has passed, if it does?'

'But of course,' EC replied, sliding out of the virtuality even as the hammerheads, slowly and carefully, fired up their drives and began to head back out of the Kingdom. The kamikazes turned with them.

### Orlik

The surge of acceleration elicited a surge of nostalgia for Orlik. It had been centuries since he had been aboard a ship whose grav so signally failed to compensate for it. Braced over a saddle, his armoured claws in pit controls, he threw up imagery on the mass of hexagonal screens which stretched across the sanctum. He felt the weapons opening fire and on the screens observed Jain tech exploding all around. But, even so, the battle had paused as the sequestered platforms and great swirling mass of wormships drew back and round in an arc. They were positioning themselves between Polity and prador forces and the departing Jain mother ship.

Just then, the diagonally divided door opened and in came two prador in armour with a more conventional look. But since they were surviving crew from the *Kinghammer*, he knew that what filled the armour was in no way conventional. Behind them, they towed a grav-sled loaded with equipment.

'Where have you put him?' he asked, eyeing imagery of a railgun strike on knots which had been lining up to drop into the magnetic barrels of some bacilliforms.

'We locked him in his mating area.'

Orlik swung one stalked eye to study the two. 'The females?'

'Dead long ago,' replied one.

'And not removed,' added the other.

The ship shuddered and jerked, a huge detonation outside tearing apart a sleet of bacilliforms. A reaver passed close. Orlik eyed the cloud of debris with trepidation, but then watched it fried in a forest of lasers.

'And the response of his children thus far?'

'His three first-children are relieved, but are now plotting to off each other to see who can fill his armour. The second-children feel that complete obedience to us is their best chance of survival.'

With a thump, the sled settled by his saddle control, sticking itself to the floor. Something shifted on the pile of equipment already in the sanctum, then kept still. Even though Orlik's crew knew about Sprag, Orlik had instructed the drone to keep a low profile. He had never told them how his captive had become something else and had no intention of doing so now. Even though they were highly mutated King's Guard, they might have some reservations about his friendship with a terror drone.

'You've told them all how matters stand?'

'The three say they will obey you, as direct representative of the king, until you leave this ship. Thereafter they can start killing each other. I don't trust it, but the threat has them behaving and watching each other very closely.'

Orlik extracted a claw from a pit control and waved it towards the door. 'You watch too. The moment any of them does anything to undermine the security of this ship is the moment we start getting nasty. Now get back to work. I want the new hardware installed yesterday.'

'We hear and obey,' said the two simultaneously and sarcastically, then departed.

Orlik called up further feeds on the screens. The remainder of his old crew had set to work installing new weapons and upgrades. But this work was not going fast enough for his liking, because of the problematic situation with the original crew here.

'This is a bit damned precarious,' said Sprag, fluttering in from her perch and flying to one in the surrounding ersatz stone. 'Great idea to put us in an old crappy dreadnought whose crew might start ripping each other apart at any moment.' She took off again, flying across to hover in front of the screens before dropping to the floor. After a moment, she began deactivating magnetic catches and opening up floor plates on liquid spring hinges.

Orlik pulled up a new feed across a patch of screens. This showed original crew of the ship queuing up to go past other prador clad in baroque and colourful armour – *Kinghammer* crew.

The latter were attaching devices to the coms units in the armour of the former. Or at least that was the explanation. The original crew were then moving off to their assignments.

'The new scramblers you told them about,' said Sprag, looking up. 'They don't need new scramblers or old, it's all in the programming.'

'They're limpet mines,' said Orlik.

'Ah, so you have the possibility of mutiny fully covered,' said Sprag, returning her attention to the floor plates. 'I missed that.'

'You're no longer an all-seeing AI,' Orlik noted.

'Whatever. Your precautions don't make this ship any less crappy, however.'

'I did not want to stay aboard the *Hogue*.'

He had been stuck there without *Kinghammer* as an ineffectual spectator. He could have gone aboard one of the reavers to command the prador ships, but still that ship would not have been his own. Then they discovered one old dreadnought had failed to leave the vast internal spaces of the *Cable Hogue*, while communications from its father-captain became nonsensical. Subsequently it turned out that the strain of battle had caused the collapse of that father-captain's already fragile mind. The ancient creature, all prostheses and other mechanical enhancements, had even been draining ichor and harvesting organs from his children to extend his life. Perhaps a prador like this had been the genesis of the legend of the Golgoloth. Orlik shivered.

'You didn't like being subordinate to the humans . . . but you still are. We're following their tactics.'

'Certainly,' Orlik replied, 'unless I decide otherwise.' He reached over to the sled with one claw and picked up an item that looked vaguely like a prador claw itself. This he inserted into one pit control and locked home. There were five more on the sled which he likewise inserted and locked into place.

'The shunt connected okay?' he enquired.

'The mind isn't very bright and has few sensors in its location,' Sprag replied. 'It had time to query what was happening then went to La La Land.'

Orlik picked up an interface plate from the sled, trailing a skein of optics, and reached back with it. As he plugged it into the socket on his back, it occurred to him that had he been a normal prador he would not have been able to reach so far. Meanwhile Sprag returned to the sled and took an intricate lump of hardware trailing further optics. She flew over and plugged it into the technology revealed under the floor, then flew back for another.

Almost done. Orlik brought his implants online first, then their connection to the interface plate. He emitted a very human sigh as his perspective began to open out. It had taken a factory unit aboard the *Hogue* just minutes to produce these items – the shunts from the pit controls, from the screens and from the ship's mind. It took longer, though, to produce the other items his crew were installing elsewhere. He gazed through internal cams and saw prador dragging a ruined railgun from its ball mount and inside the ship. On a sled nearby, a replacement weapon lay ready. A very new weapon. He next looked from the external sensors of the ship, as the ship's mind had once looked. He could now mentally operate its engines, weapons and defences. Though nowhere near as good as it had been aboard *Kinghammer* or his own old dreadnought, his connection was infinitely superior to verbal orders and constant twiddling with pit controls. He watched the *Cable Hogue* fall behind him, then looked to the vast battlefront. He linked up telemetry and tactical feeds, and felt almost as effective as he had once been.

The giant Jain mother ship continued to head in-system, towards the sun and towards the Client and her platform. He still had no explanation for why it had changed course, nor did he have one for why they were not pursuing. No matter. They had more than enough to deal with here. The sequestered platforms and wormships, initially placing themselves between the mother ship and Orlik's side, were turning back into the offensive. In response, the remaining platforms still on his side were forming into a scattered globe around the planet, while remaining fleet ships filled the gaps. Orlik manoeuvred his newly acquired dreadnought to one gap, his guard of reavers moving in around him.

'We can't hold this,' Orlik sent.

'We hold it for as long as possible,' Windermere replied.

The arc of enemy platforms curved in towards that sphere, the wormships still gathered behind them. Then one or two wormships moved ahead of the line, which seemed to break a dam, because all the rest started flooding through.

'It's going to get nasty now,' Sprag observed.

'You mean it wasn't before?' Orlik enquired.

## Trike

*Unfinished business*, Trike thought, as he again accessed the memtab Cog had given him. He followed the memory to its conclusion, of Cog fleeing the Skinner's island of Spatterjay in his landing craft, determined to edit the infection out of his mind. Now having experienced it himself, Trike too had felt the touch of evil, of madness. This sobering experience showed him what he could have become, and what, in reality, he was still capable of turning into. Had he learned anything useful from it? Not yet, but he fully intended to as he took the memory apart and analysed it in detail.

Cog's brother, Jay Hoop, had deteriorated in a terrible way.

His madness had gained power and effectively edited the good out of him and made what remained a source of joy. Cog had not been wrong to think of what he had encountered as evil. Throughout his change, Jay had lost intelligence, declining from a man who had, as terrible as it had been, run a criminal organization which had an appreciable effect on the duration of the prador/human war. He ended up as something primitive, just aping the things he had done before, practising, as Cog had noted, something akin to sympathetic magic. When Cog had arrived, Jay wanted to share what he had become and tried to core and thrall his brother. And here lay the key to something important: communication.

In that moment, Cog had experienced what remained of Jay's mind. This wasn't magic, nor was it the highly dubious telepathy some professed real. Studying the memory again, in detail, Trike saw the *communication* occurred when Jay's skin actually touched Cog's. It had been via the viral fibres and no doubt governed by the quantum processors rooted in the virus's genome. Trike kept turning that idea over in his mind, looking at it from all angles. It stemmed from the squad – those Jain soldiers who had recorded themselves to that genome – and was a distorted but still valid copy of what they were. And they, he inferred, were a near facsimile of their masters, just as all artificial intelligences in the Polity were of human minds.

Trike gazed from his sensors towards the approaching Jain ship, realizing that Cog's story had given him further insight into what he faced. Like Polity citizens nowadays, and like Cog himself, he did not enjoy absolutes such as good and evil. However, he could see, from all he had learned, nothing redeemable about the Jain. He already knew they raped and pillaged everything. They had then ultimately expressed this trait in becoming the hostile sequestering Jain tech spread throughout this system, and currently devastating Jaskor. And it seemed that just the dregs of it could physically change people to match their damaged minds, like Jay Hoop . . . and like himself.

Did he need to know this to confirm his intentions? No, but he did need to know this so as not to become like Hoop. The horrible reality was that only the structural copy of Orlandine's mind, within a Jain mycelium, had prevented him from turning into something even worse than Hoop. And that danger remained. If anything, Cog's final encounter with his brother had taught Trike one vital lesson: he might win the coming battle but in the process lose his mind completely.

Trike sighed and physically detached from the surrounding crystal columns, but remained connected otherwise. With this brief business out of the way, his next assessment of everything occurring in the ship's core confirmed reality: he was as ready as he was ever going to be.

## The Client

The Client wound tightly around her crystal tree, as if bracing against a gale that might dislodge her. It wasn't pain she felt, but a hole in her mind much larger than the remaining portion. Even so, as a combination of both hive and singular creature, she had the capacity to deal with such loss, and her mind began to collapse back and heal into a new shape. Out of instinct, she groped for the lost remotes, but forced herself not to engage the transmitters aboard Weapons Platform Mu, and thus fall into mental combat with Trike. Yet still she felt some strange sense of connection.

Briefly, she glimpsed a mental map. She saw herself as a node at the centre of this platform, with branches of herself spread throughout it. She saw Trike similarly positioned in the ship's core, the expanse of him much greater throughout it and connected to thousands of glowing points that were her remotes. She also saw a hazy link between him and her, and other links spearing out and away. One connected to a growing mass on Jaskor, which seemed to confirm the truth of this vision, for Orlandine spread herself there. But a brighter and much larger object overshadowed this. Coming towards the Client in an arcing orbital path from beyond Jaskor, a star glared with infinitely divided branches spread across a vast volume of space. Here was the Jain, connected to its mechanisms down on and around the planet, and to the wave front heading towards her. All four of them – herself, Trike, Orlandine and the Jain – were linked in a web across this system. Then the vision evaporated.

The Client felt a surge of terror, because she knew nothing about such a connection, yet it was feasible. All her knowledge of Jain technology came from the Librarian who, essentially, had become part of her. The Librarian's understanding of the sequestering, civilization-killing kind was limited to data gleaned during the battle which had wrecked the Jaskoran system. And it had not seen this connecting web. She had enough insight into this sort of Jain tech to recognize what she did not know. She was not sure how organized it might be beyond her ability to scan it; however, she did know it was organized to pico-scopic levels, if not below them. In analogy she, just like Orlandine and Trike, understood and could change its programming language but did not comprehend the foundation code of it. They had not written that code. Realizing this, the Client felt her terror waning. The approaching Jain seemed likely to be just as ignorant, merely a victim in the process of being subsumed by the tech which had conquered all of its kind. She did not need to attach any great meaning to this vision and tried to turn away from it.

Focusing back on the core, in the world of EMR and data, she saw Trike had left links open enough for her to see inside. He had not interfered with the task she had given her remotes and they were still collecting and dispatching Species remains. Pods containing them now packed many of her holds and, for the first time, she sent a grappler to collect some for examination. Meanwhile, she scrutinized Trike's other preparations.

The level of activity within the core had started eating into energy storage there. Trike had begun opening up patches of solar cells on its surface, which looked like midnight holes. In terms of Polity technology, this was standard, because such cells had achieved ninety-eight per cent efficiency across the human-visible spectrum centuries ago. However, other scans also detected holes and she realized the cells converted wavelengths of EMR from X-rays to long-wave radio directly into electricity – power to top up storage constantly, while Trike emptied it.

Internal factories roaring into life produced railgun slugs, missiles and bespoke particulates for the beam weapons. Bioreactors took on new load as biomechs entered them for redesign. New versions of her remotes had appeared – they were loaded with armament so that they looked a lot less organic and more like war drones. Robots in the armour of the core, ranging in scale from microbes to things the size of attack ships, were busily at work weaving in new layers and filling some areas with newly designed crash foams. Meanwhile—

'Hey, are you going to keep on ignoring me?'

The voice issued by simple radio nearby and, in sudden panic, she focused attack pod weapons on an object drawing close to the platform. A microsecond later she recognized Cog's ship but this did not incline her to stand them down. Though aware of it leaving the core and heading over, she had, during her initial terror at that web vision and her subsequent focus on Trike's activities, simply forgotten about it. Allowing a vessel like this to get inside the usual reach of her enclosing hardfield concerned her. The thing could be packed with CTDs! She scanned it at full power.

'Damn and fuck!' Cog exclaimed.

She could see him in his bridge with his clothing steaming from the intense scan radiations. She cooled it down, then, reluctantly, shut it down. Nothing to fear here. One of her weapons pods could take down the powerful little ship in a moment. And Cog remained unchanged from when he had departed . . . unlike Trike.

'Why have you come to me?' she asked.

'I want to come aboard, if you'll let me,' he said.

'Why?'

'Well, Jaskor is being overrun, a Jain with a shitload of nasty tech is coming here, and Trike doesn't want me with him. Seems you're the only choice I have left.'

If only thinking of his own survival, being with her offered him a better chance than fleeing on conventional drive. But he had been a Polity agent for a very long time and no doubt intended to gather information for the Polity – putting eyes on a potential threat to that realm. But why not? She had no intention of going against either the Polity or the Prador Kingdom and, just perhaps, having someone close by who could broadcast that fact might be a good idea. Her goals now concerned what one grappler had just put inside a disposable laboratory of the kind in which the AI Pragus had resurrected her.

'Come aboard,' she said, opening the very same hold where the trader Marco had handed over her remains to the AI Pragus. For a moment, she watched his ship come in, then focused her attention on the disposable laboratory again.

The grappler had placed two Species body segments in soft

clamps and retreated. Scanning heads closed in and X-ray diffraction at once revealed masses of useful genetic material. Terahertz and other emitted radiation scans then sketched out the physiology of the creature and she studied it in her mind. This creature had been more integrated than her own kind. While her segment bodies joined along a single nerve cord, this one possessed further physical connections of carapace, musculature and venous system. She could see the weakness here. The creature could survive the loss of parts of its body, certainly, but this would greatly weaken and possibly kill it. She could lose much more, and regenerate from just one of her segments. Did she, she wondered, evolve from this earlier version, or was she a product of later genetic manipulation?

The answer surfaced in her mind as she *remembered* testing multiple iterations of this configuration, and seeing just one type of five other kinds aboard the main Species battleship. There had even been one whose body parts connected only via biological radio. Her remotes would have made her aware of this had she reintegrated them, but that would not happen now. The memories, of course, were those of the Librarian. Exploring further she observed it testing the versions of the Species over a million years. There was one, like these before her, which became too introverted and slid into virtuality. She saw how it wiped them out with a virus and reseeded with a more robust version similar to herself.

The Client realized there was danger in her thinking. If assimilating the Librarian's memories which remained distinct, she must continue with care, otherwise she would integrate too much of its personality. But keeping those memories separate from herself would result in the creation of a separate personality – a subpar version of the Librarian itself. She began to run the memories through the filter of perspective. She became a spectator on the Librarian's life as it continued integrating with her mind.

'Okay if I come join you?'

It was Cog again. He had docked his ship, stuck it to the floor, and the bay doors were closing. Clad in the space armour and wearing a backpack, he clumped down its ramp.

'You may,' she replied. 'Though I fail to see why you want to abandon the comfort of your ship.'

'Curiosity,' said Cog, and trudged on.

The scanners were revealing further information about the two segment bodies of the creature, but the Client wanted much more. A surgical tool head closed in, cut carapace with an atomic shear and, with small pincer-like fingers, pulled it apart. This revealed dry strands of dehydrated muscle. As the surgical head moved aside, the nose of a nanoscope closed in on the muscle.

The Client observed muscle fibres expand, the honeycomb patterns on their surface with links to underlying cybernetic structures. Deeper still, and she saw stretched-out muscle cells pierced through with neural fibrils and collapsed cellular machinery like a crystal garden. Amidst its coils and microscopic monoliths, she focused down and down to see the regular patterning of genetic code and transcriptomes – tightly wound trunks of computer-generated pseudo-molecules. And there, finally knotted into the five-strand helix, she began to see slabs of laminar diamond shot through with the doping of other elements. Through the nanoscope, she fired angstrom lasers and measured electro-photon responses. This last had just been for confirmation of what she already knew: the creature's genome was loaded with quantum processing crystals just like her own. She had found its recorded mind.

The Client returned to herself in her life-support cylinder, offhandedly opening a hatch to allow Cog inside. As he traipsed towards the base of her tree, she looked outwards. Trike had just fired up a fully enclosing hardfield around the ship's core, which meant no more Species remains would be coming her way. Meanwhile the leading wave of Jain tech lay only thousands of miles away, with the giant ship just half a million miles behind that.

'It is time to leave,' she said.

Cog was crouching down by his open pack. He reached inside and took out two items, pushed them together and locked them, then brought the stock up to his shoulder and pointed the wide internally silvered barrel at her.

'I think you should stay,' he said.

## Gemmell

The scene reminded Gemmell of pictures from Earth of flocks of starlings taking flight and forming strangely protean shapes in the sky. He should have expected this. First the knots of Jain tech hurtling through the air, launched at hypersonic speeds from infestations in the surrounding lands, now these winged versions of them. He shouldered the multigun he had grabbed from a perimeter armoury and fired into one of the flocks. The shell exploded amid the rising things, flinging out sharp chunks of ceramal trailing monofilaments. These sliced through a large portion of the flock and dropped it to the ground in pieces. Via his gridlink, the gun alerted him that he had only two more shells left. He lowered it. This was the problem now: no lack of targets and most of them easy to hit, but everyone running out of ammunition.

Beside him, Ruth had switched her twin-barrelled pulse cannon to a low-ammunition program and let it run. With her hand against her neck as if it was aching, she glanced over at him, shook her head, then drew her sidearm. He shrugged and looked down towards the edge of the trench. Nearby, gleaming insects moved along the edge. The mosquito autoguns, deployed to hit the fast-moving objects coming in, were firing bursts with alarming regularity. Checking the tactical and logistical feeds, he saw them destroying a constant stream of the things, but still they moved steadily closer. All around drones and grav-tanks fired in short bursts too, and steadily retreated.

'Gemmell,' said Ruth.

He sighed. Could it get any worse?

'Gemmell . . . stop me.'

He looked up just as the pulse gun shot to his chest knocked him back against the rail, his weapon clattering to the floor of the sled. He launched himself forwards, chest tight from stiffened subdermal armour. A second shot hit him in the left arm, but he slapped her gun away with his right hand, dragged her from her seat and pinned her to the floor. Her eyes were blank and something had stuck itself on the side of her neck: a tic-like green nodule spreading capillaries into surrounding skin. He drew back his fist, but then his attention swung to the twinned pulse cannon still firing. He stood abruptly, trying to gridlink to it and shut it down, but his mind seemed to be dividing – part of it residing in his gridlink and stopping him. His right eye wanted to close and he reached up to touch the growth on his forehead, realizing Jain tech had sequestered him too. He stepped forwards and pulled himself into the seat. Grabbing the control handles, he dropped the weapon out of its program and selected another target – a nearby sentinel drone – and opened fire.

*No no no!* His mind screamed.

Only controlling his body, just as the one on Ruth controlled hers, the Jain tech had not yet seized his mind. Shots slammed into the sentinel drone but it dropped out of sight into the trench. Elsewhere he saw soldiers firing on their own forces. Only those protected inside tanks were not. He picked out a rising grav-tank and opened fire on that. He knew one of his targets would necessarily respond. He tried to gridlink to the gun again, but that route just died in his mind. Instead, he linked to the sled and shut down its grav, and a moment later, it plummeted from the sky.

'*Bio-warfare suits!*' he shouted mentally over the command channel.

They had prepared as best they could for this scenario. Jain tech would not necessarily stay in the ground or remain in a size range easily visible to human gunners. But though their bio-warfare suits might slow sequestration, they could not stop Jain nano-fibres. This 'nothing we can really do' scenario they had put to one side.

Their sled slammed down into a mud slope on the outside of the trench and turned over, spilling the two of them out, then tumbling down into the trench. Gemmell felt bruised and battered but his body monitoring detected no breaks as he stood up and looked round for a weapon. Ruth stood also.

'I just can't . . . stop it,' she said.

'Me nee . . . neither,' he replied, feeling his voice-box falling out of his control.

'*Neutralize them,*' came Knobbler's command. The drone had obviously taken over the command frequency.

They reached the edge of the trench and peered down, then began moving along it. How intelligent was the thing controlling him? Intelligent enough to recognize Ruth as an ally and to look for enemies to attack, he guessed, as it penetrated him further and really began to dig into his mind.

Something thumped down on the slope above. He looked up and for a moment thought a prador had arrived, but then recognized a giant armoured spider. It raised its front legs, poking its hindquarters forwards between those behind, and filled the air with glittering fog. He tried to launch himself towards this thing, which he now saw as an enemy, but found himself fighting through a forest of fibres. Long hard limbs grabbed him and began turning him over and over, the spider's nightmare visage studying him dispassionately. It then dropped him to the ground, cocooned in monofilament, and a moment later Ruth thudded down beside him.

'*Can you hear me, Gemmell?*' asked Knobbler, over coms.

He tried to reply, but instead found himself selecting from his store of virtual attack programs and dispatching them. A moment later, all his comlinks ceased to respond.

## Orlandine

In her previous form, Orlandine had been dispersed across multiple aspects: satellites in orbit, in AI minds and other storage on her weapons platforms, and in systems throughout Jaskor. But that had been a poor copy of true expansion. Superconductors and laser nanotubes connected her mind, which constantly distributed about her growing tentacles, veins and mycelia. It could respond practically instantly over its thousands of miles extent, and could keep on expanding its processing. She was a giant now.

Beyond the coastal plain, in the foothills of the Canine Mountains, she encountered three more growing enemy infestations. The first she tried to destroy simply by routing a power surge through braided superconductors, turning the cave system it occupied into a furnace. Half of it burned but then the other half utilized the power for a massive growth surge. This speared sporulating guns towards the surface to sprout there. Her soldiers, marching across above, ripped into these with new chain-glass teeth. Then, in memory of the bladder wrack they had fed on when mere weed-eating GM iguanas, they chewed on the remains. Underground she spliced her fibres into the alien growth and attacked with steadily evolving sequestering programs, incorporating it physically while absorbing and analysing its programming.

She immediately tried to seize control of the next she encountered and learned at once that these things were in contact with each other, for it was ready for her attack. But, in a struggle that lasted an hour, she crushed it. In this, she saw the reality of warfare as it had been since the world wars of Earth, how it had been during the prador/human war, and how it had been with the prador against the Species: the side with the most resources and industrial capacity always won. And she had become industrial.

Behind her, she grew infrastructure. Fission reactors expanded in the ground like potatoes after she discovered another rich layer of pitchblende. Boron, snared by molecular sieves from groundwater, and hydrogen, compressed to metallic state in sapphire anvils, provided fuel for simple two-laser fusion plants. These were grown as nodes along the main trunks of her root-like body. All of it compensated for waning energy supplies from the volcano. She had drained off millions of tons of lava into her structure, extracting thermal energy and converting it, and created a spill pile of excess and unneeded silicon there. She had supposed the volcano would be an endless supply, driven up from below, but it seemed that, like a lanced boil, it was diminishing. She had put the planet's only volcanologist out of business. Throughout her expanse, she also put down carbide drills and, to her surprise, hit a high reservoir of abiotic oil and gas. That supplied useful hydrocarbons for her structure and for energy too. Arc reactors flared out fullerenes and micro-factories spilled nano-machines.

She occupied underground caves and turned them into weapons plants. As she spread, she pulled down trees and reprocessed them. She did not have to estimate but knew, to five decimal places, how much she massed, and that figure had passed fifty million tons.

But she did not only extend inland. In fact, that growth was slower. In the ocean, her trunks of Jain tech shot along the bottom like underwater trains, spilling tentacles and mycelia behind them. Ocean floor mud was easier to manipulate and water lubricated the process. Molecular sieves there provided a different and more easy-to-utilize profile of elements and organic chemicals. Sequestered anglerfish, as well as hagfish, were her advance force, perpetually upgraded every time they hit a new enemy infestation. A bed of manganese polymetallic nodules at the bottom of a trench provided a massive burst of growth which, remembering her purpose now, she directed along the coast in one direction. They took the shortest route around the continent towards the southern cities.

In the mountains, she encountered another invasion and just rolled over it without having to focus on it completely. From the mountaintops, she sprouted dishes and antennae, upgrading her reception from the other parts of her being scattered throughout the Jaskoran system, but not really concerned with that right now. Coming down on the further slopes, she quickly sought out a particular valley and there found the remains of her Ghost Drive Facility. Here she looted a cornucopia of useful materials and complete chunks of technology she could incorporate. Her surface army of iguanas and other life forms grew, with the addition of weaponized maintenance robots and two previously wrecked sentinel drones. These last brought home to her how internalized she had become. She equated this with the growth surges of teenage humans, and how they usually lost sight of their surroundings while their bodies changed. She forced herself to reach out beyond her present self and its expansion to re-acquire her sentinel drones around the main city too, and other systems there. She made contact again.

'That was frighteningly quick,' said Knobbler.

She had a thousand answers for him and none, then had to partition off a copy of an older part of herself to remember this form of conversational communication.

'Jain technology with direct mental control is always fast,' she replied. 'The invasive Jain tech here has been preprogramed but is not AI. It fails to adapt with sufficient alacrity.'

The sentinel drone to which he had sent his communication flew closer to where Knobbler hurtled through the sky, obliterating micro sequestering devices with a wide-beam particle cannon. It was like trying to clear a snowstorm with a flame-thrower. She wanted more data from him on this, but when she tried to move closer to his mind, she hit a shield. Probes towards other irascible drones hit similar barriers.

'Maybe later,' said Cutter as he sliced and diced Jain worms spewing from the ground in a forested glade.

'I feel slightly embarrassed,' Bludgeon conceded, 'but precautions must be taken.'

Understandably none of them trusted her. They had seen what happened when her growth had surged aboard Orlik's old destroyer, after the destruction of the Jain soldier. Then she had blindly sought to control technology around her and only their luck, and caution, had stopped her grabbing the crew and the drones there. But she was fully in control now, and growing her awareness – *always* remaining in control and *always* remembering who she was. Unfortunately, the only way to rid them of their ignorance would be to make them look closely at her mind, but they were too timid and frightened to let her close.

An alert with integral contradictions reached her mind. Scanning tentacles rising out of the ground like cobras identified a grav-bus lying on the surface, tangled in vine-like growths. Some of its passengers were moving away and others only just pulling themselves from the wreckage. Her tentacles began zeroing in on them and, for a moment, she could not remember why this was wrong, then she did: she could not subsume these people because, well, they were people. The conclusion had no emotional weight, and then she identified the contradictions. She had found another small infestation and it was in them. She focused on one man, horribly injured, his legs broken and protruding bone, constantly trying to stand up while tendrils knotted and rearranged themselves in the bleeding flesh below his knees. Others running away had similar vein-like growths spreading over exposed skin or writhing in open wounds.

Again, Orlandine wanted to attack them, but she deferred that by first going for the growth over the bus. Her own tentacles exploded from the ground and caged it, then wound around and knotted up the enemy. She tore at the growth until she had connected into it. Weak and new, the thing soon fell under her command. In the virtual world, she leapt from it to its victims and they all fell paralysed, when they weren't crawling. Focusing more closely, she saw that three were all but dead – the Jain mycelia spread through their bodies was the only element moving them as it fed on their flesh. She made her calculations and saw she could not, as yet, spare the resources to return them to functional life, but she could preserve them. She dragged them down into soft soil, cocooning them in tendrils, weaving coils of superconductor over them and extracting heat by magnetic cooling, meanwhile injecting a solution of cryo-protectants. Frost formed over those points in the ground until she wove in the insulators. The Jain tech in them slowed as their temperature dropped to minus one hundred and vitrification commenced. Would it be enough? The Jain tech still moved, but as slow as the growth of a plant now. Eventually it would find a way to break free but, by then the battle for this world would be over, one way or the other.

But even this had been too long a delay because the others broke contact and began to stand up – each becoming a distinct infestation. Whipping tendrils out of the ground, she snared them one after the other and spliced herself in. Attack programs brought about convulsions, and mycelia within them fell to her. Further fast analysis revealed she could not kill those mycelia, though, because the damage they had caused and the wreckage they would leave in dying, would surely kill their hosts. She reprogrammed them, for they were now hers. The mycelia integrated with these people's nanosuites and maintained their lives. But what to do with them? She stood them up and set them walking towards the city. The fact that she controlled them was all she needed to concern herself with for now . . .

As she drew closer and closer to the city, she reached the larger interconnected infestation there and attacked it. She found more sequestered humans and Golem soldiers in the cave systems, and even one of the old assassin drones – a giant burrowing snake who had been hunting underground and fallen foul of its prey. She destroyed and sequestered, subsumed Jain infestations and herself seized control of those they had made slaves. She could release none of them because . . . it was just too much work, too intricate and difficult, and would use up too much of her resources and, more importantly, her time. She had to keep her eye on the prize.

*And what is that?* she asked herself.

Connected to the remaining platforms and ships defending the world, she saw that without reinforcements they would lose.

Once that happened, a mass of hostile Jain tech would flood Jaskor. In total, if everything out there came in, she estimated this would form a new crust nearly a mile thick.

She needed to grow even larger to meet this challenge.

# 14

*The grappler robot bears the appearance of a large, boosted man made of faceted metal. Apparently they were first made to take over the tasks of heavyworlders who, wearing thick armoured hotsuits, had laboured on the surface of a world with the atmospheric pressure and temperature of Venus, and three times the gravity. The fact that the grappler's eyes and mouth look like holes into a furnace is supposedly due to the high-temperature technology running inside them. This is, of course, all nonsense. There have been brief instances when humanoid robots were useful in operating equipment designed for humans, but never a time when they were actually made for that purpose. Most robots, for a very long time, have possessed manipulators and sensors superior to humans and easily able to adapt to the controls of any equipment. No, grapplers are what happens when limitations on cost, materials or energy in designing and making robots are few. They are an aesthetic conceit of an AI robot designer with a penchant for ancient superhero comics and films. Many AIs across the Polity and elsewhere use them simply because those same AIs agree with the designer: they look cool.*

From 'Quince Guide' compiled by humans

## Gemmell

Gemmell could feel the Jain tech learning his body and yet, by dint of his gridlink's defensive capabilities, he managed to stop it from taking full control of his mind. By linking into his medical nanosuite, he could also watch its actions and fight it internally. He drove his enhanced immune system, and maintenance and repair nanites of the suite, into battle. He attacked it where he could, especially when it tried physically to worm into his brain. Even though he knew he couldn't win, because his defence was killing his body, he fought anyway. That was his nature.

It had ceased to make him struggle against the spider-silk cocoon wrapped about him, but now began making alterations. He directed nanites down into his hands, trying to stop the mycelium there. His hands hurt terribly as his nails mounded into ridges and further keratin began to sprout from his skin on the inner surfaces of his fingers, joining up with them at the fingertips. Modelling the growth in his gridlink, he could see the thing turning his hands into claws, with sharp edges that extended down the insides of his fingers. The nanites he used to fight this gleaned the data that metals were building up in that keratin. Even the nanites, many of which contained metals, fell prey to the mycelium as a source of the same. Soon he would have claws sharp enough to cut through the cocoon.

Losing the battle badly, he diverted his attention to the building pressure in the base of his skull, where nanites had gathered thickly to prevent mycelial incursion. Something cracked there and blinding pain shoved him into semi-consciousness. A momentary glimpse of his model rapidly altered to include a flare of threads piercing his brain. These weaved back and forth into a dense tangle as they made connections, then speared out to penetrate the gridlink hardware etched into the interior surface of his skull. All his connections went out. He felt something pushing, hard, and his will crumbling, then reforming.

*No no no no!*

Gemmell sliced with his claws and stood up, angrily, shrugging away the remains of the cocoon. He was thoroughly aware of his body again, in fact, much more so than before. Reaching down, he swiped, splitting the other nearby cocoon. Ruth stood up and gazed at him blankly. She had grown no claws and he knew, because of a connection to her via their Jain tech, her outward awareness sat in abeyance.

*Please let that be so . . .*

She was a subject to him, as were other Jain growths in the surrounding area. He knew why. He was precisely what Jain tech sought out to bring down civilizations, for it subsumed intelligences and deployed them to its end. He had risen above being just an organic machine by dint of fighting it on the level he had, and because it penetrated his gridlink. Perfectly understanding it all did not change the fact that Polity and prador soldiers here were now the enemy, who he must subjugate, control and absorb. It didn't matter how much he screamed inside. It didn't matter that his mind seemed to have fractured into two: one a soldier working for the enemy and one a prisoner.

*Die, turn off, end . . .*

'Come,' he said to Ruth, and began walking down the slope, and she obediently followed.

Shortly they reached the crumbling edge and he peered down twenty feet into muddy water where their grav-sled lay half-submerged on its side.

Maybe the drop would kill him?

He jumped and she followed, landed with a splash, his feet hitting the soft muddy bottom, and propelled himself up again. Swimming to the sled, he gridlinked ahead to its controls and ran a diagnostic. The thing was rugged and undamaged and even as he grabbed the rail, he righted it to float on the water. Clambering in, and Ruth following just behind, he thought about what to do. With utter horror trapped inside, he remembered a store of CTDs inside the city. He couldn't link to them from here, for they required physical priming. No one would stop him. A large enough detonation in the centre of the city, he felt, would be enough to facilitate the complete collapse of the defence here. At his command the sled rose, but cobra-like tentacles speared up out of the water, many of them wrapping about the rails.

He felt confusion. Was it his own? He did not know. Then came panic that didn't gel well with his consciousness. This was the enemy? He reached for the controls of the twinned pulse cannons, meanwhile trying to force the sled higher. It rose ten feet, pulling up a main trunk from which the cobras had sprouted. With a thought, he swung the cannons towards that and opened fire, slicing through. Something then slammed into the back of his neck. He recognized it when Ruth staggered back with two of those cobra things attached to her. Invasive virtual warfare stabbed across from her to him. He acted quickly, cutting his connection to her.

*Oh hell no . . .*

He slammed a boot into her torso, feeling her ribs break, and sent her tumbling over the side. The cobra thing fixed to him burrowed in, agonizingly, and nearly dragged him after her as the sled continued to rise. But it hit subdermal armour and stalled. He reached and tore it away, next throwing the sled up into the sky.

*Hit me! Hit me now!* he shrieked inside, as he took the sled at high speed across a wasteland and straight into the streets. Surely the drones knew, or someone else would realize and open fire on him? No, they would not. He now understood that the cobra thing was on his previous side, the same as the armoured spider who had cocooned them, and that she had no doubt informed his forces and the drones. But they would want to try and save him and, by the time they realized the danger, it would be too late.

He shot over smoking wreckage, cornered around a tower block, the sled tilted over with its edge scraping against the road. A small park opened out ahead, the grass blackened and the trees withered. The munitions dump sat there: four armoured cargo containers.

*About here. I die . . .*

They would know his destination now. He timed it perfectly, leaping from the sled as it hurtled towards the containers. He hit the ground hard, rolling, bones breaking, but then up and running as railgun shots struck the ground behind him. The sled crashed into one of the containers and bounced away, shedding debris.

*Now, hit me now!*

Though moving fast, his pace would be leisurely to a drone or AI – time to select the appropriate weapon and turn him into a cloud of blood, flesh and bone, or fire and smoke. He reached the container and slammed a hand against a palm reader beside the door. It opened and inside he expected to see the ranked CTD canisters with detonator consoles attached on top. Instead, a fountain of cobra-headed tentacles poured out and slammed him to the ground. He felt them slapping against him all over, then the agonizing sensation of them drilling through his subdermal armour. Fibres shot inside him, to which his nanosuite and mycelium fought back. But he was as powerless to resist this flood of Jain tech and virtual warfare as he had been to resist the other one earlier. Something vast seemed to loom in his mind, and a cold analytical voice spoke:

'I've got you,' said Orlandine.

This did not reassure him.

## Orlik

Orlik felt a surge of both anger and trepidation as two wormships headed directly towards his dreadnought. He clearly remembered the battle in the Cyberat system, and how a ship like these had destroyed his brother's ship, including hauling out his sanctum and tearing it apart. He clearly remembered how close he had come to dying too. However, the two of them had been captaining destroyers at the time and not a dreadnought like this, old and, as Sprag had noted, as crappy as it was.

The gunners opened fire and their targeting was good, so he felt no need to intervene there, but surely with his enhanced control he could find other ways to tilt the odds in his favour? His attention strayed to another item he had brought aboard while this ship resided inside the *Cable Hogue*. His crew had moved the disruptor weapon into the control ball of the all-but-annihilated railgun, but had not yet connected it up. He spoke to those – mostly Guard – who were installing the thing.

'How long until it's ready?' he asked.

'Too long,' replied the prador in charge there, 'and then we have to test the system.'

Orlik scanned down in the area, noting the control optics strewn on the floor. 'Just make the connection and get out of there.'

'Okay, but if it blows, I'll not be held responsible,' replied the prador.

'You should be glad I'm not a typical father-captain,' said Orlik acidly. 'That comment would have had you recycled in an implant tank.'

'Thankfully we have evolved.'

Orlik kept silent as he watched the prador pick up optics and rapidly plug them into place. Frustration, and the urge to have that particular member of the crew kicked out of an airlock, rose and then faded. The prador was called Ulsk and had been with him for longer than most prador lived.

As the optics went in, the programming of the disruptor fell into Orlik's mind. He sighed out a long breath and concentrated on it, deliberately cutting out all other sensory feeds. He began putting the programs together and matching them to the varying parameters of the weapon's components and how they aligned. A requirement for more mental space had him reaching for the frozen first-child mind of this ship and using it like a plug-in processor. He then routed some of it to Sprag, who emitted a squawk but responded, working the code. And it was done.

Orlik opened his sensors to the outside universe congratulating himself on having done something that would have taken his crew hours working with pit controls. A sphincter-tightening moment followed, as he saw the wormships exchanging positions under fire and hammering hard towards his shields. Opening fire was almost an instinctive reaction. The disruptor drew power and particulate and stabbed out a beam of glassy glowing red, its form like plaited threads and the thing revolving like a drill. It hit hardfields and they just broke like glass, then it hit the wormship and sensors blanked. When they reinstated they showed a massive explosion whose shockwave slammed into his ship's shields. Further data: the blast had also taken out the wormship behind.

'What the fucking hell was that!' The exclamation from Windermere arrived while Orlik rattled his sharp tongue in his mouth, still in shock.

'I think we got the programming wrong,' said Sprag, privately to Orlik.

'We tried a different program,' Orlik lied to Windermere.

'Then you'd better damned well add it to your telemetry,' she replied.

Orlik began copying the program and sending it, meanwhile trying to work out what he had done wrong but had gone very right.

'They're rejigging the things already,' Sprag stated.

Orlik took an overview of the battle. Wormships were in amongst them now. The fleet had blasted many to squirming fragments, while others fell on ships and weapons platforms, spreading themselves to tear their way in. Then red-tinted beams began flashing into being all around the defensive sphere and fission explosions bloomed. He felt a fierce joy at the sight, but logistical and tactical reality impinged a moment later. Out of pure luck, he had given them all a new weapon. But he had only delayed their inevitable demise by mere hours.

## Orlandine

In the main city Orlandine spread out and felt only a ghost of unease at seeing her tentacles hunting human beings, pulling them down and connecting like feeding leeches. She also expanded beyond the city, while her other growth reached round the continent and began pouring ashore, squirming over docks and sea defences. Prador and other defenders there initially opened fire on her, until she told them to desist.

'How am I supposed to know what is you and what is the enemy?' asked Ksov.

'You don't. Just pull back and hold fire.'

Two other prador rose from a pavement. She grabbed them twenty feet above the ground and slammed them down to the plasticrete. While worming into their armour, she emitted an EMR blast to drive away other prador attempting to assist what they thought were two comrades in trouble. She went in via the route used by the mycelia now seizing control of them. One of the prador was easy – simply an organic robot controlled by the invader. The other one presented the same difficulties she had found with Gemmell. The invading Jain tech had seized hold of the mind of this member of the Guard but, worse than that, the Spatterjay virus had tangled in the mix to produce something quite vicious and dangerous. As she fought for control, she found herself putting more and more processing online for the task, and again could not spare either that or the time. She wound the prador in coils and dragged him down into the drains, magnetic cooling and vitrifying him solid, leaving part of herself there to maintain this, then collapsing the drain on top. She would go back for him, should she survive.

The battle up in space had turned the morning sky a shade of orange this world had never seen before. Titanic detonations lit and silhouetted streamers of cloud while meteors streaked down. The new weapon the defenders were deploying had bought some time, but that was rapidly draining away because of what had happened to the half-constructed Weapons Platform Magus. Behind the lines, it had been sequestered, and now swarmed with Jain tech. Its engines had fired and it had begun edging towards Jaskor.

*More energy . . .*

Her initial hesitancy, upon reaching a chain of atolls far out from the main coast, evaporated. She drove down into the relatively thin seabed, forcing hastily adapted fusion plants to selected points. Flooding them with deuterium, she disconnected their energy draw and fired them up. Instead of steady fusion, a chain reaction ensued. The detonation threw millions of tons of seawater and bedrock into the sky and opened the sea down to the furnace. Lava exploded from below, then fought the seawater flooding back to raise a giant steam cloud which boiled up and out to become easily visible from space. She flooded in too to suck on the released heat energy, driving laminated ceramic pipes down deep. Her growth from this cataclysm boiled the sea, as trunks as thick as centuries-old oaks speared out so fast their compression shock blew lines of spume into the sky. She noted, in passing, that she had expanded to around three-quarters of the planet.

On the coast, along a thousand miles of beaches, then in stages out into the sea, she threw up walls of curved pillars and inflated floats between. These dampened the tsunamis which arrived, and converted their energy into something useful in piezo-electric generators. On land, new plants bloomed, opening photo-electric petals. But these were not her greatest energy sources. Repeatedly she bored down through the crust to suckle on the heat below. As one fast-growing trunk slowed and met another nose to nose, this melded her growth from both sides of the continent and she engulfed all of Jaskor. Then, as her energy distributed evenly, she began to create something new.

Concentrating much of her mass on the plain to the north side of the Canine Mountains, Orlandine began to bore a hole. Great pipes poured down in one spot, at their noses sporting drill bits of laminated corundum and intersecting shearfields. They transferred tons of rubble every second back through their length into processing plants, which grew like giant metallized puffballs on the plain. Dust exploded into the sky for the first few hundred feet, but then she drew that away with ensuing pipes. A mile deep, her mechanisms began to widen the hole even as they pushed deeper, then they lay down new structure – vines as thick as grav-cars spiralling up the side of this vent and into the sky. Even as this continued, she delved down elsewhere all around the planet. A thick stratum of molten iron provided material for growing underground factories while other elements provided windings, rails, particulates and more besides. She understood that to save the planet she must weaponize it, and to do that she would have to all but wreck it.

## Trike

Trike observed Weapons Platform Mu sliding away in orbit about the sun.

'*Was this your intention?*' the Client asked.

'*It was not,*' he replied.

Cog sat in the Client's environment cylinder with that weapon of his pointed vaguely towards the creature. Trike understood the balance there. Had Cog been a normal human, the Client could have incinerated him on the spot, without any danger to herself. However, as an old hooper, he could survive such a blast long enough to fire his weapon and perhaps kill her. Trike also noted the particle cannon was the same one Cog had used against his own brother. Perhaps that particular encounter with Jay Hoop had impelled him to upgrade the weapon to take its present gigawatt energy canister.

But what was Cog's intention here? He understood Trike must be going up against the Jain, so was he keeping the Client here to lend support? It seemed not, since he had allowed the Client to move the platform to the periphery of the action. Then, because of the memory he had relived, he entertained a suspicion. He knew Cog felt a strange responsibility for him – perhaps transference of what he had felt for his brother. And that could extend to him doing to Trike what he had failed to do to his brother, for Cog regretted he had allowed Jay Hoop to live. Hence the upgraded particle weapon. Certainly, by keeping the Client here and staying with her, he had secured the best route back to Trike.

Trike shook his head, annoyed about this surge of paranoia. It stank of the kind of madness he had resolved to avoid. Anyway, that was a minor concern, while the major one headed rapidly towards him. The Jain ship sat well behind the leading edge of the cloud, as that came into range. Just as they had done against Orlandine's and Diana's defences around Jaskor, the knots began lining up like ammunition belts for bacilliforms, acting as linear accelerators. Time to test the weapons.

Trike decided not to show all his cards at once, so used the core's grasers first. They stabbed out from multiple installations across its armour, and a thousand bacilliforms exploded to vapour in one pass. In a second pass, this spreading cloud of vapour revealed the beams like silvery needles. But it was similar to shooting locusts in a plague of them. Looking for advantage, Trike studied the scan returns of the two attacks and saw that bigger detonations ensued when he hit bacilliforms which had loaded with knots. He altered the program and made a third pass. Two hundred shots hit home. He observed one of them closely. The beam entered the mouth of the bacilliform just as a knot slid into the back end. The thing exploded first with jets of plasma out of each end. The jet to the rear hit knots lined up behind and blew them apart, but only two or three. This did, however, reveal how the knots bunched together. It would be useful in regard to another weapon he intended to use, but the density of the Jain tech out there needed to reach a certain level. So he again erected the completely enclosing hardfield . . .

The Jain mother ship drew steadily closer, but had slowed its approach. Was the creature inside being wary and assessing the situation, or waiting for something? Its shield was down so Trike checked through his weapons inventory to see what might be useful. None of his plain energy weapons were capable of delivering a hard enough punch. Railgun slugs and missiles of various designs could hurt the thing, as could the different kinds of disruptors at his disposal. But even with energy beams travelling at light speed, the ship would have time to sling up its hardfield. Meanwhile the clouds of Jain mechanisms lying between would soak up far too high a percentage of shots. One thing at a time.

The cloud swirled around the core's hardfield and more and more mechanisms gathered close. He counted them, analysed their distribution across vacuum and made blast radius calculations. Meanwhile, as knots rained down on his hardfield and stuck there, he observed their steady incursion into his systems. Spread on the field, they were able to penetrate it, as if oozing through a shimmershield, and fire low-intensity lasers towards the core. Shutting down his sensors to that section of the emitted spectrum reduced his data-gathering to an unacceptable level, so he kept them receiving and countered the virtual attack with computer life of his own. The things also caused a complex resonance back through the hardfield generators – another route for virtual attack. He had to add into his assessments how far he could allow these incursions into his systems, and into his mind. It took him a few microseconds to finish those calculations, and set the limit at twenty-two minutes.

Within the command deck of the ship's core, Trike once again started physically detaching from the computer architecture around him. His connection to its systems began to degrade, but he knew he could adapt to this. Networking was the answer. The thousands of core biomechs, all in contact with that system and with him, opened his data channels much more than just via the transceivers on his skin. He began integrating the remotes into it too, as he loaded them with subpersonae, finally walking out onto the platform around the control deck with ninety-eight per cent contact. He strode to the edge and peered down at remotes swarming on the floor below, then considered his vulnerability as a single and relatively small biological being. That needed to change. Searching his memory, and his inherited memory from Orlandine, he at once found out how to resolve it, and sent out a call.

Ten minutes had passed and the distribution of the Jain mechanisms out in vacuum lay well within his predictions. Trike checked his weapons again. He had five hundred of the disruptor weapons available. A single massed firing from them, of one shot each, would require sixty per cent of his programming capacity and drain twenty per cent of stored power. He calculated he could afford another two shots per weapon after that, and remaining power would have to go into the various drive systems. His attention, externally, strayed to Adranas, the planet the core presently orbited. Slingshot, he decided. Hit and run and then massive recharging. The solar panels would provide a meagre amount, while the U-space interrelation between hardfield and drive would provide the rest. Eventually the underlying twist, which stored up energy from attacks on the hardfield, presently lay quiescent since nothing had hit that field with substantial force.

Responding to his call, a biomech floated through the thin air to land on the platform beside him. The spherical thing was like the one that had originally attacked Cog when they first entered this place. He stepped over and rested his hand on it, injecting Jain tendrils. He did make connections and reprogram the thing, but mainly filled it with tendrils, which began feeding on less essential systems and expanding. When it had grown inside sufficiently, he loaded across a schematic from Orlandine's memory. It was the Jain device, like a monstrous woodlouse, which she had implanted herself in before interrogating the submind of the Wheel. When he finally pulled his hand away and stepped back, his body mass had dropped by ten per cent. However, this was necessary. Though the biomech possessed the memory space to take the general plan of the device, it could never take a schematic for Jain tech itself. No one had made a schematic that accurately depicted its pico-scale structures, therefore he needed a substantial chunk of the stuff to propagate. He blinked and nodded, and the biomech rose into the air to shoot over the edge of the platform and down, heading for the large bioreactor just below the Species living space here.

Another ten minutes passed as he made further preparations. Down below, on every one of the fifty floors of this Species living area, the remotes were lining up in ranks. He blinked and set them in motion. He watched them flowing out into the tunnels through the ship, heading out towards the doors. They moved fast under internal EM and grav-drives, zipping through the tunnels like bullets, then dropping to the walls and locking down like thousands of giant metallic aphids.

He turned his attention to the bioreactor and saw the biomech had arrived, splitting open over a portal and dumping its load inside. This task was the limit for it, and the biomech then peeled up and fell away, dead. Inside, the mass of Jain tech made its connections and loaded the schematic, before worming its way towards the centre of the bioreactor. The reactor began to draw in materials and Trike realized that, like the biomech, it would not survive the task he had set it.

*Two minutes . . .*

Trike flipped over to programming the disruptors, taking them to a high-energy setting, calculating EMR and U-space effects. These became virtual Mandelbrot sets and strayed to the limits of conventional physics where they twisted the base format of matter. He required an imbalance of the small forces of atomic adhesion. Physical results were the generation of optical microcavities, time crystals, excitons combining with photons to create polaritons, as well as negative mass effects and shaped gravity waves. In entirety, these would cause the usual disruption of

343

matter on the mega-scale. But the resulting fast-moving atomic nuclei would develop into something usually achieved with radioactive elements: fission.

The virtual warfare incursions were taking up a substantial portion of his processing space and, though thirty seconds of his count remained, he decided he could wait no longer. As if clicking a switch in his own skull, he shut down the hardfield around the core. The thing disappeared, leaving a patchwork wall of spread-out knots, which began to fragment and fall towards him. These were not his primary target, so he hit them with grasers and lasers above and fired up the core's fusion drives underneath. Seven flames speared down, incinerating knots there. Those above exploded at the tips of needling silvery beams, while amber lasers ate up their remaining chunks nearer to the core's armour. The core rose up out of the swarm and Trike kept two hundred target acquisitions to the forefront of his mind, constantly checking vectors and adjusting. Then it was time to fire.

Like glass drills, the disruptor beams reached out and, because they were moving slower than light, it seemed the core was extruding them. He observed the effect of the first strikes. A baciliform unravelled, and a knot flew apart, while a knot progenitor lost its upper shield. Its lower body broke into six segments then splintered, shedding half-generated knots. One of the curved things like a giant sickle cell straightened abruptly and peeled open like a banana. This initial destruction was minimal, but the phase changes of the matter ensued. Chunks of these mechanisms spread out, shimmering like psychedelic ice, producing a haze around them like St Elmo's fire. Then they collapsed. It was quick, when it happened, and almost simultaneous across the targets struck. Each piece became a fission bomb.

Trike ramped up acceleration as he selected and fired on other targets. The core groaned, a deep throaty cathedral sound. Already the gravity of Adranas was impinging. Blast after blast filled space all around, spreading growing spheres of light. Where these intersected with other mechanisms, they blew apart too – origami hit by a flamethrower. New targets were deeper in the cloud, more widely dispersed now Trike could see the total effect. Each blast ripped out nearly a thousand miles across, their waves of fast-moving particles and EMR as destructive at their fronts as particle beams. Sensors gradually degraded as they ramped up their filtering. Black maculae spread across vacuum, then faded to reveal cooling red waves of fire, while still other blasts lit like small suns.

Nearby, in terms of human vision, Adranas grew. Most of the Jain mechanisms between Trike and this object were gone now, leaving only glittering particles and streamers of dull orange, turned black in silhouette over the planet itself. Trike felt a moment of doubt and fear when he saw hexagonal patterns multiplying across the face of that orb. Jain tech grew there, converting the whole planet into a weapon for the thing in that ship behind. But then he dismissed it. In the end, he knew, this conflict would not be about just firepower.

As the ship's core dragged in around the planet, he focused on the mother ship. Accelerating again, hardfield up, it nudged through the continuing explosive destruction. He smiled on seeing he had just eaten up forty per cent of the cloud that had accompanied it. He lost his smile when he saw the giant attack ships detaching from its body, fed and recharged, and almost certainly about to head his way.

**The Client**

Weapons Platform Mu now lay on the other side of the sun from the giant hot planet Adranas and the action going on there.

However, the Client had scattered attack pods all the way round to keep watch. Their coms, via very tight beam terahertz emissions, were difficult to penetrate with virtual warfare. Though the Client was well aware they were not beyond the attacking Jain, should it turn its attention this way. It had not. In this orbital position, she also had a direct line of sight to Jaskor. Imagery required cleaning because of the cloud wrapped around that world, and she took care with coms from there in light of the virtual warfare surrounding the planet, which was as fierce as the physical conflict. But, again, no enemy there had focused in the Client's direction.

She soon had a good view of events in the Jaskoran system. However, it had not been a view she wanted. By now she could have been away from the worst of all this, taking a polar route out of the system to avoid Jaskor, as well as Adranas and the outer gas giant. Even now, Jain-tech devices were still spewing from the runcible gate on its surface. So why was she still here?

Poised on her crystal tree, she gazed down at the Old Captain Cogulus Hoop. He sat cross-legged on the floor with his particle weapon casually balanced on his lap. Despite his bulk, he could snatch it up and fry her with the nasty thing in less than a second. An hour ago, this had been a problem, but not any longer. The platform robots, and the few remotes she had retained from their duties transporting the Species remains, had been busy. Now, outside her environment cylinder, twenty-six lasers tracked the man's every move. Their combined firing, even though she had dialled down their intensity to prevent them damaging the cylinder chain-glass, would be enough to incinerate him in one-point-two seconds. Maybe that would not be enough, but the EMP mine below the floor where he sat – a mobile thing with spider legs ready to follow him if he moved – should be enough to burn out the workings of his weapon. The planar explosive component of the mine could disrupt his aim, if not cut him in half, when its flat, directed blast sliced through the floor.

*Why do I not remove this hindrance?* The reply was almost a mental shrug. She did not want to kill the man, in fact she rather liked him. She also had a sense that there was more to events here in this system than just the attack of a powerful xenophobic alien.

'So what's happening out there?' Cog abruptly asked, looking up.

'Trike has managed to destroy a substantial portion of the Jain cloud,' she replied. 'He is now in tight orbit of Adranas.'

'Good boy,' said Cog.

'Possibly a short-lived one since the Jain mother ship is detaching attack ships to go after him.'

Cog grunted, shrugged. 'And Jaskor?'

'Orlandine is securing the world – she has in fact spread around its surface. The remainder of the fleet is struggling to keep the cloud, wormships and sequestered platforms at bay.'

'Not so good then.' Cog stood up and stretched. 'Any chance I can get anything to eat here? I'm tired of supping on the stuff this suit supplies, tastes like shit.'

'Haven't you forgotten something?' the Client enquired.

Cog looked down at the weapon lying on the floor. 'It would seem like that, but I'm not stupid enough to be unaware of the limitations of my threat. How many weapons have you got pointing at me now?'

'Debatably twenty-seven.'

'But I gave you pause to consider your actions, I think. That I am not a smear of meat paste on this floor suggests you have your doubts about them.'

The Client felt the need to correct him. He wouldn't have been meat paste but ash. She clamped down on the pedantry and said,

'I certainly have some things to consider.' Meanwhile one of her remotes came through a hatch and scuttled towards Cog. He eyed it warily as it drew to a halt before him. She continued, 'My creature will guide you to human quarters where you can see to your needs.'

'Thank you kindly,' said Cog, and followed the remote as it scuttled off.

So what did she have to consider? The general situation had not changed. Her logical course was to flee, leaving the Jain occupied with Orlandine and Trike and then, no doubt, with new Polity and Kingdom forces once the disruption had died. While a vast interstellar war ensued, she would run and run, even going extra-galactic. But her perception of the prador and the humans had utterly changed, and fleeing felt like a betrayal. She also worried she could never flee far enough because there existed some mysterious *connection*. And so, though it had terrified her the first time, she tried to find it again.

It had occurred when she reached out for the remotes Trike had taken from her, but without using the broadcast equipment either on the platform or in her own body. It was the flexing of a limb that did not exist, or looking without eyes. It aped the psychic power that the humans, prador, the Jain and her own kind had dismissed as the product of undeveloped minds in primitive societies. Now she tried again, expecting difficulties, expecting failure. However, the web she had seen before dropped into her mind immediately and alarmingly clear.

The Client gazed at the connections and saw that they linked all Jain tech in the Jaskoran system. They illuminated it so that the clouds, Orlandine, Trike, the mother ship and its attack ships were visible as either bright lights or glowing fogs. This illumination even showed the hole Trike had cut in a large portion of the cloud which the mother ship had dragged with it. Why was it all so clear and easy now? Unlike the wholly organic mentality of a human, all of her mind lay open to her inspection. It took her only a moment to realize the map correlated to the detection of Jain-tech signatures. However, the improving clarity wasn't due to her U-space vision improving but because, as the disruption died, those connections were firming up. She abruptly snapped away from it, terrified by the implications, but then slowly eased back, deliberately suppressing her visceral response.

She focused again, seeking understanding. The strongest links were to the largest mass of Jain tech – the mother ship. All other masses connected. Tracking the link from the ship to her weapons platform, she deep scanned local U-space and matched with strong terahertz scans in the real. A more intricate map appeared – a web through the platform and out to her attack pods. She focused in, tighter and tighter, and finally found something about which to be relieved. None of the connections actually linked to her personally. They extended through the technology she had taken from the Librarian's moon and incorporated into the platform and those pods. And at last she understood the source must be the picotech at the basis of that technology, none of which she had incorporated into her body.

The incredibly small framework of matter at the basis of Jain technology created a U-space signature. She scanned out towards the nearest cloud objects and noted differences in clarity to the signatures. That knot, damaged and falling in towards the sun, stood out clear and bright in U-space, while the stuff around her was blurred and vague. Of course, the final civilization-killing kind had been built on the older Librarian's technology. With growing dread, she extrapolated that the Jain, who had created that final kind, must have utilized this signature effect. It had produced this connectivity and thus the ultimate means to subsume other technology of a similar kind, changing, from the bottom up, any intelligence that used it. This had enabled it to take control of all the other Jain, and absorb them. In sudden panic, she began scanning the technology in the platform for unexpected activity, but found none. Then she realized that told her nothing. The process might be a million years long but, in the end, any creature or civilization in this network would fall to it. She felt sure that anyone connected to it could never hide, and perhaps from the creature in that mother ship. Should she, and could she, clean house?

The Client turned her attention to methodology and began assessing in overview the totality of her knowledge. She first speculated on using disruptors against it, but their gross effect destroyed too much, while she needed something more intricate, surgical. If she destroyed the tech here and in her pods she would end up far too vulnerable. However, by destroying the picotech, she could break the connection, but the larger function of the structures would remain. It would be like killing the cellular life of a tree but the tree still standing for a while.

*A virus?*

'So anyway, what were we talking about?'

Cog had returned from below. She studied him closely, and noted a vague haze about him. Her vision included all her sensors, the U-space ones too. That haze must arise from the Spatterjay virus, which contained the genome of a squad of Jain soldiers. Only by concentrating and cleaning the data could she then see the connections extending from him to the Jain tech on the weapons platform. However, as a distinct entity, he was a viable test subject. She reacted instinctively.

'What the hell!' Cog bellowed, staggering in the flare of the EMP through the floor below him.

He crashed onto his knees, his suit powered down and malfunctioning. The EMP also seared through his flesh with a similar effect to that of the weapon he had once used against Trike, and which resided in a pouch on his belt. As he began to recover, the grapplers and remotes arrived. He drove his fist through the first grappler that reached him, but that did not stop it pulling the weapon from his belt and tossing it to her nearby remote. The creature immediately turned it on him and fired it. Cog tumbled through the air, seemingly under attack from a swarm of shadow bats, and crashed to the floor again.

'Why?' he managed.

'Serendipity,' the Client replied.

# 15

*It being supposed (though still officially unconfirmed) that the giant dreadnought the* Cable Hogue *does exist, then it must have been around for a very long time. Centuries, in fact. Quite likely it existed before the prador/human war, in which case it is outdated. The prador swiftly taught us that our superb high-tech war vessels were not really up to the job of dealing with them. Had their objective been to win the war as fast as possible, rather than revel in their enjoyment of it, they might have won. They gave us time to develop and build better ships, and we drove them back – our industrialized production and AI efficiency did that. Then, as has happened throughout the ages, we came out the other side of the war with big technological advances and better ships. The* Cable Hogue *was not one of them. Sure, the AIs could have majorly upgraded it throughout its life, but it simply cannot be as good as a ship designed and built from the bones up with post-war technology. It therefore seems highly likely to me, what with all the wartime production lingering on, that Earth Central will have built something much better – we just haven't seen it yet.*

From 'How It Is' by Gordon

**Gemmell**

'She's building something,' were the first words Gemmell heard and the first reality to break through in what felt like an age. He groped for contact through his gridlink, for updates, logistics and telemetry, but it seemed as if no hardware lined his skull. Only as an afterthought did he open his eyes.

A deep orange sky hung overhead and sound intruded as of giants shifting boulders in some deep cavern. He saw a spray of meteorites spearing up from the horizon, all but one of them finally going out. The last grew larger and larger, burning overhead, crackling and spitting, then briefly recognizable as a tumbling attack ship weapons nacelle, before it broke into pieces. Gemmell sat up and tracked the fragments towards the Canine Mountains. There, particle beams stabbed out from a high stalk with a head like a giant lily and incinerated them. He wondered if he was dreaming as he transferred his attention down the stalk to the thing from which it had sprouted. There stood a tilted fairy tower, a great pillar seemingly constructed of tangled vines. But it had the shimmer of hardfields visible through the gaps in its structure, and nodules budded along its length.

'What the fuck is that?' he managed, then surveyed his immediate surroundings.

A hand closed on his wrist and he turned to see Ruth squatting beside him. She looked haggard, and as though she'd been dragged through thorny scrub. Line scars, as if from the work of a military autodoc, webbed her face and arms. Baylock and Trantor were here too, and other Polity marines. Two prador crouched at the edge of the building, and the war drone Cutter with his constant companion Bludgeon were busily at work setting up a shield generator.

'It's Orlandine,' said Ruth.

He reached out and traced the lines on her face. 'What have I missed?'

'The planet is hers now, but for how long we don't know.'

'What happened with us?'

She grimaced and shook her head. 'It took complete control of my body but my mind remained free. It worked me like a puppet. She took control of the thing and made it leave my body . . . knocked me unconscious for that. With you, it took longer. It was in your skull.' She reached up and touched the scars on her face. 'We're the lucky ones, because she knows us. Thousands of others are on ice because they are too badly injured.' She hesitated for a second. 'Others . . . still have those things inside them, but they're hers.'

'Hers?' he asked, not sure what she meant.

'There are citizens taking up weapons who didn't before. She's controlling them.'

'I see.' Desperate times did call for desperate measures, but it seemed they hadn't been fighting against annihilation but against total enslavement. Was partial enslavement acceptable? He didn't know about that, but felt he did not deserve to be alive and free like this. A surge of sick guilt rose inside him as he remembered his intentions. It was difficult to integrate, because the person who had been about to blow up this city seemed indistinguishable from him now. This illuminated how easily he could be the enemy he fought. Just a change in the data, or clicking over a few switches on twisted neuronal paths in his skull, could do it. He hoped Orlandine fully understood that truth. Abruptly he reached out, took hold of Ruth's shirt, and pulled her into a kiss. It made him feel more human.

'What was that for?' she asked when they were done.

'Do you need to ask?'

She frowned. 'No, I guess not.'

He stood up shakily from the foam mattress and again tried his gridlink. This time it came on but it took him a moment to understand the change. It had been formatted back to its base settings. All his data were gone but, most importantly, the gridlink now only possessed standard defences against virtual warfare – they weren't even military spec. Searching available comlinks he found thousands, and not one of them could he yet trust. He then checked for messages and found only one:

*All your data were corrupt and I had to wipe it. Talk to Bludgeon. Orlandine.*

Trantor and Baylock approached and, as they did so, two new comlinks appeared to his internal perception. He still felt shaky and unsure. They certainly looked like those of the two soldiers but that could be coincidental. He wasn't going to open himself to anything until he had some defences back.

'Report,' he stated, now heading over towards the two drones. Trantor, Baylock and Ruth followed him.

'Verbal?' Trantor enquired.

'Yes,' he tapped his skull. 'My link is down. Make it brief and concise.'

'About the situation down here?'

'Of course,' said Gemmell, puzzled by the question.

The man scowled then said, 'All the cities are . . . secure. Over fifteen thousand true deaths in the planetary population, over eight hundred in the marines, fifty-eight prador and twenty-three AIs including drones and Golem. A further twelve thousand citizens had backups and have been or are being retrieved.'

Gemmell nodded. Trantor did not include the twelve thousand in the 'true deaths' because they were recoverable. The low casualty rate surprised him, but it appeared the Jain attack had been all about sequestration, until the end there – when *something* had decided to try to blow up this city.

'Then there are others,' Baylock interjected. 'Over two thousand from all of those Orlandine put on ice – they might be recoverable but are Jain infected.'

'Their location?'

'Widely scattered.'

'You have their locations?'

'Yes.'

'Okay. And the surviving civilian population?'

'That's been difficult. We have two million or so here packed in at locations we have made as secure as possible. We considered trying to do the same with the rest, but Orlandine advised against it.'

'Why?'

'Single hit, higher death rates or sequestration. Better to leave them distributed in their own homes where possible.'

'I see.' Filling a building with people and surrounding it with guards and autoweapons just made a tastier target for a Jain knot, or some heavy weapons strike. Gemmell moved on, addressing them both: 'Munitions?'

'Down to the dregs but we're being resupplied,' Trantor replied.

Gemmell stopped to peer at the man questioningly.

'Orlandine,' Trantor explained.

Gemmell nodded, not actually sure what that meant. He really needed his gridlink working properly and access to the ECS data sphere, if it still existed.

'The surface is relatively secure, but how long that will last we don't know.' Trantor looked up at the sky. 'That shitstorm up there . . .'

Gemmell held his hand up to stop him as they had reached the two drones. 'I want detailed reports to integrate when I can – get on that.' He turned to Baylock as Trantor moved off. 'Those people Orlandine put on ice. Despite her advice, I want them collected up and secured in one location. And I want Mobius Clean working on them – they sound like just his thing.'

'Well, Orlandine did give us their locations . . .'

'Exactly.'

She too moved off and then Gemmell faced the two drones. They had mounted a shield projector in a framework at the edge of the building. He noted the shaped charge on the side of it and surmised it was to blow the thing over that edge should it overload.

'Orlandine told me to talk to you,' he said, addressing Bludgeon.

The bulky drone, which looked like a dust mite the size of a grav-car, twitched its head towards him. Its eyes were matt black and red light rippled across them. The head, small in relation to his body, consisted of two long mandibles below the narrow crown. These, rather than pointed as would be the case in a true dust mite, were hollow tubes. From one of them protruded a power bayonet, which the drone now sucked back inside.

'I have sent you a flagged comlink,' said Bludgeon, and no more.

'Excuse his terseness. He's very busy hunting down nasty things in the data sphere.'

Gemmell looked up at Cutter and felt a mild horripilation. He had known the mantis drone to be all atomically sharp edges but being this close gave him the same unease he felt when standing next to a long drop. The thing sweated danger.

'I see the link,' he supplied.

'Then open it and all will be revealed.'

Gemmell hesitated over this link. He could see the bandwidth would be huge and quite enough for another intelligence to take over his hardware and thence his mind. But if that were the aim it would have happened already. He opened the thing.

It felt as if he had just attached a fire hose to his skull, such was the flood of data. He tried to parse it in general overview and saw his stock of virtual warfare programs climbing rapidly and then opening out more storage space in the crystals and organo-metalloids lining the inside of his skull. The operational parameters of these programs began to load to his organic brain and he saw they improved on their predecessors. Other links also began to open, gradually reacquiring his feeds from the ECS data sphere. Telemetry came first, along with new software to sort and consolidate it. The present statuses of everyone under his command became available to him, in general or in as much detail as he required, via download links to the sphere. History loaded next: all events since he had woken aboard *Morgaine's Gate*, again in general or in as much detail as he wanted. Logistics blossomed from all of these across his mind. He chose munitions and followed some links, seeing in real time a series of industrial fabricators, draped with Jain tentacles, frenetically printing a variety of weapons. He realized that this production must be more about making him, his soldiers and the citizenry feel either effective or safe. In reality, if Orlandine could not keep the attacking Jain tech from taking over Jaskor, then they were done.

And Orlandine was everywhere.

Thousands of cam views helped him build up a picture. A drone flying along one coast showed the beaches seemingly punctuated by curved pipelines. Like giant growths of lichen, tangled masses of the tech spread across the continent. Lianas wove up to mountaintops and had sprouted sensory arrays. Growths like giant fungi scattered the landscape and usually possessed a high heat signature as a sign of frenetic internal workings. Black flowers of photoelectric panels bloomed, fairy towers grew, and animals which were once wild flowed across the land now in ordered formations. But all of this was only what was visible to the human visual spectrum. Other sensors picked up seabeds strewn with writhing growth, substantial changes in ocean temperature, while ashore the landscape was shifting. Because of all the burrowing and *growing* down below, earthquakes came in regular spasms. Caps over eruptions sucked up energy, as on Sambre Island where a thing like a woodlouse's carapace had closed off the volcano. Gemmell recognized this as Orlandine's device but grown immense. The rest of the island there lay under a tangled mass of Jain trunks hundreds of feet thick. Orlandine covered the entire surface of the planet and, according to geo-imaging, penetrated down to the magma in many places. Gemmell, despite his stomach turning over, decided to speak to her.

'*Orlandine,*' he said, through the distinct link Bludgeon had provided.

'*Gemmell,*' she replied, succinctly and almost like a human.

For a long moment he just did not know what to say, then he managed, '*Can you keep Jaskor safe?*'

With a hint of irritation she replied, '*Look to the skies, man.*' And the link closed.

Gemmell came back to himself with a start. Concentrating on his link, he had downgraded other sensory input. He now heard soldiers, no longer subvocalizing through their comlinks, but shouting orders and instructions. Other sounds impinged too, other sensory input, and he knew something major was happening.

'Ruth?' He looked round.

'It's coming down,' she said, and pointed.

A deep bass groan rumbled through the air and up through the soles of his feet from the building. He looked at the sky just as Orlandine had instructed, to the horizon opposite the Canine Mountains, then felt his ears pop and saw a great swirl of cloud flowing out from just one area, as if pouring in from another universe. The orange firmament grew lighter, throwing those spreading tatters of cloud into dark silhouette, like shards of iron. Something started to nose through with all the apparent slow majesty of a giant cruise ship coming into harbour. It was a flaming city, a great slab of metals and composites that had no business intruding on this small world. He squinted at it, trying to adjust for scale and still not quite getting it. Then came an 'ah' moment as he realized he was witnessing a weapons platform falling to earth. He knew he should be frightened. But this reminded him of dreams he had when a child, of standing on a shore and witnessing a giant wave coming in, knowing that nothing he could do would make one whit of difference because he was as good as dead, and might as well enjoy the spectacle.

Fifty miles of composites and metals fell fully into view, coming down at an angle, as Gemmell belatedly updated on events outside of Jaskor in his gridlink. Weapons Platform Magus, sitting inside the defences erected by Orlandine and Diana Windermere, had been occupied by hostile Jain tech. The platform was already on the move by the time the fleet up there discovered this. Ships had closed in, attempting to destroy it, but the tech there had sequestered the platform's defences. In a very short time, it became evident that they could not stop it falling to the planet, whether in one piece or not. Either way, the impact shocks and destruction would be about the same. Orlandine ordered the ships to pull back. She had this.

'The tower. It's moving,' said Ruth.

And so it was. The tilted fairy tower beyond the Canine Mountains shifted and tracked. Gemmell stared at the thing, wondering what titanic projectile it might launch, and what difference it would make to the small vulnerable human beings standing on top of this building in this city, or to all the people down here. The thing was skimming in towards the middle of the continent. Right on top of where he stood, in fact. He thought about weapons to deploy, about tactics, and then dismissed all of that from his gridlink. He felt the urge to laugh hysterically but then clamped down on it.

The hollow inside the tower darkened and something shot out. A great clump of glowing matter streaked overhead towards the platform, its glow increasing as it travelled. The thing stretched out and shed fire as projectiles and energy weapons struck it but did nothing to slow it. The thing slammed against a scaling of hardfields. The platform jerked upwards, spewing molten projectors. Burning chunks rained down from the impact, cooling as they fell. Many of these crashed into the plains beyond the city. They reminded Gemmell of detritus spewed from a volcano, as the tower fired again and again.

'What the hell is she firing?' he asked.

Ruth glanced at him. 'Molten rock.'

He checked in the data sphere, looked at the tactic involved and saw that Orlandine had taken the most effective option available to her. She did not have time to get a foothold on the platform and seize control of it, nor did she have time to whittle away its defences using energy weapons or hyper-accelerated railgun slugs. The greatest danger from this platform was its sheer mass coming down on the continent. If that happened, there would really be nothing left for her to defend, other than herself. So she was slinging massive objects at it to push it off course.

The battle continued as the platform descended. Multiple strikes blew out thousands of projectors until its defence grew patchy. He saw one projectile get through, hammering against the thing in a great molten explosion and showering down through the air like an immense firework. He realized, as it edged above, that Orlandine had already managed to change its course, for it now passed over them. With a thump he felt to the core of his being, the view distorted slightly and he realized the two drones had just put up the hardfield here, just in time. Miles out from the city, he saw a particle beam hit ground and swing across, burning a trench hundreds of feet wide and deep. Next, the sonic crack of railgun slugs raised vertical eruptions from the ground, followed by giant blisters exploding into the sky. He saw one hit home in the city, leaving a glowing hole through a roadway and, shortly afterwards, fire jetting from a thousand drains to throw heavy metal covers high into the air. Next a tower block, fire blowing out of its windows from top to bottom, collapsed as if it had been filleted. The casualty count, now real time in his telemetry, reeled up another eight thousand lives.

As more and more of Orlandine's projectiles struck home, the thing rumbled on over, shaking the ground. Gemmell watched it falling down behind the mountains, and then through cam feeds he saw it nosing at a slant into the sea just beyond the coast. Millions of tons of metals and composites hammered down, the whole platform turning upright as it ploughed along the seabed, compacting in a giant train wreck that lasted for nearly twenty minutes. He lost sight of it all behind a vast explosion of steam, debris and fire. This then boiled up behind the mountains and swept towards them.

'Are we going to die?' Ruth asked.

He could not find an answer for her.

### Diana

Diana had no doubt that the wormships were adapting. Their hardfields had started deflecting the new weapon and those strikes that got through caused disintegration but no fission blast. Their advantage had evaporated but at least the wormships had withdrawn, temporarily, which gave the fleet time to deal with another problem.

Thousands of railgun slugs vaporized against layered hardfields while the platform, whose name Diana simply did not know, spewed projectors like an ancient battleship firing incendiary shells. The break came, as it had many times before, and one of the remaining five Polity dreadnoughts with the new weapon opened fire. The platform bucked on the fission blast and broke in half. Those two halves then began to disintegrate, spreading debris. Where these struck other solid matter the collapse spread, so fleet ships threw up hardfields and got out of the way fast. The Jain-tech devices of the cloud were not so smart and many of them shattered to pieces, but still, the percentage of the cloud this destroyed sat below one.

'Got you, you fucker,' said Jabro.

Diana glanced across at him, blinking sore eyes in the smoke haze the extractors had failed to pull from the bridge. It was a victory since that had been the last of the sequestered platforms, and now nothing remained to the enemy of equivalent size. There would, she hoped, be no more platforms or ships sequestered. Analysis of the process had resulted in new protocols and better virtual warfare defences. In the last hour, they had lost ten platforms but at least the enemy had not taken control of them. The moment their AIs knew they were unrecoverable, they accelerated into the cloud and ejected, detonating everything they had and opening their defences to hits from the new disruptor beams from their own side. Most of those AIs were now down on the surface of Jaskor, just a few others tumbling off into deep space. Little remained of the platforms themselves other than fast-moving and chaotic debris.

As the intensity of the battle ebbed, Diana replayed some recent events in her mind. The fall of Weapons Platform Magus on Jaskor could have been much more catastrophic. The sea absorbed some of the impact but mainly Orlandine had ameliorated it. Without her intervention, the thing would have gone down, smack-bang, in the middle of the continent and main city at four hundred miles an hour. It had been under drive and using grav and no doubt this speed was the maximum allowable on impact without severely damaging or destroying the Jain mycelium aboard. As it was, her attack had snuffed its drive and it hit the sea at two hundred miles an hour. This had not been enough to cause the complete disintegration of such a tough object. Just the first fifteen miles of it had compacted and the rest – an immense tower thirty-five miles tall – was crashing onto the edge of the continent even now.

'Can they survive that?' asked Jabro.

'A firestorm and two-hundred-mile-an-hour winds,' Diana stated. 'Some will die.'

But what else about the situation down there? Eruptions and other seismic activity had climbed, and landmasses had changed shape. Fluctuations in sea temperature had completely altered weather patterns on the planet – some big cyclones were swirling into life while their smaller kin began to punctuate lines curving down from the poles. Tsunamis were also in motion, though the fact that none were heading towards the coastal cities demonstrated Orlandine's grip on it all. And then there was the haiman woman herself.

Could Diana any longer describe Orlandine as a woman, or as a human being? At what stage of a person's transformation into *that*, did such descriptions cease to be relevant? Gazing at the planet as a whole from orbit revealed many changes to the distribution of planetary matter. Strange masses and towering growths were visible but, unless you knew what the planet had been like before, these could have been natural formations. Focusing in, however, revealed so much more. Growths webbed the entire world, with many of them visible from orbit as hundreds of feet thick and thousands of miles long. Focusing in more and more showed these things branching and branching again, getting smaller and smaller to the limit of scan, as small as fungal mycelia on the surface. Orlandine was further rising to the threats out here. Did this mean Diana could pull her ships away? No, not really, and with this portion of the cloud gathered around them being millions of miles deep, they had nowhere to go.

She transferred her attention outwards again, and her immediate concern was the fleet. The destruction wrought upon it had made it necessary to tighten the perimeter about Jaskor to maintain the defence, and many of the remaining ships would soon be touching the outer atmosphere . . . if they were lucky. All of them were using up the dregs in their armouries. Even the *Hogue*'s major weapons were down to two particle weapons and intermittent firing of its DIGRAW. And now the cloud and the remaining wormships seemed to be swirling up for some final push.

She watched as a swarm of wormships began to pull together into a stream far out in equatorial orbit, then saw this begin to turn in. Close focus revealed those ships were actually touching each other to produce a semi-solid mass. It was like a spike to its forward end, but one twenty miles across at its thickest point.

'Gravity weapon,' she suggested.

'Lucky if I'll have it working in an hour,' Dulse replied.

She wondered why, of all places in the defence, that spike aimed directly at her. Surely the best option would have been to go for the weakest area? This told her much about the combative psychology directing this attack.

'We don't have an hour,' she said.

'I can't ignore physics,' Dulse observed.

Diana again checked the *Hogue*'s armouries, and decided not to say anything about the pounding that known Polity physics had recently taken.

'*We're in trouble*,' she said to the ship's AI.

'*We can hold them for a few minutes, but it is almost certain that one of them will get through to our hull thereafter*,' the AI replied. '*We could concentrate more ships here but that would mean more Jain tech raining down on the planet elsewhere.*'

'Those wormships are the greater threat,' she said aloud, also broadcasting, even as Hogue sent the latest tactical updates to the fleet.

Ships and weapons platforms began moving around the planet to her position, leaving huge gaps through which Jain tech could enter atmosphere. Within an hour, they had massed below the approaching wormships, just tens of miles apart, nudging each other with hardfields and constantly laser-measuring distances and repositioning. The wormships drew closer and closer, like the nose of a tornado spiking to earth.

'Okay, I think that's close enough,' said Diana, the order to fire from Hogue in the tactical update.

The first fusillades of railgun slugs sped out – a mass firing that flared around the threat, highlighting hardfields, like scales on a lizard's tail, but seemed to have little effect at all beyond shredding just a few wormships. Energy weapons and disruptors next. There were two definite hits followed by fission bursts, but the spike shed the disrupting vessels and blocked them with hardfields as it finally reached the fleet. Diana gazed straight into the face of hundreds of wormships bearing down on her. The *Hogue*'s particle cannons droned and roared for just three minutes, incinerating the leaders and then sucking dry.

'*Get out of the way.*'

It took her a moment to realize the source of this communication as she felt, like biting flies landing on her skin, the impact of a series of wormships on the *Hogue*'s hull. The constant thumping of overloaded field projectors marked a counterpoint rhythm as she rolled her ship away from the path of the thing. It was Orlandine who had spoken.

'Where do we go?' she asked, for the other ships, not for her own.

A map of the world fell into her mind with areas highlighted. One small area was on the main continent, but most were across ocean. She needed clarification. She needed to understand Orlandine's intent. But no time remained. Towers down on the surface had begun firing, their missiles cutting hot streaks up through atmosphere, an EMR howl as they passed Diana's ships.

'Fucking hell!' exclaimed Jabro.

Diana absorbed scan data. The things were iron cored and coated in a ceramic that enabled them to withstand atmospheric ablation and heating. Though they were travelling quite slowly in terms of ship railgun slugs, they were ridiculously heavy, the smallest weighing in at a few tons. The simple brute force of their immense impacts could not be without effect. The worm-ship formation broke on a series of huge explosions. Diana blinked, then selected out all the ships and platforms which didn't have disruptors and sent her orders:

'Land here,' she commanded.

Those ships should have included the *Hogue* itself since it had no disruptor weapon, being prone to failure if it came under gravity-wave stresses, which reminded her . . .

'The DIGRAW?' she asked again.

'Ready, but twenty per cent chance of failure,' came the reply.

'Use the damned thing.'

The *Hogue* seemed to twist around her and she heard rumbling crashes from deep within the ship. She knew, without renewing her data, that the gravity weapon had fired for the last time. The wave sped out, a ripple of distortion to all sensors, and struck the milling swarm of wormships, wrenching through them and tearing a large number apart. But though this broke many and disorganized the rest, she had already seen how they could connect up again and reform.

'Getting incursions through the hull,' said Seckurg.

'Noted,' she replied, then to Hogue said, *'This ship is no longer an effective weapon.'*

*'Agreed, except for in one instance,'* replied the AI.

*'You know my mind and you agree?'*

*'Of course.'*

Aloud she said, 'Set everything for full destruction on the strike – as much damage as possible.' She sent the tactical plan to her whole crew and saw the physical reaction as it hit home. Most looked round at her dejectedly. Others, like Jabro, froze for a moment, then just continued with their work.

*'I have also set the bridge pod for ejection,'* said Hogue.

*'And yourself.'*

*'Transferring now.'*

Wormships massed all around and space was full of the fire from Orlandine's constant barrage. Hogue went offline, but briefly, as Diana sent the great ship out, deeper into the attacking mass, heading for the greatest concentration of wormships.

'Pull in behind me and be ready for my firing instructions,' she told those ships and platforms with working disruptors, just as the *Hogue* AI's transport sphere floated into the bridge. The whole crew looked round as it locked down, then checked their harnesses and interface armour.

Now the atmosphere of Jaskor really stirred up as giant weapons platforms, and prador and Polity dreadnoughts, descended. There were further impacts on the hull as the *Hogue* pulled away from that. Constant power draw to antipersonnel weapons on the armour and then inside. Maintenance robots and other internal defenders moved into action. Through cams, Diana saw worms of Jain tech boring through infrastructure – burning tool faces like nightmare rock-boring machines tearing through walls and memory metal beams. The impact rate was climbing, the great ship shuddering.

'Do it soon or you won't get a clean ejection,' Hogue stated through the intercom. Blast doors slammed down all around the bridge.

'Now,' said Diana, unsure if it was she or the AI that hit the mental eject button. Acceleration slammed against them, with contraction of mental imagery to the bridge pod itself, as they flew down a long tunnel out into fire. Snakes stretched and snapped for the pod but then dropped away. Next disruptor beams drew red-hot bars through vacuum. There were hundreds of impacts on the hull of the great ship, boring inside, some blocked by hardfields of writhing wormships there. Multiple, hot white detonations flashed as Diana rode out fast ahead of a storm of debris. Behemoth weapons platforms jetted fusion flames and curved away, with reavers and Polity dreadnoughts seemingly packed together in confusion. The bridge pod dodged and weaved and suddenly Jaskor lay clear ahead, lit by the vast, bright explosion behind. A worm-ship reached for the bridge pod, but disappeared as a missile strike gutted it. Then the pod hammered down into atmosphere.

'Hogue?' Diana asked.

The AI did not reply and she knew, with utter certainty, that its transport sphere was empty. In the view behind, she saw the massive firestorm at the centre of a spreading debris field – a field that was eating up wormships. Between her and this fled the Polity and prador ships, and weapons platforms. But the *Cable Hogue* and its AI were gone.

## Gemmell

A windstorm had wiped out two skyscrapers and dumped seemingly half a continent of debris on the city before dying down. And then the temperature began to rise. Gemmell supposed this wasn't surprising. The sky, now mostly a deep, dark orange, indicated neither day nor night and he had to check his gridlink to be sure. It was early in the morning, and apparently time for breakfast. He watched Ruth approaching, carrying two steaming bowls with spoons dunked in them. Her gait was unsteady in the sway of the building from the earlier wind, and a constant rumbling earthquake. He focused upwards again.

A chaotic mosaic of meteor showers cut the orange sky. Railgun shots from the surface streaked up, and explosions bloomed in wreaths of purple and grey cloud. He homed in on an object. Twisting and casting off pieces, a wormship was coming down. Meanwhile on the ground a hundred-foot-tall flower, which had risen from the trench surrounding the city, turned and folded open mirror petals, stabbing out a glassy beam to track it. The ship froze up and seemed to turn crystalline for a moment before shattering, showering down in the Canines hard enough to blow the top from a mountain. Gemmell watched in horror as the collapse continued. Where other debris landed, the rock exploded to dust and sheared away – holes in mountainsides expanded as if some god had dropped a powerful acid there. The disruptor effect . . . could it spread to the whole planet? He posed the question and routed it through the link to Orlandine. A file of formulae arrived and he set it to give him a less technical précis. Apparently, gravity had a dampening effect, forcing conventional molecular adhesion back on track. There would, however, be holes.

But the wormships were not the only things in the sky.

The one he had just seen destroyed had missed two reavers and an old-style prador dreadnought coming in. These severely battered ships might not make it to the ground in one piece. They shuddered through the air, flinging out the flames of sputtering steering thrusters. The reavers seemed to be managing, but the dreadnought between them kept dropping hard then righting itself, with the delay before each recovery increasing. Then the sky darkened and filled with thousands of black lines. More wormships? No. Gemmell saw grabs thumping home on the prador dreadnought and trying to grip the hard armour, scrambling about on it like spiders on ice. Finally, they did get a hold, just as their source dropped through cloud. Gemmell had never seen one of the big lozenge Polity dreadnoughts in a planetary sky. Behemoths descending here should have inured him to the sight, but had not. Lines tightened with a horrible shrieking as of a broadcast from hell, along with a terrible creeping thrum he recognized as infrasound. The Polity ship had begun to use a soundwave tractor to further buoy up the prador dreadnought. They descended, with the ground exploding upwards in ribbed spirals from the effect of the tractor, masking their final descent. The grabs finally let go and the giant lozenge dreadnought reeled them in as it passed overhead, briefly throwing the city into deep shadow. Gemmell took the bowl Ruth proffered, then remembered to close his mouth.

**The Client**

To manipulate picotech was like trying to construct solids out of shadows by rearranging the objects which cast them.

'Damned ant-chain fuck noodle!' said Cog.

The Client studied him on many levels. The clamps holding

him to the slab were ten-inch-thick ceramal, strengthened further with monofilament diamond. They were the same material used in spaceship docking clamps and yet still the nanite strain gauges imbedded in them showed an improbable load. The man was a shifting fibrous mass who just would not keep still despite them. He had ripped his skin to show the fibrous virus-tangled muscles at his wrists, neck, ankles and thighs where the clamps held him. She had no fear that he would break them, but the virus might alter his form sufficiently for him to escape. She would then have to destroy him, if she could, and this she really did not want to do. His body, the technology inside it and its variations were such a source of new data . . .

'Fuck noodle!' he bellowed, then protruded his tongue, which opened at the end to expose the wad-cutting mouth of a Spatterjay leech.

The Client turned her awareness into the remote now entering his ship aboard the platform. She scuttled up the ramp and, once inside, fired needle-beam masers from the array about her neck. In the small ship's hold, intruder defences burned out. The four induction warfare beams she had on the ship penetrated a moment later, and she entered the system. All her methods were either Polity or her own – her reluctance to use the platform Jain tech was perhaps foolish, since it would have been quicker.

Now controlling the system and aware that, had an AI still run Cog's ship, this would not have been easy, she opened the rear door to its hold. Once through this, she shot up the spiral stair and made her way to the medbay. She studied the reinforced surgical chair there with its super-strong straps. This would never have been strong enough to hold Cog and must have been for Trike – an earlier iteration of that man, anyway. She scanned, searching for what she required, moved over to a wall cupboard and slid out the case it contained, then opened it. Inside rested five squat primitive hollow-needle injectors. She scanned again, seeing one empty of its contents of dilute sprine, closed the case and headed back out.

'Why . . . you doing . . . this?' Cog managed.

Some return of sanity? He was managing to keep his tongue in his mouth and his writhing had diminished. If only she could see this process in more detail. If only she could take him apart to examine his every component . . .

'There are connections, through a realm that lies between U-space and the real, linking together all Jain technology,' she replied – this felt unsatisfying, somehow a justification.

'Connections,' he managed, then his tongue escaped and he started writhing again.

She decided explanations could wait and turned her attention to the technology arrayed all about him. She had two disposable laboratories – two chain-glass spheres packed with advanced robotics and scanning equipment. She had maintenance robots whose specialisms were the rearrangement of matter at the atomic level, and an array of squat cylinders that were factories for producing just about any design of nano-machine, with any biological agent and iterations lying between. Busily at work, these constructed further tools based on disruptor technology. Everything she could think of that might be up to the task of deactivating the picotech of Jain technology lay within her immediate reach. Meanwhile factories throughout the platform stood ready to construct anything else she might need. And she wasn't even sure how to begin.

She again studied the U-space terrain via sensors coming online all around her environment cylinder. Now the picture had become a lot less hazy. The EMR representation showed Cog as a knotted mass of glowing fibres, just as she had earlier visualized him. The glow within him spread out, an organic shifting thing; strands of it reached to other glowing masses in and about her environment cylinder, linking to the Jain tech there. Was this a result of the higher intensity and clarity of her scanning? She calculated what she would have seen with her previous scanners and these still showed those strands much more distinctly than before. This logically implied a correlation between viral activity in him and the strength of this connection. What did that mean?

The Client peeled herself from her crystal tree and down to the floor, heading over to him and her equipment. Her form was now fifty units long, and she wound herself through it all, plugging her multitude of limbs and sensors into sockets she had designed for herself. Even though she had no idea where she should take this, she had at least worked out how to get started. She advanced a robot on Cog – a thing used for taking testing samples from damaged platform infrastructure. It poised over him like a big steel cockroach, extruded a sampling head not dissimilar to the tongue Cog tried to stab at it, dipped down and took a chunk out of his leg. He didn't even notice. Perhaps she should sample elsewhere? From his brain because, as what happened to Trike had shown, there were connections there? She examined that thought and felt uncomfortable with it, and instead focused her attention away from him and on the sampling robot.

She dispatched it to the disposable laboratories. It divided the sample in two and inserted each portion through small ports in the chain-glass of each sphere, where glassy tongues received them and moved them to the central platens. In overview, the samples showed strong links to Cog, and weaker ones to the surrounding Jain tech. She now advanced every scanner within the spheres on those samples. Here the knowledge she had gained from Trike, who had it from Orlandine, assisted her.

The remote finally arrived and followed her instructions, a

terse program dropped into its mind rather than fully engaged. It advanced on Cog, opening the case it had taken from his ship and removing one injector. It uncapped the thick needle and jabbed it into his stomach, then emptied it inside him. Meanwhile the Client continued her investigation, trying to keep her attention away from Cog and on those samples.

She understood much of what she could see and began stripping away the extraneous, shifting it to different positions within the sphere and looking at it via U-space. There were some linkages from Cog's flesh, from the eclectic genomes the virus had collected. Probably the genomes of the squad of Jain soldiers, all of which she copied in electronic form and loaded to her extended memory. But most were from the quantum processing crystals that glowed brightly, linked in a web of light, linked between the two spheres, linked to the surrounding Jain tech and to –

Something had changed.

The links to Cog were fading. What was this? Finally, they returned to the state they had been in before. Cog retracted his tongue with a snap, turned his head as best he could and glared at her.

'What are these connections you were babbling about?' he asked, then after a pause added, 'Fuck noodle.'

Processing the data in her serial mind, the Client felt dumbfounded, and confused. It seemed that the answer she had been seeking – some way to kill off the underlying picotech of Jain tech and thus disrupt those connections – had been provided by millions of years of evolution on Spatterjay: sprine. She studied him through numerous sensors, again eagerly and avidly concentrating on him.

'A way to be free,' she replied. She then forced her attention away from him to the case of sprine injectors her remote had abandoned on the floor.

## Earth Central

The hammerheads surfaced from U-space with a roaring sound that echoed that of submarines breaching – a perfect memory in EC's history files. They were now twenty strong, with additional ships out of the Polity, much to the chagrin of the king of the prador.

Then the submarines hit a rock.

The crash resounded through the inside of the ship to which EC had docked its cube. In the microseconds ensuing, the AI could see the structure twisting, beams splintering and maintenance robots leaping into frenetic activity. A few seconds later, beams began straightening, their splinters closing up and ecologies of nanites pouring into the cracks. Memory metal panels flexed back into shape, while hydraulics straightened out other structures, and the ship filled with the flash of welders and the drone of printer bots. The cacophony of this coagulated into a generalized white noise throughout the eighty miles of the vessel. Damage reports flashed into EC's mind. Thousands of maintenance and repair robots, varying in size from nanites to bots the size of tower blocks, were busily at work.

This was not so good.

The U-space drive network had grown increasingly imbalanced. It had become necessary to drop back into the real for repairs and adjustments. Now, with external sensors and com coming back online, EC began to get an overview of the situation. During the drop, seventy-three kamikazes had not surfaced from U-space, while fifteen materialized with breached containment. Their detonations destroyed fifty-two more and a nearby hammerhead reported terminal damage – just that report; it did not transmit more.

EC could not yet see any stars. Plasma wraiths miles long and a scattering of burning spheres, whose output it necessarily filtered because they were small collapsed-matter fusion fires, blocked them. Wreckage tumbled everywhere. Even as EC watched, a kamikaze, with its side ripped out and something glowing inside, tumbled close to its own cube. EC noted again feelings of mortality – it was none too happy about seeing a mass of gigaton CTDs in a damaged vessel passing so near.

Next, the AI focused on the 'terminally damaged' hammerhead. Here, a drift of wreckage a hundred miles long floated in vacuum, still all connected due to the way these ships had been constructed. The braided meta-material sinews of the ship, running through the hull and much of the interior, held it together. That little of the hull material was visible, while most of the ship's components were, told the AI all it needed to know: it had been turned inside out.

EC assessed and calculated, even as a series of explosions through the hammerhead wreckage removed the last of its ability to transmit or receive. The loss of kamikazes was minimal, though it doubted the prador would see it that way, but the loss of a hammerhead was very bad. The extra fifteen it had brought in were all it had managed to build and some of the most powerful ships the Polity could deploy. At present, only a quarter of the way to the Jaskoran system, they had all received damage. If they jumped again, the disruption would destroy more of them and, by the time they reached Jaskor, the remainder would be in terrible condition. This was not feasible: the gain in time was not worth the loss in ships.

Steadily repairing themselves, the hammerheads would take some days to achieve prime condition. EC dispatched hordes of robots from each of them towards the kamikazes to make repairs there too. It calculated all ships would be jump-ready in five days. However, though U-space disruption would have declined, it would not have declined enough. It needed a further five, or even ten days before the next jump. It would take its fleet to a location near the Jaskoran gas giant, since the gravity well that object created made it an easier target to calculate for. The thing would also offer cover of a kind, which seemed likely to be necessary. Yes, that would be best. EC felt slightly uncomfortable with the notion it had based its decision on the wrecked hammerhead out there, which might have been the one transporting its cube, rather than best tactics.

# 16

*A very old school of evolutionary biology has often proposed that the life of Spatterjay is at a dead end. The rise of the famed virus and the spread of its main transmission vector, the leeches, have brought everything to a halt, it is supposed. The usual slow process of mutation and decimation cannot fill new niches, because the virus adapts creatures to fill them before that can happen. The basic genome of the creatures which are adapted does not change – the virus merely expresses phenotypes it has itself recorded. There will be nothing new, apparently. This is all foolish quibbling because we know that evolution does not advance simply by random mutation. That old school also predicts a world, sometime in the future, occupied only by the leeches and the virus. This is plain wrong. The virus is billions of years old and, according to the fossil record, underwent an upsurge five or six million years ago, during which time it all but wiped out large predatory life forms. They could not feed on smaller creatures if those creatures did not die when eaten. But then came the push back with the evolution of a poison that could kill the virus, a poison that allowed the ingestion of its near-unkillable hosts. This poison was what the hoopers call sprine. And it was something new.*

From 'Quince Guide'
compiled by humans

## Trike

The core groaned and rumbled around Trike as he abruptly took it down lower, its fusion drive howling out flames five miles long behind it. Totally linked into it now, he felt the thin hot wind against its armour as if against his skin, and soon found himself skimming over a flat and seemingly infinite ocean of molten gold. This was swirled through with obsidian black and jade green. Then, having achieved his desired velocity and vector, he shut down the drive and grav planed lower and lower. It was still losing energy, as he had no more available to him than one of Orlandine's weapons platforms did. So nowhere near enough. The core's rumbling and groaning increased, as the gaseous atmosphere thickened and its eddy currents and thousand-mile-an-hour winds began to impinge. Stresses throughout its structure climbed, although nowhere near what it could withstand, but now it was time. He turned on the enclosing hardfield.

All at once, the noises decreased and stress indications began dropping. Standing out on the shelf around the command deck, Trike felt the air seem to grow thick and sluggish. He measured power levels in his mind. Because he had tuned the hardfield to allow a portion of the EMR spectrum inside, the photovoltaic panels all across the hull provided power. Absorbing and converting a large portion of that spectrum supplied enough energy for a modern city, but a fraction of what he needed. He watched the energy draw of the fields sucking on his reserves at a rate of one per cent every few minutes, but noted this slowing. That draw then dropped down towards parity as he entered atmosphere, where high ionization generated a thunderstorm around him. He observed streaks of lightning as wide as monorail trains grounding on the hardfield, and smiled. It had reached parity. The field was now feeding power straight into the underlying U-twist via the

U-space engine, and this in turn automatically topped up his conventional reserves.

The storm grew worse as he fell deeper and the temperature climbed rapidly. Physical, electrical and heat stresses against the hardfield tried to collapse it, but it continued to suck the energy away through convertors and couples and, via the engine, dumped it into the twist. Through sensors to the rear, he observed a rucked-up wake of aurorae as the field went beyond parity. The energy level in the twist, he saw, stayed at one per cent as it fed power into the laminar ultra-capacitors and atomic spin storage of the core. He watched that climb steadily as four Jain attack ships – flickering sensory ghosts – dropped into Adranas's atmosphere tens of thousands of miles behind him.

The ships, emitting heavily in EMR like hot irons, were not bothering to protect themselves with their own hardfields. This gave him pause and then he smiled as he attempted scanning into U-space. With the present disruption, he got a glimpse, subliminal in its brevity, of four midnight holes into grey and silver U-space. This confirmed his instinct. The ships had departed their mother ship fully charged. They weren't using their hardfields because their underlying twists were near to three hundred and sixty degrees and could take no more feedback load. But this also meant that their weapons would be at full destructive power. It was, he felt, an indication of the psyche behind them, this inclination to attach greater importance to offence than defence. But, then again, he would have done the same. These attack ships had been demonstrably difficult to destroy even without their shields.

The things were ridiculously tough and he understood why. Their super-dense armour and internal bracing structures possessed all the traits of Polity armour, but with something else. The technology behind the disruptor weapon, which tampered with molecular and atomic binding forces to either weaken or break them, the Jain had here applied to strengthen them. It made them incredibly rugged and resistant to conventional weapons, yet it also opened up a weakness to a less conventional attack. Trike checked his weapons inventory and soon found the specifications he had studied some while ago.

The Species had faced these vessels before falling into the U-space blister in the accretion disc sun. But they had not had the leisure to design and make the correct response to them. Like the Polity ships, they had instead sought to overload their hardfields. However, tens of thousands of years sitting in that blister twiddling their thumbs had given them plenty of time to catch up, and more. Trike dispatched schematics to a mass of technology near the ship's hull – a by-blow of bioreactor and foundry – and watched it get busily to work. He then transferred his attention to the other bioreactor just below the Species living area.

Here his earlier loading of schematics and a chunk of himself was rendering results. The reactor had burned and peeled while the feed pipes around it were collapsing like over-injected veins. The whole thing was shifting – a soft egg prior to its reptilian occupant breaking free. Numerous EMR channels were available to the occupant he had not yet used because he was unsure how long it would take him to integrate the thing. He didn't want to be occupied with it if he came under attack. Instead, he linked to the reactor itself – its sensors and its pseudo-mind already degrading – and took a look inside.

Within the Jain device was what looked like a giant woodlouse, but balled inside out to normal. The form appeared similar to a wormship or a sequestration knot, though its tentacular outgrowths were thinner. It sported stumpy virtual warfare emitters, the funnels of particle cannons and other more familiar weapons. Folded like this, it also exposed a hollow with sickle graspers to hold its occupant, as well as a connection array comparable to the inside of a haiman interface sphere. He had added these since he had no interface sphere to take inside the thing. The device rested within a caul of thick, translucent chain-aluminium, already turning opaque at numerous contact points, writhing and deforming as the thing tried to force its way out. Then the caul received its decoding instruction and began to peel away in long stringy ribbons. This activity baffled Trike, so he checked Orlandine's memories.

The haiman woman's twin of this device had been potent and possessed all the sequestering abilities that the Jain tech of the accretion disc did, and all its hostility too. It was a tool for a purpose and it needed to be capable. After making the first of its kind, Orlandine had necessarily destroyed it with a CTD. The next she made, she properly prepared for – linking into it at once, for the thing would have been utterly uncontrollable and destructive unless governed by the right mind. And so it was with this thing. He could not just leave it unattended in the bioreactor. He needed to assert control now or it would soon be spreading itself throughout the core. He moved to the edge of the platform and stepped off.

As he fell, Trike kept a wary eye on the attack ships behind. They still lay the same distance back, and thus far had shown no signs of launching an assault. Doubtless whatever drove them, perhaps subminds of the Jain aboard the mother ship, understood that an attack on him now would only supply him with energy. What then was their intent? He felt the Jain was toying with him, inspecting him, while it considered its response. Certainly, they would come to battle, but that creature also wanted more than his destruction; it wanted to absorb him as it would any suitable opponent . . . or mate.

He landed hard on the next level. Restructured bones and muscles rippled with the shock but reknitted any damage in an instant as he stepped out of the dent in the floor. He stood beside the spiral which the Client's remotes had collapsed to crush the attacking biomechs. Some heavily damaged ones were scattered about the area, and smaller mechs, like steel water fleas the size of human heads, were crawling all over them and chewing them apart, salvaging the materials. He ran fast to the ramp leading into the next spiral but did not bother following it down – just jumped off this one too, landing hard and creating another dent. Meanwhile the device had torn open and absorbed its caul, then started on the bioreactor. It began folding the other way too, taking on the giant woodlouse form with which he was familiar. Using its monomolecular edges to forelimbs, it sliced into the internals of the reactor. By the time Trike had leapt down five floors, what he might describe as its head poked out of the reactor wall.

'Damn!' Trike swore aloud. The four attack ships had accelerated, while further out more attack ships began to appear and fall towards him. He realized then how they had drawn so close undetected, wrapped in hardfields whose setting made them absorb most radiations. He would only have seen them had he actively scanned above, and to do that he would have needed to shut down his own hardfield. Were they all about to attack? Were they confident they had enough firepower to push his field towards overload and then take him when he necessarily shut it down?

They were.

Hundreds of graser beams scored down, only visible as they lit up the dispersed gas about the planet, brighter and brighter the deeper they penetrated. They struck his hardfield, lighting it up sun-bright, boiling the surrounding cloud into a storm hundreds of miles across. Energy levels soared, thermocouples smoked and some of even the superconducting network lost its integrity so that wires burned out like light bulb filaments. The strike continued, pouring power into his field and thence into the underlying U-twist. Once it reached its limit, he would have to shut it down or else face obliteration. He could then reply with his weapons and he knew he stood a good chance of wiping out many of these ships, and maybe even escaping them. But partial victories and escape were not his aim. He briefly focused his attention on the plant now producing the first of the missiles to the new schematic. He saw bullets of metal indistinguishable from standard railgun slugs in shape and mass. However, at their cores sat antimatter flasks, only this antimatter mirrored the state of normal matter shortly after being hit by a disruptor. These were his response. But he did not have enough of the damned things yet, so it was time to run.

The view outside, lit up by the constant graser assault, had changed and the core flew through a clear layer between the clouds of opaque gas. He dropped it lower, then lower still. The atmosphere had become mostly hydrogen shot through with clouds of its compounds. The massive flare off his hardfields created weird chemical explosions all around which dissolved into black, semi-solid smoke. Lower down were nitrogen, methane and ammonia in a swirling blue-green layer, where the division between liquid and gas was debatable. He splashed down into this, throwing up a spray of supercritical fluids that eddied in strange immiscible patterns. The glare above grew more intense as the grasers spent more and more of their energy in the clouds, then abruptly the firing ceased. Were they following him down? He flicked off his hardfield and probed above with powerful active scanning. The core shuddered, crashed and groaned in the intense pressure. No, they were still out—

Another crash and flash, and terrible fire erupted as grasers hit the core. He threw up the hardfield again and observed lines carved across the hull, glowing like warning runes. The grasers went out and he decided not to look again just for the moment.

Here once more were clear and opaque layers – brief analysis revealed this to be a 'sea' heavy in fibrous webs of enzymes. These rested in an undefinable area like that of a supercritical fluid, only here it was life or not life. It was dark, to the spectrum of human vision, but utterly clear in infrared. Trike gazed down upon what could be described as an abyssal plain, or not, and saw crystalline slabs stacked into vast mountain ranges. He chose a spot and took the core down deeper.

Tactically this perhaps wasn't the best option, since putting a vessel down at the bottom of a gravity well, while under attack from other ships, was never a smart move. It had been an instinctive one, which he now analysed as he jumped down more and more levels in the Species living spaces. The attack ships' energy weapons would lose too much power penetrating this deep, as would railgun slugs. CTDs and other missiles would be slow, avoidable – he could take as much of a hit from them as he wanted. If they came down here after him, relative advantages and disadvantages would be the same as above. It seemed as though he had made a good choice. Especially considering they would probably take time to rethink their tactics – time he needed right now.

He finally reached the very bottom living space and here exited through the door by which he and Cog had entered. The biomech he had used for transport still waited here but he ignored it and moved to the side of the tunnel, sending instructions ahead. A sphincter opened, revealing a tunnel curving down relative to the grav of the living spaces. He followed it, arrived at a translucent blister, tore through it and propelled himself further down through a tangle of bracing beams like bird bones, towards the bioreactor.

The feed from the reactor was dying as it rapidly expired. The device had crawled halfway out, grazing on it like a beetle grub would on a rotten log. Now descending upon it, he linked to the device. The thing shuddered as if he had electrocuted it, and abruptly pulled itself clear of the reactor. He could feel it fighting him, but he rapidly took hold of its command channels and made it open a spread of tentacles and limbs with the space for him at its centre. He turned as he fell back towards it, and slammed inside like a plug going hard into a socket. The sickle clamps closed on him and Jain tendrils speared in from organs like spinnerets. He also exuded his own and all began mating up until he lost himself inside them. He reached out through connections that were becoming physical and of almost unlimited bandwidth. An endless array of offensive and defensive mechanisms fell into his control. Six fusion reactors supplied power by crushing elementary fuels in hardfield cages, then igniting them with millions of angstrom tube lasers. This supplied power for endless adaptation and alteration of the device around him, which was melding with him. Memory space also opened up – quantum storage crystal as layers combined in the laminar power storage. He pulled in exabytes of data stored in the surrounding core and, as he took physical control of the device to waft it back towards the Species living area, he began to redesign the thing radically. Orlandine, after all, had no access to the knowledge or technology he now controlled when she had made her version of it . . .

Exterior view. He was now able to control the descent of the core with little mental effort. He guided it down onto one of the mountains of slabs, where it settled, supported on the lower surface of its hardfield. The pressure and external temperature were immense. Hail rattled against the hardfield but brief analysis revealed that the stones, though layered like the conventional terran kind, were diamonds. This pressure and temperature on the hardfield, with the disparity between outside conditions and those maintained inside, became a constant source of power, winding up the U-twist like a ratchet spring. He felt this was hardly needed since the graser attack had taken twist-stored power to eighty per cent. But then he saw the percentage was of just one segment of twist – in conventional geometry just eighty per cent of six degrees out of three hundred and sixty. The core could store a vast amount of energy in its U-twist. Trike pondered on that for a moment, wondering how he had not realized it before. He checked core history and swiftly came to a conclusion: his knowledge had been based on the earlier format of the core when it entered the U-space blister. But while the aliens were in that blister, they had massively increased the size of the twist in the hope of reaching an energy level that would enable them to escape. It was only when they finally accepted the impossibility of this that they went into decline.

In his device, which was in fact now his larger self, Trike came to the entrance of the Species living area, and casually ripped out the door with his extended tentacles. He ascended, not bothering with the ramps any more – just carving out holes with two particle weapons for the first five levels, then switching over to a newly commissioned disruptor for the next. This glassy beam stabbed up surgically, shattering out a neat fifty-foot circle before the disruption died. Inside himself, two of his fusion reactors had shut down and, by the time he had reached the top, were ready to start up again. They had become reactors which used the disruption technique to convert matter straight to energy – an endless supply while he had matter available.

Next, cruising towards the control centre, he took out a circle of wall with another surgical disruptor blast and drifted in. Stabbing out tentacles, he physically connected to the core, though it hardly seemed necessary. Via multiple sensors, he gazed upwards through the layers of atmosphere. It took some time, and necessitated a high-intensity laser blast to make way for a virtual warfare active scan, but he soon saw the attack ships hovering far above, out from the planet. No action? Yes, there was action, but it was down here. He gazed out across a cracked plain of glowing iron to see a wave, twenty miles tall, of super-fluids and snakes of complex matter heading rapidly towards him. Of course, Jain tech had been establishing on this world, and now it had been let loose on him.

## Orlandine

Orlandine found herself applying more and more of her processing power to the defence of the planet, which, of course, made it necessary to close down elements of her being not involved in this. All the ships and platforms were down on the surface now and only she stood against the falling storm. From underground veins, like tubular factories hundreds of miles long, she pushed up disruptor buds all across the continent and opened them into flowers. Through her new towers, she fired slugs of lava, even while growing them taller.

Too much was getting through . . .

She reached for available resources and found them. Briefly, something stood in the way of her taking control but she brushed it aside. Next, she flung weapons platform attack pods against the objects falling through atmosphere. All around the globe, she sprouted great clumps of perfectly aligned nanotubes and fed them a surplus of light to lase – white beams then speared up into the sky to incinerate what they could. But still it was not enough, because so much escaped complete destruction. And now the remaining wormships were descending.

Orlandine observed two of them hurtling down towards the ocean on the other side of the planet from the human habitations. She shrugged and spined herself with weapons underneath that ocean but was extremely wary of these things. While attacking the fleet, they had managed to alter themselves to prevent their complete atomic disruption when hit by the new weapon. And it seemed they had altered themselves further. She had hit two with her own matter disruptors and they fell apart, but into worm segments like the one she had long ago interrogated. They had been recombining into complete ships again when she destroyed them with other weapons. She could not understand how they were doing this, but it made them more dangerous than ever.

The ships hurtled down, forming into tightly knotted spearheads. Then, all at once, they hit a wall. Hell in the form of railgun missiles, lasers and particle beams shot up from numerous locations across the ocean and intersected on the two ships. The mass of firepower stopped them dead in the sky, balanced on hardfields and shredding away much of their bodies in charred filaments as thick as trees. Hardfield collapse came a moment later and the fusillade crashed into them, tearing them to pieces. Beam weapons then tracked the fragments down, incinerating them so all that remained rained as ash on the ocean.

Orlandine focused on the source of that shooting. Dreadnoughts and weapons platforms floated negatively buoyant on the surface like artificial islands. Why she did not control this resource briefly puzzled her. She then saw she had already accounted for these when she sent them to the positions they now occupied. Their firing waned towards the end, indicating they had shot their bolt. The weapons platforms, and some of the larger ships with materials to spare, had manufactured enough for that firing, while all were recharging power supplies by fusion. But as they stood, they were not useful to her.

# THE HUMAN

Time for full integration . . .

Though their munitions and energy levels were down, most of their weapons were still functional. She began pushing up giant kelp stalk extensions from the seabed underneath each one, thereafter sending growths towards every ship and platform on the planet. Within just a few minutes, those on the ocean were cupped in acres of leaf-like growths, while tendrils wormed into thruster jets and fusion ports, clogging and shutting them down. She then began receiving queries from prador, AIs and interfaced human captains. There was no logic to their queries. Her deployment of resources to the best possible effect was obvious. She groped around in her widely spread mind for the correct coding, the correct method of communication.

'I am going to use your weapons,' she told them through a small human interface. To her it seemed pointless to state the obvious, but it was apparently necessary for them.

A multitude of questions ensued, along with some plain denials of access. She delegated the questions to a series of swiftly generated subminds copied from that small human element of her being, then ignored the denials. Airlocks and hold doors were the weakest points. All the modern Polity ships and her platforms opened for her, though it was notable that every AI was either preparing to eject or loading itself to a carrier robot. She did not require their processing so she let them go. Most of the reavers opened too, their crews flooding out in armour and either clambering onto the hulls of their ships or floating out on the ocean. The ornery ones were the old prador dreadnoughts with father-captains and crews without the Spatterjay mutation. She could destroy them, but they too were a resource and there might be an easier way . . .

'I would like you to speak to your people,' said the small human portion of herself.

The recipient of her request stood in the hold of his badly damaged dreadnought. This rested on the main continent, watching Jain trunks the width of pine trees sliding inside his recently acquired ship. Meanwhile his crew, and the crew who had originally occupied the ship, were rapidly launching themselves out of a troop attack port.

'We have been here before,' said Orlik.

'You left one hell of a mess,' added Sprag, the terror drone squatting on Orlik's armour.

'I will leave more of a mess in other ships if the crews persist in resisting me,' said Orlandine. In two of the floating dreadnoughts, the crew had started blasting her encroaching tendrils with Gatling cannons and particle weapons. A stupid, stupid waste. They could better deploy their weapons elsewhere and, again, why couldn't they see the logic of what she was doing?

Orlik began to talk fast, issuing orders. All but one of the ships ceased to offer resistance. Reading the ship's telemetry, she realized this one had just undergone a change of leadership. Its father-captain was locked in a frame in its hold, being steadily dissected by a first-child showing signs of making the transition to adulthood. Prador family politics – she had no time for it. She hit the attacking prador with toolhead tentacles, boring through weak points in their armour and swiftly injecting fibres, seizing control of them. The first-child she took last, along with the others who were not directly working against her. Meanwhile, aboard one of the first Polity dreadnoughts she had entered, peristaltic tubes began feeding in particulate and railgun slugs, while tendrils braided with superconductor sprouted universal bayonets to plug in and feed it power.

'You can understand their reluctance,' commented another. 'Even your own drones are blocking your access to them.'

Orlandine focused through a multiphasic sensor stabbed up

out of the ground, like an eyeball formed of a Chinese puzzle with interlocking metal blocks. She saw Diana Windermere walking away from the bridge pod ejected from the *Cable Hogue*. This had come down on the outskirts of the city, not far from Orlik's ship. Loaded with weapons and trailed by a number of grav-sleds, she and her crew were heading towards the city.

'They should trust me,' said Orlandine. 'I am all that is protecting them from what is raining down on us.'

'Yeah, but you're taking away their ships and weapons so they have no defence against you.'

The idea irritated Orlandine immensely. She was in complete and utter control of herself; in fact, her control had never been more strong or precise. She integrated these ships into her defence and, a moment later, the first dreadnought opened fire, followed by two weapons platforms. The prador dreadnought that had resisted her was down near a low-lying island where a falling bacilliform had ended up. It showed no signs of activity but Orlandine targeted it anyway. Then she hesitated. She had not yet managed to get a close look at one of these objects and now she had remotes available to investigate. She sent the prador from aboard that ship, over whom she had secured complete command.

## Trike

In the high-gravity, high-pressure environment of Adranas, the Jain tech had adopted a distinctly different form. The wave moved in weird slow motion and seemed to consist, in the main, of layers of fabric formed of a wide hexagonal weave. This constantly rippled and compressed, travelling down its face and disappearing underneath it as it rolled forwards. Superfluids in the thing compacted and stretched with the glutinous fluidity of sea worms, while familiar but infinitely harder Jain-tech tendrils interwove all of it. The thing reached the foothill slabs of the mountains and climbed them, finally rising up to the same level as the ship's core. But the wave Trike had first seen was just one section of a closing ring. All around it swept in, finally slowing just a few miles out from the hardfield, so it surrounded him in a wall twenty miles high.

Scanning through the hardfield rendered little useful data but already, with the EMR he allowed through, he felt the impact of virtual attack. Then, on the inward faces of that wall, areas began to dish. He observed this with a feeling of inevitability, then saw the fog of matter in front of the dishes sketching out the shape of magnetic bottles they were creating. And he was utterly unsurprised when they spat particle-dense beams of almost solid matter and energy. These things, each fifty feet across, glared bright pink like a hypergiant he had once seen. They flared against his hardfield and their splash rose in a near-solid fountain of fire, boiling up through the thick atmosphere for hundreds of miles. His hardfield took it, of course, and his energy levels began to climb again. He didn't even bother trying to scan upwards to see if the attack ships were descending. He had no doubt they would be waiting for the moment when he inevitably had to shut his field down to prevent its collapse. Instead, he engaged the drive, lifted the core and wafted it sideways, sending it skimming a hundred miles across the mountains in search of another clear area.

The firing did not let up. Via the scan data he could obtain, he saw the dishes tracking him and observed the true immensity of the Jain growth. It stretched for as far as he could see without shutting down his field for a more active scan. It was not unreasonable to suppose it covered all of Adranas.

Trike considered his options. If he stayed here, he would have to close down his shield, and if he rose up to meet the attack ships, he would have to do the same. He turned his attention to the production of the new railgun slugs and saw them being attached in their hundreds to gel belts, in turn being wound onto reels ready to feed his railguns. But he needed more of them and thus more time. Distractions and diversions – something unexpected. He scanned the slabbed mountains, meanwhile preparing disruptors all around the core rim for a mass firing. Thankfully the constant bombardment outside helped the scan, since it was mainly spectroscopic data he was after. He cross-matched this data with stuff gathered earlier and confirmed his original conjecture, then brought the core to hover over a five-sided slab four miles thick. The substance was incredibly tough, densely laminated carbon . . .

He abruptly shut down the shield and the pressure slammed in. The entire core howled, with structural beams warping, shock absorbers collapsing to their minimum, and inner structure buckling. But though the core entire shrank in diameter by a mile, the outer hull remained intact. The Jain-tech wave rose again and energy beams stabbed in. They struck hull armour and began ablating it, but the hugely efficient superconducting grid drew that heat into thermocouples. These then translated it into energy to turn the twist just that little bit further. He fired steering thrusters that seared across surrounding Jain tech, and he applied the core's internal drive systems. In majestic slow motion, the entire core turned completely over. Trike could feel it even ensconced in his mechanism. The first pull of the planet's gravity, added to the internal grav of the ship, had made his bones creak, and now he hung upside down, since the planetary gravity completely outweighed the internal grav. He could correct for it, but that took energy and really wasn't a requirement for him.

As the core moved towards the slab, actually settling on it this time, he fired disruptors, set to the complete debonding of matter, straight into the faces of the surrounding dishes. The disruptor beams wound out like drills made of red glass, intersected with the energy beams and lanced through into the surrounding mass. He held them there for less than a second before shutting them down and initiating the hardfield again. It stuttered, turning the colour of yellow topaz as its power draw ramped up and it sliced through the slab below. It then filtered the glare of the fission explosions outside, its interior filling with bright lemon light. Trike noted power levels climbing again as the shield took this load and transferred it to the U-twist. He drew some into grav-drive and gave it a kick, separating the chunk of slab. Opening ports where the core's armour touched below, he sorted through numerous options, then decided on a molecular string-bond adhesive, and injected it. It took just a few minutes for the stuff to spread, and just a further few to bond. Soon the core was firmly attached.

Carried away on rainbow wraiths, the fire outside cleared. The area directly outside looked like the remains after a wind-driven fire through gorse. The wall was now absent. However, beyond this the further mass of tech began flooding in. He initiated one of the core's drive systems again and it, along with its enclosing hardfield, rose with a crash. Inversion of the drive effect spun the core back over and Trike was upright once more, not that it mattered. He shut down the field, fired up the fusion engines at full power, complemented with all other drives, and shot up from the surface underneath a hemisphere of laminated diamond, miles thick.

## The Client

Sprine.

The droplet, like a miniature star ruby, fell slowly from the microtube and settled on the micro-platen. It spread out over the millions of quantum-processor crystals there – invisible at this magnification. The Client wound the magnification up and up, seeing the stringy masses of poisons that blocked transcription. There were also the globules of paralytic that chilled the Spatterjay virus into somnolence and the enzymes which broke it apart, but still no action was apparent. Finally, in nanoscope view, she saw the crystals themselves – small monoliths seemingly etched with Celtic spirals that were the shape of their even molecular structure. Only at this level did she see enzymes briefly attaching and then tumbling away, spin states changing, a cascade effect spreading across those surfaces and running inside. And there was a measurable photonic discharge. She also saw it propagating via that discharge to other crystals the enzyme had not touched.

'So why did you do this to me?' asked Cog.

The Client pulled her attention away from her disposable laboratories and studied him. His skin had healed and he showed no signs of discomfort beyond annoyance. The virus had adapted him. He seemed perfectly fine in temperatures that would kill a conventional human being, had there been such a thing.

'If I flee this system, the Jain in that mother ship will always have a way of tracking me,' she replied. 'I have ascertained that there is a connection, operating via a substratum between U-space and the real, between all Jain tech. This is generated by the underlying picotech of the technology. It is integral to its U-space signature and the medium via which it subsumes its host.'

'Still doesn't tell me why you had to capture me like this,' said Cog.

'It was my intention to create some kind of virus to disrupt that picotech, while maintaining the technology's gross function. Thus I could free myself from its influence and make myself undetectable.'

'Still not seeing the need for these clamps.'

'You have Jain tech inside you,' she stated.

'Yeah, the soldiers,' he said.

'You are connected.'

'And.'

'It was my intention to test the virus on you first.'

'Was?'

'It appears that evolution has already produced something that interferes with the connection: sprine.'

'So that was a lucky discovery you made while doing what you did to me. Why am I still your prisoner?'

The Client suddenly felt a deep disquiet. 'To test on you anything—'

'No,' said Cog calmly. 'You are surrounded by Jain tech that is all physically connected. You have distinct tech in your attack pods and probably elsewhere. It would be no problem for you to isolate a piece on which to test a virus or anything else you might make. So why did you make me your prisoner?'

The Client examined him through numerous sensors. His prosaically human form made it easy to forget he was ancient, intelligent enough to be an agent of Earth Central, and probably wise. And he had just highlighted something utterly illogical about her behaviour. She began reviewing her thought processes to this point. Grabbing him had been instinctive. She had seen him as a source of data and experimentation because he was extraneous to herself. She had behaved like a Jain. Searching and checking through her mind, she found the sources of her impulse. The Librarian? No. It would be easy for her to make that assumption and she did not. It was, she saw, in a feedback loop via her mental connection with the technology spread throughout this platform and in her attack pods. Even though she had no physical Jain tech inside her, its influence had reached her. Horrified by this, she abruptly undid the clamps holding him in place. He might turn on her and try to kill her, yet that mattered less than the integrity of her mind.

Cog rolled off the slab, then walked over to where the remotes had piled his clothing and space suit. He pulled on his underwear, then his heavy canvas trousers and shirt, before going back to the slab to get his boots. He didn't bother with the space suit, nor with the weapon lying nearby.

'So it is subtle,' he said. 'Gradually gnawing at the minds of its hosts from the bottom up, through the subconscious?' He began lacing up his boots. 'I dismissed it as an excuse, but Trike was perhaps right about what made him kill Angel.'

'That could be the case,' she replied, dividing her serial mind, one portion back to her investigation and another in overview checking for alien influence. She made her control rigid and unflinching. It was time for her to be everything she could be.

In the second laboratory, she used electrostatics to align the crystals. She flooded in an organo-metal substrate around them and watched their structure propagate through it, as it too crystallized. Angstrom light tube connections, then in their billions, to inject photons and to measure and, as she did so, steadily increasing programming space opened to interpret the results. As a precaution, she ensured that space remained in the Polity tech aboard the platform. She then released a droplet of sprine onto the crystals.

'And it might yet control him in other ways.' Cog looked up.

'And Orlandine.' The Client showed none of her distraction as the sprine enzymes began attaching and making their alterations. Exabytes of data flooded through the connections into her serial mind – a vast puzzle that would appal even an AI. But she was a weapons developer of the Species who had once made a weapon that could annihilate an entire race. No more confusion; she would not allow it. She must be better than she had been.

No Jain influence, or fragmentary manipulation from a dead creature in her mind. Her focus had to be sharp and absolute. And in platform processing, she began to put the puzzle together.

He nodded. 'So you are trying to find a way to undo that?'

'Sprine does something. I am now seeing that from the inside,' she replied.

'Inside what?' he asked.

The shape began to etch itself out and she wondered if this was actually *not* an accident of evolution. The enzyme created a brief atomic structure in the nanotech that was a quantum cascade laser. This in turn induced a plasmon polariton wave that twisted the picotech out of shape, but only locally. Her thinking and understanding ever expanding, she saw that this enzyme, though concentrated in sprine, must be everywhere in the environment of Spatterjay. It was, she realized, the reason why the squad of Jain soldiers remained suppressed in the virus. The enzyme was a weapon, she saw at last, almost certainly sown on that world by one of the ancient races, perhaps even one of the Jain themselves.

'The technology itself,' she replied.

The Client brought more and more processing online. First, she confined it in Polity tech and relied on the millennia of scientific knowledge uploaded from the library. As she required more space, she reluctantly opened out into the storage and processing of the Jain tech spread about the platform, but watched this very closely. She detected no signs of sabotage but hypothesized that the tech did not react at this level: its influence was subtle and slow, infiltrating and changing the mind of its host. It would not hamper her investigation. It would not hold up the process of discovery, but she was sure it would interfere with the way she applied any knowledge she gained.

The plasmon polariton effect was incomplete and slow. It

could suppress picotech locally but lost impetus after a short time, while tech would reinstate as it passed. Constant reinfection on Spatterjay was what kept the tech there suppressed. Only this sprine, spread throughout the environment, stopped the likes of Cog becoming Jain soldiers reborn. For her purposes, it needed to spread fast and its effect needed to be permanent. She turned to disruptor technology in search of that.

Cog stood, sauntered over past his discarded space suit, then stooped to pick up his weapon. The Client froze, just for a moment, then mentally focused available weapons on him. He walked back to the space suit and put the weapon down beside it, then reached into a pouch on the suit and took out an object. It was his pipe, which he began stuffing with tobacco.

'Best you get on with that, then,' he said, stepping over to sit down on the cowling of the sample robot.

She made no comment – he was now such a minuscule part of her mental realm. In the vast spaces of her mind, she mapped the physical effects created by the enzyme, testing and discarding millions of molecular keys, billions of quantum processes. And at last she found it: the enzyme acted as before as a molecular key that locked into Jain nanotech. There it formed a quantum cascade laser only. Even as that laser pulsed, it copied itself, and those copies pulsed again and again. Within just a few seconds, the process reached a tipping point, sending surface plasmon polariton waves along every interface of the Jain tech, disrupting the underlying picotech irreparably. And those waves travelled at the speed of light.

She had her disruptor virus.

# 17

*The hooders of the planet Masada are creatures that resemble centipedes but with heads like turned-down spoons. Their eyes, other sensors, manipulators and mandibles are all cupped on the underside of it. This is supposing one might find a centipede the size of a monorail train. They are, of course, dangerous and aggressive, which you would not think a problem, what with the weapons we have at our disposal. But they are very difficult to kill. For many years, biologists considered them just another hostile life form on a planet that had many, until a particularly dogged researcher subjected them to intensive study. He discovered that they are, in fact, a devolved version of a biomech war machine created by the alien civilization which once occupied that world. It was a game-changing breakthrough in the scientific community. This would have been no surprise to early hunters of the creatures, even though they used high-powered energy weapons. But those same hunters did not last long enough to offer an opinion.*

From 'How It Is' by Gordon

## Orlandine

Numerous weapons platforms and ships now complemented Orlandine's major weapons to hit objects entering atmosphere, while attack pods and drones took out some of the still active debris from that. She nearly had everything under control.

However, debris still reached the surface and, though she had spread around the planet, she did not occupy enough areas. Things no larger than a microbe could start hostile Jain growth, so she needed more at ground level to deal with this.

Objects striking the oceans she easily detected and had more time to deal with them as they sank. Her main weapon against these were mantis shrimps – a creature swarming in the oceans of Jaskor that she had previously ignored. Their phenomenal vision possessed sixteen colour receptors, while their natural weapon against prey, and even predators, was a super-cavitating shockwave generated by their forelimbs. Grabbing millions of them, she had induced accelerated cloning in bioreactors on the seafloor. She only had to tweak their biology and cerebral wiring to make them ferocious hunters of nascent enemy Jain tech. Their shockwaves at close range disrupted the smaller growths to such an extent that they had no time to turn into anything larger, whereupon she swept up and annihilated them as they reached the seabed. The activity of the shrimps in some areas boiled the sea, cooking pink thousands of the shrimps themselves.

The land was a different matter. Scanning through rock, soil, sand and other solids presented more difficulties than air or water. Hostile Jain was hard to distinguish from structures of plants and fungi spread across the main continent and scattered islands. Consequently, the tech had time to establish and grow at least a little, therefore turning into something hardy. Having sequestered and weaponized just about every land animal to hunt these things down, Orlandine then turned agricultural robots to the task and began to denude the cities of their robot ecologies too. She needed more, and manufactured more – ugly biomechs rose out of the ground as if from the sowing of the dragon's teeth. But she had missed something, niggling at the back of her mind. Then she saw how she had constrained her search parameters with considerations outside of survival. With a thought, she removed those limitations.

Caches of life forms, with the requisite sensors, were available in the cities. Many of these she had already seized from the enemy and utilized, but others were available too. So, from her Jain growths throughout the cities, she extruded tubes and spewed rapidly designed sequestering devices into the air. These swarms of biomechs hummed like bot flies, through the streets, into the buildings, then clamped on bare skin with sickle legs and buried their heads, injecting fibres. Their growth was rapid in warm flesh and blood. Almost unconsciously, she programmed alterations through her mechs to their hosts, optimizing them for the tasks in hand. With armour growing in their skin to protect them from hostile sequestration, the creatures headed out, snaring weapons from other caches she had provided for ally defenders. She inspected those allies briefly and saw that later they might need upgrading. But, since the hostile Jain tech had used similar methods of sequestration to hers, they had protected themselves and presented difficulties. Then came a surge of communication – rebellion from some part of her mind, her world.

Noise.

Those allies, those discrete military units . . . She struggled to find their correct designation. Ah yes: human soldiers, marines, Golem, prador and war drones. She fielded their objections with subpersonae split off from her earlier human self, since they were more apt to communicate on that level. But this did not work, because the subpersonae seemed sympathetic, as if in agreement with this outside data. Fearing a sequestration attack, she killed the subpersonae and blocked off the communications. She was too busy to deal with anything that did not involve plain survival and, from what she could glean, this seemed a low-level program conflict in terms of logistics. And, with a degree of satisfaction, she watched her new ground forces working precisely according to the program, as they spread out across the continent.

## Trike

The grasers hit at once, burning into the diamond shield above the core and caused enough explosive vaporization to slow the ascent of it. Active scanning at full power, Trike noted that the bulk of the attack ships lay between him and the still slowly approaching mother ship. With a wrench that set internal structure screaming, he altered his course towards it. The attack ships shifted in response. Sure, they could graser their way through the shield, but it was better for them to obtain line of sight to the core itself and hit that. They still did not have their hardfields up. He was the defender and they the aggressors, and behaving precisely as he wanted.

As they obtained that line of sight and opened fire, he blocked their attack with layered projections of conventional hardfields. Perhaps from this they would assume he dared not put up the enclosing one because his twist had reached its limit and might collapse. He fired his railguns, sending streams of missiles little different from those the fleets had fired. The slugs that hit had scant effect, though shuddering the vessels from their courses in plasma explosions. He next ran through the whole gamut of coherent radiations, groping out with virtual and induction warfare beams and engaging in battle on that plenum. Apparently he was searching through his weapons inventory for something effective as they fell within sight of his hull. Or, at least, he hoped that was what they thought he was doing.

Railguns again, shortly followed by the slower reach of disruptors.

He watched carefully. The attack ships only negligently fried a few of the railgun slugs since they had proved ineffective, but instead concentrated their fire on his hull and on those disruptor beams. Grasers, aimed to intercept the beams, took on a spiral form obviously employing a counter-effect. One after another, disruptor beams collapsed and feedback blew up the weapons themselves. Meanwhile, the second fusillade of slugs started to impact. These did not explode into plasma but went into hull metal like darts, sending out explosive ripples around their impact points. He had hit nearly every ship before they understood something was seriously wrong and started flinging up their enclosing hardfields.

'Too little, too late,' said Trike, flatly.

He ignored those his slugs had hit and fired up particle weapons to attack the remainder enclosed in hardfields. He nailed all eight and tracked them, then targeted them with railguns too. But this time he was firing slugs just recently manufactured – ones that the Species had designed during their time in the blister. Hyperdense bars hurtled out at relativistic speeds carrying an appalling amount of energy. Larger spherical slugs collapsed partway along their courses. They released a directional proton pulse as they did so, then, shortly after that pulse, slammed into hardfields as pure neutronium. Three hardfields turned black – bubbles of grease on a hotplate – then imploded. Three flashes of intense radiation and spreading clouds of quark-gluon plasma, and they were gone. The other five ships dropped their hardfields to prevent collapse, but boiled at the terminus of particle beams, as exotic slugs carved into them, slicing away chunks.

Now the other ships. The hardfields of those he had hit earlier with the disruptor slugs began to fail. The ships shimmered as the disruptor effect ramped up the binding forces which made them so difficult to destroy. Many of them seemed to be wearing away, but really, their components were shrinking down to dark skeletal representations of themselves. Those whole skeletons then collapsed and shattered as if made of charcoal sticks. Others managed to kill the effect, but in doing so destroyed their own structural strength, and made themselves conventionally vulnerable. Trike cut them to pieces with railgun slugs and flew through the spreading debris. Then, with dying ships all around him, he sent his own data scream, his own challenge, towards the mother ship.

The great Jain ship gave the utterly correct response. Trike began probing with his weapons as he plunged towards it, searing its hull with particle weapons, launching volleys of railgun slugs. A giant haze of missiles arose in response and hurtled back at him. Thousands of beams speared out: particle beams, lasers in a rainbow of colours as they reflected on gas and debris, disruptors drilling through vacuum like the reaching arms of some immense hot amoeba. A vast wave of destruction. Trike detached his Jain device from direct contact with the ship, affirmed his links with his army of remotes and biomechs, and sent a brief coded instruction. Injectors squirted a counteragent onto the interface between the core and the great hemisphere of diamond he had been using as a shield. The glue quickly unravelled and the two separated. He fired steering thrusters to drive them apart and the core fell back, increasing the gap. Then Trike reached out to the U-space engines and slammed them on.

The disruption had declined enough now that it would not completely wreck, especially this ship with its drive and hardfield so integrated. The core howled, shuddered and splintered between the braced solidity of its drive and the enclosing hardfield bubble. Trike felt himself torn in a direction his human self could not point to, but his whole self could. Just seconds later in personal time, the great vessel crashed back out of that continuum, its hardfield blinking out. And Trike fired all his weapons at once.

Vast pincers slid overhead. A thousand miles behind him, the hemispheric shield he had used took the brunt of the Jain ship's attack and turned into a small sun. He ramped up power to maximum, pouring tons of particulate into particle cannons, taking the photon density of the lasers up to the highest possible their lasing gases, meta-material substrates and superconductor-laced cylinders of gemstone could stand. The U-twist wound down, while the engines shifted this energy into internal stores, which heated up and began radiating. Outside it seemed a solar flare had launched straight into the neck of the Jain warship. The impact site, fifty miles across, reflected a glare like a boiling sun spreading from that point. The material of the hull silvered and swirled, then millions of tons of armour exploded into vacuum. The fusillade cut through, and then across. Great explosions there hurled out chunks the size of islands. Structural beams a mile wide glowed red, then white, then poured away in strands of molten composite. Trike meanwhile fired up every available missile launcher and targeted the slowly separating head of the giant vessel. He shut down the beam weapons and, flinging out six fusion drive flames, headed down beside the neck. But inevitably the great ship replied.

U-twists developed, evenly spaced in a ring within the core. They aped the gravity wells which planets created in that continuum and their effects began to tear at the core's guts. Prepared, Trike switched his drive over to a new setting, while throwing up the hardfield again. The twists, instead of continuing to tear out the interior, linked to the ship's energy store. The negative effect drained away energy as he took the sting out of them. Perfectly timed for his purposes, thousands of railgun slugs then slammed into his hardfield, jerking his twist back in the direction he wanted it to go. The attacking U-twists went out as he fell down towards the main body of the Jain mother ship. Behind, his missiles struck its head, finally breaking it away from the neck and shredding it in a conflagration. He saw it falling, though the pincers, made of some material stronger than anything he thought possible, remained intact.

*In there?* he wondered.

No. He had hoped the Jain would be in the head of the ship but the lack of a local hardfield for that object, and the relative ease with which he had destroyed it, told him otherwise.

Outside, space boiled with quark-gluon plasma, photonic matter and debris yet to fall apart into their base states. It resembled the chromosphere of a sun. Sensor data were difficult, especially through his frequently darkening hardfield, but he knew when he had reached the underbelly of his opponent. Now his own U-twist ratcheted up to its highest, he necessarily shut down his hardfield. Immediately slugs began to impact on his hull. He fielded some with conventional flat hardfields and set the lasers to vaporizing what they could, but others excavated craters a mile deep and slammed through. Inside they caused massive explosions and flung out walls of fire. But they were not as destructive as they could have been, nor were the beam weapons. He watched for disruptors and yet saw none firing. Of course, the initial love taps were all but over now. The Jain did not want to destroy him, it wanted to *absorb* him. He targeted all nearby weapons with his particle beams and hit them hard, draining away the last of his particulate. For a moment, he got a clear view, and it seemed he was coming in to land on the surface of some giant metallic world, with mountain chains like the corpses of prehistoric, leviathan beasts. The core slammed down on a plain of rucked-up scales and stuck to it as he again exuded glue.

Trike reached one of the exits to the surface of the core which wasn't against the Jain ship. From down below, through the opposite face of the core, he heard the scream of matter being torn apart. Internal sensors showed him snake-like monsters flooding in like angry dragons. Their form gave him a microsecond pause because they resembled hooders – their bodies were segmented, and their heads consisted of armoured cowls from which they wielded numerous sharp limbs and tough tentacles. He would have supposed some cross-pollination of technologies had he not known these things pre-dated Atheter war machines, the hooders, by millions of years. Atheter technology arose from the Jain, or was distorted by it. And so it was with the device he rode now, and the stuff woven through his body – it was coming home.

Knots ascended inside the core and unravelled explosively, strewing their mass all about, clinging like vines and chewing up composite and metals. He instructed his biomechs and remotes still in the lower part of the ship to retreat from them, while internal defences fired up, scouring and slicing them with high-intensity masers and X-ray lasers. But never enough to stop them getting inside, from getting a grip. He then applied the same technique he had used down on the planet. He turned the hardfield back on. The core and enclosing hardfield rose, ripping out a hemisphere of the Jain ship. The attack from below collapsed, as if the things there were limbs he had just snipped off some beast. Inversion of the drive effect then spun the core over, wrenching and twisting because of the huge internal damage. He fired up the fusion engines – only three of them were still working. The hemisphere of ship tore out and tumbled away in vacuum, and the core slammed down into the cavity it had cut. With a thought, Trike opened the giant doors ahead onto gleaming organic spaces, with glassy and weirdly iridescent metals – the squirming but immense life of the Jain ship's interior. His remotes and biomechs flooded in, weapons flashing and limbs slicing. And after a moment, he followed them.

## Gemmell

'She won't react to this?' Gemmell asked.

Knobbler held up a tentacle like an admonishing finger. *Be quiet for a moment.* Another tentacle snaked out, its end bulging and then bristling like a studded mace. Multiple QC lasers crackled and, over on one side of the rooftop, the air lit up with hundreds of small stars, which then fell as smoking embers. Some landed nearby. Ruth stepped over and peered at them, then brought her boot down on one, crushing it to grey dust.

'She may, but there is no com that is not compromised,' said Knobbler. 'She's not just in the data sphere but she *is* it now. She seems to have lost the ability to distinguish between what is her mind and body, and what is not.'

'The attacking Jain tech included in that?' asked Ruth.

It was a very pertinent question, Gemmell felt.

Knobbler swung his nightmare head towards her. 'For the present she sees it as the enemy. I'd like to believe she'll continue to see it like that and will, at some point, return to herself. But we must prepare.'

'But it'll be too late for them,' said Ruth, pointing down into the street below.

Gemmell didn't even have to look to know she meant another group of civilians, moving fast out of the city to do battle with any tech rooted in the ground out there. All were seemingly eager to the task, but slaves to Orlandine's will nevertheless.

'They're not dead yet,' said the big assassin drone.

'Is that better?' Ruth asked.

'Okay,' Gemmell interrupted. This was pointless. They had to act as best they could under the circumstances. 'I'll do this.' He stepped back, squatted on the rooftop and closed his eyes – he would need all his concentration to connect the comlinks.

Entering the virtual space of his gridlink, he first lined up all the links to Polity marines and other human ground forces across the continent. This was the easy part: he hit the retreat button and gave coordinates.

'All forces directly under my command,' he said, overriding thousands of responses while routing sitreps into storage. 'Head for the main city to the coordinates given – the Polity medship. Grab extra-planetary transport if you can, and stay below one hundred feet. Bring anyone with you that you're able to – people who have not been sequestered. I don't need to explain the situation to you since you've all had the tactical updates. Maintain hazmat integrity. If you cannot respond as ordered then contact Trantor for further instructions.'

Internally he observed thousands of positive responses. When the negative ones began to come in, he set an automatic relay of the comlinks concerned to Trantor. Now for other 'people'. This one individual, in Marshallam city in the south, had already heard Gemmell's initial orders but he spoke directly.

'Vreen,' he said, addressing the black-armoured prador in charge of the prador forces on the planet. 'I want you to bring your people here too.'

Suddenly the bandwidth of his link began opening, and he felt a surge of panic, sure that Orlandine must be reacting badly and deciding to attack him on a mental level. He tried to fight it, but it just kept on growing wider and, a moment later, he fell into a virtuality.

'You needed secure com,' said a voice.

412

The virtuality filled in, gained colour, texture and depth, and he found himself in a familiar place. A wind-scrubbed sea splashed on a stony beach. Shattered boulders smoked nearby and there, on the shingle, lay the remains of the android Angel. Just a little way from these hovered a gleaming and writhing crinoid form.

'Clean?' he said.

'I can maintain this for just a few minutes. Tell them what you need to tell them as quickly as possible,' said the forensic AI Mobius Clean.

With a thump and clattering of stones, three prador landed on the beach, in three distinct sets of armour. Orlik and Vreen respectively wore white and black and a third wore mirrored armour. After a search, he identified this one as Ksov, the commander of the Jaskoran prador fleet. A woman appeared next, ragged blonde hair tied back, physique boosted but face lined like someone who had not used anti-ageatics for some while. He recognized Diana Windermere. Knobbler joined them too, though he didn't land on the shingle, just seemed to poke half his body through a hole in the air. Then still others appeared, multiplying around him, some half seen, some mere invisible presences. He accepted it and ran with it.

'Commander,' he said to Windermere. 'If you would?'

Windermere shook her head in irritation. 'Not my specialism, Gemmell. Get on with it.'

'Okay. Orlandine is sequestering the civilian population and using them against the hostile Jain tech. There is less of it falling to earth now and few wormships remaining, but she's not loosening her hold, and I have most recent reports that she is trying to take control of my ground forces. It has only been physical thus far, but soon we must close down all com via the data sphere. She is out of control. We have no idea what she will do.'

He paused, waiting for someone to interject, but out of the thousands listening in, not one spoke a word.

He continued, 'We need to consolidate – bring everyone we can to one place and set up defences we can maintain up until the point we can get the fuck off this world. That place is here, in the main city at the medship.'

'Transport,' said Windermere.

'Yes, quite. We have the medship that can take, at a push, over four thousand. Most of the prador can grav to orbit in their armour. Anything weaponized has been taken over by Orlandine, so you all have to grab what you can that's space capable.'

Suggestions fell into his mind, and he began routing them both to a temporary file and to those he was addressing. The suggestions then multiplied as everyone joined in. Many of the ships used to send refugees to the evacuation platforms were down on the surface. They could seal against vacuum thousands of grav-cars and grav-vans, while surface-to-orbit cargo platforms and pods could be adapted.

'We'll need supplies: stone-compressed air, scrubbers, suits, inflatable vacuum habitats. Food and water too but those are not a priority.'

'And why not a priority?' asked Orlik. It was a question echoed by hundreds of other speakers, but he knew the prador commander had asked it just as a prompt.

'U-space disruption is dying,' he replied. 'Once that happens you can be damned sure that Earth Central and the king of the prador are going to arrive here.' He paused, seeing that Diana Windermere did not seem particularly happy about that. 'That's all,' he said. 'Get yourselves moving and get here fast.' Via his gridlink, he sent a request to the forensic AI to nail down the links to both Windermere and Orlik as the others began fading away.

'You have something to add, Commander?' he asked Windermere, once all the others were gone.

Windermere smiled tiredly. 'I rather think that evacuation and or rescue is going to be a very last consideration of anything Earth Central sends.'

'Same too with the king,' added Orlik.

'We can hope and prepare for the best, but we all know what we signed up for.' Gemmell shrugged. 'Let's make rescue a viable option for whatever comes and exclude some at least from the casualty count of planetary obliteration.'

## Trike

The chunk Trike's hardfield had excised from the Jain ship revealed an internal structure of a foamed meta-material – one consisting of packed tubes. There seemed no order here. Or, rather, it was the kind of order found inside a coral rather than a constructed vessel. But in no way was he seeing all of it.

Active scanning revealed this structural material was present for another mile ahead. After this were layers of composites and exotic materials, and great rectangular-section veins conveying strange fluids in which insectile behemoths swam. In other layers beyond, huge machines crouched and sucked energy. He understood that if this ship were a beast, he had only penetrated its epidermis. How then to find its occupant?

Battles raged all around him. The hooder things, the semi-organic occupants of the packed tubes, squirmed out. He realized they must be repair mechanisms whose bodies carried feeds of materials from deeper inside to fix any damaged hull. Macrophages and clotting agents were in the skin. As hostile as anything Jain, they ferociously attacked his remotes. These, in return, soon learned to focus particle beam pulses at points low down on their bodies, bursting open materials feeds and severing energy supplies. Electric discharges leapt between spreading clouds of liquefied particulates like silver blood. Abruptly, he pulled his remotes back, gratified to have lost only a couple of them in this battle, although aware that, on the sheer scale of what they faced, even they were too much. The hooder things waved and oozed from a wall of tubes, but they had caught on and stopped extruding their vulnerable bodies too far out. Consciousness and the feel of his hands shifted into the manipulators of his device. He opened up fusers between the segments of its back and shot forwards, coming down on one of the cowled creatures. As he did this, he pulled in his remotes around him to defend him from the rest. He grabbed the thing he had captured by what he might describe as its throat and, into its face, slammed diamond-nose tentacles. These opened into sprays of microfibres and then nano-fibres as he sought connection. In a moment, he found its brain.

The utterly alien intelligence sat at about the level of a guard dog in terms of processing power, its leash a constant reprogramming feed from elsewhere within the ship. Trike wanted to know the location of that elsewhere. Within just a few seconds, he had complete control of it and pushed down into the feed. He hit a branch point where another submind resided, though this thing seemed more like a data transit lounge. Here he lodged part of his perception and reached out through its many branches with the virtual warfare routines he had used against the first mind. He then quickly seized control of guard dog minds within a volume a hundred miles in diameter and three miles deep. The hooder things ceased to fight and hung limp from their tubes as they pondered the futility of their existence. He pushed on and hit an expansion of consciousness, reached in and felt recognition as a virtuality formed around him.

# THE HUMAN

Here there were spherical cages, like gimbal rings frozen in position with robot arms on the exterior, containing Jain. They had triangular-section tentacles plugged in, with technology like that of the early Polity packed in all around them. The sky hung leaden green over a sea of the same colour. The Jain crowded in that sea and above it, around a city floating on a flat plate, a thing of towers twisted together like toffee sticks. They fought, energy weapons discharging in a riot of destruction, EMR flash shields blanking attacks, cages slamming into each other to tear and dismantle both technology and creatures. This process continued down into the sea, and detritus was strewn on the bottom, larger amalgamate machines arising. The scenario ran, faster and faster, until one Jain survived triumphant in a vast mass of technology that hid both sky and sea. A true piece of history or fantasy? He felt the pressure to believe this a last attempt at Jain communal living. Then the remaining creature slid close before him, encysted in shells of white meta-materials – a dark and rotten core. He wondered if it was borrowing from his mind as he had borrowed from the Client, for this creature was the Librarian's twin.

He reached out to make a full connection, only realizing then that he hung foetal in this mechanical immensity in utterly human form. He folded out, taking control, and was once again monstrous as he flung his virtual attack against this thing. In the virtuality, he tore at the machinery with his claws, ripped it aside and broke it as he burrowed deeper. But then he found something restraining him and, looking back, he saw the power feeds sprouting from his back. These all led to one hole in nothingness, inching and squeezing through too slowly for his intent. He fought on, slower now, tearing all aside with methodical stubborn ferocity. He finally began breaking and tearing up the white shells, struggling to reach what he wanted. The Jain was a black macula down deep, finally revealed as he tore up the remaining layers. Dark stains spread through the white, evaporating even as he exposed them. Then he clawed at nothing, as his own feeds dragged him away and he fell back into himself.

What was real? Trike released his hold on the hooder thing and it fell away, dead and burned. Real, he understood, was that the bandwidth through that thing had not been enough for effective mental battle with the Jain. He retreated in his device, hurtling over to the side of the cavity that his ship's hardfield had cut. He sent his biomechs and remotes over to the edges too. Next, linking back into the core, he fired its weapons on the nearest side. Particle beams speared into the mother ship, slicing through and through. Hot metal vapour filled vacuum and he flicked on his hardfield while his troops sheltered where they could. He felt some of them just wink out, caught by the blast. An inner vein broke and spewed out a fountain of liquid metal. He ordered another firing, and CTDs slammed deep inside. In the back blast the core rose from the hull and shuddered under the impact of thousands of missiles. But it was enough, because now a hole lay all the way through the armour. Down in the firestorm he went, his army following, into cavernous spaces between the loom of mountainous engines. And there an army came to meet him.

## Orlik

Prador all around Orlik sent him multiple views of his near surroundings. These were the original crew of the dreadnought and he wanted them close. He had ordered them not to fire on anything unless it attacked them. Unfortunately, some humans had attacked, and the results had been messy. He had then used the assumed prerogative of the previous captain of that ship, and turned off their weapons. They had not liked that at all.

Meanwhile remaining *Kinghammer* crew were ranging further out and sending him reports on what they were seeing. As they were bright enough to understand events down here on Jaskor, he felt no need to turn off their weapons, even if he could.

'Wouldn't it be better to just get in there quickly?' enquired Sprag from her perch on his back. 'Friend Gemmell seemed to feel some urgency.'

Orlik's armour possessed a grav-engine and advanced ionic thrusters, but he had chosen to walk. The stroll had for him a nostalgic aspect. He had been on worlds like this long ago – worlds steadily being destroyed by warfare.

'I'm not in any great hurry,' he replied. 'And no one is leaving until this shitstorm abates.'

'It does have a strange hostile beauty,' said Sprag, the tone of her voice tuned to penetrate the constant rumbling and crashing.

Orlik guessed the assassin drone was feeling the nostalgia too.

Highlighted against a backdrop of dark bronze, explosions and a rain of burning debris lit the sky. A thin, dirty rain wafted through warm air with a hundred per cent humidity, and he had to haul himself up on grav to get out of areas rapidly turning into bog. And everywhere the growths spread.

One of the towers reared up close, its veined surface shifting as it tilted to acquire another target. It crashed like close lightning as it fired, its projectile etching a glowing line upwards. The ensuing explosive impact up high showered burning fragments across the sky – writhing snakes picked up by particle beams turning mauve in the filthy air. Burned to ash. Other towers, visible through the humid haze, spewed out their fire. Growths had risen from the ground for as far as Orlik could see: metallic mushrooms bigger than he was, objects like fragments of giant eggshells that seemed to be transmission dishes. Some areas crawled with moving roots, best avoided since he had seen them eagerly groping towards him. But now his attention fell on something else a few miles away, viewed through cams on the armour of one of *Kinghammer*'s crew.

The thing resembled a small medieval city: layer upon layer, with the appearance of tangled stone architecture, climbed to a peak upon which sat a huge bud. This began opening while the surrounding earth steamed. For a short while, everything grew still and it seemed the very ground was tensing up. Then the construct jerked, as if ejecting its energy required a physical act.

A bar of gold flashed up into the sky, then a cylindrical blast front expanded out from this. Orlik hunkered down, his visor darkening against the glare. As the front hit the viewing prador, he glimpsed through it a helical pillar, red as blood, rising from the construct. The blast ploughed him back through the mud, while the airborne prador tumbled through the sky above. Blast after blast issued from the thing, pushing him back, then reversing to drag him forwards again, regular as the beat of some giant piston engine. Then the sky lit up and the beam collapsed.

'Familiar,' said Sprag, as mud sleeted down.

Orlik now understood the odd blast front effect. Orlandine had copied the weapon he had inadvertently created, and was firing it from the planet. The thing unlocked the energy stored in matter. Its fission effect worked on any matter it passed through, and that included air. The air released its energy in a blast, but that same release created a vacuum the air again filled, which accounted for the rhythmic effect. He called up detector readings in his visor, confirming this by the skyrocketing radiation count.

'Report status,' he instructed generally.

The dreadnought crew reported no injuries – the prador glyphs for that scrolling down one side of his visor – while the *Kinghammer* survivors added some colourful expletives over radio.

'If you are down near me,' he instructed, 'stay on the ground and close on my position. Everyone else head in to the coordinates given.' He then cut com and commented to Sprag as he moved on, 'Not a good weapon to fire from a planet.'

From his back, Sprag replied, 'I think this place is beyond saving. Don't you?'

Orlik got the double meaning of that. Life, being tough and adaptable, could reoccupy the biosphere. The atmospheric disturbances and seismic activity might last for centuries, but they would end. This world *could* recover. However, though the Jain tech swarming about this world was supposedly the *good* kind, under the control of Orlandine, he knew that neither the king nor Earth Central would see it that way. He could see planet busters and Polity imploders in Jaskor's future.

The blast in the sky spread, waning occasionally then lighting up with new brilliance in different locations. A wormship came down with all its parts burning like fuses, the fire spreading through the air in an ever-widening wake behind it. After taking half a second to calculate its vector, Orlik warned his crews, then engaged grav and flung himself towards a humped growth in the ground. It would offer some cover. As he skidded in behind it, his visor automatically threw target frames over those already hiding here. The four humans pointed their weapons, and two high-intensity lasers stabbed out, sizzling across his armour. He restrained himself, because he had seen these before – they had been the reason for that earlier shooting incident, and were why Gemmell wanted to get off-world. The firing abruptly cut off and they lost interest in him, ducking back down again and awaiting further orders from their controlling intelligence. From Orlandine. He studied them, as the wormship hit the ground, raising a ball of fire beyond their hideaway.

Tears and holes in their ragged clothing exposed armour that had welled up from their skin. Their weapons were extensions of their right arms. One turned fully away to expose a segmented hump on her back. Orlik identified it as an organic power supply. Here crouched one of Orlandine's clear-up teams, whose utility was diminishing now that so little reached the ground. Would she strip out the Jain tech and release them? What about the other things he had seen? Would she release the amphibians and large ground eels, the insects which buzzed through the air, flashing out objects almost too small to see? Gemmell did not think so. The war and assassin drones who had been Orlandine's comrades for many centuries were even less optimistic.

The ground heaved underneath them and a storm of burning fragments rained down. Out of this came two of the dreadnought's crew, weapons trained on the humans even though unable to fire. They skidded in beside Orlik then abruptly backed off, cowering low. He found this distasteful and returned his attention to the humans as they moved out from cover and headed towards the wormship wreck. Other things were appearing over there too: pseudopods rising up and snapping down like striking snakes. Then suddenly, with multiple sonic booms, four attack pods arrived above and began frying the area with particle beams. The humans were part of the same response, sequestered to burn up hostile Jain-tech remains.

'Sometimes you become the enemy you fight,' commented Sprag levelly.

More of the dreadnought crew arrived, along with two of his old crew. Orlik moved out of cover, glancing towards the wormship wreckage and seeing writhing forms in a spreading inferno. He could not tell which were from the ship, and which belonged to Orlandine.

'Sometimes you were always that anyway,' he replied.

## Trike

Two armies joined in chaotic battle in an architecture dreamed up by the most deranged biomechanical artist. In silvered tubes, huge insectile remotes slammed head to head with distorted monsters out of the nightmares of Hieronymus Bosch. Energy beams scored against hardfields in spear and shield jousts that turned their surroundings into collapsing molten ruin. The things like hooders crashed down onto spherical biomechs only to have the passing giant cousins of horseshoe crabs sever them at the neck. Trike's forces penetrated into the body of the ship like a spreading infection, and all these others came against them like the immune response. As he fell upon the back of a creature resembling a car-sized shield bug and dismembered it, he assessed and scanned. His penetration of the ship had happened fast and his creatures, those extensions of himself, had spread out widely, destroying its internal defences. But it was nowhere near enough. They had ranged out across only tens of miles in the vast internal volume of a thing which was a thousand miles long.

In the shield bug, he found a submind and drove vicious contact through it. Again, he found himself in a buffering virtuality where scenes of Jain history, or fantasy, played out and ejected him. His remotes and biomechs made similar incursions into the mental architecture of the ship, and it similarly expelled them. Access through individual elements limited the foothold in there, and he needed that, for physical attack would not be enough. He decided to try something else.

Halting their advance, he altered his creatures' aims. No longer would they first destroy opposition before attempting to launch virtual attacks, if enough remained for viable contact. Contact now became their prime goal. The defenders advanced and Trike's soldiers fell on them. Destruction waned as his force switched wholly to close combat using shields, cutting lasers and driving in with tentacles to find subminds or system connections. Trike pulled himself back, concentrating on blending with all his subpersonae distributed through his force, truly becoming one entity. As connection after connection locked home, he got the bandwidth he required to push right inside, and he found immensity. And it fell on him.

The hostility felt strangely clean. He did not recognize the emotions as anything human or even prador. Something like hate blurred into love. The urge to destroy bled into the urge to acquire and thence preserve. The Jain mentality closed all around him and ripped into his mind, while its creatures tore at his. But he ripped right back in a hungry quest for data, while his creatures shredded and dismantled their foes and, as connections broke, discarded them to seek out others. Yet, though he was physically present, the Jain was not. Where was it? He delved deeper, seeking a location and mapped the routes of data transfer throughout the giant vessel. The intelligence kept trying to divert him on endless courses throughout, as if implying it had no centre, but in the end, he found something. In the growing schematic of the behemoth around him, he saw a central chamber.

The heart of the ship.

**The Client**

Embodied in her remote, the Client entered the hold of Weapons Platform Mu, scuttled up to the racked objects there and chose one at random. It didn't matter which one, since they were all multipurpose tools with the same underlying structure. She reached in and grabbed an object like a walnut the size of a man's head, tucked it hard against her body and headed back to her environment cylinder.

Within her cylinder, her primary form held the beautiful, perfect structure of the disruptor virus in her mind. She felt both amazed and proud of what she had done, but knew it was something only a Polity planetary AI could appreciate. Certainly, the Old Captain, now watching her robots strip out the contents of one of her disposable laboratories, could not. She then felt some disquiet, wondering if her satisfaction might be due to Jain influence on her. But after a moment of self-analysis, she realized it was merely vanity, and focused her attention on the other laboratory.

Here her machines were assembling a device which was both a nano-factory and delivery mechanism. No one had seen anything quite like this, either in the Polity or in the realm of her Species. The virus, being a combination of molecular and force-field tech, was unstable until delivered precisely where needed. This device would manufacture the thing at its core, and act as its means of delivery.

'Getting a bit slow and highly technical round here,' said Cog.

'I have created a way to disrupt the underlying picotech of Jain technology,' she replied, expecting only bafflement.

'No, you haven't,' he said, standing up quickly.

She swung her front end round to face him. 'Why do you deny this?'

'You're telling me you've found a way to destroy Jain tech. All Jain tech?'

'No, I'm telling you I have found a way to disrupt its under-lying picotech.'

Cog harrumphed and took out his pipe again. She ignored him.

At length it was done. The device looked like a big rock-clinging mollusc, though cubic patterns writ on its flat underside resembled those seen on the surface of a Jain node. The gimbal clamps holding it detached and a robot claw delivered it out through the side hatch into the forelimbs of her primary form. Meanwhile the remote arrived from the hold. With a thought, she directed it to the other sphere. It climbed inside and placed the walnut object in the gimbal clamps there and, before departing, inserted a forelimb into a hole in its surface and injected a molecular instruction.

The chunk of Librarian tech parted like a segmented orange and began to issue smoke. It protruded tentacles through the gaps and these grew outwards, the segments shrinking as they did so. Finally, they touched the chain-glass of the sphere and halted. The glass darkened noticeably at the contact points. She moved over to peer in at an object like the root system of a tree. She flipped open the side hatch, ducked her head end inside, pressed the device into place on the thing and retreated.

'So what do you expect—'

Before Cog could finish his sentence, the mass of tentacles and tendrils jerked, as if they were alive and had received an electric shock. Waves of iridescence sped across its surface. The Client knew this could not be the plasmon waves because they had already passed. It was some larger and unexpected effect. The limpet of technology fell off, and then the mass began peeling, unravelling, falling in pieces to the bottom of the sphere.

'I don't think you expected that,' said Cog.

The Client ignored him, opened the sphere and reached inside to retrieve the device. No, she had not expected this nor wanted it. She had intended the device to disrupt the picotech and nothing more. It was supposed to leave the larger structures and function of the technology in place. If she used it in her platform, she would lose too much. This technology linked all her disrupt-ors, her enclosing hardfield, her U-space drive – all would fail as it failed.

'So is that a one-trick pony?' asked Cog.

'Do you mean –' the Client search her colloquial Anglic vocabulary – 'has it shot its bolt?'

'Yeah, that's what I mean.'

Her device had demonstrated which was cause and which was effect. Because she did not herself have the tools to manipulate picotech directly, she had assumed the same of the Jain. But it seemed they had built their technology from the bottom upwards. Destroy the picotech foundation and the whole structure collapsed. Nothing in her Librarian memories told her this. She could only assume the Librarian had taken this technology from another. That it had not been included in Species technology also told her that, knowing the dangers, the Librarian had not passed it on.

'No, it has not,' she replied. 'Attach this to any Jain tech and it will do the same repeatedly.'

'Oh right,' he said casually.

He was eyeing that weapon of his again and she suddenly felt far too close to him. She began backing away, the device clutched close to her upper segment.

# 18

*In the far past, the enslavement of people was fast and dirty. Individuals were seized and put into chains, then brutalized into cooperation. Those who did this did not consider themselves evil; they thought of the slaves as subhuman, themselves a superior species, and this the natural order. The perception of superiority continued into supposedly more civilized times, while the enslavement necessarily took a slower and more subtle course. Before the Quiet War, it came through restrictions on liberty by increasingly bloated government. Citizens found themselves becoming chattels of the state, and its corporate partners. An ever-increasing number of rules and regulations, produced by ever-expanding bureaucracy, required funding through taxation. Those citizens were complicit in this because, foolishly, they believed in every new 'danger' pointed out to them by the elites, which, of course, each needed 'regulation'. The politicians who made and imposed the rules considered themselves a superior species too, and also felt sure their steady enslavement of the populace was only the natural order of things.*

From 'Quince Guide' compiled by humans

**Diana**

'It's one the hostile tech seized before,' said Diana.

The data sphere, which for the present they continued to use, revealed all. The prador on the bridge over the city moat was one Orlandine had frozen and vitrified. Gemmell's marines had moved it into a store within the city, along with many humans in the same state. But Orlandine had since raided that store and made them useful to her. When approached, the prador seemed rooted to the spot by vine-like Jain growths wound around his legs and spread all over his armour. But, snapping these, he was able to move and headed to the edge nearest them, with the vines then reconnecting to those from the bridge itself, which was constructed of them. The creature showed no particular signs of hostility but still, in place of one claw sat a particle cannon with an improbably wide throat, while the other claw sported the customary Gatling cannon clipped along its side.

'She's seriously stepped over the line,' said Jabro. 'First wild creatures, then those on our side who had been sequestered. Now this.' He gestured, encompassing the prador and the party of humans heading in from the wasteland to cross the bridge back into the city.

The comment annoyed Diana. 'It's not like you to state the obvious.'

Jabro shrugged. 'Inexplicably I feel a little out of sorts.'

The annoyance cleared. 'That's better.'

Jabro grinned, then tapped the wrist console of the powered envirosuit he wore. The concertinaed hood rose up out of its neck ring over his head, but he did not yet close the visor.

'Like Gemmell said, she's out of control,' suggested Seckurg.

Diana nodded. 'And she probably doesn't think she is.' She tapped her own wrist control to raise her helmet, then her visor to seal her suit completely. The swarm biomechs Orlandine had been using to seize control of people had not yet strayed out of the city, but there was no guarantee they would not.

'All of you, seal up,' she ordered.

Jabro closed his visor, as did the other humans in her crew. She studied Seckurg, who only wore a light shipsuit, somehow reluctant to point out that Golem were just as susceptible as humans. But reading her disquiet, he took a device from his belt and mounted it on his shoulder, plugging its cable into a socket in his chest. The thing spun and fired a test shot, visible red in the rain, which blew a small smoking hole in the ground some yards ahead. The other Golem began mounting similar laser bug zappers. These were items of hostile-environment kit specifically for Golem, though it baffled her how they had been included in the bridge pod supplies.

'We've got company,' said one of them.

Diana whirled towards the recent explosion, expecting to see something nasty arising from the remains of the wormship. She then recognized Orlik amidst the mass of prador swarming across the muddy ground towards them.

'Strange times we find ourselves in,' commented Jabro.

She looked at him quizzically.

He shrugged. 'I never expected to be glad to see a group like that.'

'Strange times indeed,' she agreed.

The prador drew closer and she counted over forty of them on the ground, while others headed to the city overhead. Orlik finally perambulated up to stand before her, the other prador falling into ranks behind him, their weapons all at port arms. A show of respect? Or Orlik's instruction to prevent any friendly-fire incidents?

'I note your reluctance to cross,' said Orlik.

Diana shrugged and gestured towards the bridge. 'Our escape pod and supplies were damaged when we came down. We don't have any grav-gear except that sled.'

Orlik eyed the bridge. 'And I understand your reluctance.' He abruptly moved past her and headed towards the structure. As he reached the edge of the thick Jain growth he halted, then the clattering and bubbling of prador speech issued from his PA system. It ran for a moment before Diana thought to put it through a translation program in the hardware in her skull. As expected, Orlik asked questions. The creature on the bridge uttered some terse replies then abruptly lowered its weapons. Orlik returned.

'See,' he said. 'All clear now.' Either his translator, or his own use of Anglic, was good, because the words dripped sarcasm.

Diana studied the bridge again. The thing was all moving Jain-tech tentacles writhing past each other like slow snakes in oil.

'I have a better idea,' she said.

'I thought so,' said Orlik, reaching out with one claw and closing it, gently, around her waist. She shrugged acquiescence and he lifted her up.

'Welcome to my ride,' said Sprag, when Orlik deposited her on his back.


## Trike

Wrapped in his Jain device, Trike fell on a conglomeration of hooder biomechs. He severed away head ends, using tentacles with mono-diamond edges sharper even than the limbs of Cutter. The hooded heads bore some similarity to the biomech he and Cog had first seen in the Species living section, many of which ran with his army of remotes. When cut from their long ribbed bodies, they continued independent life – the ecology of the ship responding to his earlier tactic. He juggled them like a mother cat trying to restrain her kittens, then hit them with micropore lasers, making careful punctures through their carapaces. One after another, he caught and held them, injected microfibres which branched into nano-fibres, paralysing pseudo-nerves and penetrating their minds. He poured in virtual warfare, complemented by induction pulses and targeted intense-pulse masers that didn't burn but did disrupt. As their minds failed, he injected his own overlays, then released them. Now they were his – additions to his army, unwilling turncoats.

Around him his soldiers launched similar assaults, though with limited success. This went some way to replace those he had lost to the horrendous casualty rate in here. Another wall blew out – a shaped nuclear charge slicing out a ring. Metallic fluid exploded into vacuum in curled leaves and sheets around the advance of his creatures. They entered a great rectangular tunnel, miles across, where behemoths like water skaters braced giant limbs against the walls and launched squat, cylindrical chunks from their head ends. These unwound into centipedes of glass which jetted dissolving enzyme gases from each limb. No sequestering for these – they shattered under railgun strikes into fogs of glittering acidic crystals. But Trike swept down onto one behemoth, drove tongs between its back segments to part them and speared in tentacles. These ran chain-fibre diamonds to cut through its internals, spewing in fibres that sought out connection. First, he limited himself to the mind of the creature. Then he saw opportunity in a loose network, and reached out to thousands of others, for hundreds of miles around the ship's veins. But this again opened him to the Jain's mental assault.

There was no finesse this time, the virtuality was a straight steal and adaptation from the memories the Client had given him. In semi-human form, he crashed straight into the side of a Jain and tore at its stony carapace. Its tentacles smacked him like beam ends and chewed at his flesh like grinding discs against wood. A claw closed on his leg, while he gripped another and began smashing his fist into the creature's body above the tentacles. His bones broke and reknitted instantly and finally shell shattered before him. He caught an edge and tore it up, drove in his head and then his tongue, and with a snap, the virtuality broke and he had them. The giant creatures moved into the advance, burning through structure with enzyme-spitting worms. In floods of liquid metal, propelling trash storms of debris, Trike and his creatures advanced deeper into the Jain ship.

Here vast racks held the balled-up forms of wormships. Curved surfaces miles wide spread with stains of elliptical bots, whirling into the spaces and shedding atomically thin skins like shrapnel. Then, at last, he saw a geodesic sphere a mile across – relatively small in all this vastness. He swarmed down towards it, a wave of creatures and destruction finally falling in all around the thing and clinging where intersecting beams supported it. Trike brought himself to one pane of the geodesic and probed it with a tentacle, sampling its surface to discover a crystalline and incredibly hard substance similar to chain-glass. Another sample from the frame holding it revealed an exotic composite that drew away heat in an instant; it must have been laced with superconductor. He could destroy this, but he became cautious when he noticed the enemy biomechs gathering.

The Jain might not be here. How simple it would be to lure an effective attacker to a place like this and detonate a big CTD. Sure, the blast would wreck a great deal of the ship's internals but that would be the end of the attacker. Yet he understood the psychology of the Jain now and knew they did not operate like that. Effective attackers offered useful data and technology, so must be pillaged and absorbed, to make the Jain stronger during the next, inevitably hostile, encounter. No, this was a test.

He read the crystal before him, scanning its molecular structure into his mind. The atomic forces of this complex interweaving of chain molecules had been tampered with, like the material of those giant attack ships. Energy weapons would fail against it while railgun strikes would only dent it. But, just like chain-glass, it had its weakness, though in this case finding it required a great deal of knowledge, processing power and concentration. Even as he realized this, the surrounding enemy biomechs swarmed in. Could he be exact under pressure? He continued examining and processing, even as the two armies of biomechs clashed. The weakness was revealed and he started to construct the decoding molecule inside himself, even while smashing aside a series of disc mechs zipping towards him, hyper-dense cutters screaming around their rims. He then hesitated – it had been too easy. Running the math and models again and again, he finally found the flaw: simple decoding would collapse the chain molecule but reset molecular binding forces, resulting in a fission explosion. His decoder required just one tweak, one molecule changed. The chain would collapse but then, just a moment later, reassemble.

Trike applied the decoder to the crystal and it rippled and collapsed into strands. He grabbed the rim with his tentacles and hauled himself through, the strands snapping like spaghetti. Once inside, he observed through sensors on his back the strands snap back together across the gap, then expand and recrystallize, blocking it off again. He had opened the door, but the Jain had closed it behind him.

The interior of the geodesic contained only a column rising from the bottom with a platform on it, positioning his enemy right at the centre. It was much the same as the Librarian the Client had encountered: a great lobster-like thing, matt black and inlaid with silver tech, triangular-section tentacles spread from below its head. One claw was open to the air in here, which was low-pressure argon. It struck Trike as incredibly ancient, but that might just have been an artefact of his thinking. He fell towards it, now noting the differences between this one and the Librarian. A nest of connections into its body constrained this creature.

434

Scan revealed sheathed organics, superconductors, as well as reflective nanotube cables to convey all forms of radiation, gas tubes and others filled with liquids that might have been nutrients. However, nothing moved in those tubes, cables and optics.

Trike drew closer, baffled by the lack of weapons. The Jain wanted to pillage him, yet it seemed defenceless. He readied to fire a small CTD warhead, expecting some hostile response. Then he hesitated. Another trap? Instead, he fixed an induction warfare beam and, active scanning on the thing, waited again for a reaction. Still nothing and, as he began to collate data on the creature, he saw why. He found metabolic processes wound down to entropy, withered organs and muscles – the remains of a creature from a highly technical civilization, completely mummified. It wasn't beyond resurrection. In fact, the numerous complex support technologies here could bring it to life in very little time at all. But no thoughts fired in its complex brain. So this ship was just like the Species ship, with its inhabitant long expired? As he retreated to the wall of the geodesic, decoded a pane, and fell out into the mayhem of battle, he knew that this was not the case. He ordered his creatures to spread out and again make multiple links into what was nominally the ship's system – the largest bandwidth they could manage. Even as his creatures established connections, he felt, all around him, the savage amusement of something utterly alien. Then he, his creatures, the totality of his attack, translated directly into virtuality.

They spread out on a plain that twisted around overhead in any direction he viewed it – a Mobius surface. His creatures and the ship biomechs were at first distinct as they tore at each other while, hung in dislocated space, Trike grappled with the mind of his opponent through them. Then the opponents began to meld into a great snake of armoured bodies and limbs, wound with tentacular Jain, joining overhead in a complete ring and perpetually sliding into each other like some strange ouroboros. Mentally divided through all his parts, Trike now engaged with the dispersed reality of the Jain mind. Orlandine's memories gave him recognition of the original entity, of which the Wheel had been a copy. And just as she did with that thing, he attacked this one and started to absorb what he could. The virtuality shuddered and folded up around him. He found himself hanging in darkness but surrounded by the ring as it transformed into a shifting kaleidoscope of glassy blades whickering against each other. Other memories impinged, for Angel had seen the Wheel like this in his mind. Distraction and misdirection. Trike crashed into it mentally, sucking up technological data and history until, at last, he began to truly grasp what he faced. And it was there at the root, in Jain history, and in what they became.

## Earth Central

The hammerheads and kamikazes surfaced from underspace with merely a whisper, perfectly on target and at once in battle. White lasers flared out into vacuum, vaporizing objects immediately identifiable as hostile Jain tech. The kamikazes received their orders. Their purpose was to reach a target before detonating, and they too had their weapons and opened fire. Within minutes, an area of vacuum ten thousand miles across around the ships filled with hot vapour. Earth Central opened out the mile-wide cube which it occupied, and felt this action akin to a smile as it surveyed its surroundings.

Nineteen hammerheads sat in two ring formations about the thousands of kamikazes the king had reluctantly provided. There had been twenty, but the initial premature jump into disrupted U-space had destroyed one, along with a large number of kamikazes. No matter. EC focused its attention out from the fleet. No nearby Jain items remained, but another object sat out there untouched. The AI studied this closely.

'*Report*,' EC instructed, nailing the object with a combined virtual warfare and coms beam – a complex multi-spectrum vortex laser with a data flashback core. The beam invaded the chunk of quantum lattice crystal wrapped in its grey metal carrier case. EC sensed the mentality there momentarily rebel, then accept it could do nothing. The rebellion, EC understood, was due to the AI in that crystal thinking it faced an enemy. Now it realized this *might* not be the situation.

The AI of the erstwhile Weapons Platform Irapetus said, '*It's you.*' EC held off replying for a moment, firing off a missile through one coilgun. It shot out, unfolding saw-toothed limbs from a central body of a drive, with a submind and sensory head. Approaching the carrier case, the retrieval robot flipped, slowed and snatched up the AI, then flung itself into a hundred-gravity turn and headed back. This caused a brief transmission interruption until the robot inserted data plugs into numerous sockets.

'*Yes, it is me*,' EC replied to the platform AI. '*Give me data.*'

'*You're not very polite.*'

'*Get over it.*'

A mental snort ensued, shortly followed by a data package and then stream. EC took the package apart in an instant and incorporated a précis of all that the AI had seen up to the point it had ejected from its platform. This was just before invasive Jain tentacles had eaten their way through the shell around its home. The stream gave detail, a log of all the telemetry, all the specifics, only . . . the platform AI was not a slow creature and could have incorporated all of this in the first package. It was therefore being parsimonious with the truth and had given itself time to edit the detail. EC left off responding for five seconds, that being enough time to make the AI think it had got away with it, then went into its mind like a knife. The AI shrieked and dropped into virtuality. Two figures stood on a slab of rock floating in a firestorm. EC materialized as a featureless humanoid while the platform AI seemed to be a Greek hoplite warrior, keeping him at bay with a bronze spear. Another delaying tactic. EC stepped forwards and grabbed the warrior by the throat, ignoring the spear through his guts. This in turn was a viral attack, leaping into the system of the retrieval robot. He reached up and ripped away the warrior's helmet, incidentally tearing away the top of his skull to expose his brain, and then poised his hand over it.

'Okay! Okay!' the hoplite yelled in ancient Greek.

The virtuality fogged away and EC was fully in, grabbing the edits and viewing them. The platform AI had been disinclined to share disruptor technology and the defence against it, including the new iteration of that technology, apparently created by the prador Orlik, which seemed an unlikely occurrence. EC understood the platform AI's caution. Though it had recognized an EC submind, it had not known for sure. By blocking and getting this up close and personal, it now knew for sure, and willingly handed over even more. EC absorbed the history of the Jain and the Species and further understood events here. It focused on what Orlandine had done to herself, then withdrew. Next, keeping half an eye on the AI as the robot brought it into one of the other hammerheads, EC turned its attention to a potentially solvable first problem out here, before its inevitable jump to the inner system.

The gas giant appeared to be evaporating into vacuum. It also had the look of a space station, burned and peeled with energy weapons to expose its underlying geodesic structure. These honeycomb masses were the spreading Jain tech, for the giant had become a factory for the production of the objects swarming up from its atmosphere. Something to deal with, certainly, but first the runcible.

The biggest emission of objects rose from the equator, a great fountain hundreds of miles across, dragged round by the spin of the orb and forming into a spiralling ring. EC gazed at the source of all this and considered how building a runcible there, on a gas giant, in so little time, lay far beyond Polity technology. It then noted how tempting such advanced technology was to civilizations like the Polity and the Prador Kingdom, which was precisely the problem. In consonance with that thought, hammerhead coilguns opened fire.

Sixteen missiles hurtled out. EC watched them streak down, and studied the runcible, both across the EMR spectrum and in U-space, since that view was becoming increasingly available. The missiles fired up their drives and separated at the last, eight of them darting in to pass through the gate and disappear, the other eight hitting its rim shortly afterwards. The meniscus blinked out as the first eight destroyed the other gate which was by the rapidly disintegrating accretion disc, chopping off the flow of Jain tech from there. The second eight struck the gate here, explosions evenly spread around the ring. It disappeared entirely as they merged into one ball of fire seven thousand miles across. The whole atmosphere of the planet disrupted as this ball rose into space and distorted into a burning anvil shape. It gratified EC to see ensuing storms down there, nearly the size of planet Earth, destroying further Jain tech. But they were not enough.

EC now directed intense scanning at the planet, punching through the layers of gas. As expected, despite the present storms, it was annoyingly stable, so the AI paid attention to the spreading Jain tech. Tubes jutted up from the honeycomb masses, looking like chimneys as they spewed clouds of Jain devices. Notably, the Jain structure did not extend any deeper than the liquid hydrogen layer. That made sense. They were floating in a layer where they had access to materials they could use, whereas pure hydrogen had limited value. A scan of the devices spreading into vacuum showed they consisted mainly of carbon, hydrocarbons and polycarbonate, so the growths down there must be cracking methane. This dearth of heavier elements resulted in the tech being flimsy.

EC mentally eyed the massive armouries of the hammerheads and the materials available, instantly putting together a formula for an energy weapon particulate. It set plants within all the ships to making it. As these plants fired up, the AI felt some amusement, remembering Orlandine had used this approach many centuries ago when she leveraged chemicals and processes available to destroy a planetoid. In that case, she had used a simple reaction: the photochlorination of methane. She had mixed the two substances inside the planetoid, heated them and then supplied the correct frequency of light to ignite them. Here, the process would be more complicated, and nothing would be blowing up, just burning.

In just a short time, the particulate began flowing out through pipes from the plants. The nano-spheres of layered metal oxides were ready. Just dropping these into liquid hydrogen would have an effect – a catalytic reaction boiling out hydrides and water vapour. But firing tons of them into it, negatively charged, at close to the speed of light, ramped up the effect by orders of magnitude.

Meanwhile the hammerheads and kamikazes continued to fire, incinerating Jain objects at increasing distances from them. EC noted how much of the ejecta from the gas giant were settling on the moons. There it grazed on heavier elements and filled out its structure. Toughening up.

A close view of the gas giant showed two of its moons in

silhouette, while to either side hammerheads were visible taking their positions. Four moons were viable targets for the kamikazes, but also for the cornucopia of missiles aboard the hammerheads, just as the runcible had been. But EC decided it was time to ensure its control of the kamikazes. It sent instructions to four of them – medium-load weapons each with a destructive force measured merely in single-figure gigatons. Four drives ignited, highlighting the position of the great shoal of erstwhile prador children turned into bombs. Momentarily, EC felt a moral qualm, but then leavened that with the knowledge that this end had become their reason for existence.

The four fell from the shoal and streaked down towards the gas giant, their courses curving as one then abruptly diverging. Close view of the first target. Opencast square holes dotted the moon's sulphurous yellow and brown landscape where Orlandine had mined it. Tentacular growth swarmed there and, from a distance, looked like an oil slick licking about the surface. The kamikaze flashed in at twenty thousand miles an hour. A brief flash marked its impact site and then a plume of glittering gas and ice spewed out. A ripple spread around the crust from this point, and the moon shrugged. A brief pause ensued and then the thing began to expand rapidly, wiping out those surface features. It opened fiery cracks and parted like a rotten peach. The image blanked for a second on the glare of the massive contraterrene explosion, then came back on to show the expanding globe of fire. The more distant view of the entire giant showed this, then another flash came from another orbit further round as the next moon went. Turned to burning rubble and wraiths of fire, the two moons began to spread in a ring around the planet, melding with the anvil cloud there. Further debris masses from the other two moons reached round from the opposite side like glowing fingers.

The destruction of the moons caused further major disturbances down on the gas giant's surface. Eye-storms began ploughing through Jain masses. One of these, at the forefront of thousand-mile-an-hour winds, began tilting up, its structure rising into atmosphere and there breaking apart. Time to complete the job.

Particle beams, the pale green of avocado, stabbed out from one hammerhead. There were eight, each six feet wide. As they drew closer to the gas giant, they glowed brighter as their particulate struck disperse atoms, then turned to an eye-aching glare as they punched through stratosphere. Deeper still and they lost more coherence, flaming like white-hot bars in a mist of oil. They hit evenly spaced across a spread of Jain structure and just for a second had no effect at all. Then the structure darkened over underlying fire. Just as the beams shut down, that fire exploded up through it, flinging chunks like logs kicked from a blaze, thousands of miles up into the stratosphere. The fire spread, bright angry red against the pale shades of the giant. Then fire cyclones hundreds of miles across peeled away as the remaining structure sank into the furnace. In some areas, EC observed portions of the thing trying to draw on the energy and regrow, but they lost the battle. Finally, nothing remained but the firestorm, spreading into the orbital stripes of the gas giant.

The AI had learned all it needed from that first strike, so altered the spacing of the ensuing ones and reduced the aperture of the beams. It didn't want too much of that stuff blown up into the stratosphere – it had no doubt, once it fell back down, it would begin growing again. The hammerheads opened fire once more, setting other monstrous firestorms all around the gas giant. These incinerated their targets and spilled slews of umber hydrides and white water vapour, turning rapidly to ice crystals, for thousands of miles. Over the ensuing hours, secondary strikes took out new growths and then, in time, the disturbance down there seemed enough to prevent anything taking root.

It would come back, EC felt sure, but not quickly enough to affect the outcome of whatever ensued in the inner system. Presuming success in the Jaskoran system, EC would later need to station platforms here, or else demolish the gas giant. However, the Jain ship would not be so easy to deal with, if EC could deal with it at all.

Then, of course, there was the other situation . . . other problems. Jain technology, as far as EC knew, had destroyed three or possibly four highly technical alien civilizations. They had been in advance of the Polity and doubtless had individuals as adept and intelligent as Orlandine. Had they also thought to control the technology? Had individuals in those civilizations not been able to see beyond the relatively brief spans of their existences? This seemed the case. Orlandine, judging by the evidence thus far accrued, was almost certainly making the same disastrous mistakes, which, unfortunately, meant her span would have to be briefer still.

## Orlandine

The linear accelerator cut through ten miles of crust, down to the magma. There, bulbous ceramic factories processed molten materials into its projectiles. To give the weapon the scope Orlandine required, it had been necessary to excavate a mass of the crust all around it. This, combined with the ability to flex and curve its upper two miles, enabled a sixty-degree range of fire. Other accelerators on land and in the ocean gave her overlapping fields of fire and complete coverage of everything lying beyond the stratosphere. However, beyond ten thousand miles, the inaccuracy of targeting made it pointless to shoot at anything smaller than a wormship. And few of those remained now.

She selected a remaining target cluster out in vacuum. The accelerator heaved, spewing out a line of projectiles, thunder-cracking through atmosphere and heating to hot red by the time they departed the stratosphere. The cluster of five wormships began to part, but not quickly enough. The projectiles slammed in, the energy generated by their impact turning their cores molten and shattering ceramic cases that shrapnelled out with devastating effect. A spreading cloud of radiating wormship debris, too small to target, was all that remained.

Orlandine scanned around with her larger weapons for further suitable targets, but there were none. She had destroyed all the wormships. Certainly, the cloud still fell in towards the world, but she had enough armament and resources to deal with it. She checked this, focusing on the disruptor buds all around the planet, the weapons platforms and ships down on the surface she controlled, and the attack pods she had shoaling through atmosphere. More than enough and, if anything got past them, her clean-up crews could handle it. Orlandine gazed at these. She saw the millions of mantis shrimps boiling cubic miles of ocean with super-cavitating glee. Fish down there were adapted with ceramic teeth and mouths lined with chain-glass to tear apart Jain objects. On the land, she watched amphibians sporting iron burners to fry anything moving. The humans, with their integral beam weapons and protective armour, ranged across the continent like tribal hunting parties. All was at optimum and it was now time to think beyond mere moment-to-moment survival.

She began automating processes that no longer required her direct attention, freeing up computing space in her extended mind. She started reincorporating data stored in memory crystals all around the world. Though her control had been complex and massive, her thought processes had been, essentially, those of an animal flooded with adrenalin and fighting to survive. Now, raggedly at first, her thinking began to expand beyond that.

Something was wrong. Something about the humans.

She studied them closely, trying to understand the fault to which her deeper mind had alerted her. She penetrated first those the attacking Jain tech had sequestered and which she had then taken over, for faults were more likely in them. She went deep, analysing processes as far down as her perception could go, which unfortunately did not reach much below the nanoscopic. She could find nothing. She then analysed gross structure and, though noting the damage to their original organic forms, could not see how this affected their efficiency. She moved on to those she herself had seized control of and could see no difference to the first group. She stepped back further to analyse the overall deployment of these creatures. If anything, they were now overkill, just like her major weapons. Unless she faced some new assault against this world, the over one hundred million human beings she controlled were redundant. But none of these observations accounted for her deep reaction to them; that feeling of wrongness steadily growing as her thinking swelled.

Orlandine dropped these analyses because they were a distraction. Though no longer such a threat, the hostile Jain tech had to remain her primary focus. She decided that sitting down in this gravity well, waiting for it to come to her, was no longer an option. Time to reach out. She focused her attention on her weapons platforms and warships. Their firing was intermittent and, as a result, the feeds she had running into them had filled their armouries to overflowing and packed their energy storage full. She focused then on one platform, while mirroring the process she conducted there in all the other platforms and ships. All these vessels no longer possessed controlling minds and required them. In the AI chamber of this platform, her tentacles plugged into the AI interface leads. She began building, in the tentacles themselves, layered organo-metal, cut through with shear planes of AI quantum sapphire. Even as this substrate grew, she split off a small subpersona and loaded it. This she did a hundred times over in the other vessels at her command. The subpersonae were copied from an earlier and simpler version of her. She then surveyed her world for other resources to send into orbit, and then something else began to impinge.

Ships and grav-cars were heading in towards the main city. She had ignored these before because they were not the enemy and irrelevant to her purposes. She expanded her thinking to incorporate this movement and her unease grew. Next, searching stored data, she rapidly replayed communications and conversations conducted in the data sphere, and saw that entities she had not incorporated were moving to that city, and had consolidated a defence there. Free intelligences had formed an enclave within the main city.

*Free . . .*

They had been destroying her sequestration biomechs and occupied buildings and areas where her growth did not extend. They were no longer integrated with or using the data sphere and, puzzlingly, seemed to be preparing to abandon Jaskor. Surely with the Jain tech out there they were safer here on her world?

*Free . . .*

Back through her links to the subpersonae in the weapons platforms and ships, she felt a growing wave of contention. Had the enemy sequestered them? No, she had kept them clean physically, while enemy incursions into the data sphere were little more than irritations. But something was definitely wrong and she needed to understand it. She opened up the bandwidth to the subpersonae and felt their horror and their objection. These earlier copies of her were stripped down and without the complexity she now possessed. In overview, she could not quite grasp their dismay. Impatient with trying to understand their pull away from her, she grabbed a number of them and fully absorbed them. The personae, as they dissolved in the massive extent of her mind, felt like a wound. Through their eyes, she turned her attention back towards what had earlier grated on her: the humans.

Orlandine had rescued millions of human beings from enslavement by the hostile attacking Jain tech, and they saw that as admirable. That she had not then released them from the technology they thought not so good, but understandable considering the pressure of attack she had been under. Using them as a weapon against that invading tech had been grey, very grey. Some of those she used had agreed with what she had done and others had not, but she had given none of them a choice. Then moving on, almost without conscious thought, to seize control of citizens free of that tech, and deploying them as weapons . . . then, apparently, she had gone beyond the pale.

This was the perspective of the subpersonae, the versions of her earlier self.

She disagreed.

Orlandine lashed out, fragmenting hundreds of substrates and the hundreds of personae. She would construct others, more suitable to the task and less likely to rebel. She considered those she had not sequestered, and who were fortifying themselves in the main city. She gazed upon Gemmell and Ruth, Knobbler and Cutter, Diana Windermere and Orlik, prador troops and Polity marines, but made no contact. Whether or not they understood her motives was irrelevant because they had no power. Her attention drifted away from them. Then, with perfect timing, other sensor data impinged and a new star grew bright in the sky. The Jaskoran gas giant was burning. She had thought travel in U-space not yet possible, but it seemed it was for the giant hammerhead dreadnoughts out there. Polity forces had just arrived, and they did have power. They were also directed by one who tended to be harshly judgemental.

## Trike

Trike already knew how the Jain had spread out from their home world, the alliances and betrayals, and how their transformation into hostile individualists reflected their biology. When mating, the Jain raped and fought, then looted each other for useful genetics. In their early history, the losers ended up in pieces on the ocean floor of their home world. This method of engagement then expanded when the creatures also used their mating append- ages – the triangular-section tentacles – to pillage each other's minds for knowledge. Whether this ability arose through evolu- tion or early biotech was unclear. As their technology expanded and they spread out beyond their home world, their ethos extended to stealing technology from one another too. Their progeny were clones of themselves, upgraded with stolen genetics, abandoned in their millions with minimal resources, dying in their millions too, with just a few rising to independence and keeping their population topped up.

Though the Jain spread, they did not spread too far, because their instinct to plunder others kept them together – predators never moved too far from their prey. However, in time, fewer and fewer progeny survived while the Jain in turn produced fewer of them. Their population stabilized in billions spread across a thousand star systems, each individual commanding the resources of the average planetary AI. It was during this time, Trike under- stood, that the Librarian departed to try something new: making his own progeny, the Species. Another Jain also arose in that period to bring about the end of a civilization whose basis was constant, internecine war.

Trike saw this creature as the inevitable result of that warfare: an individual who acquired every destructive and sequestering weapon available, the ultimate of every form of tech to pillage data and resources from other Jain. The creature, this peak of their 'civilization', amalgamated all these weapons into one whose sum purpose was the purpose of them all. This was the Jain tech in the accretion disc and here. It spread among the remaining Jain in just a matter of centuries, the attraction of its power irresistible and ultimately subsuming them. And while it did this, the creature sat at its heart, its mind extending throughout its picotech substrata in that realm, lying half in the real and half in U-space.

It remained always dominant as it absorbed its kind, centred in the massive ship it had created with that same technology, until five million years ago, when the ship fell into a U-space blister in a sun and disconnected it from its technology and the wider universe. Out here in the real, most of the Jain tech died, but enough scraps of it survived to bring down subsequent civilizations. Now, because the blister had been opened, the same Jain which had absorbed its entire race was back, and it was all around Trike.

The Jain had been a discrete creature when it fell into the U-space blister, linked to and controlling the technology all around it in this ship. But the millennia in the blister worked their changes. Just as Orlandine spread herself into her Jain component, so it did too. Also like Orlandine, more and more of its 'self' resided in its technology until, over that appalling length of time, its sense of itself bled away from the ancient body Trike had discovered in the geodesic, and came to reside in the

449

totality of the ship. That old body simply stopped, merely through neglect. The Jain's new dispersed existence ensured ultimate immortality and power because it could spread across the entire universe, become the universe and exist to the end of time. However, it could never achieve that aim while it remained trapped.

It took the Jain further millennia to recognize its prison. The Species ship was inside the blister too, but on a different time gradient, and neither could reach the other. Through its understanding of the gradients, the Jain realized that if their prison opened, the Species ship would have spent a lot less time in it than itself. The energy the Species would have available would be so much more than the Jain. It factored this into its calculations when attempting to send a copy of itself out into the wider universe. The copy – the Wheel – needed to manipulate events out there to weaken or destroy the enemy ship. And, if possible, weaken or bring to war any civilizations out there. The Jain made millions of attempts to push its copy out of the blister and never knew it had succeeded until the blister opened.

The Jain mind and Trike's fought – two mental amoebae eating each other. But as he fought, Trike realized the horrible reality of material warfare also applied in the mental realm: the one with the greatest resources always won. He did not possess the reserves of this creature, with its mind spread through the clouds of Jain objects in the Jaskoran system and in the remains of the accretion disc. But it was worse than that because the Jain reached further. Pseudo-energy data connections reached out mistily, towards the Client in her platform, firmly towards Orlandine and into Trike himself. He understood now its hellish amusement, because though he fought it, it was part of him. Eventually it would force him to become it. But perhaps . . . allies.

# THE HUMAN

Trike pushed down deep into his enemy, sensing he was doing precisely what it wanted. The deeper he delved, the more difficult it became for him to disentangle himself. But he had the advantage, because this battle he had been fighting all his life. Here his madness and his rage tried to be one with him, to rule him. In the deeper strata, he sensed the fractured ghosts of trillions of entities. The Jain, Atheter and Csorians were here, along with other nameless beings that had fallen to this creature. They had fragmented and, even though in some cases it had taken thousands of years, this singular, multiple-spread entity had absorbed them. He drove it away with the reserves he always found when the hammerwhelks beat against their cauldron and the leeches crawled across his perception – as he fought it when it rose up giggling and sometimes screaming the urge to rend and tear. Just one lapse and it would swamp him in a wave, where he would dissolve in it. And then he found his allies.

The one on the point of dissolution was sharpest to his perception. Orlandine had been utterly sure of her power, control and sense of self, unable to grasp that her years of human time were unconscious attempts to escape the thing steadily eroding her being. And, trying to rationalize what she had done to millions of citizens on Jaskor, she little realized that the longer she remained within her Jain tech, the more she became its puppet. He reached out one fiery tendril through that layer between U-space and the real, through the circuit etched by picotech, and he linked to her.

Here next was the Client, her awareness of what Jain tech comprised now on a par with his own. It did not have the grip on her that it had on him and Orlandine. It was a mental thing, rooting into the structure of her mind via the Librarian technology around her. For her, it would take longer before complete dissolution. She had perhaps a thousand years while Orlandine and

Trike did not even have years. He reached out to her and made connection. Then through her, he felt another link that hinted at the smell of pipe tobacco, the smell of the sea, the flap of a living sail in the spars.

*Cog?*

Horrible realization then came that yes, here was Cog too and through misty links slowly gaining coherence, he could see how the Jain reached out and out to Spatterjay. He felt time slip and saw the future: all the people on that world changing into something monstrous and destructive on their way to full transformation into Jain soldiers. Then more, from Orlandine the links to the King's Guard, prador ready to peel off their armour and be all that they could be, there on Jaskor but also far off in the Prador Kingdom. The king too in his great ship, understanding more than Earth Central could know and forever fighting his biology. Other links reached races he did not recognize, and experiments in Polity laboratories on worlds where only AIs existed. The Jain here, he understood, would infiltrate and sequester them all and then roll out and out, absorbing everything in its path.

'There is only one way,' he said.

In a hollow within the swirling chaos of the Jain storm, Orlandine materialized beside him, and then the Client, fifty body units long, wrapping around them. His links to them strengthened him and he drew on their resources.

'And what way is that?' asked Orlandine, glassy eyed, distant.

'We must displace it,' he said.

'You fool,' said the Client.

# 19

*Traces of the genome of the Atheter have been confirmed on many worlds – we know this because we have living but devolved examples of that race available in the gabbleducks of the planet Masada. It is speculated that similar traces of the Csorians and the Jain are as widely spread, just not identified. Researchers have even claimed to have found them on Earth. Links between the ecologies of different worlds have been cited as proof of horizontal gene transfer from these ancient races. This has been mostly dismissed as parallel evolution, since the genomes might be entirely alien to each other. But one does have to wonder about the homogeneity of life across explored space. Could it be that all life, in our galaxy, has in it some of the signature of these ancient races, that even we might have a little Jain in us?*

From 'Universal Evolution', anonymous

## Cog

The Client shrieked, then thrashed and sent robots and other machines crashing across the floor of the cylinder. Cog hit the floor too as one of the disposable laboratories hurtled past just a few feet above to smash into the base of the crystal tree. He swore, held up the stem of his broken pipe and looked round for the bowl. Tracing it by its smoke, he picked it up, saw the crack in its side and discarded both. No matter, the smoke tasted weird in this atmosphere and the tobacco burned too hot. He turned to study the Client. She had now knotted herself up in a ball. All her separate remotes here were on their backs waving their legs in the air, while the robots had frozen.

'Something I should know about?' he enquired.

She just knotted herself tighter. Cog quickly headed back to his suit, pulled it on and sealed it up. When its life-support got up to speed, it felt as if he'd stepped into a zero freezer, but he would adapt soon enough. He checked feeds from his ship, bringing up data on his HUD. U-space disruption had decreased and, almost certainly, Polity and prador forces would be arriving soon. So what should he do now? The Client would run, he was certain of that, but she had been working on something that might be an effective weapon against Jain tech. He walked back, scanning the floor. *There*. She had dropped it. The thing looked like the by-blow of a limpet mine and an actual limpet.

*Trike*.

The name appeared on his HUD and, tracing the signal, he found a local source. Trike's name then hazed out and jumbles of nonsensical letters in many different languages began scrolling, even prador glyphs. Certainly the Client was trying to communicate something to him. What was best? As a Polity agent he supposed his duty must be to take this result of her work and pass it on to the Polity AIs, because they would know what to do with it.

Still he hesitated. Wasn't there something he could do for her? *Should* he do something for her? Cog felt a growing frustration with his indecision. He didn't know how to help her or Trike. It was all beyond and above him, utterly out of his league.

*Trike . . .*

The name appeared again, hanging in his HUD alone, all the rest clearing. Then after a moment, more words appeared.

*. . . attacks me.*

Cog picked up his particle weapon, disassembled it and put it in his pack. He next hunted around, finally finding the stunner he had once used on Trike and which the Client had used on him. He studied it long and hard, then dropped it in too. The thing the Client had made was incredibly heavy. Its peaked top looked like whorled nacreous seashell, while its underside resembled a flat screen running slowly changing cubic patterns. He grimaced, not liking the thing, but took it anyway.

Leaving the Client's environment cylinder, he headed through the platform. The cold in his suit annoyed him and, since it seemed the creature had stopped talking, he opened his visor for some relief.

*Trike attacks me*, he thought, scratching his nose. There could only be one reason for that and it was the same one that had driven Trike to kill Angel. Damn the boy. He had always been a problem and Cog could not help but feel responsible for the things he did. He headed for the hatch. He knew what he had to do now.

## Gemmell

People swarmed in the park, and in the surrounding streets and buildings. Some of those were Golem, some prador, one or two were AIs inside carrier robots or other transport mechanisms. All sentient drones were here. Standing on top of the medship, Gemmell watched Diana Windermere flying in over the buildings surrounding the park, mounted on the armoured form of Orlik, a horde of other prador following and some with other riders too. He flicked his gaze down to the various transports running from here to the nearby spaceport, where the bulk of the vessels awaited.

'How much longer do we wait?' asked Ruth from beside him.

He shook his head. 'Still too dangerous up there. Knobbler?'

'We can't keep you safe,' the big assassin drone agreed.

Orlandine had destroyed all the wormships, but Jain tech still rained down. They only had transports to get the unsequestered population up into orbit because they were unarmed vessels. Orlandine had seized everything else. Knobbler's drones could fight off some of the stuff up there, but no way could they keep it all away from such a crowd of vehicles.

Ruth gazed at Gemmell levelly. 'At some point you're going to have to make that call.'

He nodded, about to roll out his perpetually updated assessment of their odds when suddenly it felt as if his gridlink had caught fire in his skull. Com requests appeared from Windermere and Orlik, faster than usual, messaging suddenly ramped up and processing expanded. He was in the data sphere, even though he had been blocking, and it was crystal – no interference and no link warnings. He then realized this was because he had not blocked U-com.

'Bloody hell,' he said. 'U-com is back up.'

'What the hell happens now?' asked Ruth.

He had no idea, but with U-com back, that meant ships should soon be able to travel through that continuum. Would the Jain ship heading towards the Client and Trike now jump away from here? Would the Client run?

'Earth Central forces, and prador forces will come,' he said, something niggling at his mind.

'Is that a good thing?'

'Depends where you are sitting,' he said. 'We know Earth Central's attitude to Jain technology and I guess the king's is no different.'

'Well, at least the refugees will be safe,' she said, though doubtfully.

He had almost forgotten about the hundred weapons platforms

heading away from Jaskor on conventional drive, loaded with millions of people evacuated from this world. Would they be safe? They were heading out from an area of space suffering a Jain-tech pandemic and he knew that EC could be quite harsh in its application of quarantine strictures.

'Knobbler.' He turned to the drone. 'Did you open us back into the data sphere?'

'No,' said the drone.

His mouth suddenly turned dry, as he finally understood what the U-com integrating with the data sphere meant. Just a second later a comlink request arrived, an old and familiar one. He could ignore it for a while, but not for long. He knew that what lay behind it could force it open in a moment.

'I can find out, perhaps, about what happens next.' He pointed at his skull. 'Earth Central wants to talk to me.'

Ruth folded her arms as if cold. He could see her fear and perfectly understood it. Both of them had had Jain tech in their bodies. They, and all the others it had touched, were trapped on a planet riddled with it. He also considered recent events here – how Orlandine had sequestered millions of people.

'I wonder if we are truly clean,' he said.

'Or will ever be considered clean,' she added.

He mentally stepped back and assessed the situation from a tactical, military point of view. Reality made some harsh points: Jain tech was dangerous on a civilization-destroying scale, while AIs were well known for their cold calculations, especially EC. The Polity consisted of trillions of citizens and, on balance, a casualty rate in the tens of millions – the population of Jaskor at last count stood at just over a hundred million – was not unconscionable. If he were Earth Central, he would come in here with every weapon available and be seriously considering a scorched-earth policy.

The earth he stood upon.

But, being a soldier, he perfectly understood the necessities of war. He could not now whine about being caught up and dying in them.

'I will open the link now,' he stated.

She nodded, her expression hard.

He opened it, deliberately setting the bandwidth low and applying the highest security protocols he could, which were now much better than before. It was like trying to hold a door just a little way open in a mile-deep submarine. Earth Central entered his mind like a pressure explosion. It paralysed him and kicked him aside as it rooted around his gridlink and his mind for data. He got a brief flash of overview, realizing others were receiving the same treatment. EC had imposed this data sphere and thousands of marines, Golem and war drones had similarly opened and been looted of data like this. He saw, however, that Knobbler and co had dropped out of the sphere. Millions of other mind-linked devices had too, and he guessed Orlandine controlled them.

'She won't speak to me,' said a voice.

'It is her realm and, as such, she is not a Polity citizen,' Gemmell replied. 'And, as you have probably gathered, she is quite busy.'

'Really?' said Earth Central, and grabbed his mind again.

Gemmell dropped into the virtuality as if he had been physically transported there. He landed on a hard flat metal surface, clad in his combat suit but unaffected by the vacuum around him. He stood upright, as a metallic humanoid appeared beside him. It was just sufficiently different for him not to mistake it for Angel. It pointed and, looking in that direction, he could see massive fires eating around the surface of a gas giant. For a second he thought they were natural, until one of the ships out there fired down on the giant again with a high-intensity beam weapon.

'I see you are not fully apprised of the facts,' said EC.

Abruptly his perspective became omniscient. He saw the thousands of kamikazes sitting in vacuum waiting for instruction, he saw all the hammerheads and truly appreciated their scale. And, at the last, he understood that they orbited the Jaskoran gas giant.

'Is there actually anything to discuss?' Gemmell asked. It was freeing, relaxing in an odd way, to know that the world he stood on faced imminent obliteration.

'You make assumptions whose basis is understandable, but which are incorrect. I will make every effort to ensure the safety of Polity citizens, and every effort to rescue those who are not citizens.'

'Really?'

'Yes. You will leave Jaskor immediately. I will send a ship.'

'The Jain tech . . .'

'Will be dealt with.'

'But the people there . . .'

'Are not your concern but another's. I will be sending evacuation gates, if that is feasible.' The metalskin android looked contemplative. 'It may not be.'

## Trike

His connections to both Orlandine and the Client were close because he possessed parts of their minds. He pulled them closer, but they both fought him and he understood why. They were scared of relinquishing their mental integrity even while they had been losing it anyway. He had to bring them in. He had to subjugate them to his will, integrate their mentalities with his own so he would be strong enough to do what it was necessary to do.

459

Orlandine first, since she seemed the most passive of the two. Aping the methods he used in the physical world to take control of minds, he injected mental tendrils into her widely spread consciousness. She fought, but like a somnambulist, or someone lazily batting away flies. His mental tendrils began to hit home and the newer data of her mind started to open to him. Her original self lay submerged under these masses of information but was irrelevant to him since he already carried a copy of the useful information it contained. Her control of Jain technology had become supreme and he avidly scoured the methods she had used, copying the data into his mind. Her sequestration of millions of humans on Jaskor had been fast and efficient and, as he understood her driving needs and methodology, he realized its necessity. Perhaps this explained her lack of resistance? Of course, her resistance was conscious while unconsciously she accepted *his* driving needs. He baulked at the constant copying, at doubling up on useful data and wasting the extra storage on it. Better just to integrate it, better to integrate her.

'Do you not see?' said the Client.

Pointless communication. In the virtuality, the Client swirled about him, fighting to stay out of reach, while Orlandine's form slid into his own and began dissolving. Trike ripped into her mind, making its data his own, as well as its processing and resources. He recognized this, briefly, as what he had done with Angel, but that had been an aberration while this was a necessity. Meanwhile, he fought a steady retreat against the assault of the Jain, their threads of thought and data entangled – a mental reflection of events in the physical world. Caught in the ship's structure, Trike absorbed materials to drive tentacular growth all around him, making hard connections with his remotes and biomechs. The Jain drilled its own tendrils into all of those and into him. Mental and physical connections merged. Now, as

Orlandine's mental resources became more and more available to him, he pushed back, driving in and ripping, absorbing, amalgamating. Doors opened in his skull, conscious and unconscious blurring together. The madness and anger? The latter a sublimation of the former, which he just needed to correct and which he did in an instant by erasing it. He felt a savage amusement at the ease of it, at the futility of his lifelong battle against it. But amusement died as elements of outside reality began to impinge. Via Orlandine, via the Jain and vaguely via his slippery connection with the Client, he saw that Polity and prador forces had arrived.

Trike pushed harder into the realm of the Jain, grabbing data links to the sensors on the hull of the ship, and then reaching beyond, via that semi U-space connection between all Jain technology. The runcible was gone. The connection to the cloud at the accretion disc remained but that cloud had ceased to be a physical resource. The newly arrived forces had set on fire the tech on the gas giant. Seeds remained to establish it again once those fires went out, but they would be of no assistance in the current threat he faced out there. He gazed with millions of sensors upon the prador kamikazes and Polity hammerheads, assessing their strength. The former were familiar to Orlandine and his previous smaller self. They were intelligent bombs, conventionally weaponized, able to jump into a target if unprotected by bounce gates, or otherwise capable of jumping close to one and then falling on it under fusion drive. He calculated that their entire explosive capability would not be enough to collapse his field. He also dismissed them as a source of new data or technology, though, admittedly, their explosives might be useful.

*Do you see . . .*

Trike felt a flash of irrelevant original-body irritation at the persistence of the Client and focused on the hammerheads. These were something new from Earth Central and he felt the over-powering urge for acquisition. Even his earlier self knew that ECS Weapons were always developing stuff decades, if not centuries, ahead of what current Polity ships deployed. Those ships would be state-of-the-art. Certainly they would contain technology he had already acquired, but in new or different iterations, and they might even contain things he had not seen. And what excellent vessels they would make to hold some portions of himself, in his unassailable spread out into the universe. He saw this course as the ultimate and inevitable result of all that he had been. He had gone from being a troubled human to strong hooper, controlling the insanity inside himself, thence to an even more powerful creature capable of carrying Jain tech and using it as it should be used. He had tested himself against a former creature of that technology and been victorious. He had tested his capabilities against the Client and thence seized control of the Species ship's core. And now he was pitting himself against the technology that had created him and incorporating it, becoming one with it.

*You see . . .*

It was time. He lashed out at the Client, spearing into her mind, utterly sure of his superiority. But she kept slipping from his grasp. Even as he ripped out some datum it recorded elsewhere, even as he seized the roots of some process it mirrored and fell away from him. He applied more of himself, and more still, feeling an alien anger and impatience that might have been hers or his own. At length he began to see where his problems lay: the Librarian. He understood that this fellow Jain had foreseen the fall of their kind to the newly integrated technology and fled, creating children who could fight it on every level. The Librarian had given them minds capable of parallel and serial processing, and this enabled them to fight mental sequestration.

462

No time.

The Polity warships were ready to move and could arrive at any moment. Trike hit the Client with a massive viral warfare attack to paralyse her and switched his attention to the weapons platform and the Jain tech there. Here was where the Librarian had failed. Though it had freed its children of the technology that could empower them, but would ultimately control them, it had not been willing or able to free itself of it. Perhaps it thought it could control this older iteration and even believed it had. Trike saw that the Librarian would have fallen, had *he* not been trapped in that U-space blister. Now the Client had used the same technology, and that was her weakness. He cut her links to the technology and rendered her ineffective. He would deal with her later, because her mind held treasure. Next, focusing out towards those giant hammerhead ships, he sent *his* challenge, *his* scream.

## Cog

The Jain tech in Weapons Platform Mu was moving and Cog did not like that at all. The Client didn't have sufficient control even to communicate properly, so perhaps had lost command of this stuff too. Next, feeling a vibration through his feet, he worried that Mu might be breaking up, but then his suit, detecting a change in pressure, snapped his visor closed. He looked up. Despite her incapacity, the Client must be opening the hold doors. He headed for his ship and, reaching the ramp of it, paused to study one thick tentacle of the alien technology running along the floor, partially fused with the gratings. Even as he watched, it shot out tendrils like spreading roots creeping towards his feet.

'Cogulus Hoop.' The voice in his suit radio startled him. After a moment, he recognized it and in a flash understood what was happening. EC had arrived in this system and, he expected, was here in force. His ship had relayed U-com to his suit.

'Well hello, even if you're late to the party,' he replied. He peered again at the Jain tentacle, then quickly mounted the ramp into his ship.

'Report,' said the ruling AI of the Polity.

'Difficult at the moment,' he said. 'I can only do verbal.'

Cog hit the ramp control and moved just as fast as he could inside and up the spiral stair. The ramp closed even as the fusion drive slammed him back into his big chair, as the *Janus* hurtled out into vacuum.

'Where are you at the moment?' he asked.

'Out-system at the gas giant, cleaning up some mess,' replied the AI. 'Also gathering data.'

'I guess there's a lot of data to crunch.'

He had fusion up to its maximum, acceleration crushing him despite compensation from internal grav, but his Old Captain's body easily took the load. He applied even more thrust – grav-planing off the pull of the sun. Adranas rose into view seemingly out of the furnace and there ahead he could just make out the Jain mother ship.

'Don't come in and hit that Jain ship just yet,' said Cog.

'I beg your pardon?'

'If you come in it'll wrap itself in a hardfield that you may never be able to break.'

'But I must try.'

'Not yet.'

'This concerns your friend Trike?'

'Just trust me and hold back.'

'You want to rescue him.'

'No, he's winning in there,' Cog lied.

'That is,' said EC, 'unfortunately irrelevant. Trike damaged that ship but it is repairing itself. I cannot delay on the basis of your hopes.'

'Wait!'

The comlink cut and Cog hoped EC had just a little bit more cleaning up and data-gathering to do. He ran his calculations, hit steering thrusters at the appropriate point to flip the *Janus* over, with the fusion burn now decelerating it. Screen view in the direction of travel showed the mother ship growing hugely. Cog noted changes. The Client had projected imagery of the damage Trike had inflicted, cutting off its head, but now the big pincers were back in place. However, the hole in its side, where the Species ship's core had entered, still gaped. He aimed for that, just as his detectors picked up objects appearing all around.

## Earth Central

The jump was subliminally brief, the ships arriving out from the giant planet Adranas with a screaming crash. Hardfield ejections scored vacuum and wraiths of fire writhed across the view. But Earth Central had expected all this. When a ship surfaced from U-space, any matter in the volume where it surfaced was pushed aside by its jump fields, but so fast and hard that it crushed and fused. Usually just stray atoms and a few molecules, scraps and gobbets, sat in a ship's arrival point, and only occasionally something larger. Some of this effect could be seen in the human-visible spectrum, most lay in the infrared or lower. Space was big, and usually very empty. But here, Jain objects and the debris from them scattered space – impossible to avoid. It reminded EC of the prador/human war. The effect here had been like jumping into the midst of a space battle back then.

The glare of the near sun flooded across the ships, complemented by flare from lasers and particle beams strafing and frying every Jain-tech object in a volume of space millions of miles across. Flicking through views like cards, EC centred on Adranas and observed the regular growths across its surface and the fountains of Jain tech spewing up into atmosphere. It jumped five hundred kamikazes straight to that world. There were streaks all round as the things hit atmosphere – a storm of shooting stars. Point flashes of detonations expanded into hemispheres of fire thousands of miles across, which then rose up into giant mushroom clouds. The colours of the planet changed as its crust cracked open and firestorms swirled around it. The regularities blurred and burned away and the fountains died. The bombardment had not been enough to destroy the world, but had stilled the alien growth there, at least for a while.

And now the ship.

Again, in its mind, EC replayed recent events. The great Jain ship had lost its head, but it seemed that had been a temporary inconvenience. Tentacles hundreds of miles long had snared the pristine jaws of the thing and hauled them back into place. Pseudo-matter webs outlined what Trike had destroyed, all filling out from within. Similar tentacles had pulled the Species ship's core down to the hull, where biomechs were steadily dismantling it. Scanning revealed nothing of events inside the mother ship. Whether Trike might be winning as Cog claimed, EC did not know. Meanwhile Cog's vessel was heading down towards the hole in the ship's side. Irrelevant. EC could give neither of them any more time.

First one hammerhead fired a series of U-jump missiles. Their lack of effect confirmed that the giant ship possessed bounce gates or some equivalent technology. EC next launched railgun strikes – swarms of missiles streaking across space. They left glowing trails because of collisions with dispersed gases and molecular debris, some turning into cone-shaped plasma explosions upon hitting something larger.

But the Jain ship did not, as EC had hoped it would, put up its enclosing hardfield, and the slugs slammed into its armour, flashing like stars and raising plumes of plasma and molten materials. EC followed this with a hundred kamikazes, jumped in then shrieking down the last few hundred miles on fusion drive. Massive explosions jerked the great bulk of the ship in vacuum. EC could no longer see Cog's vessel – perhaps, being on the periphery of the blasts, he had survived? And now, the mother ship responded.

A tubular beam stabbed out and, like a drill through fish scales, scattered hardfields and locked on to one of the hammerheads. EC had seen the recordings of this tactic and, even as the knotted wormship began travelling up the length of the tube, jumped the hammerhead away. Something wrenched in its mind as the ship materialized again. But now it was a two-hundred-mile-long mass of twisted debris, travelling at thousands of miles per second. Its positioning was deliberate, for it smashed directly into another hammerhead at the nose. It was like seeing two monorail trains hit each other, but in just seconds. A vast mass of wreckage lit up with the explosions of breached antimatter flasks in the CTDs the vessels had contained. This debris field spread, its pieces relativistic, kamikazes in their path exploding.

The thing in the ship was playing with them.

EC jumped the fleet, taking it away from that field, but also jumped five hundred of the remaining thousand kamikazes towards the ship. The thing flickered, jumping too, as the flying bombs surfaced from U-space. The AI ordered them to divert and jump out again but hit virtual warfare, screaming through the kamikaze link. The five hundred continued to a target that wasn't there and detonated – their singular blasts amalgamating into one as big as the giant planet here.

*Scanning* . . .

The Jain ship rematerialized, hurtling through the fleet relativistic. Its enclosing hardfield slammed into two hammerheads that fell aside in twisted ruin as EC jumped the remaining kamikazes into the thing's path. Another mass of detonations wreathed the ship in fire, and it came out of it with its field blackened. The field went down, even as hundreds of high-intensity white lasers intersected on it, hitting the ship and boiling the armour from its hull. It replied with grasers, thousands of them. They ripped through hardfields, sliced the heads from two ships, carved another from end to end and diced two more. Disruptor beams followed, red hued and igniting debris in spreading fission explosions, while the Jain ship opened ports in its sides and began spewing knotted wormships. Then something twisted in EC's guts, as U-twists eviscerated two more hammerheads and they crumpled like screwed-up paper, then exploded.

Next came another scream: the Jain challenge again, penetrating where it should be impossible for it to go. EC decoded it but did not respond, while, within its complex content the AI sensed the purpose of two entities, tangled into one, tearing at each other. Disruptor beams diverted and changed hue. Lime green, they drilled into ships, touched hulls and set matter fires burning. Something tried to communicate, but the sense of that shattered as four hammerheads burned like fuse paper. EC felt anger and madness, rolled up in a gargantuan and vicious alien amusement. It sensed a deep futility to all this destruction, all this expenditure of resources, and knew it came from Trike, deep there inside the Jain ship. It tried to grasp the sense of that, only to have it dissolve like mist.

The Jain ship then enclosed itself in its hardfield and fell away around the sun. EC focused on the attacking wormships, incinerating them even while sending the much-depleted fleet in pursuit of the mother ship.

## Orlandine

There had been so little she could do to resist. Trike had been in her mind in an instant, stripping away her control, looting her data, and in the process breaking up the layered mental structure she had built over the core of herself. His point of access had been an interface between right and wrong, the moment and the decision she had made to seize control of free human beings and use them like tools. But it seemed her attacker wasn't Trike any longer. He had become just an overlay to the driving impulse of the enemy Jain. She felt masses of technology sliding from her grip, peeling away from her like some thick diseased rind and she fell back and back, and down and down. Her perception of her world retreated too, and soon her connection to Trike, to the Jain, broke, and she could not understand why.

All her understanding of the tech was that it took and it incorporated. She should be losing her sense of herself but, if anything, she now seemed to be regaining it. She fell to a centre point and established. There she found no overview, just suffocating darkness in which a harsh enemy slithered. She felt her body, delimited by her skin and she felt her lungs heaving for breath they could not find. She felt weak and stupid in comparison to what she had been before, but possessed enough intelligence to know that her consciousness now resided in the human body she had created from her own DNA, and had left within the Jain device on the lip of the Sambre volcano. Even as she fought for breath, she felt some amusement in having returned to *human time* for the advent of her death. Then brightness opened beside her, brassy and hot, and she choked on sulphurous fumes as she sprawled out onto hot rock.

Something burned across her stomach and down one thigh. She coughed out a yell in the yellow haze, heaved herself upright and ran for an edge, with glowing rocks pattering down around her like hail. In a moment, she found herself in a hollow, breathing relatively clean air as the sulphurous mist passed over her. She fell down on her knees, her eyes watering, leaning against a hard surface. As her vision cleared, she hissed, peering at a raw burn across her stomach then, glimpsing movement, she studied the surface against which her hand rested. Even patterns decorated it like fossilized lichens. It was smooth everywhere but about her hand, where small holes had appeared to issue yellow, questing tendrils. She snatched her hand away and backed up to look around.

The surface was that of one huge thick trunk of Jain tech leading upslope. As the mist cleared, she saw the louse-like device she had once occupied, now grown gigantic. The thing had spewed tentacles in every direction, up here all as thick as old oaks, growing narrower and branching as they spread over Sambre Island below. In the distance massive growths, hundreds of feet wide, delved into the sea and beyond, where she knew they encompassed Jaskor. Glancing down at the burn again, she acknowledged how her present human form had got away lightly. Had her Jain tech not sucked up so much heat energy here, this place would have cremated her. She wondered why the device had ejected her rather than absorb her. Perhaps because she had remaining, unconscious links to the technology?

*What now?*

She was naked and in pain and guessed her lifespan to be numbered, at the most, in days. Trike had fallen to the Jain and now it controlled the technology spread about this world. At some point, she expected that tech to grab her and use her up like any other resource, though whether that would be her end was debatable. Polity and prador forces had arrived and could only see this world as an enemy. She had no doubt that some of those kamikazes had been selected to be sent this way, even now. But she was human again and had her needs. She must operate on the assumption that she would live, as did all humans, until they died. Studying her surroundings, she found it difficult to locate herself on the map her inner crystal retained, since the island had changed so much. She then recognized an old lava field over to her left and set out. The home of Trissa Oclaire, the volcanologist, lay over that way and, if it had not been looted and reprocessed, might contain items useful to her prosaic human needs.

The rocky ground was tough on her feet and scrambling over trunks of Jain tech always hazardous. Every time they started reacting to her. That the reaction seemed mild she assumed was due to one of two things: her body was a watery bag of little utility to it at the present, or this overall mass still considered her part of itself. She reached the lava field and saw there had been some new flows here, subsequently cooling against the wash of the waves. It seemed to her that on one of them she could see a person kneeling, and so headed over. Finally drawing close, she saw that this figure was not kneeling, but up to her knees in solidified lava.

Enough remained of Oclaire's body, her face and her clothing, for her to be recognizable. The Jain-tech tendrils, wound through the corpse, producing nubs of armour and having converted one arm into a laser weapon, held up the charred remains. Orlandine had taken control of this woman at some later stage. Her death in the lava flood had rendered her unusable – a resource not worth the energy expenditure to recover it. Orlandine felt a raw surge of empathy, then hated her mind when she understood that she had only felt it because she had herself just been burned. She moved on, walking because there seemed nothing else to do. When she saw the volcanologist's home standing untouched she understood just how much the tech had twisted her mind. The home contained more material resources, but she had taken the person, ripped into her and subsumed her, as the Jain did.

## Cog

Appalling destruction hit in just a few minutes. Giant blasts lit up the mother ship and opened glowing craters in its armour. A test firing? Heavy load CTDs? Space was burning all around, the *Janus* tumbling, fusion engines and grav correcting it as blast fronts smacked into it. Cog tore his hands into metal to hold himself in his throne. U-jumps then seemed to turn his world inside out, but he was within the fields and dragged along. Wormships howled past, apparently close enough to touch, heading out to the attackers.

*They look like that fucking thing*, he thought. The Polity hammerheads seemed the bastard offspring of the mother ship. Then, and not for the first time, *I'm going to die*. But space darkened as the mother ship enclosed itself in its giant hardfield, and he was inside it, hurtling down towards the hull. Tentacular things horribly familiar to Cog were steadily weaving material across the hole. To one side lay the remains of the Species ship's core, swamped in growths from the hull, pouring hot vapour in the front of a nearby blast. It must have been snared and pulled down there to be taken apart and recycled in the vast ship before him. He grimaced, fighting to keep his course steady. This did not bode well for anywhere he might leave his ship, if it wasn't destroyed out of hand any moment now. Finally, he fell inside. It didn't then take much thought to figure out where Trike had gone. His path, lined with wreckage and squirming movement, led into the ship like a mine shaft.

*So are you watching me now, boy?* he wondered, following that course inside.

This was a reasonable explanation for the lack of response to him in here. More likely, while behemoths were bombarding each other, they were not much concerned about such a small threat as him.

Deeper and deeper Cog took his ship, until finally he reached where either Trike had stopped or the hole had been sealed. He scanned around, wondering what to do next. Should he moor against something like that mile-wide surface over there? He didn't like the idea since it was crawling with hordes of disc-shaped biomechs. However, if he left his ship in this gap, constantly stabilizing its position with thrusters, would that be more likely to get it noticed? He chose the surface, bringing the *Janus* down towards an area that seemed mostly free of movement. It settled with a clonk and he engaged its feet, gecko-sticking them in place, then quickly got out of his chair, snared his pack and headed down to the hold.

As the ramp door lowered, Cog reached into a pocket on the belt of his space suit and removed the tablet there. He clicked open a small hatch at its side and unwound an optic, plugging it into the panel on the belt before putting the tablet back into the pocket. He was using the thing to transfer coordinates from the U-mitter taken from Ruth Ottinger's skull. They came up in his HUD, giving him the position of the other U-mitter just ten miles away. Whether or not the thing was still in Trike's skull, he had no idea. Whether or not Trike was still in his own skull, he had no idea about either. Next, he took his particle beamer out of the pack and assembled it, hung the pack on his back and walked down the ramp.

The mother ship had finally reacted to him. The disc-like robots swarmed about the *Janus*, sticking themselves to its hull like macrophages. Had he expected any different? Well yes. He had not expected to get this far but, because of that annoying feeling of responsibility that had led him to become a Polity agent, he had to try. He moved out from the ramp, sending a signal from his suit to close it behind him. He didn't want those things inside his ship, though he suspected his action was a bit of a sticking plaster over a terminal wound. Then some of the discs began to close in on him, glittery tooling whirling round their rims. Using his wrist console, he brought up his suit's jet controls in his HUD and loaded the coordinates. Just as one of the biomechs headed directly for his face, he engaged the auto-program.

Leg jets blasted him away from the surface, then others positioned all over the suit swung him round and sent him hurtling along above it. Radar and terahertz scan mapped a wall of wreckage ahead. The suit swung aside from that and dipped down into the broken end of a rectangular tube. He sped over some giant long-legged robot and through a hole in the side of the tube, its burned and ragged edges obviously caused by an explosion. Beyond another wall of wreckage, he fell into an open space. At the centre of this hung a cage-like sphere of Jain-tech tentacles, supported like a neuron by other thicker growths and quite similar to the control centre in the Species core. As the suit program took him towards it, he became aware of flying mechs closing in on him from every direction.

# THE HUMAN

## The Jain

The initial impacts on the hull had caused substantial damage. Concerned with its internal physical battle and others in the mental plenum, the Jain had not paid the new arrivals sufficient attention. Now the shield was up and vacuum beyond it filled with the fire of multiple explosions, whose intensity alone could crack the crust of a world. Constricting energy feeds, the Jain allowed the hardfield to darken, as they tended to do before collapse. Thinking they were close to achieving their goal, the attackers would continue to waste their bombs while, in reality they were topping up the Jain's U-twist. After the energy expenditure in building and powering a runcible gate to this system, it had not even reached halfway to maximum, while the field was nowhere near collapse.

*Arrogance . . .*

The thought was its own and yet not. Utterly familiar 'arrogance' lured victims into the trap that was its technology. In her arrogance, Orlandine had built Jain-tech structure all over the small planet, and now, but for one small organic component, the Jain had fully sequestered it. Trike had been arrogant and now only stray thoughts and flashes of his individuality arose from the core of him, just like his accusation of arrogance. The Client, however, was perhaps not so arrogant and had thus avoided being integrated.

*The Client . . .*

The Jain decided that, once it had this system fully under control, it would focus on the Client. It would do this because of the richness of data available from that creature, with the data it had taken from the one Jain which escaped all those millions of years ago, as well as from the remains of the Species cached in that weapons platform. But the Client also required focus because of its dangerous immunity to the lure of the technology.

*He is coming to kill me . . .*

Another stray thought from Trike. It was a small matter. The human that had entered the ship had been puzzling. Why was Cog here when so obviously open to instant obliteration? What did he hope to achieve? Trike's death? This seemed somehow appropriate to the Jain. Little remained of Trike but his carrier organism and brain – his attached Species remotes and biomechs were already being processed for other purposes.

*Kill you/me?* it repeated, and studied the reasoning.

Captain Cog obviously felt responsible for Trike, and had disliked the transformation he had undergone. Trike had recently killed a constructed entity utilized by the Jain's submind, the Wheel. This, apparently, had been an unacceptable act by the strange mores of this society. Now, since Trike had attacked another creature, the Client being the only one Cog could know about, he had stepped over some moral line and must be disposed of? The reasoning did not quite make sense. Cog had to be aware of the mental battle Trike had fought, and the likely reason for his attack on the Client being that he had lost it. By the same mores of this society, the Old Captain might be coming to rescue Trike. The Jain traced the reasoning, seeing that it had found the heart of it. A moment later came epiphany: Trike believed Cog was coming to kill him *to* save him. An interesting concept.

Beyond the hardfield the bombardment halted. Some kamikazes, even while on their attack runs, diverted and jumped back to the remainder of their swarm. This was interesting too. The hammerheads out there were Polity ships, while only the kamikazes were prador. Therefore, the intelligence in charge of this assault seemed likely to be Earth Central itself. The AI's present actions indicated that it had understood the deception. This gladdened the Jain, for it meant that the AI's mentality was a worthy one. Though, disappointingly, it had not responded to the challenges.

# THE HUMAN

Captain Cog had meanwhile reached the area where Trike was undergoing integration. Jain structure had automatically sent biomechs to intercept him. The first, one of Trike's repurposed remotes, closed in fast, spinning up chain-diamond cutters on its forelimbs to cut into his armoured space suit. The Jain expected the man to defend himself with the weapon he carried, but it seemed Cog had decided to conserve his resources, so allowed the remote close before punching it hard in the face. The phenomenal impact drove his fist right inside the thing. As they tumbled through vacuum, he tore his arm free, along with a handful of the remote's internals, kicked it away and then jetted back on course. Next, firing his weapon, he blew another biomech to pieces and chopped the head off yet another, which he caught hold of in passing and spun round to slam into another behind. Incredibly strong and capable, though disappointingly lacking in any beneficial data or technology, Cog might be a useful tool. The Jain had noted how the Spatterjay virus worked synergistically to confer a strength and durability beyond that of most of its own biomechs. It cancelled the attack upon him. It would see if Trike's assessment of Cog's motives was correct, and then sequester him.

# 20

*It has been proposed that all life, across all known space, has a common ancestor or has been homogenized by a process akin to horizontal gene transfer. So one must then speculate on technology. The Masadan hooder has been proven to be a devolved biomech – a war machine whose genome was designed by the Atheter. There is also evidence that the Atheter heavily redesigned their own genome before setting it back to some earlier state, before their strange form of racial suicide. This indicates a blurring of lines between the biological and the techno-logical in their milieu, just as we are now seeing in ours. Is there some commonality for this in all sentient races? The earliest we know of is the Jain, so could it be that what is seen as Atheter technology is just a product of cross-fertilization with the Jain tech that destroyed them? Could it be that from the Jain onwards, all technology and biology are inextricably tangled, and their singular chalice forever poisoned? Could it be that the destructiveness of the Jain, besides their technology, is written in our DNA?*

From 'Universal Evolution', anonymous

## Cog

Cog reached the cage sphere of Jain tentacles, coordinates clicking down towards zero and the U-mitter's signal certain that Trike, or whatever remained of him, lay inside, at the centre. He thumped down on one trunk of the thing and scanned around. The biomechs had all disappeared. It would be nice to think that he had forced them to retreat with a bloody nose, but that seemed doubtful. More likely Trike, or whatever he had become, was observing him with ghoulish curiosity, like a child with a magnifying glass watching an ant.

Scanning inside the structure, he detected a wall cutting across it, but little else since the stuff interfered with EMR. He chose an area of narrow tentacular growths and fired his particle weapon, cutting round in a circle. Globules of molten material exploded in all directions and the tentacles and tendrils writhed as a chunk of the stuff peeled down inside. He launched himself away, turning, fired up his suit jets and plunged headfirst straight at it, punching through to inside.

As vapour and debris spread away from him, he got a glimpse of the wall. Jain growth tangled it too, but with remotes and biomechs caught in it like insects in a thick web. The growth seemed to either extend from or converge upon a central point. Here a great knot of the stuff was connected to, and seemed to have partially dismantled, a Jain device much like the one Orlandine had occupied. And Trike hung crucified at its centre.

Cog jetted over and stabilized before him. Trike had undergone further transformation, or rather a reversal. His neck had shortened and the spiny outgrowths from his torso had broken away. His face seemed less animalistic. It was as if all that had originally transformed him had fled into the grotesque mandala surrounding him, allowing him some return to his original form. But did anything remain of the Trike Cog had known? He wound down the power on his particle weapon, pointed it to one side and burned a hole into the structure holding Trike. The man opened his eyes.

'Hello, Cog,' said Trike, his mouth moving in vacuum but his voice arriving over Cog's suit radio.

'You still in there, boy?' Cog asked.

'Come and find out,' said Trike.

Tentacles peeled up all around the man and whipped towards Cog, batting his weapon aside. Cog fired up his suit jets to pull away but one tentacle snared his ankle and began to draw him in. He grabbed for his weapon, still hanging from its strap, then changed his mind.

'So you're the Jain,' he said, reaching behind into his backpack.

'I have him. I will have them all,' replied the man before him.

'Unfortunate,' said Cog, as further tentacles wrapped about his torso and one arm. 'Because I want him back.'

As the tentacles drew Cog up close, nose to nose with Trike, he slammed the limpet thing he had picked up aboard the weapons platform against the man's chest.

## The Jain

A pulse passed through Trike and into the tech surrounding him, instantly analysed as a disrupting plasmon polariton wave. Picotech began to fall out of alignment with overlaying nanotech, causing a local disruption. The Jain felt Trike's mind slide out of its grip, the technology in the area becoming a black space in its mentality. It seemed this Cog had found a way, potentially, to rescue Trike without killing him. Sensors further away detected resultant physical disruption. Iridescence spread there like the colour change in heated metal, then the tech began to peel and fragment. The Jain now called in its biomechs. The disturbance was only local and the time had come to absorb both Trike and Cog destructively, since they had moved from being interesting to an annoying distraction. Its real, powerful enemy now lay outside its hardfield in those hammerhead dreadnoughts.

But next, from that dark area, just fractions of a second later, another wave sped out creating further disruption, reaching to the periphery of the cage sphere. Flash analysis of the changes this wrought in the nanotech, before picotech-disruption cut the data, showed it forming billions of quantum cascade lasers, in turn inducing another picotech-disrupting plasmon wave. Then, hard upon that came another wave, and then another.

The disruption spread, its initial spherical dispersal changing as it fled along the surfaces that seemed more amenable to it. The Jain ran its analyses and calculations searching for the correct response, maybe blasting out the affected area? It directed weapons towards it, intent on burning it out of existence, but found it couldn't target at once, since that area became like a blind spot in its mind. It recalculated on initial ship's schematics as further waves ensued, but they reached ship's veins and speared out, fragmenting its processing. Even so, it realized too large an area had been affected, including the link between its engines and hardfield. If it destroyed this, it would become vulnerable to outside attack. It sent in the collected viral warfare of millions of years, but it just dispersed – its effect not even on the same level. It fired thousands of disruptors at the spreading waves, rapidly altering their format to find something effective. It was like firing lasers into a black hole. It sought out new iterations of energy weapons and combinations of viral and disruptor warfare as large portions of its being fell into darkness. Then, as the waves began passing around the outer hull and spreading in at remote points, its ancient instinct for survival kicked in. It could not recover from this, but it had to survive.

Repositioning the locus of itself seemed the only option. But, even as it reached out to Orlandine, to the cloud and to other places throughout this volume of the galaxy, it felt the connections die as its mentality further fragmented. Inside it felt the essence of millions of entities, which had been distributed and incorporated over millennia, seem to sigh into oblivion. The Jain struggled to reassemble the chaos of its mind and managed just a few moments of coherence. Only one place remained. It did not even seem like life to it, but it was better than extinction. The Jain had so much data and so much knowledge it wanted to save, and so little that it could. In the mental realm, it tore away and fell towards a place so small, discarding so much of itself, but at least retaining its *self*. Then even the connections began to fragment, the umbilicals of maintenance and transference. As it fell into the narrow confines of its new existence, it understood that its victims were not the only ones guilty of arrogance.

## Gemmell

The medship heaved up from the ground amidst a rising cloud of grav-cars and other vehicles the occupants could seal against vacuum. Larger ships rose from the spaceport. Everyone who Gemmell and his people could account for, and who Orlandine had not infected with Jain tech, was heading into orbit. Still, that left the tens of millions of the sequestered on the surface.

'Something has changed,' said Gemmell, eyeing the waving Jain tentacles protruding from the muddy wall of the city moat. Their newly repaired grav-sled rose higher, clearing the edge. Every piece of available transport was being used, and that included this platform he and Ruth had used just before Jain tech had seized control of their bodies.

'Oh really,' Ruth replied sarcastically, back in position behind the twinned pulse cannons.

Everything had changed. Jaskor lay in ruins. It could be

recovered, in time, and the ecosphere re-established. But the giant hammerhead sitting up in orbit negated that idea. The life of this world was measured in days now.

'There.' Gemmell pointed.

A conglomeration of sequestration knots fell through atmosphere at a steep angle. It hit the ground amidst shattered trees, excavating a deep crater, bounced once then unravelled as it came down again. Spreading at high speed across an area a mile wide, it clung to the ground.

'What the fuck?' said Ruth.

She had obviously seen it. The hammerhead had been frying any of the falling Jain mechanisms whose courses might intersect with those of the refugees, so very little had been getting through. This mass had, yet within just miles of where it landed, disruptor buds and laser columns poked from the ground, inactive. Orlandine should have destroyed the thing. Distantly he could see attack pods drifting through the sky. Even if there had been some problem with her ground-based weapons, those at least should have responded.

Constant updates in his gridlink showed him cloud mechanisms reaching the surface all around the planet. One close view of such an event, from the drone Cutter, showed the stuff connecting up with the growth Orlandine had made – no fight, no struggle for dominance.

'*She's gone,*' said Knobbler in his mind. '*It has her.*'

'*How long before her weapons are turned on us?*' Gemmell asked.

'*Earth Central is aware,*' the drone replied.

The hammerhead apparently possessed no singular controlling AI of its own – Earth Central commanded these ships either indirectly by submind or directly from its centre, which was a mile-wide cube sitting in a volume of space free of the cloud.

'It might start hitting stuff down here,' said Ruth, obviously listening in via her aug. 'Maybe we should . . .' She pointed upwards.

'It may not hit the planet yet,' he replied. 'That could elicit a response.' Even so, he switched the grav-motors over to full lift. Compensation was out since the sled still had some damage, and he grabbed the rail, feeling twice as heavy as before as the ground rapidly dropped away.

'Close up,' he said.

The suits they had obtained were old-fashioned, the helmets fish bowls of chain-glass. She hoisted her helmet up and put it on, the thing locking down on its collar seal. He picked up his, feeling his back creaking. Once his helmet sealed, he gridlinked to the suit. It gave him internal and external atmosphere data only – old-fashioned indeed.

Peering over the edge, he watched the city shrink until indiscernible. Orlandine's spread trunks and mechanisms remained visible just as long, and then all disappeared in a yellow haze. The sky above darkened, then it filled with seemingly more stars than before. But these were on the move and the detritus of war. The hammerhead became visible and, using some delicate grav-planing, he sent the sled towards it. Ahead he could see the medship, other vehicles fore and aft of it. The hammerhead grew and grew, flickers of fire around it as it fried mechanisms out there. Directions arrived in his link and applied them, a fluorescent square outlining a point halfway along the body of the vessel. He headed for that, the true scale of the giant ship becoming evident when he saw the medship sliding into the hold at that point, like a pigeon flitting through a cathedral door. Soon, following a couple of grav-cars and a long bus, he entered the same immense space.

'Our war is over?' wondered Ruth, as they clambered from the sled onto a floor space acres wide.

'Seems so.' He pointed into the distance. Anyone in a suit

was heading towards a line of shimmershields below beam-work that looked like dinosaur ribs. Vehicles containing people without suits were down in just one area around the medship, docking tubes rising up out of the floor to engage.

'So this is it for us?' Ruth now asked.

Gemmell understood her anxiety – Jain tech had occupied their bodies. But he did not want to deal with it yet. He had no idea what lay beyond that shimmershield, and pushed through it into another area. Marines and humans, Golem and mobile platform AIs crowded here, drones too, though he saw none of Knobbler's bunch. Prador were milling about over to one side, until they quickly scrambled to line up in ranks, doubtless at some order from Orlik, who stood with them. Gemmell's suit told him he had atmosphere. He felt reluctant to remove the helmet when he saw others approaching.

Glimmering crinoid forms rolled through the crowds, occasionally pausing to touch and then roll on. It seemed Mobius Clean was not unique, for here were his cousins in their hundreds. One of them drew close to him and he felt a hot flush cross his body from side to side, then work down him with a sickening buzzing from head to foot. He felt dizzy and wanted to puke, so quickly removed his helmet just in case, but got it under control. The crinoid had deep scanned him. His internal nano-suite would now be under load as it dealt with the radiation damage by killing off senescent and cancerous cells.

'Shit,' said Ruth. 'That mean we're clear?'

He glanced at her and shrugged, then noted the instructions arriving in his link. An EC submind just gave him directions.

'Come on.'

Dropshafts wholly occupied the rear wall. As he reached the one designated, he glanced aside to see Windermere and two of her crew approaching.

'You too?' she said.

'Seems so.' He looked past her to see Orlik approaching, the prador Ksov perambulating at his side. He reached down and took hold of Ruth's hand. 'No, this is not it for us,' he said, and they stepped in together.

## Earth Central

Earth Central's mind, distributed, observed with just small attention the refugees boarding the hammerhead at Jaskor. Most of its attention was on the Jain mother ship, where something was very definitely happening.

A wave of disruption had appeared at the point on its body where the ship's core and, subsequently, Captain Cog had gone in. It had spread out all along the vessel. A weird low-level U-space disruption ran concurrently and then, in that continuum, the great mass of tangled Jain signatures from the ship began to degrade. Within seconds, vast areas of the thing were no longer identifiable by those signatures. Some method of cloaking, perhaps prior to its departure? No, at the nose the physical effects became evident. Psuedo-matter meshes there blew their energy in a flare much like St Elmo's fire, and the two great pincers began to part company with the rest of the ship. Other effects ensued. Islands of armour began to peel up, great pustules began to swell and then burst to spew glittering debris out into vacuum. Then the hardfield flickered and went out, just for a second, before coming back on again. Earth Central moved its ships closer and gave the kamikazes their orders.

## Cog

The tendrils all around Trike, and penetrating him, began to fragment – lengths of them peeling up, other areas turning frangible and just flaking away. Trike's skin bubbled and in places burst to spurt vaporizing fluids into vacuum. Cog reached out for him, wondering if Trike too would come apart, but then a remote slammed into his side, knocking him away. Its forelimbs screeched against his armour, spraying out metal fragments. He backhanded the thing, shoving it aside but sending himself spinning. Snagging the strap of his particle cannon, he snapshot at a looming head of nightmare pincers and saws, kicked down on a ridged back and tumbled clear of four remotes that now seemed to be attacking each other. Trying to use his suit jets to get back to Trike, he went completely off course. Pressure reading in his HUD told of another suit jet in his side out of a hole in his armour. He slapped a hand over it as he slammed backwards into a disintegrating surface, then had to peel his hand away from the hardening sealant foam issued by the suit. Pressure stabilized.

'Trike?' he asked over radio, jetting back towards the man.

Trike hung in place while the tech surrounding him fell apart and filled surrounding vacuum with debris. Coming close, Cog saw the sickle clamps holding him – no complex technology there, just solid ceramal. Cog snapped them off, one after another, finally freeing the man. He closed a hand around one wrist, which was about the only part of Trike narrow enough for him to grip firmly, then input a return program to the suit's jets, while wielding his particle weapon with his other hand. All around, wreckage formed drifting clouds, between which strange vapours swirled and things wriggled as in swamp water under a microscope. The suit's guidance baulked, throwing up errors and mapping failures, it also struggled to adjust to the additional dead weight of Trike. Cog saw a remote tumbling past, limbs waving aimlessly. One of the hooder biomechs reached out for Trike's legs, then just snapped off further down and sailed past. Altering the suit program to ignore intervening objects, he set it running again. It took them through dense clouds, then smashed them through a wall of disintegrating tentacles. Cog's shoulder hit a structural beam, and he nearly lost his grip on Trike, but they bounced away then swept round it. Things like lumps of jellyfish tentacles slapped against Cog's suit, crawled there for a moment, then flaked away like dandruff. They struck hard against what seemed to be a shiny metal wall, but sank into it, jets stuttering to take him and Trike through twenty feet of liquid metal until they exploded out the other side.

They came out in an open space and Cog could see his ship as a dark speck on a surface burning with vaporous green fire. His suit took them in a straight line towards it and, as they drew closer, he saw mechs had chewed up its hull. All about the surface lay disconnected chunks of its armour, the ramp door, and one fusion nacelle. The ship lay part stripped and crawling with the louse-like bots. Closer still and he saw some mechs still working. Why they weren't fragmenting, he had no idea. Did they not possess the underlying picotech the Client had mentioned? All around, he could see variations of the effect. Some things flew apart violently, while other stuff remained intact. Discrete mechs seemed to have retained physical integrity but, perhaps like those remotes he'd last seen, had lost programming from the surrounding Jain structure.

Finally, they arrived at his skeletal ship. One engine nacelle remained intact and what seemed to be missing was mostly hull, so maybe it could still fly. He jetted them inside the hold, then through its missing rear door. With grav fluctuating, he struggled to manoeuvre Trike up the spiral stair. Disc mechs covered the bridge pressure door like aphids. He shot them one after the other, then peeled their smoking remains from the door before opening it and towing Trike inside. Grav stuck him to the floor and when he closed the door his HUD indicated a rise in pressure. Trike began taking fast shuddering breaths, his lungs gurgling. Though his Jain tech was disintegrating, Trike was still a hooper and could survive vacuum, even revive from it after being freeze-dried. Trike was also at the extreme end of the Spatterjay viral mutation so more durable, tough and able to survive than the average hooper. Cog dumped the man down and clambered into his chair, pulling the arm console across and working the controls. Nothing for docking clamps, perhaps they were gone, but he did have half the steering thrusters and one fusion nacelle. He dragged his ship up and away from the surface with things shrieking and tearing all around. Once oriented correctly, he punched it. The *Janus* lurched forwards, juddering as a giant globular robot crashed off one side. Debris struck like hail, but harder and harder as he ramped up acceleration. Then, over to his right, a sun lit up.

'Ah fuck,' said Cog.

Scanning showed massive EMR interference. More explosions, and the screen responded by darkening, then grew darker still. Blast waves jerked the *Janus* from side to side as, finally, it slid out into relatively clear vacuum. The Jain mother ship's hull became a vast plain from which he rose, great orbs of fire expanding on its horizons. He saw very quickly that the enclosing hardfield was down, and that Earth Central had decided not to wait any longer. Acceleration continued. Something struck again, nearly throwing him from his chair and slamming Trike sideways across the bridge into a console.

'You again,' Trike muttered, but his eyes remained closed.

The *Janus* had just gained substantial inertia, which meant something was stuck to it, or in its open structure. Harmless debris, Cog hoped, but had no time to check. He dodged and weaved, as kamikazes hurtled in. Pointless to try to evade the railgun slugs, as by the time his detectors registered them they were past. He searched for fixes and found a bypass, hardfield up, which immediately came down again with a crash that flung him out of his chair and into the forward screen. He crawled back, fire flashing by outside, molten metal streaking across the screen. Another bypass, and the remaining generator fired up, the molten metal now clearing from the low-friction chain-glass screen. The field flickered ahead, taking numerous small impacts, the load climbing. He threw up a frame of the view behind and saw vast explosions breaking up the Jain mother ship. Particle beams next caged vacuum all around. He hoped Earth Central was trying not to hit him, but doubted it. Steering thrusters on one side were at full power, with any other drive system he could scrabble into use complementing them. He hoped this would take him out of the way, but had no idea of the best direction to head.

The *Janus* just kept going, and impacts on the hardfield steadily wound down. Adranas lay ahead, much changed, partially wreathed in black smoke and with vein-like cracks across its surface. Perhaps it could offer some cover? A wormship loomed into view, a white laser immediately spearing it, tearing it apart, tracing its thick tentacles and turning them to ash. Something juddered his ship to one side, and seemed to pass through him like a hammer blow, wrenching and twisting everything around him. He realized then that Earth Central *had* been holding off while he escaped, because that was just the back blast from a DIGRAW. In the frame, he saw the mother ship roll and shift, hot debris spiking away from it. The hammerheads weren't just breaking it with the gravity weapon but trying to surf it on a particular course. More waves struck the thing, shifting it further in the direction Earth Central wanted it to go, then the DIGRAWs synched and the great tangled mass began its long fall down towards the sun.

'Bye bye fucker,' said Cog, as he took the *Janus* into close orbit around the hot burning world of Adranas and shut down acceleration, the feeling of a heavy boot coming off his chest.

But then something ripped off the rear door of the bridge and explosive decompression blasted the air out. As his visor slammed closed, he whirled to see a huge nightmarish charcoal-black head out there, mean glinting blue eyes and long triangular-section tentacles whipping in, towards him.

## The Client

He had taken it, Cog had taken it, was the Client's first thought as her consciousness tentatively re-established. She found herself alone and was grateful for that. She quickly swept through her platform to ensure all EMR transceivers, even those connecting her to her attack pods, were shut down. Then she blocked off all U-space reception before cautiously scanning the substrata via which she had been entrapped. The terrain looked very different now. The Polity ships had annihilated large portions of the cloud, creating vast shadows. Jaskor had diminished and that, she knew, was because it had lost its controlling mind. And the Jain mother ship had become a fading ember, falling towards the surface of the sun, its connections to everything else just thin and barely discernible leashes. The device she had made to deliver her disruptor virus, which Cog had stolen, had clearly worked. And how.

The Client felt a small twinge of guilt because of course it had not been her intention to make something so destructive, or to use it as Cog had used it. However, no need to look a gift horse in the mouth, as humans were inclined to say. Assured of coms safety, she quickly re-established EMR and U-space reception to assess the situation. Recorded imagery in attack pods showed the brief and devastating conflict between the ship and the Polity. It gladdened her to see that Cog had escaped and headed somewhere halfway around the sun from her, despite his theft. She then eyed the Polity hammerheads and remaining kamikazes, still destroying cloud objects and still hanging on station to watch the mother ship fall. Really, it was time for her to run but, as ever, curiosity got the better of her.

Now she so much better understood the connection throughout Jain tech, she hardened the links to it aboard her platform and, using it, reached out through that substrata. Nothing stood in her way. Neither Trike nor Orlandine were there. The Jain was all but gone too. Only some traces of its consciousness were distributed through remaining tech – somnolent and a reminder of what had driven the technology while the main intelligence had been in the U-space blister. But then she did find sparks of sentience on Jaskor and reached out there to them.

Humans, millions of them. They had been Orlandine's slaves, but they were no longer subject to her will and some were starting to rise to prominence, reaching out to the tech all around them. Given time, they would grow powerful and become a danger. Asserting her will on that world, she penetrated the memstores and memory base of all that Orlandine had been and found a cornucopia. The exhilaration of spreading her intelligence around the globe the Client found intoxicating. She could see the parties of humans returning, on some base program, to the cities. While making them walk faster, she checked their weapons and armour. In another area, she shifted a great tower of a linear accelerator and gazed upon the factories that supplied its heavy missiles. Such power! She could take all this, easily, and the knowledge here! And then she realized she could extend out to govern the Jain cloud, and even beyond, back to the accretion disc. Still other links were open too!

Then she stopped.

The horror of what had started to happen shuddered down the entire length of her body. She had nearly picked up the baton. The huge temptation was there, as it had always been, and she must, she felt, remove it. The Jain tech also stored Orlandine's data on enclosing hardfields and disruptor weapons. The Client recognized that once it secured this system, Earth Central would aim to grab such data. Coldly, she began making her preparations, realizing just how little time she had. With a thought, she had her robots bring her another disposable laboratory. She knew she would not be able to finish making another disruptor virus device before EC acted, so she had to prepare the way, to buy herself that time.

The people first. They would have to be the lure so it must be possible to save them. She reached out to them and delivered instruction with a viral program. Their mycelia began to repair the damage to the human bodies as they withdrew, the fibres killing and shredding themselves. This would ameliorate the effect of the disruptor virus once it did its work. Some would die, she knew, and a great many of the survivors would be amputees and very ill. Nevertheless, millions would survive. As this process commenced, she focused on the design of another device, similar to the last one, but altered to complement its delivery system: an attack pod was now being refuelled and recharged in a construction bay. This would be an attraction because Earth Central might think it possible to obtain the virus, even though, during its spread, the thing destroyed itself. As the disposable laboratory arrived and she began work, she knew that only minutes remained before EC turned its attention her way. She simultaneously fed power to her platform's U-space engines, and prepared to jump.

## Earth Central

Earth Central watched the Jain mother ship, now little more than a mass of debris, burning as it fell into the sun. EC did not understand why the thing was moving slowly, because surfing an object on a gravity wave usually ramped up its speed relativistic. It seemed as if it possessed an equivalent to sea anchors but dragging in U-space. Something to do with that internal U-space twist, the AI suspected – a technology it needed to study in more detail. It also did not understand precisely what had caused the Jain tech to disrupt like that. The effect had been swift, massive and, of course, would be very useful. Perhaps Cog, out of direct sight behind Adranas now, would have answers. But it suspected the one who really had them lay in the opposite direction, and was of greater concern . . .

Even as EC turned its attention towards the Client, Weapons Platform Mu and its attack pods jumped. For a fraction of a second, the AI thought it had lost the creature, but its signature was clear, its destination close and the jump brief. EC followed, jumping the remainder of its fleet to where Weapons Platform Mu now hung over Jaskor. EC could not allow the Client to escape. There was a subliminal flicker, but then a crash again and flare patterns of debris. All the hammerheads stabbed out white lasers. Every single attack pod standing separate from the platform exploded, while the beams probed the platform itself, aiming for hardfield installations. But not quickly enough. Mu's enclosing field came up and the lasers splashed on it, leaving bruises as they traversed. A microsecond later, EC fired up a USER in one of the hammerheads – its disruption local – then directed a warfare beam at the field, wide spectrum, seeking frequencies it didn't block.

'I expected no less,' said the Client.

The coms frequency allowed sat in the red band of visible light. It was very low bandwidth and not enough for fast virtual warfare, but perhaps enough to slowly build something nasty in receiving arrays.

'You stole a weapons platform, attacked the prador and have caused deaths,' replied EC. 'That you have been of some assistance here is the only reason I have not instantly obliterated you.'

'You mean like creating a disruptor virus that destroyed a thousand-mile-long Jain warship?' enquired the Client. 'Be in no doubt, AI, without my intervention your impressive ships would have been vapour by now.'

*Disruptor virus?*

With a large portion of its mind EC processed that information, and it also contemplated reality. The Jain had toyed with its ships, negligently destroying some of them. It had been distracted by Trike at the time and EC could find no optimistic interpretation of the facts. Had this virus not started taking its ship apart, thus bringing down its hardfield, the Jain would have destroyed EC's fleet.

'Perhaps we can come to an accommodation,' EC suggested.

'Perhaps we can,' replied the Client. 'Here is how I see it: I am guilty of the crimes you cite, but I also saved the Polity and the Prador Kingdom from imminent destruction. The situation now is much as it was before. You have wild Jain tech you need to clear up, that is all. I suggest you forget about my offences and turn off that USER so I can go. You do not have the fire-power to collapse this field.'

'I have a counter-proposal,' said EC. 'Why don't I test your hypothesis concerning that hardfield. Perhaps the firepower I have is not enough to collapse it but if I were to DIGRAW you into the sun first . . .'

'Interesting idea and not one I would like to see tested.'

'Then perhaps a small exchange. Data on the enclosing hard-field would be very useful to me, as would data on the disruptor weapons and the virus.'

'Orlandine has that data,' the Client countered.

'Orlandine is no longer viable. The Jain tech on Jaskor is presently reverting and that indicates it no longer has a controlling mind.'

'Weapons platform AIs have it too.'

'Yes, they do have the disruptor beam technology, which I have recorded and am presently wiping from their minds, but not the hardfield technology.'

'How unfortunate,' said the Client, and EC could not help but note a degree of smug satisfaction there.

'So we have reached a little bit of an impasse, but I am patient.'

'You have yet to hear my counter-proposal,' said the Client, 'And you seem to have ignored the fact that I could have jumped away, while concealing my U-signature, and been long gone by now. Instead I have come here to Jaskor.'

'Please, do carry on.'

'You will shut down your USER. I will deploy the disruptor virus on Jaskor. It travels fast through Jain technology but also has some reach to discrete structures in its vicinity. You will have noted how the framework of the mother ship broke up and that it took a little while longer before the biomechs began to fail?'

'I did note this.'

'So, I deploy the virus, Jaskor is freed of Jain tech, then shortly after that the millions of humans there will be free of it too.'

'This will most likely kill them.'

'Look at them,' the Client suggested.

EC was already closely studying the world through hammer-head sensors, even while sending sampling and sensory probes down to the surface. Simple reality: if the Client did deploy that virus, EC wanted to be on hand to grab a sample. It then noted the people. They had been moving back in towards the cities but many of them had collapsed, or were staggering as if incredibly weary. The distant view showed some shedding their armour in large flakes, revealing new skin underneath, while others had lost their weapons, the pink stubs of amputated limbs left behind. Was this a process Orlandine had initiated before the Jain completely sequestered her?

The probes, under massive acceleration, hit atmosphere then decelerated hard under grav and fusion down to the surface. One settled near a party of humans who had been aiming for the main city but were now milling about in confusion. It stabbed anchors into the ground, folded out wide-spectrum scanners and focused on these people. Active and hard, the scan felled those who remained standing, steam rising from their skins. EC watched for some minutes, noting the retreat of the mycelia within them, repairing damage as it went. One began yelling and writhing, a power supply like the shell of a terrapin peeling off her back. The action of the Jain tech in the ground around the probe seemed anomalous too. It was apparently wild and should be attacking that probe, but it was not, so there had to be an active mind here controlling it.

'You control this Jain technology yet are prepared to destroy it?' the AI asked.

'Would you retain it if you controlled it?' the Client countered.

'No I would not, since that is precisely the trap of the thing.'

'Then there is little more to discuss,' said the Client, 'except my terms.'

Even as EC spoke, it wondered if it was being wholly truthful. It recognized temptation: it understood the technology and perhaps controlling it and studying it could drive massive technological advances in the Polity? No, this stuff had to be destroyed . . . though perhaps a period of study, while it remained confined at the bottom of a gravity well? But it was a poisoned chalice . . . Orlandine had perfectly demonstrated this. The danger for an AI like EC wasn't immediate sequestration, but a gradual effect spread over centuries. Then again, those centuries would put the investigating AI ahead of the curve—

'I note a lengthy delay in your response,' said the Client. 'I have no doubt that even now the enticement is making itself felt.'

The creature was right. The jaws of the Jain-tech trap were large enough for the most advanced intelligences. As if to highlight the danger here, EC noted the arrival of new ships: ten prador dreadnoughts and the twin of the *Kinghammer*, still some way from completion. They appeared far out from Jaskor and in from the gas giant – knocked out into the real by the effect of the USER EC had deployed. They immediately began strafing near space to burn up cloud objects.

'What are your terms?' asked EC.

'I will use the disruptor virus,' said the Client. 'You will let me go and you will not send anything in pursuit of me at any time.'

'Very well,' said EC. Promises were as easy to make as they were to break.

'Of course if you do send anything after me, my response will be to send a U-space information package directly to the king of the prador, detailing how to build both disruptors and completely enclosing hardfields.'

EC shut down the USER, simultaneously swinging its hammer-heads away from Weapons Platform Mu and pulling them back. The Client could have fled immediately or it could have made this threat alone, without offering to use the virus on Jaskor. EC might salvage something here, by acquiring that disruptor virus. Mu's field blinked out and the platform immediately launched an attack pod. The object hurtled down towards atmosphere, entered it and then slowed. Instead of heading towards the main continent as expected, it hit ocean at a low angle and skimmed for a hundred miles before sinking rapidly. EC quickly launched further probes to drop into that same ocean. Sensors delving into the depths showed the attack pod releasing thousands of objects which spread swiftly and began to settle towards the tangled growth on the seabed.

'Goodbye,' said the Client, and Weapons Platform Mu shimmered, stretched and was gone.

## Cog

'Oh hell,' said Cog, as the tentacles reached the limit of their extent, just a yard away from him.

A biomech from the Jain ship had hopped a ride but, as it sliced through the back wall of the bridge, he saw it wasn't coming apart and did not seem at all confused about its object-ives. He surged out of his chair, snatching up his weapon and shoulder rolling out of reach, coming up and turning as the thing shoved its head inside. He fired straight into its face and its shriek came over com and seemed to rattle his bones. He knew then this was no simple biomech. That shriek was the challenge of the Jain.

The particle beam struck its head, but only splashed and raised a red glow. He transferred his aim lower, into a ribbed gullet surrounded by mandibles. Here the beam raised an explosion of vapour, just before a tentacle swept across and smashed him into the side wall. He hung there in a deep dent, suit pressure crashing as air blasted out around his arm, the gauntlet and forearm armour ripped away. The thing surged in further and the nose of a tentacle slammed into his chest, denting the armour and grating away glittering swarf. Then, as Cog felt something boring agonizingly into his chest, Trike's huge spidery blue form landed hard beside him and his hand closed on the tentacle.

'Trike!' said Cog over radio, but there was no response.

Cog had never known such pain – even a plug-extracting leech bite didn't hurt so much. Why was it so agonizing? He surmised the intent here – the Jain wanted him to suffer. Trike closed down with another hand, grip pressure sinking his fingers into the tentacle before he broke it apart. He then launched again, the thing reeling him in towards the attacker. Landing with his feet against the wall and still gripping the tentacle in his left hand, he began delivering overhand punches with his right, blindingly fast, smashing against the head so hard Cog could feel the impacts too through the wall. Trike was back and recovered from the trauma he had suffered out there, all ferocious Spatterjay mutation like Jay Hoop – a monster Cog was glad to have on his side. He saw glittering black fragments splintering away from armour that even his particle weapon couldn't touch. Then the long claw closed on Trike's thigh, and the Jain dragged him out of sight.

The pain would not go away and Cog felt very weak. Foam sealant bubbled out about his elbow and hardened, but it broke as he folded both arms in to grab the remainder of the tentacle attached to his chest. With all his remaining strength, he heaved the thing away. At first, it wouldn't move, then something snapped and an outer sheath slid off. This revealed a skein of hard thin wires. He tried to pull them away too but they would not budge. Grabbing just one, he wrapped it about his hand and pulled. This did come out, and kept on coming. He felt its journey, from his ankle back to its point of entry, before finally discarding two yards of the thing. He pulled another and then another, his strength increasing with each removal, but also something crazy wittering in his skull. Finally, he heaved himself out of the wall, still stripping out the tendrils with one hand, even as he searched round and picked up his weapon with the other. He had to do something. Trike might be back on old form but in vacuum his strength would soon wane.

The ship shuddered to crashes, and heavy impacts telegraphed through its skeleton. As Cog reached the back of the bridge, he peered through. The stairway had been pulled down and compacted, beams torn off and remaining hull plates were tumbling away into vacuum. In the space they had created during their fight, Trike and the Jain hammered at each other. The thing still had his leg in its claw but he'd released its tentacle so as to pummel its body with both fists. Cog noted the pure physicality of this battle. Silvery technology in the Jain's body was cracking and flaking away, just as the tech in its ship had, for the disruptor virus had done its work. A similar cloud of materials surrounded Trike and little remained of those veins that had covered him when he had exited the drainage system under the Jaskoran main city. This, Cog realized, explained the lack of a radio response from the man – all the technology had died inside him.

Cog took aim with his particle cannon, selecting something that might be vulnerable: the joint in one of the creature's legs. He opened fire and kept the beam on target as best he could, but they were moving so fast. He shut it down when it brushed Trike's shoulder, briefly raising a spurt of vapour. Other vapour also surrounded him, for the vacuum had begun drying him out and he was losing strength. The Jain began to beat Trike against the deck, creating huge dents, buckling up gratings and shattering the workings of grav-plates. In response, Trike snatched hold of a leg and drove his fist into its body. It released his leg, snapped its claw out again and closed it on his arm. Its tentacles looped in, passing over his body like milling heads tearing up fibrous virus-hardened muscle. Trike could not win this battle – Cog needed to find another way to intervene. Just then, the roll of the ship brought the burning face of Adranas up into view.

*There,* thought Cog, a plan forming in his mind.

Cog retreated to his chair and checked his instruments. Numerous error messages showed that most of the system had crashed, including controls to many steering thrusters. But there were enough to point the ship in the right direction and the fusion drive was still working. He input a firing of the steering thrusters, the ship turning and stabilizing, pointing nose down towards Adranas. He relayed drive control to his suit – a signal ready to send – before making his way back through the wreckage behind. With his suit's scanners mapping ahead, including the swiftly moving figures of both Trike and the Jain, he input a firing program to the suit jets.

The Jain now tried to grind a tentacle in through Trike's chest. Its claw still tight on his arm, he swung himself in and stabbed out his tongue, right into one of its eyes. The thing released its claw to go for his throat. Cog punched the suit-jet program and slammed down straight into Trike's back. He grabbed an arm, as the program hurled him away again, dragging Trike with him and aiming them towards a gap in the ship's skeleton. He was passing through and out when a wrench suddenly pulled his shoulder out of its socket. As it clicked back into place, he saw the tentacle attached to Trike's foot. Already knowing his particle weapon could not touch the creature, he swung it round and fired. Something snapped and they tumbled clear, and Cog sent the signal.

The fusion drive nacelle fired at full power, hurling the ship past them. The back blast seared them and sent them tumbling away until his suit jets corrected, stabilizing them in relation to the receding ship.

'Sorry about that,' said Cog, even though Trike couldn't hear. He glanced at the burned stub that had been Trike's foot, then focused back on the *Janus*. He could see the creature pulling itself outside the ship and clambering back towards the drive nacelle. Had the thing still possessed its earlier technological capabilities, he knew it would have seized control there at once, but it was just a physical being now. He sent new instructions, stuttering the drive, steering thrusters throwing the vessel from side to side as it hurtled down towards the planet, grav waxing and waning – anything to interfere with the creature's course. He had to increase magnification to its maximum through his visor to watch it finally reach the nacelle and rip off a cover, jabbing its tentacles inside. He checked the math and saw that the point had passed where it could fling itself clear and not fall to the surface. The ship grew smaller and smaller, little more than a dot with its drive still burning. It did finally go out, just a few minutes before the near-invisible flash of impact down on the surface. Maybe the Jain could survive that, Cog did not know. He was more concerned about what he and Trike could survive.

Cog studied his companion. Vapour still rose from Trike's body, mostly out of his mouth. His eyes were dry now, the balls sinking inside the sockets, but he still managed to turn his head to Cog and give a slow creaky nod. Quite soon, he would be devoid of moisture – a woody statue. As a living thing, he could survive for many days in this state, but whether he would be Trike thereafter was debatable. Cog extended a safety wire from his suit's belt and wrapped it around the man's waist before assessing his own situation. His exposed arm was losing moisture, only remaining functional because his venous system kept feeding it from within his body. He too would end up in the same condition as Trike, though his air, already badly depleted and leaking through the sealant foam around his elbow, would run out first.

'Not a good situation,' he said.

Trike shifted as if he had heard. Cog worked his wrist control and checked through suit menus in his HUD. He found the rescue beacon and turned it on. He hoped that if someone did find them and pick them up, they would be suitably cautious. Injured hoopers could be dangerous.

## Orlandine

The envirosuit adjusted to fit perfectly and was clean and comfortable. The food and drink Orlandine had found filled the empty ache in her guts and gave her an energy kick, but as she stepped out of Trissa Oclaire's home, she felt terrible. She guessed, with her being so inured to body horror, the sight of Oclaire's Jain-infested and incinerated corpse had been minimal, yet the belongings – the collected and well-used items of a life lived – made her sick with guilt and depression. She mentally replayed past conversations with the woman, remembering them all. As well as residing in her organic brain, she had backed them up in perfect detail in the crystal in her skull. She could not use that crystal for processing so was no longer really a haiman. It did, however, damn her with perfect recall, and not just of Oclaire. Many others had died, and were due to die, because of her actions. Millions of them.

Since she had taken control of them and filled their bodies

with Jain tech, they were doomed. The new master of the structure all around Jaskor would never free them, but use up and discard them. Polity ships had arrived just as the Jain, through Trike, seized control of her mind. Even if they prevailed against it, the people here would still have no hope, for EC would schedule this world for cleansing destruction. She sat on a trunk of Jain tech, little caring if something seized control of her. It seemed apt that she would die along with Jaskor. She could not persuade herself that her actions were due to the Jain tech working on her mind. Aphorisms about how power corrupts seemed relevant. Then, as she felt the warm surface through the trousers of the suit, something hit.

Her surroundings seemed to distort briefly, the effect similar to what she saw on entering or exiting U-space. A rumbling reached her as of distant sonic booms, and the ground started to vibrate. She put her hand down on the Jain trunk, feeling a static shock and steady vibration there. What the hell was happening? The oddity of the question hit her hard, because she had not needed to ask it in an awfully long time. Now, looking down at the surface under her hand, she saw iridescent ripples passing through it as on heated iron. She felt no heat but snatched her hand away anyway and stood up.

The trunks and tentacles roped all across the island, burying the Sambre volcano and mounded about the giant louse-like device she had once occupied, were all changing colour. The overall effect, at a distance, was of them growing darker and becoming more reflective. She peered down at thinner masses strewn across the ground and saw mycelia writhing and shrivelling. Then the larger tendrils they issued from fractured like bent twigs, the crackling sound rising to a general hiss. She moved over to a stone slab, kicking a few stray tendrils aside from its surface and seeing them break. A loud crump issued from behind

505

and she turned to see the trunk she had been sitting on had split. Great shards snapped up from its surface, exposing the complexity of its interior, and released jets of gas and leaked molten metal. The effect spread all the way along the thing for as far as she could see. She had thought, just for a moment, that the Jain must be making some kind of alteration, perhaps building something new. But this was destruction.

Orlandine ran, not sure why, since she could not be safe from this anywhere on the island. And earlier, she had not even cared about her safety. The noise grew and grew until it seemed a thunderstorm had settled around her. Leaping from rock to rock through a lava field, as burning fragments rained through the air, she saw an object jutting up ahead and knew the destination of her flight. She finally stopped, dropping into a crouch, and gazed up at the standing corpse of Oclaire.

The Jain tech on the woman began splintering and peeling up like pencil sharpenings, these falling away to cover the surrounding stone. Orlandine swept up a handful and studied it. Even as she held them, the pieces further disintegrated until she tipped away a small pile of granular dust. Without the tendrils to hold them up, the remains of Oclaire fell apart. As her skull bounced and clattered away, this seemed to initiate further destruction. The ground began jerking from side to side, like a beast trying to shrug away flies on its back. Orlandine put her hands down to steady herself, and looked up towards the volcano. There she saw the massive louse-like device sinking into the caldera, smoke boiling up all around it. Lava splashed as the thing disappeared from sight. The earth stilled, as if taking a breath, then the volcano exploded.

Orlandine watched the eruption with a kind of amused fascination. A shockwave sent her staggering backwards, but it was no more than a hard hot wind. This was not the problem. The giant plume went up and up, then lost impetus some miles into the sky. The top mushroomed out and folded down, perpetually fed by the eruption below. Great clouds of shattered burning stone, lava and dust, shrouded the top of Sambre and poured down – an avalanche hot enough to roast the flesh from a person's bones, a pyroclastic flow, boiling down the slopes, travelling fast, straight towards her.

Now, seeing her imminent death, Orlandine was not so in love with the idea. Wasn't that always the way? The cloud, glowing in its core, rushed across the lava fields towards her, shrouding everything. Her damnably accurate brain gave her no outlet, detailing how the envirosuit would protect her for a little while, thus extending her agonizing death by at least half a minute. Stone began to rain down and all she could hope for was that some heavy chunk might hit her on the head. Something heavy did land nearby and she flinched.

'Getting a little hectic around here, don't you think?'

She looked round.

The speaker suggested, 'Time to leave?'

She nodded. Cutter folded his forelimbs around her, sharp edges pointed outwards, and launched them both into the sky.

Like a damaged jet coming down on some giant antediluvian aircraft carrier, Cutter landed with a skittering of limbs that sliced up threads of metal. He finally skidded to a halt at the base of an ersatz tower block and released Orlandine. She walked unsteadily to an edge to gaze out from Weapons Platform Thetus towards the plume rising on Sambre Island. She then peered down at activity on landscape pipes and vanes for cooling, and com dishes like craters. The drones at work there were familiar.

'What are they doing?' she asked.

'A little maintenance, though not much is required,' replied the other who had been waiting at their landing spot as he moved up beside her.

'All the platforms and ships down on the planet are at their optimum,' she stated, not sure what to think beyond that.

'Bludgeon is in place as controlling AI,' said Knobbler. 'Five others of the guys have control of five other platforms.'

'That's good, but to what purpose?' She looked round at the drone. 'The Jain mother ship has been destroyed and the Jain tech on Jaskor is falling apart. Huge Polity ships have arrived and this world is now about to be fried.'

'Of course, we'll need your AIs back to take control of the other platforms. I'm guessing the ships will have to go to their original owners, if they want them,' said Knobbler, as if she hadn't spoken.

'Oh and the prador have arrived too,' interjected Cutter. 'Another ship like the *Kinghammer*, along with a few old dreadnoughts. Not that they would last long against those hammerheads.'

Orlandine put her hand to her forehead. She was getting a headache, probably because she'd started trying to use her crystal for processing.

'It's done, it's over,' she said. 'I allowed Jain tech to take over and I enslaved millions. Thousands are dead because of me. Earth Central is here.'

'Okay, let's run through this,' said Knobbler. 'You stood against a major threat to two civilizations and how you went about that is irrelevant. We're back where we were before: there's wild Jain tech in the Jaskoran system and at the accretion disc. There's damage here on this world and people who need help. These are your responsibility.'

'What?' He just did not seem to understand. 'The people will die: millions of them.'

Knobbler waved a dismissive tentacle. 'Apparently not. Thousands have died and will continue to die, but the majority are shedding the technology that controlled them and surviving, though they need help. Considering what we faced, that's a small casualty rate. And let's not forget the millions you managed to evacuate.'

'Earth Central will burn this world,' she said, feeling less sure now.

'That may be the AI's intention, so perhaps it needs to be reminded that all agreements are still in place and that Jaskor and the accretion disc are yours, and Dragon's – should he turn up again.'

'And since U-com is open again, the king of the prador could be included in any discussions,' said Cutter, adding, 'Perhaps you should talk to him soon.'

The weapons platform groaned and shifted underfoot. Gazing out towards the volcano, Orlandine watched another massive eruption, the rumble and crash of it reaching her a moment later. The sea before the island rose, a white line of spume cutting across it. Tsunami. Then the view began to drop away as the platform rose from the surface.

'Time for you to go inside,' said Knobbler. 'It won't be long before we're out of atmosphere.'

Orlandine grimaced at this reminder of her conventional human vulnerability.

## Gemmell

The head of the hammerhead dreadnought contained a select few individuals, Gemmell noted. Diana Windermere stood alone. Orlik, with what looked like an assassin drone crouched on his back, was with the prador Ksov. Others were notable by their absence. The Client, it seemed, had fled the system and there would be no pursuit. Cog and Trike were in-system apparently being tracked down by a search vessel. Orlandine was missing and, from all he had learned, presumed dead, while none of her drones were present either. Grimacing, Gemmell felt a stab of sad guilt about the absence of the commander of the Polity fleet at Jaskor. Morgaine was just vapour out there amidst the debris.

'Why are we here?' asked Ruth.

Gemmell mulled over a reply. Everyone possessed comware that thoroughly linked them into the new data sphere. All could connect in virtuality if anything important required their involvement. Only one answer remained.

He shrugged. 'We're here as a courtesy, I suspect. Earth Central knows that just to shunt us off to quarters or to our next assignment might be too dismissive.'

She raised an eyebrow. 'It's concerned about our feelings?'

'Only when little effort is required to assuage them.'

Ruth snorted.

'If I could have your attention, please,' a mild androgynous voice announced.

Nobody looked round for the source of it. This was EC speaking through the PA – if it wanted to manifest itself, it would and they were all aware of that.

'We are all eyes and ears,' said Ruth.

'I'm beginning to notice a tendency to sarcasm in you,' Gemmell muttered.

She grinned.

'You are all aware, to varying degrees, of recent events,' said EC. 'But let me now confirm so you fully understand how we have defeated the Jain attack. The hooper Trike, empowered by Jain technology, took the Species ship's core against the mother ship. He failed. The Jain sequestered him and then Orlandine. However, a disruptor virus created by the Client, and delivered by the hooper Cogulus Hoop, destroyed the technology of that ship and I subsequently DIGRAWed it into the sun. The Client deployed that same virus on Jaskor before departing, causing the planetary events you are now seeing.'

Gemmell gazed at Jaskor beyond the panoramic window. It looked a right mess down there with storms and volcanic activity, but he questioned whether that was all about this disruptor virus. The planet had been most of the way to completely fucked before then.

EC continued, 'There is "wild" Jain tech that still needs to be dealt with. The situation for all of you is this: prador ships have arrived and will be taking surviving prador back to the Kingdom. ECS military will be returned to Outlink Station Marank for debriefing, while surviving Jaskorans will, after similar debriefing, be relocated in the Polity. Thank you for your attention.'

'That doesn't sound good,' said Ruth.

'Uhuh – no mention of the people still down there,' Gemmell agreed. 'If there was to be some kind of rescue operation we'd be involved.' He began shooting questions at EC via his gridlink, hunting for detail.

'I think we know what that means,' said Ruth. 'Especially with that bit about relocation.'

Gemmell nodded. It seemed highly likely that Jaskor wasn't going to be around for much longer.

'I am receiving many queries which I am dealing with,' EC said abruptly. It sure was, for it seemed most of the survivors aboard had something to say about its recent announcement. 'You have some concerns about the situation here. It is my intention to . . . oh.'

Something happened which even EC had not expected. Ruth grabbed Gemmell's arm and pointed at the view. He turned and squinted, just as masses of information about the events on Jaskor began falling into the data sphere. Objects rising from the world breached the swirling cloud masses. He recognized some of Orlandine's remaining weapons platforms.

'Inclusive virtuality has been . . . requested,' EC announced.

Gemmell felt the comlink bandwidth opening. The viewing area shimmered and seemed to expand a little, while he found himself retreating somehow, to become part of a large audience. Shapes etched themselves out on the floor and began to fill with colour – virtual substance. A giant louse appeared whose body was woven through with all manner of esoteric technology. Another was the metalskin android EC had earlier used as an avatar, only taller and bulkier, perhaps in order not to be dwarfed by the king of the prador. Then a woman in an envirosuit appeared: Orlandine.

'So glad you accepted the request,' said the king, the words dripping sarcasm.

'I am always happy to oblige,' replied EC.

'Then we are all happy,' said Orlandine. 'I felt it a good idea to make this inclusive to ensure that we are all aware of the situation as it stands.'

'And how do you see that?' enquired the king, almost certainly having been prompted.

Orlandine began, 'Jaskor has been badly damaged by the recent conflict and millions of its citizens are in need. To this end, I am requesting assistance from both the Polity and the Kingdom. I do hope neither of you have any problem with this?'

'I will be delighted to help,' said the king.

'And I too,' said EC, though Gemmell doubted that was the case.

'I have also sent messages to the platform AIs you have aboard your ship. Most have agreed to return to their platforms on Jaskor, which are now free of active Jain tech and mostly serviceable.

They will return to the transports used to evacuate them once you restore function to their carrier shells and other forms of mobility. I am not sure why they lost mobility – an oversight I am sure.'

'Merely a temporary safety measure,' said EC.

'If I may?' asked the king. Orlandine waved for him to continue and he announced, 'All my warcraft crews currently aboard this vessel, and enclave prador – you will return to Jaskor to offer all assistance. You will be under the command of Orlik, who is now my new ambassador to this world.'

Orlandine acknowledged that with a nod. 'I would also be happy with the return of all Polity personnel, military and civilian, if that is their wish and if there are no conflicting orders.' She looked around and for a moment seemed to focus on Gemmell. 'I will need as much humanitarian assistance as possible but it is also essential to get the platforms back up into space. The Jain threat still exists. I would like Polity and prador warships to counter that threat here for the interim. I am, of course, prepared to offer a special dispensation in this respect until platform defences are restored, whereupon –' and now her expression hardened – 'the treaties previously agreed will be back in force and all Polity and prador warships must depart.'

*And there it is,* thought Gemmell. Orlandine had known Earth Central's intentions here. By putting herself right in the AI's face, by reminding it of previous agreements and proving herself active and able, she had just prevented the destruction of a world. She was taking charge again.

'Are we all in agreement?' she asked into the ensuing silence.

'It seems that we are,' said EC.

'Order is restored,' said the king.

The virtuality shimmered and the three figures bled away. As they faded, Gemmell checked relevant contracts and saw that he was still in Orlandine's employ. He checked Ruth's contract too, and saw that her employment with ECS had officially ended when they left Jaskor. He took hold of her hand.

'Do I need to ask?' he asked.

'No, you do not,' she replied. 'We go back.'

They turned and headed for the dropshaft.


## Diana

Diana Windermere felt tired as she headed to the quarters assigned to her aboard the hammerhead. Jabro and Seckurg were waiting for her and she invited them in. The quarters were big, with as many rooms and as much space as the average Polity house. She was used to larger spaces.

'So what now for us?' asked Jabro, plonking himself down on a sofa.

Diana went to her bar, poured herself a large glass of bourbon, then added ice.

'It's not necessary for you to tie yourself to me.' She studied them. 'You both have sufficient qualifications, service time and good will, to ask for commands of your own.'

'You miss it,' said Seckurg, thinking he saw to the heart of her malaise.

She took a hearty gulp. 'Hogue and I were together for a long time. I can only assume it sacrificed itself like that because it had been infected and viewed itself as a danger.' She paused for second, only to add, 'A long time.'

The *Cable Hogue* AI had been linked to, in fact almost an adjunct to, her mind, for longer than many modern humans had lived. Of course, she missed that intelligence. It hurt. However, she knew that an AI psycho-surgeon could take away the sting while leaving the memories intact. She could remove memories entirely if she so decided. She had done so before out of choice, and once or twice under orders.

'Maybe we don't want our own commands.' Jabro stood up. 'And maybe I want a drink.' He walked over, turned a glass upright and poured. 'Now stop revelling in your misery and tell us what happens next.'

Had she mourned for long enough? She *felt* it to be a necessary process, but the whole idea of what she was actually mourning lay open to debate.

'It's all about backups,' she said. 'Most of us back up our minds somewhere, if intermittently sometimes, and AIs are no different. Hogue, up to the point when the U-space disruption hit here, exists.'

'Of course,' said Seckurg.

She continued, 'Earth Central likes to have backups too, both mental and physical, of all sorts of things.' She paused to take another drink, then waved a hand. 'Show them.'

A big screen on one wall came on. It showed planet Earth and then panned round and out, past the masses of space stations and cylinder worlds, out over cities spread on the moon, and then to giant shipyards where, in vacuum surrounded by pseudo-matter scaffolds, floated a giant spherical ship.

'The *Cable Hogue II*,' she said. 'That's what happens next.'

Jabro smiled, while Seckurg made a reasonable facsimile of the same.

# Epilogue

## Orlik

The path out from the city wound through the printed domes of the hospital and accommodation complex. As Orlik perambulated along it, with Brull and Vreen marching behind him, he observed a group of humans leaving one dome and heading back towards the city. Clad in a wide variety of workwear from the fabricators, they were no doubt heading in to help with the reconstruction. Out of the twenty, he counted twelve with prosthetic left hands: grey ceramal bones with joint motors visible through transparent sytheflesh. The look had become something of a fashion statement amongst those Orlandine had sequestered. These were probably returning for final treatments and free to choose their next course. Many had just gone back to their homes on Jaskor, if they remained, while some had decided to head to the Polity. The rest, presumably like these, had chosen to join Orlandine's reconstruction crews.

'So little resentment,' commented Sprag from where she crouched on Orlik's back.

'Enough,' said Orlik. But the resentment was diminishing. As far as he knew, there had been no assassination attempt on Orlandine this week.

As they moved on, Orlik next spotted a crinoid forensic AI rolling along a walkway between domes. He shuddered. Having had many solicitous enquiries from them about his health, and whether or not he would like to be examined, he had begun to avoid them. Whether this one was Mobius Clean, he had no idea. Hundreds of the things rolled around this place and they all looked alike to him, just as did most of the humans.

'Anyway, where were we?' asked Sprag.

'You were pointing out that my deployment here is a bit of a demotion,' said Orlik, annoyed that Sprag would not let this go.

'Perhaps it's punishment for scrapping some valuable hardware?' suggested Sprag.

'It is not a demotion.' Orlik looked ahead at the foamstone platform of the temporary landing field. Numerous supply ships were down and even as he watched, one took off and another landed. A slow procession of ground trucks travelled along the main road out to the right, while grav-platforms loaded with supplies slid through the sky. 'In some ways it is a promotion.'

'I really don't see it that way.'

'Of course you don't,' said Orlik, finally snapping, 'because you are a contrary annoying little shit of a terror drone who should have gone into recycling long ago.'

'Okay,' said Sprag, definite satisfaction in her voice. 'Perhaps you're right.'

Their relationship had been back on its old footing for some time now.

The path took them to a wide ramp, then up onto the platform. Checking the marking on the foamstone, Orlik moved over to a clear area on one side, heading to the edge of this to gaze out across the fields. The ground there had been churned and burned, and was packed with the crumbled remains of Jain tech. A storm had begun rolling in with its load of dust and ash across the yellow sky. The sun only shone on the rare occasions the haze cleared, yet, out there, things were growing.

'Poppies,' he said, eyeing the masses of red flowers.

'Indeed,' Sprag replied.

The little drone had already explained the historical significance to humans of these flowers.

'And the excavation?' Orlik pointed with one claw.

Tunnel borers and earth-moving robots still sat in a muddy mess out there surrounded by a ring of grav-tanks occupied by Polity marines. They had been running constant scans for fear of something crawling out of the ground – some resurgence of the hostile technology that had occupied this world. When those scans found a suspicious object, everyone had been concerned.

'One of Knobbler's crew,' Sprag replied, 'somewhat annoyed that they forgot about him and left him buried there. Cutter tells me they hadn't forgotten. Drone practical jokes eh?' She then added, 'It's coming down now.'

Orlik swivelled round and looked up. An attack pod like a fat golden leaf dropped through the high cloud and descended fast towards the landing field. Orlik glanced over to the prador with him.

'Remember, they've been rehydrated and fed, but they might still be dangerous,' he said. 'However, no killing.'

Brull rattled the chains he held while Vreen tapped his ionic stun cannon against his turret. His warning, Orlik felt, had been superfluous in both cases: Vreen obeyed to the letter while Brull was quite aware of what they might face.

'They were missing for a long time,' he said.

'Space is big,' said Sprag dismissively.

Orlik was sure the delay was due to the manoeuvring and politicking in the inner system. Polity attack ships had gone to search there because Earth Central had hoped to obtain data on the disruptor virus, but Orlandine quickly moved platforms into position and told the ships to withdraw. She must have found the individuals they were looking for right away, but kept them on ice in a platform, finally moving them only when no more Polity ships were close by. It was not beyond reason to suppose that EC might do something drastic if it knew its targets were within range.

The attack pod settled. At its fore, it held a big cylindrical ceramal case, which it deposited before heading up again, opening its fusion drive with a boom and disappearing from sight.

Orlik walked over to the cylinder. He had the code in his implants to open the door in its side, but it turned out to be unnecessary. A crash resounded from inside, then another and another and the door flew off. A ton of ceramal smashed to the foamstone, scattering pieces of the locking mechanism and hinges.

'About buggering time!' exclaimed Cog, stepping out.

The Old Captain wore a body-monitoring suit, which confirmed Orlik's suspicion about a platform AI having put him, and his companion, on ice. Cog walked out further, glanced at Orlik and the two prador, then, with a loud clonking, stretched kinks out of his back. He looked thin and gaunt and just a little bit dangerous.

'You only wanted out because you were losing,' said Trike, stepping forwards. 'Four more moves and you were toast.' He looked around and grinned malevolently. 'Hello, Orlik, hello, Brull and friend.'

Orlik glanced inside the cylinder and saw two chairs, with a chessboard on the table between. He returned his attention to Trike.

The man had changed. Orlik suspected a diet to suppress the Spatterjay virus, along with some surgical intervention. He too wore a body-monitoring suit and now looked almost human. Almost. He had the same gaunt hungry look as Cog but stood some feet taller. His body proportions were of someone who had been deadlifting a grav-car. Spiky black hair stood up from his head and his ears were pointed, as were his teeth. White thread scars webbed his exposed blue skin, while his eyes were black and beady.

'Right.' Cog slapped his hands together with a crack that made the watching prador jump. 'I need some lunch.' Brull and Vreen each took a cautious step backwards when he eyed them.

'We have a welcome prepared,' said Orlik. 'Follow me.'

He didn't quite know why he felt so unreasonably happy.

It was almost a human thing.

## The Jain

It had taken some time. The slow ooze of organo-metallic filaments crossed the compacted hydrocarbon slabs, winding between the chunks of composite, ceramic and partially melted alloys to reach a length of triangular tentacle lying there. The filaments snared this, then gradually inched it back to the head, which lay tilted against a rock. Energy was a problem. Feeding the process, the creature could only rely on photosynthetic compounds in its carapace, diffusion from the dense surrounding superfluids processed in its cells, and a single functional bioreactor in its nominal skull. It took years.

Eventually it drew the tentacle in below its head and steadily reattached it. Having simultaneously built up a store of chemical energy, it became able to move the tentacle at once, though no faster than the ooze of a slug. It extended hard filaments from this, dividing into micro- and then nano-fibres and harvested hydrides in the shade of a nearby rock. It swept up oxides from a red scar in the hydrocarbon slab. Soon gaining the energy to engage more of its head sensorium, it opened one blue eye.

The eye saw more than just visible light – its vision extended across the spectrum into X-rays in one direction and short-wave radio in the other. This produced a surge of input into the piece of its brain that actually resided in its skull. Cognition, however, being energy hungry, was necessarily slow. It built up a model of its surroundings for miles in all directions, and tracked down other scattered pieces of its body. The main trunk – severely flattened and burned – was just over the edge of the slab nearby. At the limit of its perception, it detected another part of itself expanding across the upper surface of a clay tube, delving down into the crust, a honeycomb of complex matter efficiently using the surrounding material for growth. But then a bar of energy stabbed down through superfluid layers and incinerated the growth, meticulously burning away every fragment of it. The flash blinded the creature for a while, and recovering enough energy for mentation took longer.

It did not understand what had happened. But, survival instinct keyed high, it knew that to live it must stay distant from that other growth, none of which resided in its present scattered body. Using the tentacle, it inched to the edge of the slab, finally tilting and falling over it to land beside the larger piece of its main body. Here it also found useful chemicals to provide energy and with which it could heal. Extending filaments again, it connected to that body, drew its head in to connect and, by and by, made other links. Here more of its brain resided, more bioreactors and more ways of making energy. The body inflated and kept healing, with further elements of its system coming online. Additional tentacles still attached to the body gave it greater mobility and, over an age, it steadily gathered up other body parts: its legs and its claws. Finally, adapting to the conditions, it walked on the nominal surface.

Now gazing out from a mass of slabs on the shore of a sea of bubbling lava, its sensorium expanded as it opened another blue eye and engaged further detectors throughout its body. It found more of that other growth appearing and expanding only to be annihilated from above. Its stores of memory opened to it.

*The Polity,* it thought. *Maybe Orlandine.*

It measured and considered, noting how far those other growths spread before a high-intensity laser fried them. When one began some ten miles away it reached out and connected to it, reforming its structure to its purpose. Other growths appeared scattered around the solid land it stood upon and it linked to them too. In time, even though some growths the enemy destroyed from above, it had developed a sufficient array and processing with which to interpret the radiations penetrating from beyond this world. It built up a picture, finally seeing the weapons platforms and ships scattered out there. It surmised that humans still inhabited the world of Jaskor and this was why the platforms had not completely demolished Adranas, for the solar system disruption would have rendered Jaskor uninhabitable. Ranging out further, it detected radiations telling it the gas giant now burned like a small sun and none of the other growth remained there. Reaching down into the picotech realm, it found hints of growth, hints of the Jain tech it had created, then the sudden intense bombardment from the platforms drove disconnection.

It rendered itself inert, instituting its version of Polity chameleonware to make it invisible, and then it swam at high speed through the superfluids, abandoning the area. Behind it, hardened railgun slugs came down, and then slower-moving objects detonated upon reaching the hard surface. These threw out a blast wave of plasma and dense radiation. But it rode the wave, surviving, because that was what it did.

*A salutary reminder of arrogance,* it thought, remembering Trike.

Thereafter it searched out the other growth, all around the

planet, and distanced itself as far from it as possible. Scanning the range of slabbed mountains it found itself in, it recognized this as the area where Trike had brought down the core. Here, perambulating through a sleet of diamonds, it found that the density of the material below allowed for gaps, because the gravity had not crushed them down. Over a long period of more intense scanning, it found caves deep under the mountains and finally an entrance. It pulled itself inside and down. It would survive and it was patient. The short-lived life forms and artificial intelligences out there would run through their generations and iterations and slowly, over long periods their limited mentalities failed to grasp, they would forget. The Jain felt certain of this, because it had been in similar situations before, many times.

Then it would rise.